MOONSHADOW

Jessica wrenched herself from Fletcher's grasp. "You flatter yourself indeed, Mr. Danforth, if you think I'd submit to you at all."

"Freely?" His eyes took on a cynical cast. "Perish the thought. Of course I'll pay you, since that's what you're used to." He brushed his knuckles over her heated cheek.

She knocked his hand away and took a step back. "I'd like nothing better than to slap that lascivious grin off your face, Mr. Danforth, but I won't," she said. "I wouldn't sully my hand on your arrogant face."

To her utter chagrin, he laughed. "I know why you're angry, Jessica. You liked the way I kissed you. Your mouth opened beneath mine like a bud unfurling."

"You caught me off my guard, Mr. Danforth. It shan't happen again."

He caressed her chin in the curve of his finger and smiled _____ "We'll see about that, Jes___

MOONSHADOW

SUSAN WIGGS

AVON BOOKS ◆ NEW YORK

AVON BOOKS
A division of
The Hearst Corporation
105 Madison Avenue
New York, New York 10016

Copyright © 1989 by Susan Wiggs
Published by arrangement with the author
Library of Congress Catalog Card Number: 88-92112
ISBN: 0-380-75639-0

First Avon Books Printing: February 1989

AVON TRADEMARK REG. U.S. PAT. OFF. AND IN OTHER COUNTRIES, MARCA REGISTRADA, HECHO EN U.S.A.

Printed in the U.S.A.

K-R 10 9 8 7 6 5 4 3 2 1

For Joyce Bell, Alice Borchardt, Arnette Lamb, and Barbara Dawson Smith, with heartfelt gratitude.

And for my husband, Jay—again, and always.

My thanks to Pat Jones of the Houston Public Library, Harvey Arden of the National Geographic Society, and the Regional Information and Communication Exchange of Rice University.

Special thanks to Diane Brown for her proofreading skills.

Some there be that shadows kiss;
Such have but a shadow's bliss.

—Shakespeare

MOONSHADOW

Prologue

" 'Tis plenty I know about whorin'," the girl insisted, puffing out her emaciated, ill-clad chest in a show of bravado. More fiercely she added, " 'Tis all I bloody know."

Disgruntled at the late-night intrusion, Adele Severin pierced the waif on her doorstep with the look she used to intimidate her most hard-bitten girls and hell-bent patrons. But this scruffy visitor showed no sign of shrinking back.

"*Tiens,* I do not allow such language in my establishment. This is a place of gentlemanly entertainment."

The girl shrugged and tossed her mop of corkscrew curls. A bony shoulder poked through a gaping hole in her ragged shawl. "Whorin', entertainment—I ain't here to split hairs. A man wantin' 'is poke ain't of a mind to spend time pettifoggin'."

Madame Severin drew a horrified breath and took hold of the door, ready to slam it in the guttersnipe's face. Just then the girl flung her head back, whipping a stray coil of hair from her eyes. The kitchen lamp illuminated her face.

Adele felt an unfamiliar squeezing where her heart used to be. She pursed her lips and drew her hands to her bosom. "*Bon Dieu . . .*" she whispered, staring. Those eyes . . . they were *extraordinaire*. So huge they seemed to swallow up the rest of the small, hollowed-out face, so deep Adele felt compelled to look away; she had the uncomfortable sensation of staring straight through to the girl's soul.

What was it she saw in those unsettling pools of gray mist? A softness totally out of character with the razor-tongued

1

urchin's brash manner. The eyes held a subdued glimmer of distress, a vulnerability only one as perceptive as Adele Severin could discern.

Stepping forward, she put out a gnarled and manicured hand and brushed a dirty ringlet away from the pinched face. Instantly the visitor flinched, baring her teeth. And then the answer came to Adele. Suddenly she knew with terrible certainty what she was seeing. *Innocence.* Innocence which, despite a generous splash of mud and soot, looked as pure and untouched as a budding flower with the dew still clinging to its folded petals. Staring deeper into the gray eyes, Adele discerned terror. Suppressed, but evident. *Nom de Dieu,* the waif was no more than a frightened girl. . . .

Letting her bejeweled hand drop, Adele asked, "What are you doing here, child?"

The visitor gave a sharp laugh, as if she'd never been called a child before. She probably hadn't. She thrust her hips from side to side in a pitiful imitation of a wharfside doxy. The mop of ringlets bobbed. " 'Cause I got somthin' men'll pay for."

Adele winced at the bitterness in the low, somewhat throaty voice. Shaking her head, she opened the door wider. "You presume to tell me my business?" she asked bluntly. "Are you experienced?"

The mist-colored eyes narrowed. "Only as far as me eyes an' ears've taught me. Mum didn't let none o' the buggers near me." The girl's shoulder poked further out of the shawl; her amazing profusion of dirty curls danced. "But I ain't no Nice Nelly, missus."

"But . . . why do you want the life of a courtesan, child?"

"Because I'm a right poor cutpurse and no good at beggin', neither."

No, Adele silently agreed. This one definitely lacked a thief's guile or a beggar's self-pity. *"Entrez,"* she commanded. "I shall determine whether or not you will suit."

In minutes the girl was seated at a small table jutting out from the kitchen wall, a bowl of soup and a piece of bread set before her.

Adele drummed the table with her long, lacquered nails and watched, drawing her lips into a thoughtful pout. The child showed admirable restraint. Her street-waif's pride kept her from wolfing down the meal as quickly as possible. She took small bites, chewing slowly and deliberately.

La barbe, but the girl was filthy. She smelled of sour laundry and neglect. Her mass of tight corkscrew curls was dull, matted and probably home to a variety of vermin. The small, thin hand clutching the crust of bread had grime in its creases and a black substance embedded beneath the well-chewed fingernails. Yet despite the dirt, those hands held a strange look of fragility, creating a riddle of contrasts that tugged at something deep within Adele Severin.

"What is your name, *mon enfant?*" she questioned gently.

"Jessica." The answer came from around a mouthful of food.

"Just Jessica? No surname?"

Again that harsh, bitten-off laugh. "Oh, I got me a surname, right enough. Me mum coulda named any number o' blokes as me sire. But she didn't. Made up a name special just for me, she did."

Adele tried not to smile at the childish pride in the girl's voice. "And what is this special name, Jessica?"

"Darling," the girl replied, careful not to drop her *g*. "Me name's Jessica Darling."

"Where is your mother now, Jessica Darling?"

She shrugged. "Ain't rightly sure. In some pauper's grave. Died last month of the French pox, she did." The large, golden-fringed eyes glared a challenge.

"I take it your mother was a . . ." Adele paused, searching for one of the delicate phrases she used when forced to speak of her brand of commerce. But she'd been in the business for so long that all the figurative euphemisms sounded as crude as the basest terms to her.

"She was an 'ore," Jessica Darling readily supplied. "A beggarly bawd in Billiter Lane."

"How old are you, Jessica?"

"Fifteen, close as I c'n reckon."

"And you think to join my establishment."

The grimy head bobbed and a lock of hair dropped onto a smudged cheek. "I 'eard talk o' this place. Mighty swell by Mum's reckonin'."

"And if I turn you out . . . ?"

For just a moment, Adele saw a flicker of doubt in the

large, heather gray eyes. But, like an iron veil dropping into place, resolution replaced uncertainty and Jessica compressed her lips into a firm line. "I'll make my way."

Yes, she would, Adele realized. The girl would survive like so many other of London's poor, by plying her body for a gill's worth of gin until she grew too dissipated to command a price from a toff and too defeated to care.

Responding to a sudden jolt of long-buried compassion, Adele Severin knew she didn't want that fate for this girl. A dim memory stirred in her mind. She recalled herself at Jessica's age, on a boating excursion with her wealthy, indulgent parents. The Norman cliffs had been awash with sunlight that day, the sky so bright that when the Spanish pirate ship bore down on them, its sails blotting out the light, the darkness took on the sudden eeriness of an eclipse.

Only Adele had survived the attack. But it was survival such as Jessica spoke of—an existence not quite as fulfilling as living, not quite as peaceful as dying. The pirates had taken a dark fancy to Adele, subjecting her to . . .

No. Adele wouldn't think of that now. What mattered was that she'd escaped, had managed to make her way in a world gone topsy-turvy through a tragic squall of fate. She looked again at Jessica Darling, who was busy devouring her second portion of bread and soup.

Smiling wistfully, Adele realized she'd probably made her decision the first moment she'd laid eyes on the half-starved *épave*. A project, that was what Jessica Darling would become, a way for Adele to grow old doing good. *Que Dieu sait*, the waif was a challenge. Raw and unschooled as a dockworker, she probably had the morals of an alley cat.

Adele looked at her guest like a gem cutter regarding an uncut stone. Rough but precious. Jessica Darling would never be a prostitute, Adele vowed. Using all her considerable education and resources, the aging madame resolved to transform the child into something decent, something Adele had never had the chance to be.

"Well?" Jessica demanded rudely, wiping her mouth on her sleeve and jutting her jaw forward. "Am I in, missus?"

Adele folded her elaborately manicured hands on the table and drew a deep breath for patience. *"Tiens*, Miss Jessica Darling. First, you will address me respectfully as 'madame.' '' Jessica mumbled the word. ''Second,'' Adele continued, ''you will remember to look at me when I am speaking to you.'' The gray eyes snapped to attention.

''And third, you may return the silver scissors you pilfered from the sideboard while I was getting your soup. I have few possessions of sentimental worth, but that happens to be one of them. Someday I shall tell you about it.''

Jessica looked momentarily defiant. Then, with absolutely no trace of sheepishness, she brought forth the scissors from a fold in her tattered skirt.

''Brush that lock of hair from your eyes, *copine*,'' Adele said. ''I must see your face if I'm to make a lady of you.''

Jessica Darling smiled for the first time, shedding the facade of defiant bravado and giving Adele a glimpse of an amazingly healthy row of teeth. Sounding almost like the child she never had been, she asked again, ''So I'm in?''

Holland Hall, New York, 1759

''You're in it, all right,'' the British officer barked. ''I've all the proof I need—almost.'' He nodded at his men.

Fletcher Danforth's breath escaped with a great heave as two pairs of red-clad, brass-buttoned arms slammed him against the wall in the entrance hall of his Hudson Valley mansion. The force of his broad body hitting the walnut paneling caused the crystals of the chandelier to jangle violently.

''Out with it, Danforth,'' said Captain Singleton, bringing his beefy face close. ''Who's your supplier?''

''Take your hands off me,'' Fletcher snarled at the burly guards holding him pinioned. The guards pressed him still, their hands trembling against Fletcher's furiously straining muscles. ''Call off your dogs, Singleton,'' Fletcher said. ''I'm not fool enough to fight you, not with my children asleep upstairs and a half dozen bayonets poking at me.'' He nodded meaningfully at the soldiers crowding into the entrance hall.

At Singleton's gesture the guards fell back and stepped away, flexing their hands.

''Now, Captain,'' Fletcher said, forcing himself to remain calm, ''suppose you tell me—in a civilized way, if you please—what brings you to Holland Hall.''

"I think you know why I'm here, Danforth. But I don't mind refreshing your memory."

Fletcher heard a feminine gasp and turned to see Sybil gliding down the staircase. His wife emitted a strangled cry when she spied the soldiers with their weapons poised.

"Fletcher! What are these men doing here?"

"Go back upstairs, Sybil," he said curtly.

Fastening a paduasoy dressing gown at her throat, she said, "I'll stay here, thank you, so these gentlemen can apologize to me for the indignity of invading my home."

"Sybil, go back upstairs," Fletcher repeated, "and for once in your life see to the children."

"Let her stay, Danforth," the captain taunted. "She's bound to hear about your crimes soon enough."

"Crimes! What crimes? Fletcher . . ."

He shot Singleton a look of loathing and strode into the library. Sybil fluttered down to a settee while Singleton sat in a leather armchair. Two guards stationed themselves by the door.

Fletcher rested his elbow on the mantel and faced the redcoat. "Just what is it you're accusing me of?"

"Selling guns to the Indians." Singleton paused as Sybil gave a cry of horror. "Don't bother denying the charge, Danforth. Running Wolf told everything."

Fletcher sprang forward so swiftly the guards didn't react until he had Singleton's stock clenched in a deadly grip, the officer's gorget pressing into his ruddy neck.

"What did you do to him, you bloodthirsty son of a bitch?"

And then the guards were upon him, clamping his arms while Singleton clawed frantically at the hand at his throat. Fletcher relinquished his hold.

Singleton straightened his stock and cleared his throat. The look he gave Fletcher glittered with venom. "Running Wolf held up admirably for a time," he said. "But I've yet to meet the man who can withstand the branding iron. Most effective when applied to—ah, in deference to Mrs. Danforth I must decline to elaborate."

Fletcher's face tautened as he was gripped by horror at what had befallen Running Wolf. His fists clenched as he was assaulted by fury at what the soldiers had done. He spared no thought for Sybil's sensibilities as he muttered a curse.

"At any rate," Singleton went on, "we finally realized where the Mohawk were getting their firepower. Pity we had to resort to . . . persuasion . . . to find out."

"You damned butcher," Fletcher exploded. "Those guns were for defense against the Hurons and French. The Iroquois are our allies, for God's sake, though they know better than to trust redcoats to defend them. They're winning your damned war for you. If your bloody department would do its job for once there would be no need—"

"Never mind my department," Singleton said. "The fact is you violated His Majesty's law. Now Running Wolf expired before he could give a full ac—"

Shocked, Fletcher nearly broke free of the guards. *"You killed him?"*

Sybil rose from the settee, her beautiful face annoyed. "Fletcher, please," she said. "Who is this Running Wolf?"

Singleton chuckled and slid his eyes over Fletcher. "Fancy keeping such a secret from your wife all this time. Right crafty, *Shadow Hawk*. Even for a bloody half-breed."

"Shadow Hawk . . . ? Half-breed!" Sybil shrieked.

Fletcher closed his eyes and clenched his jaw, groping for patience. Emotions battered him as he raked a hand through his cropped black hair. He was grieving for Running Wolf, he was furious at Singleton, and now Sybil was forcing him to bare the secret he'd kept from her for eight years. Although fiercely proud of his heritage, Fletcher had guarded the truth carefully in order to protect his children and serve the clan's needs.

"Fletcher," Sybil said plaintively, "I demand to know what this is all about."

His icy blue gaze moved to Singleton and the guards before resting on his wife. "A pity we must give our secrets a public airing. Shadow Hawk is my Mohawk name. Running Wolf was my uncle. My mother was a full-blooded Mohawk." He explained this in rapid-fire fashion, knowing no amount of cushioning would soften his wife's reaction.

Sybil gasped and crumpled back on the settee, fanning her aristocratic face with a long-fingered hand. Brimming with self-disgust, Fletcher stared at his wife, watching her head sway back and forth in mute denial.

With exaggerated solicitousness Captain Singleton went to her side. "Shall I send for a maid, madam?"

Sybil turned her dazed eyes to the officer. The sight of his immaculate uniform seemed to bring her to herself.

"No, Captain," she said in her usual well-bred tone. "That won't be necessary." She came to her feet in a sudden surge of willfulness, crossed the room quickly, and stood before Fletcher, her face twisted with loathing. Drawing her hand back, she landed a ringing smack on his cheek. He didn't flinch from her blow, nor did he flinch from her scathing dark-eyed glare.

"Savage!" she exclaimed. "You lying savage! Why did you never tell me?"

A chill crawled through Fletcher. Even though he had made the mistake of marrying her, had learned over the years how shallow she was, he was disappointed at her unhesitating denunciation. "You never cared enough to ask," he said quietly. "You never questioned my ancestry once you learned the extent of my fortune."

She winced but bore herself haughtily. "I'm going home to England. Without delay." Incensed by Fletcher's lack of reaction, she added, "I'm taking the children, Fletcher. You'll never see Gabriel and Kitty again."

A killing rage gripped him. Sybil had used the one weapon she knew would cut him down. But for the guards holding him in check he would have throttled his beautiful wife with his bare hands.

Sybil smiled at the wild fury in his eyes. Then she looked at Singleton. "My hus—this prisoner keeps a safe in that wall, behind the hunting scene. Perhaps you'll find the evidence you need there."

"So loyal," Fletcher said through gritted teeth. "I always could rely on you, Sybil."

Her eyes blazed with loathing. Absurdly, Fletcher found himself thinking his wife had never looked more lovely, although she left him cold. Hatred was so much more becoming to Sybil than indifference.

"Loyal?" she queried acidly. "Why should I be loyal to a man I and my children fully intend to forget?" She swept from the library without another glance at Fletcher.

Feeling curiously relieved that their sham of a marriage

was over, he stared at the door she had slammed. The years of coming home to her empty conversation, her feeble excuses at bedtime, would become but bitter memories.

Yet at the same time he battled a frantic feeling of loss. Sybil had never been able to love, but he now realized she could hate with a venom. He had no doubt she would try to make good her vow to alienate his children from him.

Singleton chortled with satisfaction over the papers he found in the safe he had wrenched open. "Ah, 'tis all here, right enough: receipts, bills of lading, customs notices . . ." He jerked his head at the guards. "Take him away."

As they dragged Fletcher back through the foyer, he heard a faint cry from the top of the stairs. He looked up to see seven-year-old Gabriel sitting on the landing, his favorite blanket clutched in his small hands. The lad's dark hair was rumpled; a sweet, quizzical expression puckered his face. Fletcher's heart gave a sickening lurch at the sight.

"Papa . . . ?" Gabriel said in a small voice. Then, as the soldiers hauled Fletcher toward the open door, Gabriel's voice rose in a plaintive, high-pitched scream.

"Papa!"

Chapter 1

London, 1764

"Wherever did you *find* the woman, Hester?" Mrs. Dunstan asked, looking up from her perusal of the cakes on the tea table. Her fleshy chins quivered like the wattle of an overlarge bird. "She's an absolute *gem,* that's my opinion. George and Amy have positively *flourished* under her tutelage. The little darlings have such lovely manners." At a nod from their governess, the pudgy girl and her reed-thin brother paid their respects to the visitor and withdrew to the schoolroom.

Hester Pynchon set down her teacup and patted her powdered coiffure. "I confess 'twas serendipity. I'd just dismissed the other governess when Miss Darling presented herself at our door."

Listening from her station on a nearby stool, Jessica hid a smile. Serendipity. Adele had all but pushed her into the Pynchon house.

"She came well recommended?" Mrs. Dunstan asked.

Lord yes, Jessica remembered. Adele had made her sound like a veritable paragon of virtue.

"Of course. Miss Darling had a letter of introduction from Madame Severin, a French lady of impeccable quality."

Yes, Jessica agreed. Everything about Adele is impeccable. Even the brothel she runs.

"Well, she's worked *wonders* with your children, that's my opinion." Maude Dunstan turned to Jessica, who was cutting a silhouette portrait from a sheet of black tissue paper and

10

listening to the praise with wry amusement. "Tell me, Miss Darling, where *did* you take your training?"

Jessica smiled politely, as she duplicated Mrs. Dunstan's lofty coiffure with a clever curve of her scissors. "Madame Severin arranged for my schooling at Miss Tolliver's in St. Martin's. Miss Tolliver schooled me in the classics and Madame herself saw to my deportment and French." Jessica angled the scissors downward, judiciously omitting a few of the lady's multiple chins.

"Oh, that speech," Mrs. Dunstan said effusively. "It's almost *too* perfect! I tell you, Hester, there is no substitute for breeding, that's my opinion. Surely Miss Darling comes from a fine family—"

"Here you are, Mrs. Dunstan," Jessica said quickly, gluing the silhouette to a card of cream stock. "You've been a most interesting subject."

Hester admired the overflattering portrait. "Lovely," she murmured. "Miss Darling has managed to capture the very essence of you, Maude."

"Yes," that lady said, taking the card. "Yes, I quite agree. My Lionel will be so pleased." She selected a tansy cake from the tray, murmuring, "Miss Darling's a gem, Hester. An absolute gem, that's my opinion . . ."

While Mrs. Dunstan prattled on, Jessica excused herself, placing her scissors and tissue paper in a fruitwood box and starting toward the schoolroom. She was hard pressed not to burst into laughter at Mrs. Dunstan's flattery. The self-important woman couldn't know how far she was from the truth. The good lady and Hester Pynchon would need a bale of burnt feathers to revive them if they ever found out the "gem" of a governess had been raised by a wharfside moll and her training paid for by a notorious madame.

But Miss Tolliver and Adele had schooled her well. After five years Miss Jessica Darling bore no trace of the brash, razor-tongued urchin who had presented herself on Adele's doorstep, demanding a job. With evangelical fervor Adele had worked to bring about the transformation.

Once Jessica realized that a decent life dangled within her grasp, she'd developed a hunger for learning that gratified Adele and amazed her teachers. She learned to speak French and English with perfect articulation. She labored tirelessly over her sums and the tenets of logic. She pored over poetry and history. Most important of all, Jessica learned how to behave. She knew every nuance of deportment and could rattle off a dozen forms of address in two languages. By the time Adele launched her into her governess post there in Dover Street, Jessica could walk, talk, think, and act like a lady.

Now, in the schoolroom, as she helped George and Amy with their sums, Jessica felt a surge of gratitude. Because of Adele Severin, she lived a life the urchin from Billiter Lane had never dared dream of: an immaculate room of her own, a wardrobe of serviceable dresses, and the security and respectability of her governess's post. Every other Thursday she was free to go off on her own, usually finding herself at Adele's, joking with the girls and creating silhouette caricatures of some of Madame's more notable patrons.

Yet despite Jessica's comfortable way of life, a traitorous stab of restlessness occasionally pricked at her. Training the Pynchon children was hard work, and Mrs. Pynchon's demands often exceeded the children's rather limited abilities. Some nights as Jessica lay in her pristine little room off the nursery, she couldn't help longing for something to break the day-to-day monotony of the schoolroom.

But always she caught herself. She'd had her share of adventures, like the time one of her mother's "callers" had set fire to their garret room. Jessica could do without that sort of excitement. She was safe and secure here.

A sudden shriek from George brought Jessica from her musings. "Miss Darling! Amy spilled ink all over my copybook!" The boy reached over and gave one of Amy's ringlets a sharp tug.

The girl howled. Jessica quickly subdued them both with a promise to withdraw the privilege of an outing to the pleasure gardens at New Wells. The children ceased their squabbling, well aware that Miss Darling gave one warning, and only one.

Jessica was helping George blot the ink when the schoolroom door burst open. Hester Pynchon stood in the doorway, clutching a letter, her handsome face pale.

Dread leapt in Jessica's throat. Deep within her lived the fear that somehow the Pynchons would learn the truth about her and send her packing.

Lines of tension deepened around Mrs. Pynchon's humorless mouth. "I must have a word with you, Miss Darling."

Jessica hastened the children from the room. "Tell Cook to give you a biscuit and a cup of cider," she said. "You can have it in the garden." The children scampered away.

Hester lowered the letter, running thin hands over the figured velvet of her dress. "I've had some rather distressing news," she said, although she sounded more annoyed than distressed. "My sister Sybil has died, leaving her two children orphaned."

"I'm so sorry." Jessica didn't know what else to say. The only person she'd ever lost had been her mother. All she remembered feeling then was the gnawing hunger in her belly.

Mrs. Pynchon didn't look hungry, nor did she look terribly grief-stricken. She seemed merely . . . preoccupied. Calculation flickered in her pale eyes like the pages of an account book being rapidly turned. "I'm the children's only surviving relative. I suppose there's nothing for it; I'll have to take"— she glanced at the letter—"Gabriel and Katherine in. They should be arriving from Lincolnshire soon."

A loud crash sounded in a distant part of the house, followed by even louder shouts. Fearing that one of the children had met with some accident, Jessica lifted her indigo skirts and followed Hester from the schoolroom and down the front steps to the entrance hall.

Jessica stopped beside Mrs. Pynchon and gaped at the scene before her. A Ming Chinese-export porcelain urn, one of Charles Pynchon's priceless antiques, lay in shards on the marble floor. Nearby, a little girl dressed in traveling clothes and clutching a rag baby was trying to hide in the folds of a footman's cloak.

The door hung open and an angry curse drifted in, followed by the sound of running feet. "Get the devil!" a man's voice shouted. The running ceased. "There, I've got 'im now . . ." Two more liveried footmen appeared, faces flushed with exertion. One held a disheveled boy by the scruff of the neck. Jessica guessed he was the culprit who'd broken the vase.

"I'm Ambrose Wendell." The man huffed, clutching with white-knuckled hands the struggling youth's collar. "Lately of Mrs. Sybil Danforth's employ. Forgive us, Mrs. Pynchon, for arriving unannounced, but the dev—er, the lad's already tried to run off a half dozen times.''

Ambrose tugged roughly at the boy's collar, forcing his head back. His hat fell, baring a tousled mass of coal black hair. The eyes of a dark angel, set in a face that was handsome to mythical proportions, glared around the room.

Jessica gasped at the naked hatred blazing in the boy's narrowed blue eyes. He focused his attention first on Hester, then Jessica. That look cut into her heart like the honed blades of a pair of scissors. She took a step back, wondering how on earth a boy so young had learned to hate so fiercely.

Fort Orange, New York, 1764

''This *is* an honor,'' Fletcher Danforth said sarcastically to the guard who yanked him from his cramped barracks. ''Colonel Macon wants to see me, eh? He must be desperate.''

''Never mind your backhanded remarks, Danforth,'' the guard retorted. ''Try showing a little respect for a change.''

Fletcher smiled humorlessly as he followed the guard across the place of arms in the stone and timber compound. What little respect he'd had for the British militia had completely disappeared over the past five years. Their tortures—those of the mind as well as of the flesh—made living a nightmare; their corrupt and sluggish legal system stung like salt on his scars.

He stepped inside Macon's office and lounged against the door frame, noting a table off to the side which, altarlike, supported the Union Jack and a gilt-framed portrait of King George the Third in his coronation robes. God, he thought, England has had a new king for three years and I'm still a prisoner.

''You wanted to see me . . . *sir?*'' He added the title belatedly, letting it roll off his tongue like an insult.

For once Macon seemed too agitated to order the usual flogging for his least favorite prisoner.

''Get in here and close the door, Danforth,'' he said, pacing up and down the creaky wooden floor. Fletcher did so, watching Macon. His wig was askew and his stock undone, as if he'd slept in his clothes. He stopped pacing and looked at Fletcher, his gaze devoid of the expected disdain.

"Great Knife has captured my son," he said.

That didn't surprise Fletcher, for Great Knife was a Mohawk war chief and Emory Macon the captain of a patrol in the region. The officer wasn't noted for his compassion for the Indians he was sworn to protect. Fletcher raised an eyebrow. "What's that got to do with me?" he asked, although he'd already guessed.

"I want my son back, Danforth. You're thick with the Mohawk; you can treat with them."

It had been so long since anyone had placed any sort of value on Fletcher that, absurdly, he felt complimented by the man who'd spent five years hating him, thwarting his every effort to clear his name and gain his freedom. Fletcher didn't doubt he could do as Macon requested. But he held back. "Why should I help you, sir? Your son murdered an Indian child with his bare hands in that last raid up in the Oberon County."

"By God!" Macon roared, slamming his fist down on the desk. "If you don't help me, Danforth, I'll have you shot!"

"Very impressive," Fletcher drawled. "Another injustice like that might be just the thing to earn you a court-martial."

Macon's face flushed scarlet beneath his powdered wig. Apparently the reference to his growing reputation as a petty frontier dictator wasn't lost on him.

"You're lucky to be alive, Danforth," he blustered. "Your half-breed neck would have been stretched five years ago if your Indian friends hadn't killed Captain Singleton and destroyed the evidence against you."

"Evidence?" Fletcher asked mildly, wishing the war party had managed to free him as well. "What evidence?" He narrowed his eyes and leaned across the desk, knuckles whitening against its polished surface. "As far as anyone knows, you've been holding me under false arrest. You've spent a fortune trying to buy evidence and paying off those who would help me. Frankly, I'm getting a little tired of waiting for you to come up with a charge that sticks."

"Your sniveling York City solicitors and that Indian-loving William Johnson have been able to keep the hangman at bay," Macon said viciously, "but they can do nothing about the charges of insubordination and assaulting an officer of the Crown—crimes you've repeated five years running. You're mine," Macon proclaimed, his jowls shaking. "For as long as I want you, you're mine. And don't forget it. I'll kill you myself if you don't do as I ask."

Death, Fletcher reflected, would be welcome after what he'd endured at this miserable frontier fort. His life of endless work details and humiliating punishments was not an existence he valued. But then an image of Gabriel, screaming for him that last night at Holland Hall, resurrected a fierce desire to stay alive in the hope of escaping this hellhole and being reunited with his children. He slid a glance at Macon. "A dead man can't negotiate with Great Knife."

Again the colonel's fist pounded the desk. "Damn it, man, what the hell do you want from me?"

Fletcher indulged in a slow, lazy grin. At last Macon understood. "I want out of here," he said. "I want all charges against me dropped. Holland Hall is to be restored to my full control. I'll take all the conditions in writing, duly subscribed to and witnessed. You're good at that sort of thing, Colonel."

He was amazed at the officer's hesitation. The man was actually calculating the benefits of his complicity, even when his son's life was in jeopardy.

"If you turn me down," Fletcher said casually, "you'll have sold your own son for the sake of the money you've been trying to extort from my estate."

Macon expelled his breath with a snakelike hiss. "You carry the day, Danforth," he said at last. "But if I lose my son, you're a dead man."

A small contingent of redcoats hung back cautiously, clutching their Brown Bess muskets and looking terrified of the ominous thud of Indian sentry drums reverberating through the dense woods. Macon gave the order to make camp on the south bank of the Mohawk River.

"You have two days, no more," he warned Fletcher. "If you don't deliver my son by then, we'll lay waste to the entire clan."

Fletcher clenched his jaw. Imprisonment had made him vicious, had darkened his soul, yet the threat against his people revived a fiercely protective feeling. "In that case," he said softly, "your son wouldn't live to appreciate your actions, Colonel." Pivoting on his boot heel, he went to his horse, mounted, and approached the Indian encampment alone.

Hand raised in salute, he greeted the Mohawk in the aspirated gutteral tongue of his mother's people. Silent children and yapping dogs gathered on the path to the settlement. A little boy crouched in the shadows of the palisades, erecting a fort of sticks and mud. He paused to grin proudly. It was a smile Fletcher recognized. No doubt the lad was yet another of Kayanere's kin, and kin to Fletcher as well. God, but five years was a long time.

"Shadow Hawk," an aging man called, hurrying to embrace him. A brown face, wizened like a ripe walnut, cracked into a grin. "I thought the *tiohren:sha'* had killed you."

Fletcher's lips tautened, freezing his smile. "Their laws bound me for five winters, Grandfather. But their laws could not kill me."

Between folds of rugged, aging flesh, Kayanere's eyes probed Fletcher. "But I was so certain . . . The manitous showed me the Shadow Hawk's death in a dream, and yet you live and breathe as ever before."

Fletcher swallowed. Kayanere was a shaman; his dreams were portents from the other world. "The manitous were not entirely wrong," he suggested. "A part of me is dead, Kayanere. The part of me that was betrayed by the *tiohren:sha'* and my wife. A man who has lost his children is a man half alive." His throat ached as his eyes swept the village, seeing the charcoal color of Gabriel's hair in that of the boys who gathered near, seeing the small oval of Kitty's face in that of a sleeping babe strapped to its mother's back.

Handsome, broad-faced women in cotton petticoats brought food and tobacco to the bark-clad council house. Resplendent in beaded buckskins and a snakeskin girdle, Great Knife left his flirtation with a young squaw and joined them. The name Shadow Hawk dropped from his lips in a way that filled Fletcher with pride.

Kayanere muttered curses as he fumbled with flint and steel to light his pipe. Fletcher suppressed a grin. For all his mystical powers, the old man was a Mohawk who never could light the calumet. Gently taking the feather-decked pipe, Fletcher lit it after a single strike.

He talked with his grandfather and Great Knife, the war chief, whose vermilion-streaked face remained impassive as he listened. They spoke of the seasons and the rivers in general terms, skirting the issue that quivered like an arrow in the tobacco-hazed air of the council house.

The day progressed as Fletcher had predicted. The Mohawk were domineering diplomats, never rendering a decision in haste. Fletcher enjoyed the delay. A meal of venison stew revived a palate gone dull from prison fare. Fletcher swathed himself in Mohawk regalia, joined in their dances, sat indulgently through their long-winded orations. Being among these people, who so valued their personal freedom, soothed Fletcher's long-imprisoned body and soul.

At nightfall, Kayanere lounged in his lodge, sucking on his pipe and regarding Fletcher curiously. "Tell me, Shadow Hawk, how the *tiohren:sha'* treats his prisoners."

"I was stripped of all that matters to a man."

"Even women?" Kayanere sat forward, gaping.

Fletcher gave a dry chuckle. His grandfather, whose offspring numbered more than a score, had once been legendary in his prowess with females. To such a man, the deprivation was unthinkable.

"Even women," he stated and watched with amusement as Kayanere's pipe dropped to the floor.

"The Thunderer preserve you," the old man whispered.

Bemused, Fletcher stared at the low-burning fire. Something in this way of life called to him despite the fact that he had been raised an Englishman and trained abroad as a solicitor. The lot of the Mohawk was hard; he endured seasons in which survival itself was uncertain. But, fed by his own skill at hunting, warmed by his own fire, protected by his own bravery, he received the ultimate reward of freedom.

Freedom. Fletcher took a long, smoke-scented breath and pondered how the world had changed during his imprisonment. The long years of the war for empire were over; the British were supreme from the Floridas to the Arctic. But somehow he sensed a wind was rising. Energy and restlessness took root deep inside him, drawing him toward a new destiny.

* * *

The revelry of welcome ended the following morning. The clan now knew that the bonds of blood and friendship had endured five years of estrangement.

With a jerk of his grease-anointed head, Great Knife referred to the redcoats still waiting in the woods.

"They want you to release Emory Macon," Fletcher said. Great Knife's nod told him the request had been expected.

The chief grimaced and grumbled, "The Thunderer's curse on them. Macon deserves no mercy."

"That is true, my friend. But if you take your vengeance on the colonel's son, you'll bring the *tiohren:sha'* down on our people like a pack of wolves."

"We are warriors, Shadow Hawk."

"What good are warriors against an enemy so cowardly that he hides behind the palisades of a fort? You know the British never seek battle unless they have the overwhelming advantages of numbers and guns."

Pulling absently at his scalp lock, Great Knife nodded. But he set his jaw. "Emory Macon must die."

"His death will be the beginning of the end for all of you, Great Knife." Fletcher studied the solemn, hickory-tough man who had devoted his life to defending his people. "In freeing Macon, you will also free me. I can help you once again." Fletcher was suddenly desperate to convince his friend of his utility; Sybil's betrayal and the years of imprisonment had battered his sense of self-worth.

After considerable discussion the war chief relented, unable to ignore the warning and pleased at the idea that his mercy would buy his arms supplier's freedom. He uttered a quick order and Emory Macon was brought forth, a noose looped around his neck.

The limping man seemed dazed by pain, unable to comprehend what was happening. Fletcher saw that the braves had already taken some of the revenge they craved. The scarlet uniform blew in tatters around a thin, pale body. A small portion of his hair had been ripped out; the new growth was pure white. One of Macon's eyes was a runny mass of pulp, probably put out by the heated flint of a spear.

"You've finally learned the meaning of an eye for an eye," Fletcher muttered as he slung Macon over his own saddle.

The young captain could only shudder and gulp convulsively as Fletcher led the horse and its burden into the woods.

Colonel Macon's relief quickly turned to rage when he saw what had been done to his son.

"By the devil," he shouted, "he's blind. Blind!"

"Your son has one good eye," Fletcher said quietly. "That's more than he left most of his victims."

"You'll not have your freedom now," the colonel vowed.

Fletcher was prepared for the officer's recalcitrance. While the other men in the party were securing Emory to a litter, he mounted and sidled his horse over to Macon.

"Hand over my release forms, Colonel. If I don't ride away from here unharmed, the Mohawk will slaughter you."

As if to confirm the threat, the cold round eyes of Indian muskets appeared in the nearby bushes.

Macon swore. Snarling, he thrust a packet of papers at Fletcher, who examined them briefly and carefully placed them in a pocket inside his long surtout. Then he wheeled his horse and thundered eastward, toward Holland Hall.

Only when he'd put a good distance behind him did Fletcher allow himself to consider the idea that he was free. *Free.* After five years of enforced detainment at Fort Orange, he was actually going home.

Home? Fletcher felt a painful jolt at the thought. Holland Hall wasn't a home anymore. It was a fabulous house surrounded by acres of rich, river-watered lands and palatial forests. But Gabriel and Kitty were gone. The very heart of his home had been ripped out by a vengeful woman.

Fletcher stayed only long enough to ascertain that his agent, Jasper van Cleef, had managed the estate adequately in his absence and shielded the greater part of his fortune from Macon's greed. Within a week he'd arranged his business affairs and then he was off to England.

To get his children.

And nothing, not even his beautiful, vindictive wife, would dare stand in his way.

Chapter 2

Humming softly, Jessica descended the back stairs to fetch a posset for Kitty, who was down with the grippe. A smile touched Jessica's lips as she fingered the smooth Venetian glass beads of the necklace the little girl had strung for her. Kitty was as sweet as her brother was surly, as loving as Gabriel was hateful.

Hearing voices in the passageway around the corner, Jessica stopped. Gabriel's smooth, cultured voice drawled out a hideous obscenity.

Flesh cracked against flesh, the sound as vicious as a snapping whip. Jessica stifled a gasp and squeezed her eyes shut. Her hand crept up to worry a coil of hair that had escaped her snood.

"You're a fresh young pup, Gabriel Danforth," Hester Pynchon spat. " 'Tis only because of my poor sister that I abide your presence at all."

Jessica's throat tightened as she imagined the proud youth braving his aunt's wrath. In a voice that sounded years beyond his age he said, "You'd best take your hand from my collar, madam. My trustees wouldn't care to hear that I've been mistreated."

"You disgust me," she said. "You deserve to be shipped back to the colonies to live among the savages that spawned you."

A frown furrowed Jessica's brow. Colonies? Savages? But Gabriel had always lived on the family estate in Lincolnshire . . . or had he?

"You won't send me away," Gabriel retorted. "You're too

21

bloody greedy. You and your fop of a husband wish to control my inheritance from Grandfather.''

Hester's slippered foot tapped in agitation. "I see you're determined to make matters unpleasant for everyone.''

Jessica heard the sound of running feet. "Come back here, you hateful brat!'' Hester shouted.

But Gabriel didn't stop. He rushed into the stairwell where Jessica stood. Shooting a murderous glance at her, he pushed past, pounding up the back stairs to his room.

Drawing a deep breath, Jessica tucked the strand of hair behind her ear. Since he'd arrived four weeks earlier, Gabriel had applied his considerable intelligence and stubborn will to infuriating his aunt and uncle. They'd branded him troublesome, but Jessica knew better.

Something about him made her ache inside with remembrances of her own harsh childhood. Gabriel's bitterness was just as intense. He lashed out and withdrew as she had. He hid behind a wall of fierce bravado as she had. And Jessica didn't doubt that he hurt, just as she had.

Putting Kitty's needs aside for the moment, Jessica marched back up the stairs and made her way to Gabriel's room. George was retreating down the hall, his face pale, his throat working. Jessica could only imagine what Gabriel had said to drive his cousin from the room they shared.

She knocked lightly on the door. "Gabriel? Gabriel, it's Miss Darling. I'd like to speak to you.''

"Go away.'' The reply sounded muffled.

"But Gabriel—''

"Miss Darling?'' A tiny voice interrupted Jessica. She turned to see Kitty Danforth standing nearby in her lacy bedgown, her brown eyes wide as she clutched her rag baby.

"Kitty!'' Jessica pulled the child into her arms. "You shouldn't be out of bed.''

"I heard quarreling,'' Kitty said in a trembling voice. "Why was Auntie so angry with Gabriel? And why is Gabriel always so disagreeable?''

Jessica carried the child back to her bedroom. "Gabriel is angry, love,'' she explained gently.

"At what, Miss Darling?''

Jessica tucked Kitty into bed and leaned down to hug her. How could she tell the child about the ghosts that haunted her brother? The boy was consumed by guilt over his mother's death. From the bits and pieces Jessica had been able to extract from him, she'd reconstructed a nightmare that would chill the blood of even the most phlegmatic adult.

Gabriel and his mother had been arguing about his expulsion from Harrow when Sybil had lost her temper and slammed her fist into a heavy plate standing mirror. The cheval glass had shattered, severing an artery in her arm.

"No one could stop the bleeding," Gabriel had said, masking horror with indifference. "The blood soaked every piece of linen in the house. Later the doctor said we should have pressed above the artery, but we didn't know about that. She called me names I never heard before, told me I was just like my father. And then she died."

Jessica breathed in the warm, babyish scent of Kitty's sable hair. "Try not to worry about your brother. He's not angry at you." He just needs to learn to live with himself again, she added silently. Pray God he can.

Mrs. Stearns, the housekeeper, arrived in a rustle of starched skirts. "Mr. and Mrs. Pynchon wish to see you in the library, Miss Darling," she said.

Guessing the meeting had to do with Gabriel's latest outburst, Jessica rose. "See to Kitty," she told the housekeeper. "She needs a posset for her cough."

Mrs. Stearns's usual dour expression softened. "Poor lamb," she murmured, crossing to the bed and laying her palm on Kitty's forehead. "Chamomile tea," she prescribed.

"Can I have honey in it, Mrs. Stearns?" the child asked.

"Of course, lovey. Anything you want . . ."

Smiling to herself, Jessica left the room. Kitty was ripe for a little spoiling. Her smile faded. Gabriel, too, needed love. But he wasn't likely to get it from the Pynchons.

Stone faced, Hester Pynchon sat in a wing armchair. Charles was at his French desk, inhaling a good portion of snuff from the back of his pale hand.

"Come in, Miss Darling," he said with a cough. "We've something to discuss with you."

"Gabriel?"

Charles nodded sternly, nostrils narrow and whitened by snuff. "Ahem. Quite so. The boy's been with us a month and his conduct continues to be intolerable. It'll be uncommonly difficult to place him in a decent school.''

''I beg your pardon, Mr. Pynchon, but I feel Gabriel is in no condition to reenter school just now,'' Jessica said carefully. ''A boy as troubled as he can hardly be expected to tackle Latin declensions and classical history.''

''He needs a good whipping,'' Charles Pynchon declared, fitting a gold-rimmed lorgnette over one eye.

''You've already given him that, more than once,'' Jessica ventured boldly, letting her distaste show. ''I can't see that the beatings have done any good.''

Hester gasped in surprised indignation. ''Remember, Miss Darling, you work for us.''

''Yes, but my first responsibility is to the children.''

''You mollycoddle the boy,'' Charles accused. ''I insist that you take a firmer hand with him.''

Jessica winced at her employer's caustic tone, but she felt strongly enough about Gabriel to voice her opinion. ''He behaves in a hateful way because he hates himself. He needs all the love and acceptance we can give him.'' She placed her hand on the doorknob. ''Let me talk to the boy. Please.''

''Ahem. Very well,'' Charles grumbled. ''But if I don't see an improvement soon, Miss Darling, I shall take matters into my own hands.''

She hid a rueful smile. Those pale, moist-looking hands didn't seem capable of subduing a mosquito, much less a rebellious young man. ''Yes, sir,'' she said, and ducked out of the library, leaving the door ajar. As she turned toward the stairs, her string of Venetian beads came undone and scattered over the marble floor. Muttering an appropriate curse from her childhood, Jessica knelt and began gathering the colorful glass beads.

A knock sounded sharply at the front door. Unwilling to let a caller find her groping around on the floor, Jessica straightened. The knock came again. Jessica waited, but the butler didn't come. The elderly Sedgewick was probably napping again in the winter parlor. The third knock sounded distinctly impatient.

Jessica crossed to the door, stepping around the rolling beads. She pushed a curl behind her ear and opened the door. A shadowed figure blotted out the afternoon light.

She found herself staring at a lace-frothed chest. A very broad lace-frothed chest. Her gaze climbed to the caller's face. It was an extraordinary face, all planes and angles and strong lines, coming together in a stark harmony that her artist's senses instantly appreciated. But the blue eyes seemed to blast a bitter chill into the entrance hall.

"Yes?" Jessica's voice held a faint tremor of surprise. This man, with his unfashionably cropped black hair and storm-tossed eyes, was very unlike most of the Pynchons' friends.

He leaned down slightly, peering at her. "Amy?"

A stubborn ringlet dropped across Jessica's cheek, which warmed with sudden color. Flustered, she gave him a quizzical smile. "I daresay this is the first time I've been mistaken for a twelve-year-old girl."

His furrowed brow smoothed. He waved his hand as if distracted. "Of course. I've quite lost track. . . ." Without waiting to be invited, the man strode into the foyer. Before Jessica could utter a warning, his boot encountered a scattering of glass beads. The beads rolled beneath the man's foot.

With a little cry, Jessica grasped his arm. His unbalanced and considerable weight nearly caused both of them to fall. She heard him curse softly as he regained his footing.

"I'm so sorry," Jessica said, awed by the knotted strength in his arm and alarmed by the humorless look he aimed at her.

He removed her hand from his arm as if it were distasteful to him. "Hasn't anyone ever taught you not to leave your playthings lying about?" he asked unpleasantly.

"Actually, I—"

"Never mind, girl. I'm here to see the Pynchons."

Jessica bristled at his imperious manner and felt a sudden wave of dislike. For this man and for males in general. Men were proud, deceitful creatures—that much she'd learned from her mother and from Madame Severin. "I'll see if they're in," she said coldly and started toward the library. The man followed, looming behind her like an ominous shadow. Voices drifted from the partially opened door.

"Miss Darling's judgment has always been impeccable," Hester was saying to her husband. "But she's wrong about Gabriel."

Embarrassed to overhear herself being discussed, Jessica raised her hand to knock at the door.

Strong fingers closed around her wrist, stopping her. She turned back, a protest on her lips, but the look the man threw at her chased the words from her mind.

"One cannot shower a savage with love," Hester snapped. "He'll fling it back in your face. Blood will tell, Charles. The boy is no better than the criminal who sired him."

Mortified that a stranger should overhear the conversation, Jessica wrenched free of his grip and stepped into the library. The Pynchons looked up, surprised; then both pairs of eyes fastened on the man behind Jessica.

"Murder happens to be one sin I haven't been accused of," came a scathing voice from the doorway. "Although at the moment I feel a sudden urge to experiment with that particular crime."

Jessica's mind whirled with confusion at Hester's talk of savages and the stranger's iron-voiced threat. Hester blanched and sank back into her chair, blinking, her mouth working like a codfish. Charles stumbled to his feet, clearing his throat and groping for his lorgnette. "Danforth . . ." he said faintly. "By God . . ."

Jessica swung around to face the newcomer whose name was suddenly very familiar to her. Staring, she retreated a step. His grand height and breadth seemed to fill the room. *Danforth* . . . Good Lord, was this overbearing creature Kitty and Gabriel's father? Surely not; Mrs. Pynchon had said her sister was a widow, the children orphans. But Jessica saw the truth now. This man's eyes were mirrors of Gabriel's—a cold and angry blue, filled with a distant, suppressed pain. The features were a harsher, more mature version of the boy's. An excess of handsomeness, she decided, must be a family trait. Danforth stared back, his face hard with fury. His mouth twisted into a mockery of a smile.

Jessica felt suddenly afraid, not only for the children but for herself as well. Against all reason, she was struck by the idea that this man's arrival could somehow disrupt her secure life.

"What?" he said, looking past Jessica. "No welcoming embrace from you, Hester? Not even a handshake, Charles?

Good lord, man, it's been thirteen years!'' With a sharp bark of laughter, he returned his frigid gaze to Jessica.

"Who are you?'' he demanded.

Somewhere, she found her voice. Incredibly, she managed to sound coolly proper as she inclined her head. "I'm Jessica Darling, the children's governess.''

His glare nearly made her wince; it was like looking at a too-blue sky. He studied her keenly, his frosty eyes moving at leisure over the curves concealed by her navy gown, up to the peach-blond cap of her hair pulled back into a snood. Jessica had the uncanny and unpleasant sensation of being taken apart, inch by inch.

One eyebrow lifted, a dark slash on his tanned brow. "The governess? I'm afraid you're not terribly convincing. You can't be old enough to hold a responsible position.''

Indignation replaced Jessica's nervousness. "My age needn't concern you, Mr. Danforth. I've had the Pynchon children in my charge for a year, with great success.''

The mention of children drew Danforth's attention from his frank appraisal of Jessica. "I want to see my son and daughter,'' he stated.

"Really, Fletcher,'' Hester said, opening and closing her hands in agitation. "This is a shock. We never expected—''

"I daresay you didn't,'' he shot back.

"You mustn't force yourself on the children,'' Hester continued. "You see, they think . . . Sybil told them . . .''

"What?'' Fletcher Danforth's voice crackled in the tension-heavy air. "Never mind, I can guess. My loyal wife has allowed my children to believe me dead.''

"No doubt Sybil thought she was doing them a kindness,'' Hester said, looking defensive.

Danforth fixed a murderous gaze on Hester. "I've been six weeks getting here from New York,'' he said. "I've driven three good horses into the ground riding back from Lincolnshire after finding the house there closed.'' For the first time, Jessica recognized fatigue in the lines around Danforth's eyes. "Send for Gabriel and Kitty now,'' he ordered, "or I shall take this house apart until I find them myself.''

Jessica glanced at Charles, but the man seemed barely able to breathe, much less speak. Hester, however, had recovered sufficiently to give the barest of nods.

"I'll fetch them," Jessica murmured. Leaving the library, she passed close to Fletcher Danforth. His nearness made her skin prickle and she avoided his eyes, resisting the urge to run.

"Mind the beads," he murmured. "It wouldn't do for the governess to find herself on her backside."

Jessica stifled a retort and marched across the foyer, kicking a few beads aside as she progressed. She wondered if there were more to the man's taunt than mere rudeness. She had the strange and unsettling sensation that, despite the fact that he knew her not at all, he knew her well. But how? She recalled her vivid and unrefined curse when the necklace had broken. Could he have heard her? Or did this Fletcher Danforth have what Adele would call *l'éclaircissement,* the ability to see beneath a person's surface, no matter how well polished that surface was?

She hurried upstairs and knocked on Gabriel's door.

"Go away," came the familiar reply.

Jessica leaned her forehead against the door. Sweet Lord, how could she tell him? How could she inform the troubled boy of his father's presence? "You're wanted in the library," was all she could bring herself to say.

A long silence.

"Gabriel?"

"I'll come."

Relieved that there wouldn't be a battle for once, Jessica went to Kitty's room. The little girl and Mrs. Stearns were sitting on the bed, holding a mock tea party. Amy and George sat on the floor, scowling at each other over a pegboard.

Mrs. Stearns, who often neglected her housekeeping duties to entertain Kitty, looked guilty as she stood up, but Jessica barely noticed.

"Get her dressed quickly, Mrs. Stearns. She's wanted in the library. And take Amy and George out into the garden." Jessica forced an encouraging smile for Kitty, thinking, my God, that man down there will eat this child alive.

Five minutes later she had both children assembled outside the library door. She heard arguing within as she tried to adjust Gabriel's stock while he pulled away.

"—not let you take them," Hester was saying heatedly.

"I wonder just how compassionate you'd be," Fletcher Danforth snarled, "if the boy weren't worth a fortune."

Gabriel's fidgeting stilled and Jessica saw a look of confusion darken his face. Although she knew the boy disdained affection, she put her arms around both children. As she embraced them briefly, a fierce feeling of protectiveness welled up in her. An image flashed through her mind—her mother shooing a leering customer away from Jessica, years ago. She squeezed them tighter.

"Everything will be all right," she said. "I'll make sure it is." Then she opened the door. "Behave yourself, Gabriel," she whispered, knowing the admonition was useless.

The three adults in the library turned. Jessica watched Fletcher closely, wondering what was going through his mind as he saw Kitty and Gabriel for the first time after their long estrangement, and wondering also why Sybil Danforth had deemed it necessary to keep them from her husband.

Fletcher didn't move a muscle, but his eyes seemed to devour the children, drinking in the sight of them. Only a tiny tic at his jawline betrayed his nervousness.

Jessica felt her throat tighten as she watched. There was something profoundly poignant about this sundered family that touched her heart. When the silence grew oppressive, she forced herself to speak.

"Children," she said softly, trying to smile in Fletcher's direction, "say hello to your father."

Gabriel didn't move. Kitty gave a small whimper and hid her face in Jessica's skirts, her little hand closed tightly around the arm of her rag baby.

"There now," Jessica said soothingly, prying Kitty away with one hand while giving Gabriel a nudge with the other. "Your father's come a long way to see you."

Fletcher continued staring at his children. By now the aching supplication in his eyes was so evident that Jessica caught her lip to stay its sudden quiver.

Gabriel took a deep breath and advanced a step. Encouraged, Jessica went weak with relief. But she'd misread the boy's action.

He stamped his foot with all his might and directed a look of pure loathing at Fletcher.

"He's not my father!" the boy screamed.

Kitty began to sob. "Don't make me go to him, Miss Darling," she wailed. "I'm afraid! Mama used to say he was a savage!" The child was hysterical—all wide, tear-drenched eyes and small, clutching hands. Jessica lifted her up and looked over the sable head at Fletcher.

"I'm sorry," she said, her heart bursting at the pain and shock she saw on his face. "I'll talk to the children."

"You do that, Miss Darling," Fletcher said stonily, raising his voice above Kitty's wails. "It's obvious they've been trained not to talk to *me*." He strode to the door and paused. Fixing a stare heavy with meaning on Hester and Charles, he added, "I'll be back."

"Gabriel, let me in," Jessica said, trying the door. "I want to talk to you."

"No."

She pursed her lips and thought for a moment. "I was hoping we could have a game of piquet," she ventured. "Your cousins are out, so we won't be having lessons."

After a considerable pause, Gabriel opened the door. Spying Kitty, who still clung to Jessica's skirts, he said, "What's she doing here?"

Jessica hid a smile. Despite his attitude, she knew Gabriel preferred having her undivided attention.

"Kitty just wants to watch," she explained. "Perhaps you might teach her a thing or two about piquet."

Somewhat mollified, Gabriel got the cards and sat on the floor. Jessica watched him closely, but for once he didn't deal from the bottom. They played quietly for a time while Kitty curled up on the bed with her doll.

Jessica could tell Gabriel's mind wasn't on the game. He played halfheartedly, his eyes wandering about the room. Finally he said what she knew had been on his mind all along.

"I thought he'd been hanged for treason."

Treason? Jessica swallowed, wondering what stories Sybil Danforth had put into the boy's head.

"You were mistaken," she said carefully. "Perhaps he's committed no crime at all. You should have asked him."

"What does he want with me?"

"I'm sure if you'd been the least bit civil he'd have told you that too."

"I don't care," Gabriel said caustically. "I want nothing to do with him."

"You may not have a choice, Gabriel."

"I won't go with him. I'm going to school soon."

"Is that what you want, Gabriel?"

His eyes were as chilling as his father's. Jessica wondered if the boy knew how much he resembled Fletcher Danforth.

"I just want to be left alone."

No, you don't, Jessica found herself thinking. You want someone to love you, to ease your mind about all the shadows that haunt you. But she said nothing.

"Miss Darling?" Kitty sat up on the bed, her brow puckered by a small frown. "Why is everyone so cross?" Her little hand twisted the wool hair of the rag baby.

Jessica rose and went to the little girl, tousling her silky hair. "Your father arrived unexpectedly. It was a great shock to everyone."

"If that man is my father, why didn't he sit me on his knee and tell me stories like Uncle Charles does for Amy?"

"I'm sure he'd like to, Kitty," Jessica said, trying unsuccessfully to conjure up such a scene. She couldn't imagine Fletcher Danforth being so gentle and playful. "Perhaps the next time he comes you won't behave so badly."

"But I was afraid! He was so—so big and fearsome looking."

"Just give him a chance, love. You might find that you like him."

Kitty looked dubious, but she nodded slowly. "I'll try, Miss Darling. Really I will."

Behind them, Gabriel snorted and dealt a new hand of cards. A footman, carrying a letter, arrived just as they started playing again. Jessica took the letter from him, instantly recognizing the elegant hand of Adele Severin. She read the message quickly.

"We'll play again tomorrow, Gabriel," she said. "I must go. A very dear friend of mine is ill and she needs me." The Pynchons knew nothing of Adele's true vocation and were generous in allowing Jessica to visit her on occasion.

"In the meantime," she added, "I want both of you to become accustomed to the idea that your father is here in

London. I think he wants very much to get to know you again.''

Feeling empty and frustrated, Fletcher walked across Dover Street to a small, well-kept park surrounded by a wrought-iron fence. The manicured arrangement of lattice-trained yew trees and clipped box hedge grated on nerves, reminding him of his preference for the unkempt splendor of the upper New York wilderness. Still, the prospect of returning, childless and empty hearted, to his lodgings at Gray's Inn appealed to him even less.

Reaching down, he plucked a boxwood twig and idly mutilated it as his dark thoughts took flight. He'd been a fool to come to England with such high hopes, nursing a gilded dream of a happy reunion with his children. Sybil had poisoned their minds against him; her ideas had been augmented by her greedy sister Hester. The memory of the stark hatred in Gabriel's eyes—eyes that used to sparkle with youthful merriment—made Fletcher's insides grow cold. Gabriel had become a product of Sybil's vengeful tutelage.

And Kitty was simply . . . afraid. She'd been an infant at the time of his arrest; she couldn't know the joy he'd experienced the first time he'd held her, almost paralyzed with love for his baby daughter. She couldn't know his pain at being robbed of watching her take her first toddling steps, hearing her chattering her first words.

He stripped the twig bare and wrapped it tightly around a finger, wondering if he could ever win back his children's affections. Sybil no longer stood in his way, but her venom lingered in their malleable minds. The Pynchons, too, were difficult. Gabriel was heir to his maternal grandfather's fortune as well as to Holland Hall; his aunt and uncle wouldn't readily relinquish control of that wealth.

But Fletcher needed his children. Without them his life had no meaning. He held his land and fortune in trust for them. Perhaps once they were at Holland Hall he could break down the barriers of Gabriel's resentment and Kitty's fear. The task wouldn't be easy. Fletcher would have to learn the art of fatherhood all over again. He no longer remembered how to do the things that had once come so naturally to him: how to soothe a scraped knee or explain why the sky was blue or chase away nursery demons at night. But the demons that now plagued his son were more insidious than the childish monsters the boy had once conjured up, so long ago.

Fletcher's gaze wandered to the elegant town house across the street. The shadows of evening crept across its facade, and he remembered his children as he'd last seen them—fearful, angry, being shepherded out of the library by that cheeky little governess. Miss Darling. A rueful smile crept across his lips. A charming name, to be sure, but what the woman was doing as a governess was beyond him. At first impression he'd thought her a clumsy, ingenuous girl. But when he recalled her speech and demeanor, her swaying hips and lush lips, he realized she was a mature woman.

Her prim, high-necked gown and the modest way she wore her hair did nothing to hide a maddening womanly allure. The stark cut of her navy dress silhouetted a wealth of frankly feminine curves. The severe coiffure accentuated her enormous soft eyes and arresting features. She didn't belong in a schoolroom but in a grand salon, attended by a half dozen servants. She had the face and body of a seductress, the manners and speech of a duchess. . . . And, surprisingly, she genuinely seemed to care for Kitty and Gabriel. Fletcher was amazed the Pynchons had the good taste to employ such a capable governess.

A hired coach rolled to a halt in front of the town house. Immediately suspicious, Fletcher sat forward, tensed and ready to intervene if the Pynchons had the temerity to transport his children out of his reach. Presently a figure emerged from the mews leading out of the tradesmen's entrance at the rear of the house.

Jessica Darling.

A gray cloak enfolded her slight form, a hat shadowed her face, but an unruly peach-gold curl betrayed her identity. Oddly, she seemed to have a furtive air about her as she spoke briefly to the driver and entered the coach.

Intrigued, Fletcher watched the vehicle roll slowly away. At first he began to walk idly in the same direction; then, as a decision took shape in his mind, his steps quickened. Hester and Charles had erected a wall of greed in front of him; fear and confusion blocked his way to Kitty and Gabriel. Though it seemed unlikely, perhaps he'd find an ally in Jes-

sica Darling. As governess she would know more about the
children than anyone else, and she might be willing to help
him win back their love.

Gripped by a sudden sense of urgency, Fletcher reached
the intersection of Dover and Albemarle Streets and hailed a
coach.

"Where to, sir?" the driver inquired.

Fletcher pointed. "Wherever that coach leads us," he instructed, overpaying the surprised driver by several shillings.
Inspired by the generous tip, the driver urged the horse to a
lively pace.

Presently Fletcher felt the vehicle slow down and leaned
out to look ahead. Vaguely he recognized the brick and marble facades of North Audley Street. Two blocks in front of
him Jessica stepped from her hired vehicle, cast a quick look
around, and disappeared toward the back of a house.

Moments later he stood in front of the same building, eyeing a faded fringe of violet curtains in the window. His vague
memory sharpened. *He knew this place.* The salon had been
popular among the young solicitors and barristers he'd studied with at Gray's Inn. His heart jumped to his throat.

My God . . . He shook off the thought. Surely the neighborhood had changed in fourteen years. . . . His legs devoured the
steps in two long strides. He rapped sharply at the frosted pane
of the front door.

The door opened slightly; the heavy scent of perfume and
expensive spirits wafted out. A large male face stared mildly
at him. "Yes?"

The butler, Fletcher thought wildly. Please be the butler.
His throat was dry; he swallowed. "Is this the establishment
of"—he paused, sifting through his memories—"Madame
Severin?"

"Might be. Does Madame know you?"

Fletcher shook his head. "It's been a long time."

"I'll just check with her; then—"

"I'd like to see . . . Miss Jessica Darling."

The beefy face split into a smile. "Wouldn't we all." The
door started to close.

Fletcher wedged his boot between the jamb and the closing
door, at the same time producing a gold crown from his

pocket. "Am I to assume Madame is turning away customers?"

A big fist closed around the coin and the door opened further. "She's busy," the man said, hedging.

With a grim smile, Fletcher slipped inside. "I'll wait."

"I suppose you've paid for *that* privilege," the doorman said, his small eyes flicking over Fletcher. "And you seem to have civil enough manners, as well as a heavy enough purse." Nodding, he indicated a parlor to the left, over-decorated in shades of rose and gold. Gentlemen sat hunched over gaming tables or stood smoking long-stemmed pipes at the sideboard, gaudily dressed women clinging to them. A crimson-carpeted staircase led to a dim hallway flanked by polished doors. Somewhere up there, Jessica Darling was "busy."

The civil manners the doorman had approved of took a sudden savage twist inside Fletcher.

"Finish your soup, Adele," Jessica said, her scissors busily rounding a curve of a silhouette. She tried, with minimal success, to capture the profile of a chimney sweep she'd passed on her way to North Audley Street. She couldn't for the life of her keep from giving the humble sweep's chin an arrogant tilt, a feature that more properly belonged to the man whose face had lingered in her mind all day. Setting aside her artistic paraphernalia she added, "You won't get better if you don't eat."

The older woman sniffed and sat up straighter against a pile of brightly colored chintz pillows. "I needn't be coaxed like one of your young charges," she said tartly. She tasted the soup and set it aside. "The new chef, *quel souillon!* Somehow he has managed to burn even the soup."

Jessica pitied the cook; Adele had a demanding palate. "At least have a biscuit," she said.

"I am not hungry. Nor am I sick. I only sent that note because you haven't been around to see me in so long. Are you becoming too fine for the likes of me, *copine?*"

"Nonsense, Adele; you're my dearest friend. I haven't been to see you because I've been busy. The Pynchons' nephew has been most difficult. It's all I can do to keep him from running away."

"Why would the boy wish to run away?"

"Gabriel's troubled. And just today his father arrived from the colonies to take him home."

"*Bien*. Then you'll soon be rid of the rascal."

"I don't think it's that simple, Adele. The children knew nothing of their father until today. The reunion was far from happy."

Adele sat forward. "Have you met this man, Jessica?"

"Briefly."

"And . . . ?"

Jessica looked down at her hands as she formed a mental image of Fletcher Danforth. "I can't say I blame the children for being afraid of him. He's terribly tall and quite devilishly dark. He was dressed like a gentleman but . . . Mrs. Pynchon called him a savage, of all things. I suppose he does look rather exotic, with coppery skin and a great shock of coal black hair. He has the face of a Renaissance sculpture and eyes so blue and cold . . . I shivered, looking at him."

"It sounds like the man has fascinated you, *copine*."

Jessica frowned. "He was unpleasant to me. I disliked him as I dislike all men."

Adele shook her head, her nimbus of snowy hair bobbing. "*Pauvre p'tite*," she murmured. "You know so little of men. They are not all like the scoundrels who abused your mother, nor the pathetic patrons of my establishment."

Eager to pull her mind from Fletcher Danforth, Jessica said, "Speaking of pathetic . . . I thought I heard the Sultan bellowing for more wine."

Adele smiled indulgently. "You did, of course. His Grace of Claremont is much with us these days, and constantly in his cups. You see, he is so despondent over his failure to win Parliament's approval for his bill to levy larger fines on convicted prostitutes."

Jessica shook her head at the irony of it. By day the elderly duke of Claremont labored hard on behalf of decency; by night he came to Adele's to swath himself in silk trousers and a jeweled turban to play the part of a lusty Eastern sultan. More than once he'd tried, with slurred promises of lavish payment, to entice Jessica into his "harem." "How terribly upsetting for His Grace," she murmured.

"*Doucement*, Jessica," Adele cautioned. "His patronage

brings a bit of amusement to the girls and a great deal of money to my coffers. My house in St. Paul's is a gift from him, you'll remember.''

Jessica nodded. ''I suppose his eccentricities must be indulged, then.''

''*Assurément.*'' Adele put a handkerchief to her mouth and coughed into it. ''A touch of *la grippe,*'' she muttered.

''I'll get some fresh tea from the kitchen,'' Jessica said, leaping up. She stepped out into the long, dim hallway. Subtle trills of feminine laughter and a rumble of masculine voices wafted to her ears. Accustomed to the familiar sounds, she made her way toward the back stairs.

''Jade!'' a familiar voice called from behind the double doors at the end of the hall. ''Where in the name of Allah is Jade? Not like her to keep me waiting. . . .''

The doors swung open, and Jessica found herself staring, half amused, half disgusted, at His Grace the duke of Claremont. The paste jewel in his lopsided turban winked at her; his wizened and drink-slackened face split into a grin. ''You're not Jade,'' he said, grabbing her wrist with surprising speed. ''But you'll do.'' He yanked her into the room. His attempt to kick the doors shut with his pointed silk slipper was only partially successful.

More exasperated than alarmed, she said, ''Your Grace, it's me, Jessica.''

Still holding her with disconcerting firmness, the duke took an oil lamp from the bedside table and held it up, peering at her through bloodshot eyes. ''Jessica, eh? Madame's chaste little ward?'' He set down the lamp and hauled her against him, assaulting her with a fog of wine-scented breath. ''You look to me like a woman grown and ready,'' he declared.

Were he anyone but Madame's best-heeled patron, Jessica would have dispatched him quickly with a well-aimed kick. Unfortunately for her, Claremont had the means to close down Adele's business, so Jessica couldn't afford to offend him.

Speaking to him like the harmless eccentric he was, she said, ''If you'll let me go, I'll fetch Jade for you, Your Grace.''

''You're fetching enough yourself, my dear,'' he said with a bark of besotted laughter. Bringing his hands up, he fit his fingers into her collar and ripped downward, rending her dress from neck to waist.

Fletcher scowled down into his glass of *pêche* Williamette. An exotically beautiful Oriental courtesan had been trying to capture his attention for the better part of an hour with sly, sidelong glances. He summoned a grin for the blatant suggestion she whispered in his ear but shook his head. Her brazenness was distasteful. Would he never have a decent woman? Was he ever destined to find pleasure only for the brief span of time his coin provided?

The woman moved away, her jade-colored harem trousers rustling, the chain around her naked middle gleaming. She turned her attention to a blond man who lounged at the sideboard, smoking a clay pipe.

Fletcher longed to end the life of celibacy prison had forced on him, and Sybil's death had freed him to do so with whomever he chose. But only one woman interested him tonight. Jessica Darling. He raised his glass of brandy to the lamplight. The rich color of the liquor, shot through with golden lamplight, reminded him of the unusual color of her hair. The notion triggered more images, of large, misty gray eyes; a sensitive mouth; a ripe, supple body. . . . What manner of woman was she that she'd play the governess by day, the courtesan by night? His gaze drifted to the open staircase.

His patience at an end, Fletcher surged to his feet. He'd followed the woman in order to talk to her, but his body needed relief as much as his mind needed answers. Yes, he decided, he'd do a damned sight more than just talk.

Her cheeks flaming, Jessica stared at her ruined gown, which had fallen in a navy pool around her ankles. "Really, Your Grace," she said impatiently, leaning down to retrieve the dress, "you're not behaving with your usual refinement."

"You're not my usual companion either," he said with a laugh. "I think I like you, Jessica Darling." He grabbed her by the forearms, catching her off balance, and brought her tumbling with him onto the bed.

"And I like you too, Your Grace," she forced herself to say. Exasperated, she shoved his hand away from her breast. His other hand appeared instantly in its place. She tried to squirm away. "Let me fetch you something to eat; Madame has laid in a supply of your favorite figs from Smyrna."

"Ha!" he said. "You're sweeter than any fruit." He caught her around the waist and buried his face in her bosom.

Standing in the hallway, Fletcher heard what was obviously their lovers' talk, saw their equally obvious bed game through the half-open door. Jessica Darling was beautiful, even graceful as she grappled playfully with the duke. Somehow she managed to appear both naive and cultured; he guessed that was part of her appeal.

Like a sluice of briny water over raw wounds, a sense of deep devastation washed over him. Nothing was as it seemed; nothing was right in the world. His children were strangers, their governess a fraud. Every sound from the lamplit room betrayed his first impression of her and confirmed his new-formed suspicions. When the duke's overfed body moved to cover the girl, Fletcher turned away in disgust.

So much for Madame's prize patron, Jessica thought wildly, as she felt the unwelcome weight pressing on her.

The besotted duke was obviously beyond mollycoddling. She struggled, reared back, and tried to pull away. Her motion upset the bedside lamp and sent it crashing to the floor.

Instantly the burning oil ignited the bedclothes and—"Oh, dear God!" Jessica cried—the duke's silk trousers as well. Her hands fell upon her discarded dress and she used the garment to beat out the flames. She succeeded in preserving the duke's person, but now the curtains had caught fire as well.

"Get up, for God's sake," Jessica cried, dragging him away from the bed and toward the door. Smoke gagged her, stung her eyes, blinding her as she shoved Claremont out of the room. Fanned by fresh air from the hall, the fire roared higher and hotter.

"By Allah, you set a man aflame." The duke laughed, too drunk to appreciate the incendiary danger.

Her eyes streaming, her heart hammering, Jessica felt herself brush against a tall male form.

"Don't get any ideas about *her*," Claremont slurred to the smoke-shrouded man. "She's—" He broke into a fit of coughing.

"Get everyone out, damn it," Jessica screamed at the

stranger. The smoke snaked thickly through the hallway and heat poured from the duke's suite. Taking Claremont by the arm and pounding on doors to alert the others, she led the way down the front stairs. Nan Featherstone emerged from another room, lumbering behind them and swearing fluently as she lifted her petticoats around her ample form. From the sounds of tramping feet, Jessica assumed a parade of other people followed.

She pulled the duke across the parlor, empty now save for a suffocating fog of smoke. Hearing Claremont begin to wheeze, Jessica pushed him out the front door. She rubbed her stinging, gritty eyes until her vision cleared enough to discern his ducal crest on the door of a waiting coach.

A bevy of footmen scurried forward and, gratefully, Jessica gave Claremont into their care. The duke had fallen to drunken grumbling; his turban had unfurled and hung limply down his back. Dismissing him, Jessica turned to look at the house. By now the entire upper story was engulfed in a tower of flames. Coughing, she staggered over to join the girls standing across the street, chattering and cursing.

Jade Akura shook her fist at a fleeing man and called out, ''Run, then, ye white-livered nidget!'' Her Cockney speech made a jarring contrast to her delicate Oriental beauty. Her almond-shaped eyes flashed. ''Cowards. I suppose they expect us to piss the bleedin' fire out.''

A watchman with his lantern and pole scurried down the street, his long, narrow whistle shrilling an alarm.

Jessica crushed her fists into her eyes and sagged against a wrought-iron fence, wondering how in God's name she was going to get herself home wearing only her shift and petticoats.

Like vermin from a sinking ship, Fletcher thought wryly as he watched the patrons flee, trailing assorted articles of clothing in their wake. Not particularly concerned about his reputation, he stood on the front walk, ready to pitch in when help arrived in the form of leather buckets and canvas hand squirts.

He glanced across the street at the tense, silent huddle of women and recognized Madame Severin, who had aged nobly since he'd last seen her some fourteen years ago. The lady looked resigned as she watched her house burn. The Oriental beauty spoke in flat Cockney tones to an enormously fat woman who, despite the eye patch she wore, had a motherly look about her.

Finally, Fletcher gave his attention to Jessica Darling. She looked small, confused, and oddly vulnerable standing there in her white petticoats. The way she was rubbing her eyes lent her the aspect of a lost child, a beauty lost amid a bevy of courtesans.

No, he reminded himself, shaken by a deep sense of shock and betrayal, the beauty, too, was a whore.

Chapter 3

The smell of wet cinders tinged the night air; a sense of profound loss settled like a cloud over the bedraggled group looking at the charred rubble. A drizzle had begun to seep from the sky, dampening the unsalvageable remains of Madame Severin's once fine house.

"So," Jade said, trying to lighten the mood, "Jessica's sacrificed her dress to save the Sultan."

Jessica scowled. "I suppose I'll be awarded a medal for bravery, but accolades for satisfying the duke are yours, Jade." Her frown deepened. "The fire wouldn't have started if Claremont had kept his damned hands to himself." Staring gloomily at the ruined house across the street, she said, "I think they're finished now, Adele."

A sooty assortment of watchmen, wardens, and sweeps who had doused the fire began to leave. A few veered across the street, teasing the girls with ribald comments and hoping for a reward of the most tangible kind. Disconcerted by her state of undress, Jessica tried to shrink into the shadows. Madame, looking regal and calm despite her loss, put the men off with her most imperious glare.

The servants and all the girls save Nan Featherstone and Jade Akura dispersed. Jessica watched them leave, remembering her own feeling of displacement on losing her mother and being turned out onto the streets. Such things didn't happen to her, not anymore, thank God.

Adele's lips were set in a characteristic concentrated pout. "Do you have the keys to my house in St. Paul's, Nan?"

"O' course, mum." Brushing aside a bright yellow curl,

42

Nan extracted a cluster of keys from her tightly packed bodice. "I never even go as far as the privy without me keys."

"*Eh, bien,* we can be off. *Alors,* where does one find a coach at such an hour?"

"Madame," said a deep voice from the shadowed street, "allow me."

Jessica whirled, hands flying to her cheeks as she recognized the rich, distinctly accented speech of Fletcher Danforth. He stood on the wet brick street, his magnificent figure swathed in the night mist and silhouetted against the whitish glow of a watchman's lamp.

Unsmiling, he swept a bow in Adele's direction and then raised a commanding hand. A coach appeared, springs creaking, the horses' hooves clip-clopping on the damp cobbles.

Jessica stood frozen with astonishment and dismay, arms crossed over the flimsy bodice of her shift.

Adele inclined her head. "How very kind of you, er, Monsieur . . ."

"Danforth," Jessica said faintly. "Fletcher Danforth." Mortified, she made the awkward introductions.

Adele pursed her lips. "So. We have a slight coincidence here."

"So we have," Fletcher agreed. The gaze that raked Jessica's indecently clad figure was frosty with distaste. "Miss Darling, may I offer you a ride as well?"

She felt like a butterfly pinned by his sharp glare. "Thank you," she said shakily, stepping to Adele's side.

Fletcher moved into the circle of light cast by the coach lamp. It was then that Jessica noticed the state of his clothing. His frock and waistcoat gaped unbuttoned, his singed stock was loose and hanging unheeded around his neck, his boots were dull and wet. His hands and face bore dark smudges.

Jessica had a sudden flash of recognition, a picture of a tall, smoke-shrouded figure in the hall of the brothel. She swallowed. "You were . . . you must have been helping with the fire," she said stupidly.

He shrugged at the ruined building. "For all the good it did."

"*Merci,* monsieur," Adele murmured. "I am in your debt."

Again he shrugged, extending a hand to help her into the

coach. With faint amusement, he did likewise for Nan. The coach sagged under the woman's weight. Jade Akura followed, shaking off his hand. "You're a damned decent bloke to do this," she quipped, "but I'll thank you to keep your hands to yourself. I'm in retirement as of tonight."

Fletcher chuckled, then turned to Jessica, one eyebrow lifted mockingly. "You look charming, but hardly like the proper governess I met this afternoon."

Surprise and indignation tumbled through her as he draped his smoke-laden frock coat around her shoulders. His fingers closed around hers and she braced herself for the familiar wave of revulsion a man's touch always evoked in her. But all Jessica felt was the warmth of his skin and the strength of his arms. Although his face was obscured by shadows, she had the distinct feeling that the stunning smile he'd given Jade and Nan was gone.

"Thank you," she said faintly.

His hands found the curve of her waist and lingered there. "My pleasure," he murmured. Then the light caught his face. Despite his words, his face was taut with savage anger.

She sank onto a cushioned seat, drawing back into the darkness, wanting to hide. Fletcher spoke briefly to the driver, then joined him on the outside seat. With a creak of leather springs, the coach surged forward. Always one to take advantage of comfort, Nan shifted heavily and began to snore.

Adele stroked the plush upholstering of the seat. "Very nice," she murmured conversationally. "This Fletcher Danforth does not seem like such a monster to me."

"So you know the bloke, do you, Jess?" Jade asked. "I ain't one to waggle on about a man's looks, but that one's right easy on the eye."

"His children are in my charge."

Jade gave a low whistle. "Blimey, now, is that right? A nice mix this is."

Before she could stop herself, Jessica uttered a vile phrase. Then, ignoring Adele's disapproving sniff, Jessica said musingly, "How in the world did Mr. Danforth happen to be at the fire?"

Jade snorted. "How does any man come to call at Madame's? Follows his special purpose, he does!"

Feeling inexplicably disappointed, Jessica folded her mouth

into a thin line. She shouldn't be surprised that Fletcher Danforth would seek companionship at Madame's; he was a man like all men. After being rejected by his children, he would naturally turn to a place that offered complete acceptance, even the kind he had to pay for.

"An odd lot, that one," Jade continued. "Seemed like he needed company, but he wasn't buyin'. . . ."

Jessica closed her eyes and cursed the turn of fortune that had brought them together in such an unlikely place. Displeasure had been clearly written in his cold gaze and unsmiling countenance. A sudden unwelcome thought, heaped with suspicion, pushed into her mind.

"Adele," she said, "he's going to think I was . . . receiving gentlemen."

Jade laughed softly. "There's a fancy for ye, now. I wouldn't sweat blood over *that*. The man ain't blind, Jess. Only an idiot'd mistake you for a moll, with your Nice-Nelly speech and Miss-Prissy manners."

"You're wrong, Jade." She opened the frock coat to reveal her underclothes. "Look at me, for God's sake! He saw me running out of the duke's room; I know he did." Horrified, she faced Adele. "What if he tells the Pynchons? If they knew where I was tonight—"

"If he stoops to such a level, you would be dismissed immediately," Adele replied matter-of-factly. "You shall have to do your best to explain, *copine.*"

Nervousness quickened Jessica's pulse and dampened her palms. Her future depended on the discretion of a man who, thus far, had proven himself to be brash, domineering, and clearly of the opinion that no lady—especially one responsible for his children—would be found in a brothel under any circumstances.

They left Adele, Jade, and Nan at the house in St. Paul's and drove to Dover Street. As Fletcher helped Jessica down and paid the driver, dozens of questions tore at his mind.

Somewhere in the distance a clock belled out the hour of four. Fletcher watched Jessica closely. Stiff backed and silent, she led the way to the tradesmen's entrance.

Fletcher let out his breath with a soft hiss. Jessica Darling certainly had a tidy arrangement for herself. By day she

played the prim governess; by night she entertained dukes at
Severin's. A pity the brothel had burned before he had the
chance to sample her considerable charms.

The thought made him scowl. She was intriguing, yes, and
desirable, and he'd never been one to gasp at her profession.
Except for one important fact.

She was in charge of his children. Determination welled in
him. The sooner he took Kitty and Gabriel from her dubious
tutelage, the better. If the Pynchons proved recalcitrant, he
was prepared to fight them all the way to the Lord Chancellor's court, if need be. Satisfied with that resolute thought,
he followed Jessica into the house.

"Thank you for seeing me home, Mr. Danforth," she said.
Her embarrassment looked genuine as she handed him his
coat. She began edging toward the back stairs.

"Not so fast, Miss Darling," Fletcher said softly. "I think
you should know I followed you to Madame Severin's this
evening."

She eyed him distrustfully. "Why?"

"I wanted to speak to you about my children, of course. I
still do, but . . ." His gaze touched her tousled curls, her
bosom, her nervously twisting hands. "Now I have some
additional questions to ask you."

He heard her swallow hard. "May I get dressed first?"

"That might keep the conversation on a more professional
level, Miss Darling."

She melted into the darkness of the back stairs, kept him
waiting for two minutes, and then reappeared. She wore a
dark gown, not recognizably different from the one she'd
taken off for the duke. Her hair was only slightly less tousled,
as if she'd tried to scrape it into some sort of order and then
given up.

"You're very prompt," Fletcher said.

Sending him a nervous look, she stirred the embers in the
kitchen fireplace. The coals flared to life, illuminating a face
that made Fletcher want to forget all he knew of her. The
firelight lent a tinge of gold to the curls framing her lovely
features. She looked delicate and damnably sweet. If he
hadn't known better, he might have revised his opinion of
women in general and Jessica Darling in particular. Instead
he sent himself a stern reminder. Although unfairly favored

by beauty, she had no business shaping the minds of his children.

"There's water for tea, Mr. Danforth," she said, lifting a heavy iron kettle. She had a low, somewhat throaty voice, far more suited to bedroom invitations than to tea. "Shall I serve you in the dining room?"

"Only if you'll join me." Fletcher grimaced. Now why had he made it sound like an invitation? He wanted answers, to be sure, but did he really want to greet the dawn sipping tea with this deceiving woman?

Indeed he did, he admitted. But not to titillate himself with the sight of her and the sound of her voice. He meant to have an explanation from her.

In minutes she was pouring the scalding brew into cups and setting out a plate of scones and butter. Fletcher marveled at her uncanny ability to appear so completely proper. Innocent even. Good God, she'd just been discovered half naked in a bawdy house and seemed no more contrite than if she'd been caught in a white lie.

She set a candle on the dining room table and sat down to sip her tea, looking absurdly demure as she brushed a stray drift of hair from her cheek. The gaze that met his over the rim of her teacup was steady and determined. "I believe, Mr. Danforth, that you're wondering what I was doing at Madame Severin's tonight," she stated.

By now Fletcher was a little in awe of her coolness, her self-possession. But why not? She would know better than to mince words when her job and reputation were at stake, which they certainly were. "The question had entered my mind," he said slowly.

Jessica bit her lip. It was the first sign of worry Fletcher had seen her betray. "I lost my mother five years ago, Mr. Danforth," she explained, "and was left with no other kin. Rather than begging in the streets, I sought help from Adele Severin. We became great friends. She was ill tonight so I went to visit her."

Fletcher almost laughed at the flimsiness of her explanation. "Oh?" he said cynically. "But it wasn't Madame you were visiting, not when I saw you. It was . . ." He paused, considering the snippet of conversation he'd overheard when he'd gone upstairs in search of her. "Ah, I remember. His

Grace. If I recall correctly, he wasn't behaving with his usual refinement.''

"Oh, God," she said faintly.

He hardened his will against her kitten-soft whisper of distress. "I must say, though, setting him afire was a rather unusual reaction . . . even for you."

She moved restively beneath his mocking gaze. "This is terribly hard to explain, Mr. Danforth, but I was fetching some tea for Madame when the Sult—His Grace assaulted me in the hall."

Darkly amused, he said, "Assault? In that case, your reaction was on the mild side. You should have screamed for help."

She worried a tendril of hair between her fingers. "I forebore to do so because Madame values his patronage. I was hoping to slip discreetly away."

"Ah. Was that before or after you disrobed for him?"

"I did *not* disrobe for him." She clutched at her starched neckline. "He tore my dress."

"Even a torn dress is better than none. Yet you'd discarded yours completely."

She drew a long, unsteady breath. "I used it to try to beat out the fire."

"My, my. How utterly valiant of you." He gripped the edge of the table and sat forward. "Your convoluted defense amuses me, Miss Darling, but each lie only entangles you more, and I'd hate to see you trip and fall flat."

"I am not lying!"

Leaning back, he crossed his ankles. "You seemed on fairly intimate terms with Madame Severin and her . . . ladies. How often do you manage to visit them?"

Jessica said nothing, only glared at him with what he considered unjustified indignation.

"Miss Darling, has it ever occurred to you that there might be something decidedly improper about your nighttime escapades? You are, after all, in charge of four children."

She drew her pretty mouth into a stubborn line. Her gray eyes narrowed. "I tend your children and I tend them well. What I do with my own time is none of your affair."

"I'm afraid it is, Miss Darling. You see, I must insist that your behavior be above reproach."

"And what of *your* behavior, if I may be so bold?" she queried suddenly. Spots of pink tinged her flawless cheeks. "I know very little about you, sir, but Gabriel insists you were arrested for treason."

Fury clutched at Fletcher's heart. "That, my dear Miss Darling, is none of *your* affair," he said, flinging her own words back at her with a vengeance.

"My point is, Mr. Danforth, that you seem confident of your ability to raise your children despite what you may or may not have done in the past." Apparently certain she had outreasoned him, she regarded him coolly.

"Because I love them, damn your eyes!" The words fell from his lips before he had a chance to consider the unseemliness of revealing so intimate an emotion to a stranger.

A lovely expression crossed Jessica's face then, an expression both sentimental and satisfied. Staring at him across the table, she said, "I've grown very fond of them too, Mr. Danforth. I'd never do anything to harm Kitty or Gabriel."

He searched her face, seeking a telltale gleam of deception in her mist-colored eyes. Although she'd given him scant reason to trust her, he found himself on the brink of believing she truly cared for his children.

"Mr. Danforth?" Her voice was soft, almost pleading.

"Yes?"

"Please don't—that is, I hope you won't find it necessary to inform the Pynchons about tonight. It would be rather awkward if they knew—" She broke off, flushing.

He sat back and curled his lip into a humorless smile, making her wait for his reply. Jessica Darling had made a serious error in asking for his complicity in her secret, a serious error indeed.

Because she'd just given him power over her. Power to use her in any way he saw fit and she might prove extremely useful in his fight for his children. If the Pynchons tried to keep him away from Gabriel and Kitty, he could call upon Miss Darling to remedy that. He suspected her post here meant a great deal to her. He wondered just how far she would go to protect her reputation.

Years ago, before betrayal and imprisonment had embittered him, Fletcher might have balked at using a woman. But not anymore. Determined to regain his children and hardened by five years of hell, he decided that scruples were for those too naive to know how to get what they wanted.

But he wasn't going to test Miss Darling just now. Later he would decide how she would repay his discretion.

"I see no need to make things awkward for you, Miss Darling," he said. Not yet, anyway.

Looking relieved, she cradled her teacup to warm her hands. "Thank you, sir. I do value my friendship with Madame Severin. We've grown quite close over the years."

The admission didn't surprise Fletcher. Severin undoubtedly prized Jessica. What man wouldn't pay dearly for a few hours with her? Surely, with her demure manner and subtle beauty, she had satisfied many a fond male fantasy.

"I'm sure you have," he said meaningfully. "Any madame would value your . . . assets." His eyes strayed to her bosom, which swelled enticingly beneath the bodice of her dress.

Her smile disappeared like a candle being snuffed out. Fletcher didn't realize how much he'd been enjoying that smile until it was gone.

"Mr. Danforth." Her voice shook and her cheeks flushed. "You must believe me. We are friends, that is all."

"As you wish," he replied wearily. He was too tired to challenge her clumsy lie. Another time, perhaps, he'd force the whole truth from her. He finished his tea and glanced across the table. "I'd like to see my children now."

She looked startled. "But it's half four in the morning, Mr. Danforth."

"I just want to look at them, damn it." Jesus, he thought, hearing the ragged emotion in his voice, she must think me a sentimental fool . . . or a desperate man.

"This way," she said, rising from the table. She picked up the candle and led him up the back stairs.

Although anxious to see his children, Fletcher was momentarily captivated by a matchless view of Jessica Darling's trim waist and swaying hips as she preceded him up the stairs. A light fragrance like spring violets corrupted by a hint of smoke wafted in her wake. By the time they entered the bedroom, he felt overwarm and restive.

While Jessica held the candle, Fletcher stared down at his daughter. The child's sable curls had escaped her nightcap and were fanned out on the pillow. One hand clutched the ever-present rag baby while the other lay palm up beside her face, slack fingers curled inward. Long lashes shadowed her cheeks and a tiny smile curved her lips.

Fletcher swallowed hard. He saw traces of the cherubic infant Sybil had spirited away, but he was overwhelmed by the idea that he didn't know this child at all. God, how he wanted to know her, to hold her curled in his lap and let her whisper her little girl's secrets into his ear. . . .

He cleared his throat and looked at Jessica. "Tell me about her."

Jessica smiled softly. "Your daughter is an angel, Mr. Danforth, a ray of sunshine about the house. She adores stories about princesses, especially the ones with a particularly loathsome stepmother."

"A perfectly happy, normal child," Fletcher concluded a bit ruefully. He was grateful, but at the same time it hurt to know his little girl had fared so well without him.

Jessica nodded at the doll. "That's Esme. She talks to it constantly. She was . . . troubled when she first came here a month ago. Often I would get her to talk to me through the doll. She'd tell me that Esme was afraid, that Esme missed her mama, that Esme's father was . . ." Her voice trailed off.

"Go on," Fletcher prompted grimly.

"I'm afraid Kitty was led to believe you were dead."

His jaw ached from holding it so tightly to stave off a rising tide of pain and rage. "Trust Sybil to lie," he said. His eyes burned as he bent and brushed Kitty's brow with his lips, inhaling a soft scent he'd only imagined during the past five years. "Your papa's here, baby," he said in a shaky whisper. He kept his eyes averted from Jessica, dismayed at having given her a glimpse of his powerful yearning and aching vulnerability.

They left Kitty slumbering peacefully and went to Gabriel's room. Like his sister, the boy was utterly beautiful. In sleep his mouth lacked its usual derisive sneer and his brow was calm and untroubled. Fletcher remembered him as a bright, athletic seven-year-old, bounding across the sloping acres of Holland Hall on foot or astride his favorite pony. The boy had loved his father with the uncritical and adoring heart of

a child. But Gabriel was a different boy now. He'd made that
painfully clear the previous afternoon.

"The Pynchons say he's troublesome," Jessica whispered,
brushing a lock of hair from the boy's brow. She looked up
at Fletcher. "But he isn't. He's deeply troubled."

"Tell me, Miss Darling."

"I wish I knew more about the situation. Gabriel rarely
speaks of himself. I've been able to glean a little about his
difficulties at school. He was at the top of his form at Harrow
and excelled at sports. Then, it seems, some rumor about his
background was started. . . . You know how unkind schoolboys can be, Mr. Danforth. Gabriel isn't the type to sit still
and let himself be tormented. He was sent down when he
broke another boy's nose in a fight."

"Lord," Fletcher muttered. "It's happening all over
again."

"What is, Mr. Danforth?"

He glanced at Jessica, realizing he'd spoken aloud. "Nothing, Miss Darling. Just a long-forgotten memory." He, too,
had been sent away to school. And he, too, had been tormented by boys who had learned of his parentage. He hadn't
broken a nose, but somewhere here in England was a young
man whose right forefinger would forever be crooked because
he'd pushed Fletcher Danforth too far.

"Surely Gabriel has gotten over his problems at school,"
he suggested. "Why is he still so troubled?"

Jessica swallowed. "He's still overwrought about his
mother's death. He was present when she died, you know."

Shocked, Fletcher stared at her. "No, I didn't know."

"Gabriel had come home from school to find his mother
none too pleased with him. They argued, and Mrs. Danforth
broke a cheval glass and cut herself. Gabriel watched her
bleed to death. His description of the experience was rather
. . . graphic, Mr. Danforth."

Consumed by guilt and pain, Fletcher raked a hand through
his hair. He hadn't been there for Gabriel. His son had borne
the suffering alone.

Gabriel's sleeping face drew into a frown and his limbs
began to twitch. He started to whimper and thrash.

Her beautiful face awash with compassion, Jessica set down
the candle. "He's plagued by nightmares," she said. She

placed her arms around Gabriel and laid her cheek against his soft hair. "Hush, lamb," she crooned softly. "Hush . . ." But the boy continued to whimper and fling his head to and fro. "I feel so helpless with him," Jessica whispered. "I wish there were some way I could chase his demons away."

Fletcher knelt on the other side of the bed, his face twisted in agony. "Son," he said with gruff tenderness. "Son, it's all right. There, now . . ."

Gabriel seemed to respond to the deep voice and broad, firm hands stroking him. He muttered and then relaxed, peaceful again.

Encouraged, Fletcher looked across at Jessica. His eyes burned with tears of regret. His heart wrenched with a fierce, protective love. To his amazement, Jessica's own eyes had spilled over, wetting her cheeks.

Lord, he thought, the woman was an enigma. He knew her to be a whore, a member of a profession that required a certain hardness of heart. Yet she wept for a boy she'd known only a month.

"The boy's too damned young to be slaying dragons on his own," Fletcher whispered.

In the bed across the room, George stirred. Jessica tiptoed to his side and tucked the counterpane around him. "We'd best be going, Mr. Danforth."

With a final look of longing at Gabriel, he followed her downstairs. At the back door, he shrugged into his coat. He turned to see Jessica watching him curiously. Her candle flickered across features gone soft with compassion. She stepped forward and folded down his lapel. A faint, clean fragrance of violets opened a wellspring of desire in Fletcher.

Discomfited, he tried to bury the feeling and moved away. "Miss Darling, my sister-in-law will do her damndest to keep the children away from me," he said.

"I expect you're right, sir. But try to understand. Mrs. Pynchon is protective of those she cares about."

"Don't tell me you believe that," he said coldly.

She lifted her chin. "The Pynchons have treated me well. I've no reason to think ill of them."

"Your loyalty is admirable, but I'm afraid you may just have to compromise it on my behalf."

The misty eyes widened. "What?"

"I mean to see as much of my children as I please, Miss Darling. And I'll need your help."

"But I can't deceive my employers."

A few moments ago he'd glimpsed tenderness in Jessica: her gentle hands soothing a child's brow, her lovely face soft with concern. Now those hands clutched, white-knuckled, at the folds of her skirt and her features were set in an aspect of implacable stubbornness.

She'd been living a lie for a year; her sudden reluctance to cooperate angered him.

"But you're so adept at deception," he said. Her chin rose a notch; he could not resist cupping it with his hand. His errant thumb moved slowly over her chin and the tiny hollow beneath her mouth. The unsurpassed smoothness of her skin, the inviting shape of her mouth, nearly made him forget his train of thought.

She gasped, and her eyelids fluttered downward, half closed, seductive. To Fletcher it was the response of an experienced woman, a woman accustomed to manipulating men with her charms. She was a whore, he reminded himself, and defensively he summoned back his purpose.

"If you don't cooperate," he forced out, "the Pynchons will hear about tonight. Do you understand?"

The startled, provocative look left her face. She jerked away. "I understand you're trying to blackmail me, Mr. Danforth. And I don't care for it one bit."

He smiled humorlessly. "Nevertheless, you will do as I ask. Don't worry, Miss Darling. If things go the way I plan, I'll be taking my children home soon, and you can go about your night games as before."

"That can't happen too soon for me, sir," she informed him, and yanked the door open to expedite his departure.

Chapter 4

Some hours later an aging butler was trying to turn Fletcher away at the Pynchons' front door. "I'm sorry," he said, quailing before the tall man's stormy gaze. "Mr. and Mrs. Pynchon are not at home to you."

Fletcher pushed past him and strode into the house. His tall boots clicked on the polished marble floor of the foyer.

"Where are my children?"

"Er, in the schoolroom, sir, with Miss Darling."

"Tell the Pynchons I'll meet with them in the library. After I've seen Kitty and Gabriel."

Muttering, the butler shuffled away.

Fletcher went upstairs to find the schoolroom door ajar. He stood outside for a moment, composing himself. He didn't want his children thinking him perpetually angry.

Gabriel sat on the recessed windowsill reading a book. Kitty was daubing with watercolors nearby. The Pynchon children were at their lessons, with Jessica supervising.

Despite a lack of sleep the night before, she somehow managed to look fresh and rested . . . and infernally lovely. Rather than masking her vibrance, her drab gown accentuated it. With her shining peach-gold hair and misty heather eyes, she had a soft, ineffable beauty that needed no enhancement.

As she helped George with a sum and complimented Kitty on her picture, it was hard to believe Jessica Darling had a darker side to her, a secret hidden behind her prim, ladylike manners and soft, cultured speech. But her duplicity was the Pynchons' problem and her charms were not for Fletcher. Before long, he and his children would be leaving London— and Jessica Darling—behind.

He took a deep breath and stepped into the room. Jessica's head snapped up. She masked her surprise and nodded a composed greeting.

"Amy, George, come and say hello to your uncle."

Fletcher barely felt his nephew's limp handshake and almost missed the curtsey executed by his awestruck niece. Vaguely he heard Miss Darling excuse them, but he didn't watch as they scampered fearfully from the room.

He was watching Gabriel and Kitty. His son pretended indifference, turning his eyes toward the window. Kitty set down her paintbrush and looked at Miss Darling, who smiled encouragingly. Fletcher knew he should be grateful, but he felt bitter at the idea that the governess should have to train his children not to fear him.

Smiling, he sat down on a low bench beside Kitty. "You've made a fine picture, sweetheart. You must like the color blue."

Kitty nodded shyly. "Blue's my favorite."

Fletcher gave the picture a moment of grave study. "It's the very color of the sky over the mountains in America."

The little girl looked pleased. Her brown eyes sparkled as she gazed up at her father.

"You haven't introduced me to your friend," Fletcher said, nodding at the rag-baby.

Kitty brought him the doll. In a moment as natural as her sweet smile, she climbed into his lap. "This is Esme. She had strawberry jam for breakfast."

Fletcher closed his eyes and breathed in the soft, sweet scent of his daughter. Inwardly, he shuddered.

Glancing over Kitty's shoulder, he saw Jessica expel a relieved sigh. No doubt she'd spent a good part of the morning preparing Kitty to accept her father. Apparently the governess understood the situation all too well, and that angered Fletcher. It was one thing to lack confidence, yet another to have it discerned by the likes of Jessica Darling.

He saw Gabriel edging toward the door, placed a kiss on Kitty's head, and reluctantly released her. Reaching into his pocket, he took out a parcel. "If you and Esme aren't too full of strawberry jam, perhaps you'd like some sugared almonds."

Kitty's eyes gleamed as she took the parcel. Impulsively

she placed her arms around his neck and kissed his cheek
with a resounding smack. "Thank you, Papa! I'll take some
to Amy and George right now." Grateful for the child's sweet
nature, Fletcher watched her scamper away. Gabriel, however, seemed unimpressed and intent on following his sister
out of the room.

"Son," Fletcher said firmly, "I'd like to talk with you."

The boy glanced at the door, but he stood still, lowering
his brows in a hostile angle. "As you wish . . . sir."

Fletcher winced inwardly at his son's belligerent tone.
"You used to call me Papa."

"You used to *be* my papa."

"I still am, Gabriel."

The boy curled his lip. "Do tell, sir."

Lord, Fletcher thought, he's more his mother's son than
mine. Sybil's sour look was stamped on Gabriel's features;
her imperious voice was echoed by the boy's. And, as Sybil
often had, Gabriel kindled Fletcher's temper.

He flashed a stormy gaze at Jessica. She bit her lip and
fixed him with a pleading look. Don't, she seemed to beg.
Don't. He's only baiting you. Hearing the message as clearly
as if she'd spoken, Fletcher glanced away. He composed himself quickly and reached into his pocket again.

"I brought you some of your arrowheads from Holland
Hall," he said mildly, holding them out to Gabriel. "Do you
remember, you used to collect them?"

Gabriel kept his hands at his sides. "I don't want a lot of
silly bits of rock carved by some savage."

Fletcher swallowed hard. He'd always dreamed of the day
his secret work for the Mohawk would be over and he could
reveal his heritage to Gabriel. He wanted the boy to feel pride
in being a *kehro:non'*. But obviously Sybil had fed him
enough falsehoods about the Mohawk to destroy the boy's
regard for his ancestry.

Masking his hurt, Fletcher forced a smile. "I'll keep them
for you, son. In case you want them later." The sharp-honed
flints bit into his flesh as his hand closed around them, but the
real pain stemmed from Gabriel's rejection.

Jessica felt her insides melt at the look on Fletcher's face.
His smile was genuine, but shadows of desperation haunted
his eyes. His desire for his son's acceptance was powerful

and obvious. Despite his outrageous threats the previous night, Jessica understood Fletcher's behavior. He needed Gabriel, and whether the boy realized it or not, Gabriel needed Fletcher.

Clasping her hands tightly in front of her, she fought an overwhelming urge to grab Gabriel by the shoulders and shake him. Can't you see how you're hurting him? she wanted to yell. But she held her tongue. It was up to Fletcher and Gabriel to grapple with the animosity between them.

"May I be excused now, sir?" Gabriel asked coldly.

Fletcher seemed about to protest, but Gabriel wore his anger like battle gear. At his father's slight nod the boy marched from the room.

Fletcher stared at Jessica with those too-blue, pain-filled eyes. "Is he always like that, Miss Darling?"

"More or less. Mr. Danforth, you mustn't take it personally. Gabriel is angry at the world. And at himself."

Fletcher gave a small, humorless laugh. "Of course I take it personally. The boy is my son."

"Please, give him time. He's still not used to the idea that you're back in his life."

"I am back. Permanently. I'm going to the Pynchons about the matter right away."

Jessica knew the Pynchons would resist but said nothing. Her employers treated her well and were a decent family, although from overheard arguments and snippets of conversation, she realized Gabriel's wealth meant more to them than the boy himself. Hester never missed an opportunity to belittle Gabriel or point out his shortcomings.

"I expect, Miss Darling," Fletcher said icily, "that you'll support my right to take my children home."

She felt herself go cold inside. His words were civil enough, but she detected a threat in his tone. The message was clear: if need be, he would use what he'd learned about her last night to ensure her cooperation.

"Of course, sir," she said with soft resentment.

"I was hoping you wouldn't be so foolish as to resist me in this," Fletcher said, swirling his brandy in his glass.

"And we," Hester said imperiously, "had hoped you'd be reasonable, Fletcher. The boy might have been born a colonial, but he's been raised as an Englishman. He's renounced his savage roots; it would be cruel to take him away from the life he knows. The *family* he knows," she added pointedly.

"Why is it, Hester, that I doubt your sincerity?" Fletcher's voice shook with quiet rage.

"Ahem—See here now," Charles blustered, reaching for his snuffbox. "You cannot speak to my wife that way."

Fletcher leveled a cold gaze at Charles Pynchon. "I'd talk to you, Charles, if you didn't have your nose constantly buried in your snuffbox."

"By God!" Charles coughed. "You've the nerve of the devil to come into my house and insult me like that. I ought to throw you out—"

"Will you, Charles?" Fletcher smiled darkly. "Would you pit yourself against a man who's spent the last five years fighting for his life at a military post?"

Charles's nostrils began to twitch in alarm. "See here, Danforth, no need for us to be at each other's throats. We all want what's best for the boy."

Hester nodded emphatically. "It's not the inheritance, no matter what you say." She gave a slow, feline smile, looking so like her sister that Fletcher's breath caught. "But perhaps it *is* the money after all. *You* are the one who covets it, Fletcher. Just to prove your greed, why don't we settle this?" She tapped a long fingernail on the arm of her chair. "Name your price. What will it take for you to go back to the colonies and leave us in peace? Five hundred pounds? A thousand?"

Fletcher surged to his feet. The murderous gaze he sent Hester made her recoil in fear. With an effort he controlled his rage. "I could offer you ten times that amount," he said through clenched teeth. He thought he saw Hester's breathing quicken. "But I will not," he added. "A father need not buy children who rightly belong to him."

"Then we are at an impasse," Hester retorted.

"For the time being, perhaps. Gabriel and Kitty may stay on here while I . . . make arrangements. I intend to settle an annuity of two thousand pounds on each of them, regardless of the outcome of those arrangements."

The avid look that crept into Hester's eyes sickened him. "I might add that the annuities will be administered by trustees of my choosing. And you know better than to expect I'd choose you.''

Hester's eyes narrowed, but she said nothing.

"I intend to visit," Fletcher added. "Frequently."

"See here now," Charles began in his tiresome way.

"I won't allow it!" Hester burst out. "Those children are terrified of you, Fletcher, and with good reason. You are not welcome in our home."

Fletcher started to rise in anger against his sister-in-law's interdict, but he decided not to embark on yet another argument. There would be plenty of time for squabbling later, if it came to pressing his claim in Chancery Court.

Glaring at his wife's kin, Fletcher realized he didn't want to visit the Pynchon house any more than they wanted him there. But he would see his children. He had an ally, albeit an unwilling one, who would help him accomplish that objective. Jessica Darling wouldn't cross him in anything he did.

Because she had a secret. And she'd do anything to keep the Pynchons from finding out about her other life.

Kitty's childish laughter trilled up from the bank of the pond in New Wells, mingling with the liquid cooing of pigeons and the soughing of the spring breeze through the water poplars lining the banks. A few moments later Gabriel's low murmur took on a musical tone.

Both Jessica and Fletcher, who were sitting on a tattersall blanket some yards distant, looked expectantly at the boy. But he wasn't even smiling. Instead he merely seemed to be explaining something about the boats he'd fashioned from the flower-de-luce plant.

Jessica went back to her cutting, adding a few last flourishes to the silhouette she was making. Taking a card from her fruitwood case, she brushed a thin film of paste over the surface and affixed the silhouette.

"Does my son never laugh?" Fletcher muttered.

She looked up to see him glowering at Gabriel. Despite her resentment at having been forced to deceive the Pynchons to meet Fletcher, her heart wrenched at the pain in his voice. "Not really. Not since I've known him." Boldly she added, "You don't laugh much either." Seeing his dark brow descend, she added hastily, "But Gabriel is good to his sister. They squabble often enough, but that's normal."

Setting her scissors and paste aside, she held up the pair of cards she'd just completed. "Do you like them?"

Still staring at his children, Fletcher said, "Of course I like my own children, Miss Darling. Did Hester lead you to believe—"

"The silhouettes, Mr. Danforth," Jessica interrupted, trying not to smile.

"The what?" He swiveled around and for the first time gave her his full attention. His blue eyes focused on the silhouettes and she heard his breath falter. His face became a study of silent longing and urgent need. The uncompromising fierceness of his features gave way to poignant vulnerability. At that moment Jessica almost forgave Fletcher for using her. His need to be with his children was more powerful than her need to conceal her past.

"My God, Miss Darling. They're beautiful."

"You have beautiful children, Mr. Danforth."

"Yes. Yes, I do." He took the cards from her and studied them closely. Jessica felt inexplicably nervous as he perused her work. She wanted him to be pleased, perhaps because she sought in him a sensitivity that would excuse his high-handed use of her.

"Lovely," he pronounced at length. "I can't explain it, but you've managed to capture their very essence—Kitty's chubby chin, Gabriel's fine nose and the way his hair falls over his brow. And they weren't even sitting for you."

"I've a whole drawerful of silhouettes of Kitty," Jessica explained. "Gabriel never would sit for me, but one time I managed to pit him against the butler at chess to keep him still for a while."

Fletcher nodded and Jessica was gratified that, at least for a moment, he seemed to relax. "May I keep these?" he asked.

"Of course, Mr. Danforth. I meant them for you."

His smile sent a rush of warm, fluttery sensations through her. Nonplussed, she took up her scissors and tissue to occupy her hands. Fletcher went back to watching the children. He leaned against a water poplar, giving her a sharp view of his profile.

As of their own accord, her fingers began to shape his portrait. Idly she wondered if she might discover more of his quiet personality in this way; silhouetting often gave her a new perspective on her subject. Her artist's eye appreciated the utter perfection of his features—the strong line of his jaw, the unexpected curve of his lips, the straight angle of his nose. With growing interest she shaped the spill of hair over his brow, then angled her scissors back down to the cropped locks in back.

As she worked, warm sensations seeped through her blood. He was more than simply a series of curves and angles; she caught herself looking beneath the handsome exterior of Fletcher Danforth, seeking the man within. She wondered what lay beneath his tanned skin, behind his cold blue eyes. And suddenly, so suddenly she nearly severed the portion of his stock her scissors were busy outlining, she began to wonder what it would feel like to touch that coppery skin, that rumpled spill of ebony hair.

A breeze lifted from the pond, cooling her flushed cheeks. He's a man, she told herself firmly. Little different from the men who had used her mother; very much like those who threw away small fortunes at Madame's.

With a quick clip, Jessica finished the silhouette and affixed it to a card.

Fletcher was still gazing at his children in that intense, devouring way.

"Here you are, Mr. Danforth," she said, handing him the portrait.

Distracted, he turned to her and took the card, scowling down at it. But when he looked up, he began to smile. The stern lines of his face softened; his mouth curved, transforming a merely handsome face into a visage of dark beauty, arresting and impossible to resist. Her heart fluttered; it was a smile she'd thought existed only in dreams.

"I . . . I hope you like it."

Fletcher studied the portrait again. "Do I really look like that?"

Jessica cocked her head. "I think it's rather a good likeness."

He laughed and the sound rippled over her like liquid

warmth. ''That mop of hair?'' he asked. ''That thunderous brow? My God, I look like the very devil himself.''

''A very handsome dev—'' Appalled at herself, Jessica clamped her mouth shut. She knew better than to comment on a man's looks. Indeed, she'd never thought to say such a thing to any man. She glanced at the portrait again. The likeness was there, but something was missing, she realized. Often in depicting a subject, she came to know the person within. But not this time. Fletcher Danforth's silhouette was on the paper, but his unique essence had eluded her skill.

He was looking at her oddly. ''Miss Darling, you're a talented artist. Where did you learn your craft?''

''I . . . Madame Severin taught me. She was adept at silhouettes before her joints stiffened with rheumatism.'' Jessica flushed and looked down at her hands. More than once in the past two weeks Fletcher Danforth had used what he thought he knew of her association with Madame Severin to force her to arrange meetings with his children. He was wrong about her, of course, but the Pynchons would never tolerate even a hint of scandal. ''These were Madame's scissors,'' she said nervously, showing him the silver stork device. ''She's left-handed, as I am.''

''The lady has given you a thorough education, then.''

Jessica looked up. His smile had disappeared behind hard lines and icy blue eyes. Defensively she drew herself up. ''As a matter of fact, sir, she did.'' She pursed her lips, remembering all the hours she'd spent perfecting her French and poring over volumes of Rousseau and Rabelais.

''I see,'' he said tautly. ''Then you are a woman of many talents.''

Jessica frowned at the derision in his voice. Why was his disapproval of her so pronounced? Surely by now Fletcher Danforth had realized her role at the bawdy house was completely innocent.

''I like to think so,'' she said, unnerved by her thoughts.

Fletcher picked up the scissors and examined the emerald eye of the stork. ''Have you ever done a self-portrait?''

''I . . . no, of course not.''

''Why not?''

''I suppose I don't consider myself a very interesting subject.''

He handed her the scissors. "Why don't you try it?" She balked, and he added, "I'm sure Kitty would like to have a memento to take to Holland Hall. She seems fond of you."

Jessica glanced over at the little girl, who was still watching with delight as her brother's lateen-rigged flower-de-luce boats scudded over the pond's surface. Suddenly the idea of losing the little girl—and even her troubled brother—made Jessica wistful. Feeling somewhat foolish, she selected a piece of tissue and set her scissors to the delicate paper.

She smiled shyly at Fletcher, who leaned back on one elbow. And, strangely, she felt comfortable.

"I'm afraid I don't know where to start," she said, staring at the paper.

His smile was slow and lazy. "Come now, you can't mean you don't know what you look like. Women spend hours studying their faces in the mirror until they've memorized every pore."

Annoyed that he considered her shallow and vain, as he seemed to believe all women were, and angered that he was being arrogant and superior, as all men seemed to her, she scowled. A curl strayed from her hair net; self-consciously she tucked it back into submission.

"Are you an authority on women?" she asked tartly.

"Hardly. Your species baffles me, Miss Darling. However, some habits are easily observed."

"I confess I haven't the time to stare at my reflection. Even if I did, I can think of many more interesting pursuits."

"I don't doubt that you could," he said meaningfully.

She bristled at his sarcastic tone. "Think what you will, Mr. Danforth. Far be it from me to try to change your opinion." The curl stubbornly reappeared on her brow.

"My, but you're prickly, Miss Darling. You shouldn't be. You may be surprised to know my opinion of you has improved, because of your obvious concern for my children." He nodded at the scissors and paper in her hands. "Humor me with a portrait now. Perhaps you could start with that ridiculously stiff-looking lace collar."

Jessica tossed the hair out of her eyes and set to work. The collar and throat were easy; her neck was hardly unique. Having executed that part of it, she hesitated.

"You look baffled, Miss Darling," he said. "Perhaps I

can help . . . Your chin is, if you'll pardon me, rather pedestrian. Slightly rounded, quite firm. A bit stubborn."

Jessica's hands worked independently of her mind, which was preoccupied with the fact that Fletcher's voice had dropped to a soft undertone and he was examining her with an assessing eye. She took a deep breath and finished the chin.

"Now your lips," Fletcher murmured.

Her scissors began sculpting a mouth. He stopped her with a light hand on her arm as she began drawing the paper toward her in an inward curve. "Not so fast, Miss Darling. Your lips are much fuller than that." He lifted his hand and let his finger trace her mouth with a feather-light touch. "You see," he explained, seemingly oblivious of the mortified flush staining her cheeks, "you're no thin-lipped spinster, despite your prim manners."

At his touch Jessica went numb all over. She tried to will herself to slap his insulting hand away; instead, she merely continued cutting.

His hand traveled upward over her astonished face. "You've a pert little nose," he said, tracing its contours. "Just a tiny upturn here." His finger paused. "Suitable for holding high in the air to indicate distaste. Ah, yes, you've perfected the attitude."

Jessica's throat constricted. "Mr. Danforth. . ."

"Just keep working, Miss Darling. I'm rather enjoying this art lesson." His finger moved on. "A high, clear brow," he remarked. "Reminds me of a medieval lady. Oh, and don't neglect to include your eyelashes. They're quite remarkably long, you know."

Jessica resisted the urge to sigh with relief when, mercifully, his hand left her face. She was amazed at how steady her hands were as they finished cutting.

"A pity you neglected to capture those charming wisps of hair around your face," Fletcher said. "I'll wager you've a veritable tumble of curls beneath that confining net."

Feeling self-conscious, for she'd always regarded her wild hair as a flaw, Jessica put down her scissors and glued the silhouette to a card, waving it to dry.

Fletcher took it from her. "Very nice," he murmured, but he wasn't looking at the portrait.

Feeling flustered, Jessica gathered her things into her case and stood up. She glanced over at the children, who had begun squabbling about the little boats.

"They're tired, Mr. Danforth. It's been a long day."

He nodded and stooped to fold the blanket. "I trust you'll be able to arrange another meeting."

Jessica swallowed. "I shall try, Mr. Danforth. For the children's sake. If you mean to take them off with you, I would have them go willingly."

"As would I, Miss Darling."

"The Pynchons seem intent on making it difficult."

He looked at her sharply. "They've discussed it with you?"

"I am a trusted member of the household," she informed him. "Matters that concern the children are often brought to my attention."

"I mean to take Kitty and Gabriel home, where they belong, Miss Darling." His voice was taut with determination. "And I am not a patient man."

Jessica stifled a gasp. "Surely you wouldn't simply . . . spirit them away."

He chuckled. "Such scruples," he said, a mocking bite to his words. Before she could form a proper retort, he waved his hand. "Don't worry, Miss Darling, all shall be done in accordance with the law. I've already retained a barrister and instigated proceedings. Although I hardly need the Lord Chancellor to confirm my right to my children, I want no shadow of impropriety hanging over them."

Legal proceedings could take months, Jessica thought with a sinking feeling. Months of secret outings, of enduring Fletcher Danforth's disturbing presence. Her settled way of life was in peril because of this man. And yet, as she watched him amble down the bank toward the pond, she caught herself thinking that the outing had been a good deal more agreeable than an afternoon in the schoolroom with the Pynchon children.

"Miss Darling, I'd like a word with you," Mrs. Pynchon said.

Jessica froze in mid-motion, then rose slowly from the table where she'd been sitting, listening to the children's grammar lesson. "Carry on, Gabriel," she murmured, feeling a burn of guilt in her cheeks. The boy glanced at her sharply, blue eyes narrowed. So far he hadn't revealed their secret outings to his aunt, but Jessica couldn't fully trust his discretion. Gabriel's complicity was due more to his animosity toward his aunt than to loyalty to his father.

Stiff-legged, she joined Mrs. Pynchon on the staircase and followed her into the parlor. Her mouth felt dry and her mind worked sluggishly. Silently she cursed Fletcher Danforth. She wasn't made for deception, yet these past weeks he'd forced her to live with it. Would she now be called upon to defend her actions to her employer?

The pale-eyed gaze Mrs. Pynchon leveled at her didn't look accusatory. Still, Jessica braced herself. "Yes?"

"We're going to Lincolnshire tomorrow," Mrs. Pynchon said. " 'Tis long past time I settled my sister's affairs there. The house will undoubtedly need attention as well."

A sigh of profound relief almost burst from Jessica. Instead she held her expression benign. "Yes, ma'am."

"Have the children packed and ready to leave in the morning." Mrs. Pynchon frowned. "I don't relish a trip of several weeks with that infernal boy, but there's no help for it."

Jessica pursed her lips. Mrs. Pynchon's dislike of Gabriel grew more pronounced every day. The boy tried to bear her petty, stinging comments with equanimity, but Jessica knew he'd wear the scars for a long time.

As always, the thought of Gabriel triggered a feeling of compassion. And the feeling gave birth to a reckless idea.

"Mrs. Pynchon," Jessica said hurriedly, "with all due respect, perhaps you'd best reconsider taking Gabriel and Kitty to Lincolnshire. Seeing the scene of their mother's death would be painful for them. Kitty has just begun to overcome her nightmares."

Mrs. Pynchon hesitated, toying with a bead on her dress. "Your point is well taken, Miss Darling, but I'm afraid they must accompany us."

"Not necessarily." Jessica flushed at her own boldness. "I could remain in London with Kitty and Gabriel, while you and your husband could take Amy and George to Lincolnshire."

"No; it wouldn't be proper."

Suddenly Jessica felt a desperate need to convince her em-

ployer not to take Kitty and Gabriel to the place where they'd
seen such horror. She was aware that another reason lurked
in her mind, but she refused to acknowledge the benefits
Fletcher would derive from the Pynchons' absence.

"We'll be fine, ma'am, truly. Mr. Sedgewick and Mrs.
Stearns can manage the household, while I see to the children. And think of Amy and George. For six weeks now
they've had to share their rooms and your attention with their
cousins. They're too young to understand that Kitty is fragile
and needs coddling, that Gabriel is hurting and needs attention. They understand only that their rooms have been in-
vaded by uninvited strangers and that I must divide my
attention among four children instead of two. Surely they'd
be glad to have you to themselves for awhile."

"You nearly have me convinced, Miss Darling," Mrs.
Pynchon said. "But you are forgetting one matter of impor-
tance."

"Yes, ma'am?"

"Fletcher Danforth." She spat the name insultingly.
"Thank God he hasn't troubled us these past weeks, but I'm
not convinced he's given up. I don't trust the man, Miss
Darling, don't trust him at all."

"He'd not do a thing to harm those children!" Jessica's
hand flew to her mouth; the defensive words were out before
she could stop them.

Mrs. Pynchon looked at her curiously. "You sound quite
certain."

Jessica wove her fingers together, willing herself to meet
the lady's eyes. "I just . . . had the impression Mr. Danforth
loves his children deeply."

"That, perhaps, is the most dangerous thing about him."

Jessica nearly laughed, but quickly realized Mrs. Pynchon
wasn't jesting. "I'll watch the children closely, ma'am, and
the Dunstans are just two doors down. . . ."

Eventually Mrs. Pynchon agreed. Jessica realized it had
been easy because her employer had really wanted to be convinced.

Jessica was satisfied yet hardly content. Fletcher Danforth
would undoubtedly be overjoyed to be rid of his wife's rela-
tives. But the deception made Jessica nervous.

*   *   *

She knew the moment Fletcher arrived. She was in the schoolroom on the second story, but the footsteps on the stairs were too heavy to belong to Mrs. Stearns, too quick to be those of Mr. Sedgewick. She was aware of a vague inner fluttering, a feeling akin to the one she'd had in the park two days before when Fletcher had traced her profile with his finger.

A flush stole to her cheeks and she tore her mind from the memory, trying to concentrate on a sample of Gabriel's penmanship. His paper was a mass of blotted scrawls. As Jessica set out a clean sheet of foolscap and prepared to summon the boy back to his practicing, a frown furrowed her brow. Nothing had been the same since Mr. Danforth had arrived. Lessons used to be pleasant affairs; Kitty and Gabriel were gifted learners and Jessica a competent teacher. Now each was distracted, each in a different way, by Fletcher.

She felt a sudden wave of compassion for the Danforth children. Their lives had been turned inside out, first by their mother's death, then by their father's reappearance.

She moved across the room to Kitty. The little girl had propped her rag baby in a chair and was sitting a few feet away, doggedly chopping away at a piece of paper with blunt-nosed scissors.

Kitty looked up, beaming. "I'm making a silhouette of Esme," she said importantly.

"Very nice," Jessica murmured, keeping her smile grave. Kitty took her artwork seriously and expected others to do the same. Jessica stroked the child's silk-spun hair and moved to the window seat where Gabriel sat, slumped as usual, reading a book. His pose spoke of withdrawal. He hugged his knees to his chest and poked his nose deeply in the pages.

Jessica recognized a volume of Swift's essays. Gabriel enjoyed them, she supposed, because he was precocious enough to appreciate Swift's ascerbic wit and subtle parody.

Gabriel glanced up at her. His eyes glittered with anger and something Jessica recognized as fear. "He's here," the boy said tonelessly.

Jessica caught her breath. "Yes," she said.

"Why does he keep coming? Why doesn't he just go away?"

"Gabriel, he's your father. He wants to be with you."

He snorted and turned his face toward the window. Jessica clasped her hands behind her back, resisting the impulse to reach out and stroke his tense shoulders, to soothe the bright red weal on his cheek. Hester had struck him with her lilac switch the day before, when he'd likened his uncle to a certain part of a horse's anatomy. Although the Pynchons' timely departure for Lincolnshire created problems for her, she was pleased Gabriel had gained a reprieve from his aunt's punishments.

"He left us five years ago," he muttered. "Does he expect everything to be the same now?"

"I'm sure your father knows better than that. But you're not being fair to him, Gabriel. You've hardly given him a chance to—"

She saw the boy's eyes grow hard and broke off, knowing without turning that Fletcher had stepped into the room.

"Hello, Papa," Kitty piped.

Slowly Jessica faced him. The hands clasped behind her back began to twist with nervousness.

Kitty set down her scissors and stood up slowly, crumpling her paper against her chest with one hand and seizing Esme with the other. She glanced back at Jessica, who gave her an encouraging smile. The child walked toward her father.

Fletcher went down on one knee and stretched his arms out toward Kitty. "Hello, sweetheart," he said, hugging her. Jessica watched him dip his head into Kitty's soft curls. He breathed in the fragrance and seemed wracked by emotion. Jessica still found it hard to believe that a man so strong and sure of himself could look so uncertain.

He appeared to gain control as Kitty showed him the jagged silhouette she'd made of Esme.

"You'll be as good with those scissors as Miss Darling one day," he commented, and looked at Jessica for the first time.

She stared back, startled by the warmth in his eyes. Spring had arrived in those frost-colored depths. Smiling, she inclined her head.

With Kitty clutching one of his long brown fingers, Fletcher crossed the room. "Hello, Gabriel," he said.

" 'Lo," Gabriel grunted and looked away.

Fletcher's smile seemed to stiffen, but his voice remained

pleasant as he strolled to the writing table and picked up
Gabriel's copy sheet. "That writing looks like a mouse has
been playing in your ink." Kitty giggled; Gabriel scowled.
"I never wrote with a good hand myself," Fletcher admitted,
as if imparting a grave secret. "When I was reading law at
the Inns of Court I had to hire a clerk to put all my notes in
order." '

For a moment, interest lit Gabriel's eyes. Quickly he
snuffed it and looked back at his book.

"Really?" Kitty asked. "You used to live in London?"

"Aye. Years ago. My father sent me over to board at Harrow and I didn't go home for a very long time."

Jessica listened, as fascinated as Kitty. She felt a little wistful too, envisioning Fletcher as a youth, thousands of miles
from home. If Gabriel's appearance was any indication,
Fletcher Danforth must have been an uncommonly handsome
boy. His looks as a grown man were no less devastating.

Warming to her father, Kitty pushed a book toward
Fletcher. "We've been reading about the savages in the colonies. Have you seen any savages, Papa?"

Gabriel's derisive snort cut through the air. Baffled, Jessica
turned to see the boy staring at his father with a thoroughly
unamused grin.

"Aye, Kitty, I've seen many of the natives of America,"
he said. "Even though England has claimed the land, the
Indians are its true lords and masters." He bent to page
through the book.

Jessica detected a flush in his cheeks as he looked at Sam-
uel Colby Smythe's history of the American Indians. Mystified by his abrupt change of mood, she watched him peruse
the volume. A tic leapt in his jaw as he contemplated a wood-
cut of a half-naked, paint-streaked savage, tomahawk raised
over the head of a white infant. His fingers nearly rent the
page as he paused to study a caricaturelike drawing of a chief-
tain, teeth bared, rings in his ears and nose.

Although Kitty exclaimed delightedly over the pictures,
Jessica had the distinct feeling that Fletcher was offended.

"Oh Papa, look!" Kitty squealed, pointing at a drawing
of Indians circling a stake where a bearded man was about
to burn. "Is that what Indians do?"

He snapped the book shut. "I'll tell you all about the Indians one day, Kitty, but now I must speak with Miss Darling.'' His smile looked forced, although the kiss he placed on the girl's head was affectionate. ''I thought I smelled seed-cakes baking. . . .''

Grabbing her doll, Kitty bounced from the schoolroom. Fletcher eyed Jessica coldly, then approached Gabriel.

The boy rose. ''Good-bye, sir,'' he mumbled and started for the door.

Fletcher's hand shot out. ''Stop, son.'' He held the boy's arm and bent close to study the welt on his cheek.

''What's that?'' he demanded tautly.

Gabriel wrenched away, his eyes as cold as his father's. ''Nothing,'' he retorted. ''At least, nothing I didn't deserve.'' He ran from the room, slamming the door behind him.

Jessica felt the outraged blast of Fletcher's gaze and for a moment words failed her. He stood there like a great, avenging archangel, obviously thinking she'd struck his son. She wanted to explain, but she was pinioned by that frigid glare staring out of a face gone dark with fury.

He stepped toward her; she stepped back.

''Mr. Danforth. . .'' There. Somewhere she'd found her voice, and somehow she didn't sound as flustered as she felt. ''Please, let me explain—''

''I'm not interested in your explanations.'' His voice was quiet and calm, yet heavy with threat. Jessica was coming to associate his quietness with fury. Here was a man whose anger was too intense for bellowing.

''But—''

''I said I'm not interested, Miss Darling.'' His jaw tightened and his hands gripped the rim of a ladder-back chair. A lock of midnight hair fell over his tanned brow. He looked magnificent . . . and menacing. ''I want nothing from you,'' he continued evenly. ''You're a fraud of the worst sort, Miss Darling, yet it seems I'm the only one who's discovered that.'' His gaze shinnied insolently down the length of her. Feeling violated, she folded her arms.

''You begged me to keep your secret the night of the fire,'' he said. ''But I will not protect a woman who abuses my son.''

''A . . . abuses your . . . But I . . .'' Emotions seethed

through her, not the least of which was indignation at his insults, but for the life of her, Jessica couldn't find words to combat his mistaken accusations.

"Aye, Miss Darling. Unless you agree, right here, right now, to keep your ignorant attitudes about Indians to yourself, and to keep your damned lily-white hands off my children, all London will know your secret. Is that clear, Miss Darling?"

"I . . ."

"Is that clear?"

Anger pounded through her, banishing all hesitation and all good sense. "You have made yourself perfectly clear, Mr. Danforth."

"Excellent." His face closed. He pivoted and strode toward the door.

"Just a moment, Mr. Danforth." Jessica was pleased at her steady, imperative tone. "I demand that you listen."

He glared back at her, his hand on the doorknob. "You forget your place, Miss Darling. A paid servant, especially one who intends to keep her position, may demand nothing of me." He jerked the door open.

Outrage lent wings to Jessica's feet and stripped away the ladylike ways she had worked so long and hard to acquire. She flew across the room and planted herself in front of him, barring his exit. "Well, I got somethin' to say to you, you bleedin' high-handed sod!" Only after the words were out did she realize her speech had degenerated into the crude accents of her childhood. But she was too angry to care about the astonished look on his face. "You aren't so bloody smart," she raged. "Did it ever occur to you that you might be wrong about some things?"

"But I wasn't wrong about you, Miss Darling, was I?" he asked scathingly. His furious gaze took her apart.

"You bloody well—"

Insolently, he placed a finger over her lips to silence her. Outrage rocketed through her, heating her blood. "Careful," he said mockingly. "Your lack of breeding is showing."

Before she could muster a dignified reply, he picked her up by the waist as if she were no more than an annoying puppy and set her aside. Then he strode from the room.

Jessica laid her hands on her cheeks, feeling the flames of

anger there, and sagged against the doorframe. She became aware of the tumble of corkscrew curls around her ears. Like her voice, her unruly hair had betrayed her.

Not for years had she slipped into her childhood speech patterns when someone was listening. But this man, this rude, arrogant colonial had ignited a fury in her that drove her past all caution.

As her agitated breathing evened out, she sought to reason with herself. Why should she care that Fletcher Danforth thought ill of her? He was obviously the sort to draw conclusions without bothering to check his facts first. The man's opinion didn't matter a blessed whit to her.

But as she turned back to the schoolroom, to lose herself in the mindless task of scrubbing slates, she vowed to prove herself better than the kind of woman he so erroneously and unfairly judged her to be.

Chapter 5

Jessica bent and tied the bonnet ribbons beneath Kitty's chubby chin. "Adorable," she pronounced, dropping a kiss on Kitty's brow. Gravely the child held out Esme; dutifully Jessica kissed the doll as well. "You'll both be the prettiest girls in all London," she said, and Kitty beamed.

Watching them in the foyer of the Pynchon house, Fletcher was assailed by conflicting feelings. Jessica's every gesture toward his children spoke of affection and caring, yet the knowledge that she'd raised her hand against Gabriel filled him with angry distrust.

She turned to hand Gabriel his gloves. "Do behave for your father today," she admonished. She spared a brief glance for Fletcher, her eyes the color of winter mist.

"Please have them back before dark, Mr. Danforth," she said. "London at night is no place for children."

Her coldness had an odd effect on Fletcher. He missed the luster of her smile. Using anger as a hedge against regret, he said, "Your authority on that topic is already clear to me, Miss Darling."

She glared. He moved toward the door before regret could take hold of him again.

Kitty clutched at Jessica's hand. "You mean you're not coming with us, Miss Darling?"

Still glowering at Fletcher, Jessica said, "No, Kitty."

"B . . . but I *want* you to come," the little girl said, pressing against Jessica's skirts and casting a worried look over her shoulder.

Gabriel began shifting agitatedly. "I don't care to go at all, then," he stated. Then, as if to correct any wrong impression, he turned to his father. "I'm not afraid of you, but Kitty'll whine all day for Miss Darling."

Fletcher gritted his teeth. He drew a deep breath, then said, "Get your things, Miss Darling. It appears you must come along if we're to go at all."

She bristled visibly at his imperious tone. She hesitated; then as she looked at the children, Fletcher saw her sense of duty win out. "Of course," she said crisply, "far be it from me to forget my place. I'll fetch a wrap." As she left the foyer, anger stiffened her narrow back and imparted a regal tilt to her head. And unaffected femininity lent a graceful sway to her hips.

Hugging her rag baby, Kitty lifted huge brown eyes to Fletcher. "I'm sorry you're angry, Papa."

He knelt beside her, suffused by love for his daughter. "It's all right, sweetheart," he told her gently. "We just need time to get used to each other, don't we?"

Behind them, Gabriel made an unpleasant snort.

"Just like I got used to Miss Darling," Kitty said. "You're not going to take us away from her, are you, Papa?"

Fletcher swallowed hard against a sudden upsurge of resentment. Miss Darling must have done some serious manipulation indeed to make his little girl so dependent on her. "I'll do as I think best, Kitty."

"But we *need* her, Papa," Kitty insisted. "Esme and I can't go to sleep until she tucks us in. And she's the only one who can stop Auntie Pynchon from punishing Gabriel."

"What?"

His harsh inquiry made the little girl flinch. "Well, when Auntie switched Gabriel, Miss Darling stopped her. She took the switch away and broke it right over her knee."

Fletcher straightened up and stared at Gabriel. The imprint he'd seen on the boy's cheek the day before had faded to a faint pink. "Is this true, son?" Fletcher asked tautly.

Gabriel shrugged and turned away. "I'd rather suffer Aunt's switch than Miss Darling's blather."

"You're just cross because Miss Darling made you apologize for calling Uncle Charles a . . . a . . ." Kitty paused, searching for the correct phrase. ". . . a horse's ass!" she chirped, puffing up with childish pride.

Fletcher choked, battling a storm of laughter. He suddenly

felt light and airy as his anger abruptly disappeared, to be replaced by warmth for Jessica and regret that he'd accused her. Never had he been so pleased to find himself in the wrong. "Gabriel," he said, "is that what happened?"

The boy shrugged. "I guess so."

Although gratified by his discovery, Fletcher felt deeply concerned that someone other than himself had disciplined his son. No longer, he decided with sudden urgency, would he keep his visits a secret. The Pynchons would return home to find him fully in control of his children, as he should have been these five years past.

"Are we ready, then?" came a clipped voice from the hallway. Miss Darling appeared, drawing on a pair of kid gloves. A somber gray cloak fluttered around her trim figure. Without waiting for an answer, she sailed to the door. She stood there, staring pointedly at Gabriel until he held the door open for her. Fletcher suspected from Gabriel's shuffling gait and his recalcitrant attitude that he and Miss Darling had clashed more than once over his manners.

Taking Kitty by the hand, Fletcher followed them out. With surprising finesse, Gabriel handed Jessica up into the hired coach. When they were all settled, Fletcher tried to catch Jessica's eye, to somehow communicate to her that he now knew he'd been wrong. But she pointedly kept her gaze fastened on the staid elegance of Dover Street and the festive sights of Shepherd Market in the distance.

"Where shall we go?" Fletcher asked.

"St. Bartholomew Fair," Gabriel said immediately. He always made the same suggestion.

And Jessica always disputed it. "I think not, Gabriel. St. Bartholomew Fair is no place for a family outing."

"But I've never been. I'm bored with the pleasure gardens and teahouses. We always go there."

"The fair can be dangerous," Jessica said. She knew that all too well. Years ago her mother used to take her there. The fair was a likely place to cut a purse or two, perhaps to find a well-heeled toff to bring back to the garret for an easy hour's work. Jessica had been too streetwise to land in any serious trouble, but she'd had a few close scrapes with the rogues who frequented the area.

"It's not a good idea to go there without proper protection," she explained.

"Actually," Fletcher said quickly, "the children might enjoy St. Bartholomew Fair. It could prove quite educational." So saying, he signaled the driver and the coach turned.

Jessica scowled at him. Damn the man, she thought bitterly, seething. Damn him and his overblown male pride. He'd undoubtedly taken her comment as a personal challenge. Under different circumstances she might have been amused to see just what sort of protector the fine Mr. Danforth would make, but bringing the children to St. Bartholomew Fair was foolishness.

While Jessica scowled, Fletcher smiled. The expression was so rare and so damnably appealing that she almost forgot to continue frowning. She wondered at his sudden change of attitude. Perhaps at last he realized the absurdity of his belief that she'd abused Gabriel.

At the entrance to the fair they were greeted by the sounds of Belphegor's concert; the rumble of drums mingled with the squeak of penny trumpets. Kitty clapped her hands with delight at the kaleidoscope of color and sound. Gabriel perched on the edge of his seat, peering at the rows of booths and strolling performers in the crowded streets.

As they stopped at Hospital Gate, Jessica began to think she was the only one who noticed the lottery pickpockets scurrying furtively through the crowd, darting in and out of convenient houses.

A sly-faced youth eyed Fletcher's pocket, took one look at its owner, and hurried off as if eager to choose an easier victim. Jessica found herself staring thoughtfully at Fletcher. As he lifted Kitty down from the coach, she realized his fluid strength and quickness of movement were enough to put off the roughest of thieves. She was safe with him.

Then Fletcher turned to her. She had no time to escape his grasp. Holding her by the waist, he brought her to the ground. Jessica tried to move away, but he held her fast.

"Just a moment, Miss Darling." He was so close his breath warmed her ear. She caught a whiff of the fragrance she was coming to recognize as uniquely his: the spice of his cologne mingling with a less tangible scent, which brought to mind forests and trees.

Feeling unsettled, she looked at him. "Yes?"

"Why didn't you explain about Gabriel yesterday? Why did you let me believe you'd taken a switch to him?"

Jessica's eyes widened. "If you'll remember, Mr. Danforth, you hardly gave me a chance." Again she tried to move away; his hands tightened around her waist.

"I'm not so reluctant to apologize to you as my son was to Charles," he said gruffly. "I'm sorry, Jessica."

She didn't know which stunned her more—his sincere apology or his easy use of her given name. The feeling that stole through her was oddly pleasant. "Mr. Danforth, I—"

"The Merry-Andrew!" Gabriel called suddenly as he caught sight of the actor dressed in the multicolored costume and cap of a jester. He grabbed Kitty's hand and moved into the surging crowd.

Jessica found her own hand in Fletcher's, and once again a warm, protected feeling crept through her. They followed the children toward the Merry-Andrew. The air was tainted by tobacco fumes and singed with the smell of overroasted pork.

Dressed in tinsel robes and golden leather knee-high buskins, the "quality" of the fair strutted in a sly imitation of royal stateliness. Then appeared the Merry-Andrew himself. His first jest was a singular instance of cleanliness. Leaning over the rail, the imp-faced player blew his nose on the crowd, pleasing the raucous onlookers mightily. Gabriel guffawed. Kitty giggled into Esme's woolen head. Fletcher looked faintly amused. Jessica was disgusted.

The Merry-Andrew clapped his hands. "Walk in, walk in!" he cried, inviting them inside the theater tent. "Take yer places, while ye 'ave 'em; the candles are lighted and we are goin' to begin."

They found a bench near the back, none too clean. Fletcher smiled at Jessica's outraged expression. He took off his frock coat and spread it on the bench, inviting her to sit. She grinned. "Apologies and gallantry too, Mr. Danforth? My, but you *are* contrite."

"I don't mind admitting when I'm wrong."

A shrill cry of "Nuts and damsons!" reached them as the vendor passed by. At Kitty's excited request, Fletcher bought a basket of the treats. He took the little girl on his lap and cracked filberts two at a time in his strong brown hands. To Jessica he offered a damson plum from the round basket. She declined and waited for the play to begin. Gabriel made short work of two plums.

The farce consisted of a parade of particolored fools, singing dwarves, dancing devils, and drooling idiots. Old Prate, the archetypical evil stepmother, evoked a wave of hilarity with her antics.

The only pleasure Jessica derived from the play was in watching the children. Gabriel enjoyed the outrageous jests immensely, devouring fruit and filberts and laughing uproariously. Kitty looked content and comfortable on her father's lap, shedding her reticence like a shy bird uncertainly sampling seed from the palm of a human hand.

A rag-clad man scampered up, holding out a sheaf of papers. "Tabloids from Grub Street," he offered. "Gossip! Court news! Tuppence'll get ye enough for the whole family."

While Fletcher cheerfully parted with his coin, Jessica's mind fixed on the hawker's words. To an outsider, they were a family. Content in her settled, unmarried life, Jessica had never mourned the lack of kin. Yet for the first time she wondered what it would be like to be a wife and mother. An absurd notion reared up, a notion that there were worse fates than having a husband like Fletcher and children like Kitty and Gabriel.

No, she thought frantically, clinging to her dislike of men and her vow to live as an independent woman. No.

They left the Merry-Andrew's theater and with a great deal of elbow labor scrambled through the throng. Cries rose up from vendors and the many stalls crowded together on every side: "Flag brooms! Knives to grind! Cucumbers to pickle! Here's rare Holland socks, four pair a shilling!"

The crowd was thickest at Pie Corner. Fletcher lifted Kitty up, holding her with one arm. His other hand rested at the small of Jessica's back, warming her with its firm pressure.

At Pie Corner, cooks stood sweating in the doorways, slapping at the flies buzzing around crocks of sticky sauces. They bellowed to the crowd, each extolling the excellency of his pig and pork. Carcasses, already half-baked by the sun, hung on hooks in the shop windows.

Peering into one of the kitchens, Jessica noticed a fat fellow who appeared to be the overseer of a roast. He stood shirtless by the pit, rubbing his neck and armpits with the same wet cloth he applied to the meat to prevent it from blistering. At one time Jessica would have been grateful even for a tainted morsel in her empty belly. But now her stomach was used to more delicate fare.

"Hungry?" Fletcher asked her in a teasing voice.

"Please, no," she said faintly, her expression of disgust eliciting a chuckle from him.

A tinkle of music sounded. "Let's go see the dancing girls," Gabriel urged.

Fletcher put a hand on his shoulder. "Not so fast, son. You're not . . . er, Kitty's not old enough."

"But they look so pretty," Kitty said, craning her neck to see the gawdy gowns of the rope and sword dancers.

"No," Fletcher said firmly. To distract them, he paused and bought cakes for the children from a wandering ginger man.

Nearby, a drink-roughened voice bawled out: " 'Ere's yer chance t'see a genuine savage Indian from America! But keep yer children close; 'e's wild as the land what spawned 'im."

Jessica had no wish to view the spectacle and was about to say as much to Fletcher. But the look on his face drove the words from her mind. A shadow seemed to drop over him, changing his congenial expression to one of fierce anger.

"Mr. Danforth," she said, "I really don't think the children should—"

"Come along," he snapped. He promptly propelled Gabriel in the direction of the canvas-clad booth and clamped his hand around Jessica's wrist. She nearly stumbled trying to keep up with his purposeful strides.

The hawker grinned as they approached; the grin disappeared as Fletcher shouldered past without paying the requisite fee. An embarrassed Jessica was yanked into the booth.

"Mr. Danforth," she said again, "surely you can spare the man his fee. He's only trying to make an honest living."

"Honest?" Fletcher bit out. "Would you have him turn a profit from enslavement?"

Jessica's eyes adjusted to the dimness. A knot of onlookers

was gathered around a raised dais. Manacled to a stool was a leather-clad, feather-decked man.

"Ooh, Papa, I'm scared," Kitty breathed, her chubby hand clutching Esme. "A real Indian!"

Gabriel studied the earthen floor. "I don't want to stay here," he said sullenly. As if he hadn't heard him, Fletcher set Kitty down. "Mind your sister, son," he said curtly, and plunged through the crowd toward the dais.

Confused by his anger, Jessica followed. People stepped aside to let him pass. Fletcher bent close to the Indian, who saluted him with a toothless grin. Iron-bound hands raised a bottle of gin; the Indian's leathery throat worked as he swallowed.

Fletcher spoke in low tones to the man. The Indian looked surprised, then hid his face behind his bottle. Fletcher spoke again. The drunken man spat a stream of gin and saliva at his feet.

The booth man elbowed his way forward. "What's this?" he demanded angrily. "The spectacle's for payin' customers!"

"Aye, move aside," another man shouted. "You're blockin' me view."

The Indian let loose with a deluge of confused syllables. To Jessica's relief, Fletcher began making for the exit. Hurrying to catch up, she said, "Mr. Danforth, I do not understand your interest in this man."

He looked at her as if just remembering her presence. "No," he said in a low voice. "You wouldn't understand. A Huron," he muttered. "Still, it grieves me to see him so."

Wondering what in the world a Huron was, Jessica fell into step with Fletcher. As one, they looked at the corner of the booth where they'd left Gabriel and Kitty.

And saw only strangers.

"Oh, Christ," Fletcher said. "Where the hell are they?" His fingers bit roughly into Jessica's shoulders. "I thought you were watching them."

Pierced by sudden fear, she looked at him wildly. "I turned my back for only an instant—"

"An instant is all it takes for them to get lost." Pausing only to grab Jessica's hand, he plunged into the street, calling

the children's names. ''How the hell could you be so irre-
sponsible?'' he demanded.

She tried to pull out of his grip. He hauled her back, saying, ''Oh no, I'm not losing you too.'' They set off through
the traffic-clogged street, eyes probing the crowd for a sign
of Kitty and Gabriel.

The next fifteen minutes were the longest and most fear
ridden of Jessica's life. Terrified visions reared up in her
mind, pictures of cutthroats, child snatchers, evil folk who
performed murder for sport. Only half conscious of her action she squeezed Fletcher's hand hard. He glanced down at
her and she saw her own terror mirrored in his eyes.

''They wanted to see the dancing girls,'' she said, suddenly remembering the children's request. Fletcher nodded
and dragged her toward the music booths. Kettle drums, fid-
dles, and trumpets clanged and scraped over a din of voices.

''Roll up,'' called a hawker. ''See the belle of the Orient
dancing with six naked rapiers! And another, English as your
mother's terrier, a-dancin' with fourteen glasses balanced on
'er . . .''

Jessica caught sight of one of the dancers. A head of
saffron-colored hair bobbed in front of the booth. Even more
distinctive than the hair was the woman's eye patch.

Jessica clutched at Fletcher's arm. ''There's someone who
can help,'' she said. She brushed past two jabbering young
women in straw hats and clog-like pattens.

''Nan!'' she called. ''Nan Featherstone!''

An instant later she was folded against her friend's sweaty,
pillowlike breasts. ''It's our Jessica Darling,'' Nan said delightedly. ''An' don't you look the lady—''

''Nan,'' Jessica interrupted, ''we've lost the children.''

Nan drew back. ''Your young charges?''

Jessica nodded miserably. ''A boy and a girl.''

''Handsome children? Nicely tricked out?''

''Yes! Have you seen them?''

Nan pulled her to one side of the booth. Jessica glanced
back to see that Fletcher was following, annoyance etched
hard on his face. But his annoyance turned to relief as, rounding the booth, they found Kitty and Gabriel with Jade Akura.

Torn between scolding and weeping, Jessica fell upon
them. ''We were so worried,'' she choked out, feeling weak.

Fletcher opted for the scolding. "Gabriel, how dare you go off like that!"

"I didn't want to stay and gawk at some drunken Indian," the boy replied, not the least contrite.

Unaware of the panic she'd caused, Kitty squirmed away and beamed at Jade. "Isn't she pretty, Miss Darling?"

"Am I now?" Jade said with a grin. "All paste an' gewgaws, truth to tell." She jangled her bracelets and fluttered her fraying skirts.

"She taught Gabriel a coin trick," Kitty said. "Do it again, Gabriel! Do it again!"

Ignoring the flare of annoyance in his father's eyes, Gabriel produced a shilling from his pocket, tossed it nimbly, then spread his hands to show they were empty.

"See, Papa," Kitty piped. "Guess where it is?"

Grinning, Gabriel leaned down and plucked the shilling from Kitty's bodice. The little girl giggled and clapped.

In spite of herself, Jessica burst out laughing. Only Fletcher's stern expression silenced her. Still, she caught a sparkle of humor in his blue eyes.

Jade smiled at Fletcher. "There now, it's all worked out for the best. I figured these two might belong to someone who prizes them."

"No doubt you hoped to ransom them," Fletcher said cuttingly, his face stern again.

Jade's almond-shaped eyes glittered with resentment. She was nothing, Jessica knew, if not scrupulously honest. "See here now, mister—" Jade began.

Ever the peacemaker, Nan stepped in. "Hear that, Jade? Our music's started. We're on." She took Jade by the hand and moved to the front of the booth.

"Can we stay and watch them, Papa?" Kitty begged, clambering into his arms. "They were ever so nice to us."

Relief had driven the fury from him. With surprising indulgence he agreed, and they joined the audience. The music rose to a cacophonous crescendo and the dancing began.

Jade performed a nimble sarabande, captivating the crowd with her exotic beauty and feats of skill and daring as she perilously wove her way between the gleaming swords. Nan bounced about with glasses full of liquor balanced on the backs of her hands.

The dancing was not a great departure from their other profession, Jessica reflected. Jade and Nan were consummate performers, whether convincing one of Madame's shy patrons that he was the epitome of masculine virility or pandering with clever moves to a noisy throng.

But Jessica knew her friends well enough to recognize the brittleness in Nan's laughter and the forced quality of Jade's pasted-on smile. After the dance, they worked the crowd for coins. "It's hack work for sure," Jade muttered as she accepted a shilling from a bystander, "but we 'ave to feather our nest somehow. Can't keep draggin' after Madame."

"How is Adele?" Jessica asked.

Jade shrugged. "Gettin' right fidgety, she is. Says she's enjoyin' 'er retirement, but I know better, I do. Age aside, she ain't ready to be countin' her pension."

"Is she planning on starting her . . . business again?"

"No, nothin' like that," Nan said confidently. "but she does need somethin' to occupy her. . . ."

"Miss Darling." Fletcher's imperative tone snared Jessica's attention. "I think we'd best be going." A muscle in his jaw began to twitch. He obviously disapproved of his children's fascination with the dancers.

A mutinous feeling gripped Jessica. He might well be disdainful of Jade and Nan, but they were her friends and she refused to discount that friendship because of his prejudice. What did he know of the kindness these women had shown her?

Jade and Nan were saying their farewells to the children. "Ain't they a fine-lookin' pair," Nan said. "Jeezuz, but the lad's got the handsome look of his pa about him. Eh, Gabe?" She gave his cheek an affectionate pinch. The boy reddened to the tips of his ears.

Hearing Fletcher clear his throat meaningfully, Jessica embraced each women heartily. "Keep well, you two," she said. "Tell Madame I'll call on her."

A barked order from the master of the booth set Jade and Nan back to the task of working the crowd.

"Ladies," Fletcher said curtly. His sarcastic tone indicated clearly that he thought of Jade and Nan as anything but ladies. He bowed and turned away, but not before he performed a coin trick of his own. Jessica was certain she saw him deposit a gold crown apiece in their silken bags. Lord, the man was a riddle to her.

Taking Kitty by the hand, Jessica started back through the fair. She caught Fletcher's eye and couldn't resist sending him a sugary smile. "You did say, didn't you, that an outing to Bartholomew Fair would be an educational experience?"

He glowered. "We obviously differ on the definition of 'educational.'"

"What would you have had me do?" she snapped. "Should I have sailed away without even a word of thanks?"

"They wouldn't have noticed the slight."

"Why? Do you think they're without feelings simply because of their profession? I will not slight my friends," she added stubbornly.

"I don't mind your association with their like," he replied with an excess of patience, "but until I take my children home to America, I'd rather you be more discreet."

She cocked an eyebrow. "As you have been, sir?"

He bristled at the obvious reference to his presence at Madame Severin's on the night of the fire. "Don't provoke me, Miss Darling," he said through clenched teeth.

Jessica tossed her head. She avoided speaking as they made their way back to the Hospital Gate. Gabriel paused before an array of knives. The grinder extolled the qualities of his wares in animated superlatives.

"Choose one, son," Fletcher said.

Gabriel shot him a look of suspicion. He seemed torn between his desire for a knife and his reluctance to allow Fletcher the pleasure of giving him a gift. Quickly, before Gabriel could speak, Jessica picked up a bone-handled penknife. "This is a fine one," she remarked.

Gabriel shook his head vigorously, seizing another knife. "This has a much better blade and the hinges work more smoothly," he proclaimed. "The best of the lot."

"Very well," Jessica conceded. She smiled sweetly at the vendor. "We'll take this one."

"One and ten," the man said, grinning at the outrageous price and clearly expecting them to haggle.

"Done," Jessica said. She glanced at Fletcher, who looked slightly baffled. "Pay the man, Mr. Danforth."

Fletcher did so, with uncharacteristic good humor. Grinning, he counted out the coins and added a few extra for a fine leathern case with a strap to be attached to a belt.

Jessica caught Gabriel's eye and gave him a meaningful stare until the boy succumbed to her silent command. Looking up at his father, he mumbled, "Thank you, sir."

"You're welcome, son. Just be careful with it. A knife can be dangerous."

"I know," the boy rejoined in annoyance.

Fletcher drew Kitty to his side. "There now, what do you suppose we can find at the fair for you, sweetheart?"

Kitty's eyes grew wide and round, and her ringlets bobbed as she looked to and fro at the crowded booths and overloaded carts. As they wove a path through Cow End Lane, she clung to Fletcher's hand. They paused at a toyman's stall.

"Oh Papa, look," Kitty breathed, pointing at a little mechanical monkey on a wooden rod. The toyman, who looked as playful and impish as his wares, obligingly demonstrated the toy. Kitty nodded politely but soon lost interest in the monkey as she perused the other toys. Undaunted, the toyman held up a doll. "This 'ere's Pretty Poll, I calls 'er. All tricked out with ribbons and knots, fine as you please."

Kitty gave serious consideration to the Bartholomew baby but clutched her rag doll against her breast. "I don't think Esme would like that at all."

"Take your time, poppet," Fletcher said fondly.

While Gabriel fidgeted beside her, Jessica watched bemused. Fletcher seemed as grave and contemplative as his daughter as they discussed the merits of a carved elephant with tiny ivory tusks, a fluffed dog, a brightly colored top. They considered and discounted each toy in turn, much to the chagrin of the toyman.

A tinkling sound from the crowd disturbed their perusal. Kitty turned and spied a grandly dressed young lady turning the handle of a music box. The little girl's eyes lit up.

"Have you a music box like that?" she asked the toyman.

His gamin smile disappeared and he folded his lips together. "Ain't never seen the like," he grumbled.

Only Jessica saw Fletcher slide a shilling across the counter. Immediately the toyman's smile returned.

"Well now," he said agreeably, "Will Bowling, up at the

top o' Cloth Fair Street, 'e gives 'em away as prizes for the stone casting.''

Fletcher led them up the street. Jessica doubted he would succeed at the stone-casting game; in her youth she'd often watched the gamesters. The ''rocks''—clay ovoids cleverly weighted to fly askew—rarely found the bull's eye at which the contenders pitched them. But then, Fletcher appeared to be a man of considerable means and doubtless his coin would make up for whatever skill he lacked.

They reached the gaming booth. Jessica remembered the proprietor from her youth; she recognized the slyness of his smile and the slight twitching of his hands when he saw the well-turned-out Mr. Danforth approaching. ''Roll up, sir-rah,'' Will Bowling called. ''A prize for castin' the bull's eye.''

Kitty bounced up and down. ''Will you win me a music box, Papa? Will you?''

He patted her head. ''I'll certainly try, poppet.'' He lifted her up to sit on the railing for a better view.

Jessica considered warning Fletcher that the rocks were weighted, but something in the supremely confident tilt of his chin warned her off. Feeling as skeptical as Gabriel looked, but as hopeful as Kitty, Jessica watched.

Fletcher removed his frock coat and absently handed it to her. Unthinkingly she moved her hands over the fine fabric and inhaled the warm, woodsy scent of it. Catching herself on the verge of fondness for this volatile, vulnerable man, she forced her attention to the game.

Fletcher selected a stone and took aim at the distant bull's eye, a painted circle centered in a leather basket. Jessica felt her cheeks grow warm at the absorption on his face and the magnificent play of muscle and flesh beneath his white cambric shirt as he drew back his arm. The weighted stone wobbled, struck to the right of the target, then tumbled to the ground.

''That's all right, Papa,'' Kitty said quickly. Gabriel snorted.

Grimly Fletcher slapped another coin on the rail. He tossed the second stone in the air, studied its flight, and took aim once again. It landed with a thunk in the leather basket of the target, exploding into shards of dull red clay.

Kitty squealed and jumped down from the rail, then hugged Fletcher's leg in a clasp of pure affection. Even Gabriel's eyes lit with admiration and he seemed to be battling an unbidden grin.

"Well done, Mr. Danforth," Jessica murmured as Will Bowling grudgingly allowed Kitty to select a music box from his tray of prizes. The children promptly bent their heads over the music box to hear its merry Maying tune.

Fletcher picked up another stone. "I believe my coin entitles me to another shot," he said.

Bowling scowled but made way for Fletcher's third attempt, which was successful. "Claim yer prize," Bowling grumbled.

Fletcher's hand found Jessica's back and he urged her forward. "Take your pick, Miss Darling." Victory seemed to have put him in an expansive mood.

Flustered, she held back. "Really, there's no need—"

"No," he agreed, taking his coat and shrugging back into it. "But humor me."

"It's not proper," Jessica said, suddenly and inexplicably fearful.

"Then allow me," he murmured and took a tiny glass vial from the tray. The vial held a nosegay of violets. "I believe," he said, stepping forward, "this is known as a bosom bottle. No lady should be without one."

Jessica could neither breathe nor move as he parted the folds of her cloak and tucked the bottle into her bodice. His nearness and the intimacy of the gesture sent shock waves thundering through her. "Thank you," she murmured nervously, ducking her head to hide a mortified blush.

And then she scolded herself for acting so flustered. Lord, only a ninny would fail to recognize that the gift was no more than a casual gesture. It was not as if he'd offered her his heart on bended knee.

During the ride home, Fletcher no longer sat alone in the opposite seat. Kitty had climbed unhesitatingly to his side and nestled her chin against his sleeve, cradling both Esme and her new music box in her arms. Brown eyes shining, the little girl leaned up and gave her father a shy kiss.

Jessica was touched by Fletcher's indulgent smile and

Kitty's beaming countenance. As the child whispered something into her father's ear, Jessica realized why she was so moved, what she was seeing. Kitty was falling in love with her father. In all her twenty-one years Jessica hadn't missed having a father as she did at that moment. The lack of a loving relationship felt like a cold, hollow spot deep within her. Blinking fast, she glanced down at the violets nestled against her bosom.

The rolling motion of the coach soon had Kitty slumbering in her father's arms. Gabriel succumbed too, his handsome face softening with sleep. "Exhausted," Jessica said. "And as happy as I've ever seen them."

"I can agree with you about Kitty," Fletcher replied. "But Gabriel . . ." His expression turned brooding.

Jessica brushed a lock of hair from the boy's brow. "His needs are much more complex, Mr. Danforth. You'll win his affection eventually, I'm sure of it. Why, he could hardly contain himself when you hit the bull's eye."

"You're very observant, Miss Darling."

"I pay close attention to the children because I care about them. Sometimes what Gabriel doesn't say is as telling as what he does say."

He looked at her closely then, studying her with no trace of insolence or mockery. She wondered what he was thinking as his eyes moved over her in leisurely fashion. His lips were poised at some indefinable point between smiling and seriousness, lending him a look of mystery. Although she could think of no name for the manner of his scrutiny, she grew warm and restive beneath his gaze.

When they reached Dover Street, Jessica moved to awaken Gabriel. Fletcher's fingers closed around her gloved hand. "Wait a moment, Miss Darling. I wonder if you'd come out with me tomorrow."

"That's not proper," Jessica objected.

His mouth twitched with amusement. "Neither of us is very proper, my dear. However, I assure you, my intentions are not what you think. I want to buy books for the children to take to Holland Hall. There's a bookstall in London Spa that I remember from my days at Gray's Inn. I'd like you to help me choose some titles."

Amazed at the thoughtfulness of his idea and flattered that

he valued her opinion, Jessica relaxed. "Of course, Mr. Danforth. What time shall I have the children ready?"

"Actually, I want the books to be a surprise. You could leave the children in Mrs. Stearns's charge for a few hours."

Nonplussed and battling a feeling of pure pleasure, Jessica said, "Very well, Mr. Danforth. I don't mind helping where the children are concerned."

The smile that had been lurking on his lips finally showed itself. "Excellent. I'll call for you at four."

Jessica stared across the arched footbridge at Fletcher, wondering if he knew how much time she'd spent getting ready for their first outing alone. Fletcher stared back at her, wondering if Jessica knew how utterly adorable she looked with that sweet, quizzical expression on her face.

She felt plain and drab in her starkly tailored dress of somber indigo. He felt glad she hadn't swathed herself in fussy lace and garish ribbons.

"A fine hour's work," Fletcher announced. "the books will be delivered to my lodgings in the morning."

"You were rather . . . extravagant," Jessica said.

"I've five years to make up for," he replied, a slight catch in his voice.

And that, Jessica realized, was what drew her to him despite his opinion of her. He loved his children with a devotion that stirred her and made her long to drive the sadness from his eyes.

"Yes, well," she said, "we'd best be going then."

"Actually, I thought we'd stay awhile. The broadsheet posted at the gate announced an illumination to begin after sunset."

Jessica started to object. It was one thing to help him select books for the children, but another matter indeed to play the companion for an evening at the spa. Still, the loneliness etched on his face tore at her heart. He had no friend in London; he was thousands of miles from his home.

"I'd like to watch," she murmured.

Fletcher crossed the bridge and they fell into step along a path shaded by climbing shrubs and sycamores. He offered his arm in a gesture she attributed to inborn gentility. Her gloved hand fit neatly in the crook of his elbow. She noted that her forehead reached no higher than his shoulder and that his strides were far longer than hers.

London Spa and New Wells attracted a diverse crowd of modish sparks and fashionable ladies, young ensigns and templars and sempstresses in tawdry finery. The walks were peopled by strutting beaux with scarlet-ribboned swords and ladies fragrant with powder of orange and jessamine.

Jessica had never found the London pleasure gardens to her taste. Before, she'd only thought of them as places where light-fingered knaves waited to relieve gentlemen of their gold repeater watches, or where a gambler with his cogged dice stood, looking cynical, at the open-air gaming table. She used to understand that type, but tonight she felt a kinship with the other strolling couples. She enjoyed the music of the fiddle and Jew's harp and admired the clever arrangement of the mazes.

"I've not had my supper yet," Fletcher said, stopping in front of a tavern on Rosoman Street. "Will you join me?"

Jessica nodded. As she waited outside, she refused to let herself consider the unseemliness of consorting with Fletcher Danforth. What harm could one evening possibly do?

A basket held between them, they returned to the pleasure gardens. Fletcher paused at a secluded green bower at the top of a sloping bank. "The fireworks will issue from across the pond," he said, gesturing.

Jessica stared at the ivy twining in an arch over the bench that sat in the bower. The springtime smells of fresh earth and budding flowers wafted to her. "Isn't this a bit isolated?" she asked softly.

He laughed. "I doubt there's a single spot in all London I'd consider isolated. I'm an American, Miss Darling. I know places where a man can ride for days at a time without meeting another living soul." He took her hand and seated her on the bench, then reached into the basket.

"Plum cake," he said, handing her a serving wrapped in cheesecloth. "And a napkin for milady?" He also took out a jar of sweet syllabub for her to drink and one of bottle ale for himself. "There's burnt port for later," he added, "in case we feel the need to warm ourselves."

His very proximity made her quite warm enough, but she merely said, "Thank you," and swallowed, uncomfortably aware that their conversation sounded absurdly formal. She knew little of how to behave in the company of a man. Fletcher's long, assessing stare and his disarming smile didn't help her in the least.

The sun slipped away and twilight purpled the sky. A nightingale called softly and doves cooed intimately in the arbors. Cherry blossoms exuded a sweet breath of fragrance as the wind stirred the branches.

"I wish I'd brought my case," she remarked. "The tea-house across the pond would be interesting to depict in silhouette. I wonder if I could capture its reflection in the water. . . ."

He looked at her curiously. "Do you always see everything with an artist's eye, Miss Darling?"

"I never took note of the fact." She broke off a piece of plum cake. "I suppose I do tend to notice shapes and shadows, the interplay of light and dark." She sipped her sylla-bub, noting that the creamy drink contained a larger measure of wine than cream. "Do you never look at things so, Mr. Danforth?"

He shook his head. "I'm afraid I lack your imagination."

She thought it an odd thing to say. Fletcher Danforth possessed qualities that would be enviable in any man, yet he appeared not to hold himself in high regard. Perhaps it was because of the charges brought against him five years earlier, which she still didn't understand; he hadn't offered to share the facts with her. Or perhaps Gabriel's continued resentment made him feel unworthy.

Feeling a peculiar sympathy for Fletcher, she drained her syllabub and let its sweet warmth creep through her veins. "Tell me about your home, Mr. Danforth. What is it like in the colony of New York?"

He glanced at her quickly, as if surprised she'd be interested in his background. "I live on a river called the Hudson, north of the town of Albany. My land is home to a number of tenants, but in the distant mountains, the forests are so thick that only trappers and Indians venture there."

Aware that Indians were, for some reason, a sore subject, Jessica asked about his house. "Is it built of logs and wattle, with a packed-earth floor?"

He chuckled richly. "I'm afraid not, Miss Darling. Happily, Holland Hall does have a few modern amenities."

Remembering that he wanted little in the way of money, she blushed. "I'm sorry."

"I understand, Miss Darling. If the library in the schoolroom is any indication, your information about the colonies is less than adequate."

"Perhaps sometime you could give me a more accurate picture of America, Mr. Danforth." Pleased that he no longer held her responsible for her ignorance, Jessica smiled.

He stared at her, seemingly fascinated. "That smile," he said, "ought to be packaged and sold as a tonic for melancholy."

She laughed, feeling happy and suddenly nervous. Unaccustomed to compliments, especially from gentlemen, she didn't quite know how to respond. He seemed distracted by the smile lingering on her lips. "You've a bit of cream from the syllabub there," he remarked in a husky voice. Lifting a napkin, he gently dabbed at the corner of her mouth.

Jessica's face warmed. She was suffused with feelings that reminded her of the day he'd asked her to cut her self-portrait. His hand left her mouth and came to rest on the curve of her waist. She couldn't take her eyes from him. His intent expression and the subtle warmth of his hand lulled her senses. When a water rocket exploded in the distance with a sudden burst of sound, she was caught off guard.

"Oh!" she cried and found herself pressing against the expanse of his chest. Instantly his arms encircled her like a warm, protective cocoon. Mortified at finding herself so abruptly in his embrace, Jessica started to pull away.

His arms tightened. "Oh no, Miss Darling," he murmured against her hair, "stay a bit. You wouldn't deny a man the satisfaction of acting the valiant protector, would you?"

Placing her hands against his chest and trying to ignore the sensation of the rippling muscles and thudding heart beneath his shirt, Jessica said, "I'm behaving like a ninny. The explosion merely took me by surprise." She felt foolish and flustered. As a girl she'd endured less agreeable surprises without flinching. Yet the nearness of this man reduced her insides to the consistency of spooned pudding.

"I'm quite all right, Mr. Danforth," she murmured, wishing she hadn't imbibed the syllabub so quickly, then wishing she'd eaten more plum cake to absorb the effect of the liquor. "Does nothing ever surprise you?"

"Aye," he said. "You are a surprise, Miss Darling." His hands began a slow, evocative movement over her shoulders and back. "I came to England expecting to battle my wife for the children. Instead I found them in the charge of a woman whose smile disturbs my sleep, whose art fills me with admiration, and whose very identity still mystifies me."

Another rocket flared, then descended with a plummeting whistle. Ignited by Fletcher's words, Jessica's insides seemed to sparkle and spin like a Catherine wheel in a fireworks display.

His fingers climbed to the downy tendrils escaping the neat confines of her snood. Encountering a brass hairpin, he frowned slightly, then removed the pin.

"Mr. Danforth!"

"Hush," he said, drawing out two more pins. "Cold metal objects have no business being embedded in something as soft as your hair." A few more pins dropped with metallic pings to the stone bench. "Besides," he continued in that soft, seductive murmur, "I've always been curious about your hair. There's no hiding its lovely peach-gold color, but this damned net keeps its texture and shape a mystery." The last of the pins fell. "A rather intriguing mystery." With a swift movement he freed her locks from the netting.

Mortified, Jessica felt a riot of curls spill over her shoulders and down her back. In mere seconds Fletcher Danforth had divested her of the hairstyle Madame had spent months perfecting to hide the unruly coils and to affect a more proper aspect. She felt as if he'd stripped her naked.

Ineffectually she tried to put her hair into some sort of order. "Sir, I wish you hadn't done that," she snapped.

He caught her hands in his, drawing them downward, allowing the curls to fall freely. "Why not?" he asked, studying her with eyes gone suddenly hot. "You look charming." He fingered a curl next to her cheek, pulling it gently to its full length and then watching it spring back into disorder. "I thought a woman considered a beautiful head of hair her crowning glory."

"This woman," she said unsteadily, "considers it her own property and not a plaything for any man."

He chuckled, looking handsome and skeptical. "What an odd thing for you to say, Miss Darling, considering you've offered much more than your curls as a man's plaything."

She gasped. He drew her closer yet, his arms unyielding, his face hard with purpose. "I should very much like," he murmured warmly against her ear, "to amuse myself as others have before me."

Before a protest could erupt from her, he brought her chin up and laid his lips over hers. Her mouth, which had been opened to deliver a stinging retort, was now open to the shocking exploration of his tongue.

Fletcher's intent to kiss her into submission continued with growing pressure. Her hands fluttered helplessly, then came to rest on his chest. Curiosity joined an overpowering range of sensations seeping through her veins. He couldn't know that this was her first kiss. In spite of her anger Jessica grew weak and pliant in his arms. She prayed he wouldn't guess the rousing effect his kiss had on her.

She tried to cling to her outrage, to use anger as armor against the sensual assault. But her ignorance in such matters was an enemy and Fletcher's kiss held all the urgency of a desperate conquest. As the sparks from the fireworks faded away, so did her resistance. Instead of fighting him she was suddenly leaning against him, intoxicated by the taste of bottle-ale he now shared by rimming her lips with his tongue. Her eyes fluttered shut; whistles and explosions and the smell of sulphur careened through the air all around them.

Her reeling senses gave birth to a sweet, burning hunger that she understood only insofar as she knew he was capable of assuaging that hunger. She became aware of him in ways she'd never been aware of a man before. Not until this moment had she ever considered the feel of surging muscle, warm and alive beneath starched and spearmint-scented broadcloth. Never had she imagined the crispness of cropped hair over a stiff collar or the way scents seemed to cling to his flesh. And never, not even in light of Jade Akura's bawdiest remarks, had she imagined a man's lips could impart such heady pleasure.

Clasped firmly in his arms, her mouth slack and submis-

sive beneath the interminable kiss, Jessica felt weak and warm
and wanting all at once. Her protests had ceased, but a thread
of reason still lingered in her mind.

Jessica clung to that thread, reinforcing it with common
sense. She'd spent four years of her life preparing for the
secure life she led. Now she was allowing this man, this
brash, rash American who thought her a whore, to turn her
into a plaything to toy with until he tired of her.

Armed with righteous indignation and fear of losing her
respectable position, Jessica freed herself from the embrace
with a great heave. Pulling away, she managed to cast herself
to the ground. "Bloody hell," she muttered.

Her skirts hiked up above her knees, the heels of her hands
braced against the cool grass, Jessica had a sudden urge to
cry. She attempted to achieve a more ladylike pose.

But Fletcher was quicker. He pulled her to her feet and
wrapped her against him. This time they were standing, and
she now felt the full force of his body against hers.

Jade had often made ribald sport of a man's body, treating
the outward evidence of masculine desire with amusement.
Unhappily, Jessica found nothing amusing in the electrifying
solidity pressing against her shuddering frame.

His fingers played through her hopelessly tumbled hair and
his lips explored her ear, teeth nipping teasingly. The warmth
of his breath ignited a fire in her and sent shivers of pleasure
shimmering through her.

"The game of cat and mouse is an old trick, love," he
whispered, "but it has never been to my liking." His tongue
curved into her ear. "Be still, my beauty."

"Please . . ." Jessica was shamed by her tremulous plea.
Infusing her words with conviction, she said, "I'm not what
you think I am. . . ."

"Oh, love," he said, running his hands down her sides,
"you do play a clever game. How many times were you
passed off as a virgin at Severin's?"

Hurt and humiliation sent her heart to her knees. "Never,"
she swore. *"Never."*

"Really?" He bent and sampled the flesh at her neck.
"Should I be flattered, then, that you've chosen to try a new
technique on me? You're really very good, my dear. If I didn't

know better, I'd flatter myself into thinking I'd had the honor of giving you your first kiss.''

Burying her pain beneath her pride, she wrenched from his grasp, planting her feet firmly and setting her hands on her waist. ''You flatter yourself indeed, Mr. Danforth, if you think I'd submit to you at all, allow you to seduce me freely right here in this garden.''

''Freely?'' His eyes took on a cynical cast. ''Perish the thought. Of course I'll pay you, since that's what you're used to. But I was afraid it might be in poor taste to dicker over pounds and pence in a moment of passion.''

She nearly choked on a great inrush of air. Only a short time ago, she'd actually felt sympathy for him. Now fury blinded her with sparks brighter than the showering fireworks. Outrage rendered her speechless but made her feel suddenly strong and glaringly alive, as if her rage could move mountains. She clenched her fists and her eyes kindled hotly. ''I won't play the cheap kitchen maid for you.''

He brushed his knuckles over her heated cheek. ''Ah, but you like to play.''

She knocked his hand away and took a step back.

Looking amazed and amused, Fletcher spread his hands in a conciliatory gesture. ''I see,'' he said smoothly. ''Time for the obligatory slap. Where would womanly virtue be without it?'' In fact, he'd anticipated her next move precisely. For that reason Jessica forced herself to relax, letting her fingers go slack.

''I'd like nothing better than to slap that lascivious grin from your face, Mr. Danforth, but I won't,'' she said with much more composure than she felt. ''I wouldn't sully my hand on your arrogant face.''

To her utter chagrin, he laughed. The low, seductive sound of his mirth bathed her senses like too-sweet wine. ''I know why you're angry, Jessica,'' he said. ''It's because you desire me, isn't it?''

''Certainly not,'' she hastened to lie.

He reached for her again; she took a step back. ''You shrink from me because you're afraid of your own feelings.''

''I am not,'' she retorted. ''I find you . . . disturbing.''

''You liked the way I kissed you,'' he said, his voice as soft, compelling, and dangerous as a sorcerer's spell. ''Your mouth opened beneath mine like a bud unfurling. I felt your flesh heat and your breath quicken.''

''You caught me off my guard, Mr. Danforth. It shan't happen again.''

He caught her chin in the curve of his finger and smiled knowingly as a hot tremor rippled through her. ''We'll see about that, Jessica.''

Chapter 6

Jessica lay in her narrow, tidy room and despaired. Deep inside her, Fletcher Danforth's kisses had spawned something frightening and unwanted, fiery longing and a mysterious, seductive ache that attacked without warning and without mercy. Sometimes the hot, humiliating feelings came stealing unannounced when she was tidying the schoolroom after lessons. Other times a wave of intense yearning surged at the very height of activity, during supper or on an excursion.

And always the new, forbidden feelings were present when Fletcher Danforth was near. She tried to exorcise the longing with stern self-lectures, declaring herself a fool for responding to the lust of a man who considered her a whore and would accept no explanation to the contrary.

Day by day she struggled to keep her feelings in check lest anyone discover the change in her. Her pride suffered greatly. She'd always considered herself immune to animal desires; she'd been proud of the fact that no man held sway over her. Yet here she was, breathless, helpless, and sleepless, the victim of the very emotions she disdained.

She shifted uncomfortably on her cot, the linen sheets rustling. At least he hadn't touched her again after that disastrous night in London Spa. He'd behaved with utmost decorum when they'd taken Kitty and Gabriel to the penny opera in Drury Lane, to view the zoological wonders at New Wells, and to the May Fair, which turned the neighborhood around Dover Street into a rowdy bazaar.

But beneath his correct demeanor lurked subtle, heated looks. Was he truly as insolent as he appeared, or had she only imagined an unspoken message in his hard blue eyes?

Did he mean to sound so sarcastic as he complimented her on her coiffure, or had she become oversensitive? Jessica could hardly object to his manners without seeming absurd or shrewish. And she was loath to cross him . . . because she couldn't trust him not to expose her past to the Pynchons.

Drawing a deep, weary breath, she suffered in silence and ached in the privacy of her pristine little room off the nursery.

"Simply outrageous, that's my opinion," Maude Dunstan declared, holding out her glass for a footman to refill with sherry. "Why, Hester, dear, 'tis a good thing you arrived back from Lincolnshire before that Danforth fellow did anything rash. The man is woefully mistaken if he thinks English justice will allow him to take those children away."

Hester expelled a long sigh. "I quite agree, Maude—"

"But I do not." Fletcher Danforth filled the doorway of the drawing room. He nodded briefly at the visitor, who looked more overstuffed than the chair she occupied. The lady blanched and her chins quivered. She seemed in dire need of a burnt feather under her nose to keep her from fainting.

Fletcher focused his piercing glare on Hester. "I've business with you and your husband," he said curtly. "Now." Turning, he stalked to the library.

A Meissen porcelain clock, festooned with cupids and ribbons, ticked annoyingly on the mantel. Trying to control his impatience, Fletcher strode the length of the Turkey carpet. For two frustrating months he'd been in London, bent on a task he'd once thought would take only hours to complete. Foolishly, he hadn't reckoned that reclaiming his children would be so fraught with obstacles. Everything had seemed so damned simple when viewed from his cell at Fort Orange.

Motivated by greed and malice, the Pynchons were determined to retain control of Gabriel and Kitty. They'd woven a strong web, a web of half-truths and manipulation designed to bind his children to them. And, damn it to hell, one of the strongest strands was that cheap, hypocritical little governess, Jessica Darling.

Her rejection stung more hotly than he cared to admit.

Fletcher thrust his hands into his pockets, certain he'd damage something in the elegant room if he allowed his thoughts and his hands free rein. He felt as taut as a drawn bowstring by the time the Pynchons arrived.

Not trusting himself to be civil, he slapped a packet of legal briefs onto the desk. "A date has been set in Chancery Court," he informed them coldly and left the house.

Mrs. Pynchon appeared in the schoolroom to inform Jessica that custody was to be decided a week hence, in the court of the Lord Chancellor.

Jessica's eyes sought Kitty and Gabriel. The girl was scrawling her name on sheets of foolscap; Gabriel was staring out the window daydreaming again. Jessica lowered her voice so the children wouldn't hear. "So soon, Mrs. Pynchon?"

"My brother-in-law has no doubt lined someone's pockets to win an early court date." Mrs. Pynchon drew her thin lips into a line of distaste. "The children will have to be present for part of the hearing, as will you, Miss Darling."

"Yes, ma'am."

"I expect you'll see to their behavior."

"Of course, Mrs. Pynchon." But Jessica wasn't worried about the children's conduct, not really. What actually troubled her was how their father would behave.

She looked away to hide her troubled eyes. Fletcher Danforth would do anything to regain Kitty and Gabriel; he'd said as much more than once. Dread settled in her belly. He might even go so far as to inform the Lord Chancellor that the Pynchons employed a woman he believed to be a whore.

"Papa hasn't been to see us in so long," Kitty said on the morning of the hearing. Her rosebud mouth pouted.

"Don't worry, lamb," Jessica said. "You'll see him today, and you must be on your best behavior."

Kitty stood still as Jessica brushed the girl's sable hair, curling the ringlets into fat, glossy sausages.

Handsome and sullen, Gabriel met them in the foyer. They were joined by Hester and Charles. Mrs. Pynchon looked immaculate and oddly earnest in expensive but somber clothing. Her usual lofty coiffure had been reduced to a neat chignon; her only jewel was her plain gold wedding band.

Jessica hoped the Lord Chancellor would see through that maternal facade. Much as she had grown to care for Kitty and Gabriel, she hoped the court would favor Fletcher. It was the only way to get him out of her life for good.

As their coach entered Chancery Lane, Jessica stiffened her spine against tremors of nervousness. What little she knew of the English justice system was grim. Her mother had once been brought up on charges of drunkenness. Jessica recalled her humiliation as she stood clutching her mother's hand in the dock among other prisoners—drunks and brawlers, hucksters and beggars. The sentence had been predictable: "Five or five," a fine of five shillings or a sentence of five days. Having had a poor week, Jessica's mother had opted for the latter, leaving her young daughter to scurry home alone to the bleak, empty garret in Billiter Lane.

Though the present situation bore little resemblence to that experience, Jessica felt no less apprehensive. The coach brought them to Westminster. The hall teemed with bewigged barristers, harried clerks, stern-faced judges. Moving through the vaulted corridors, Jessica saw groups of litigants and men of law pacing the halls in wig and gown.

She spied the object of her search near a window seat. Fletcher Danforth was conferring with a barrister. Warmth seeped through her as she admired his easy pose, one arm against the stone wall, the other holding a long leather bag in the shape of folded legal briefs. Catching herself in the midst of an unladylike perusal of the set of his mouth and the shape of his gray-clad hips, Jessica frowned.

As if feeling her gaze, Fletcher glanced up. His eyes left her to devour Kitty and Gabriel with that familiar look of love and longing. Then he glanced back at her, one brow cocking sardonically as he took in her prim gown and the modest little hat perched on her mercilessly tamed curls.

Flushing, Jessica steered the children away, to follow the Pynchons into one of the courtrooms. The room was small but lofty, with gray stone walls and oak paneling, lit by skylights. Benches crowded with people sloped steeply upward in tiers on all sides.

The Lord Chancellor Arbiter, sporting a rolled wig and robes of blue with a scarlet sash and broad yellow cuffs, sat at his raised desk. Papers littered the bench, weighted by a bouquet of dried sweet peas in a stiff perforated paper holder.

Jessica recognized the floral perfume as the ancient means of preventing the contagion of prison fever.

Kitty tugged on Jessica's hand. "There's my papa!"

Jessica turned to see that Fletcher had entered the courtroom. "You can't go and see him now, love; he has business with the Lord Chancellor."

The little girl stared at the judge. "He looks funny in that wig," she whispered. "I'll bet he has fleas in it." Stifling a laugh, Jessica took Kitty and her brother to the seats indicated by the Pynchons' barrister. Benches in the gallery were reserved for the public. Dismay welled in Jessica as she recognized the portly Maude Dunstan and her diminutive, mouse-faced husband Lionel. With fluttering hands and shaking wattles, Mrs. Dunstan was expounding on her opinion.

Jessica glanced at Gabriel and saw the boy sending a grin to another part of the gallery. Following his gaze, she saw Jade, Nan, and Adele moving toward them. Jade grinned back at Gabriel and waved. Nan blew a kiss in their general direction and Madame inclined her snow-white head with exaggerated gravity.

Quickly Jessica's eyes found the Pynchons; to her relief they were deep in conversation with their barrister.

Kitty fidgeted and swiveled around, staring at the three ladies, who had found seats behind them. A nervous-looking bailiff approached to order them back to the gallery, to sit with the public at large. A single powerful gaze from Madame sent him scurrying away, shaking his head and pretending not to have noticed the woman.

Another case was being heard. Jessica tried to concentrate on the proceedings to still the churning of her stomach. The kingdom began and ended its legal battles here, presumably with alacrity and crispness of proceedings, and with the utmost dignified respect for the law. Those attributes seemed in jeopardy, considering the nature of the current case.

Apparently the ownership of a costermonger's donkey was at stake. Jessica had no idea why the issue of a fruit-pedlar's beast of burden was being debated as a chancery matter; then she realized it was part of a larger suit involving equity. With considerable pomp, Arbiter allowed that a certain wart under the donkey's tail left no question as to the animal's identity and therefore of its ownership. Jade leaned forward to murmur her own ribald assessment of the donkey's physiognomy, eliciting a boyish giggle from Gabriel. The case was decided amid much sniggering and chattering from the gallery. A pounding gavel punctuated the cacophony.

"Order!" the Lord Chancellor shouted, his face reddening beneath his wig of elaborate white rolls. "Next case!"

As a bailiff read from a long parchment, Jessica took out a handkerchief and began twisting the thin fabric distractedly. Both children fell still, as if sensing that their future rode on the outcome of this hearing. Jessica stole a glance at Fletcher Danforth. Looking reserved and commanding in his morning suit of black and gray, he sat in conference with his barrister. Only the unnatural stiffness of his shoulders betrayed any hidden emotion.

Smug and confident, the Pynchons were seated with their well-paid solicitor and moon-faced barrister.

Guided by his barrister, Fletcher addressed the court. Jessica was fascinated by his calm explanation of all that had happened in the past five years. Yes, he had been accused of selling firearms to Indians. And yes, the charges had been dropped for lack of evidence. Relief swelled within Jessica. Unlike the Pynchons, the judge had granted Fletcher the opportunity to clear his name.

Fletcher produced balance sheets from his shipping business to prove his ability to support the children. His barrister set forth letters of reference from colonial landowners and informed the court that Mr. Danforth had already settled a generous annuity on both his children.

The judge listened distractedly, trying to be discreet as he curled a finger beneath his wig to scratch his scalp. Clearly he saw this as a petty family quarrel blown out of proportion.

Praying for a ruling in Fletcher's favor, Jessica squeezed Kitty's hand. He'd offended her, but he loved his children and had a father's right to them. A victory would mean his immediate return to the colonies, and then Jessica would be free of her unwilling fascination . . . she hoped.

The Pynchons' barrister presented his client's case, reading from statements he'd taken from high-placed friends, Gabriel's schoolmates, and Jessica herself.

In her interview with the solicitor two days earlier, Jessica had stated that she thought a father would give Gabriel the guidance he desperately needed.

"Miss Darling said Charles Pynchon is the father figure the boy needs," the barrister told the court.

She'd told the solicitor Hester was free with her lilac switch.

"Miss Darling stated that Mrs. Pynchon imparts discipline lovingly and judiciously."

Jessica surged to her feet. "That's not true," she shouted, feeling Fletcher Danforth's eyes on her. "I never said those things; he's turned it all around—"

"Order!" bellowed the Lord Chancellor. "You will keep silent, miss, or I shall have you removed from my court."

Jessica sank onto the bench in frustration. Kitty snuggled against her arm and Gabriel gave her a tight, tiny smile. Fletcher turned and mouthed something at her, something that looked like "thank you."

Perhaps, she thought, her unseemly outburst had exposed the barrister's conniving ways.

But when Hester Pynchon took the stand, her responses guided by her clever barrister, Jessica's hopes sank. Mrs. Pynchon was at her righteous best, taking the part of the compassionate aunt who feared her beloved niece and nephew would be whisked away to the colonies by a man who had neglected his parental duties for five long years.

"On a whim," Hester said in a tremulous voice, "on a whim he has decided he wants the dear children with him. Who can say he won't tire of them, leave them stranded, motherless?" The tears in her eyes looked genuine.

Fletcher's jaw hardened in anger as Hester described his children's reactions to him on their first meeting.

"Little Katherine wept hysterically and Gabriel denied that Mr. Danforth was his father. They were both terribly frightened, my lord. The man stormed into our happy home and demanded their return, as if they were no more than chattel."

Even the judge seemed to recognize this bit of melodrama for what it was. "A natural reaction, under the circumstances," he said impatiently.

Hester drew herself up. "But, my lord, it points out the fundamental problem of this unfortunate disagreement. I find it preposterous that there is any question about what should be done with the children. I can give them security. Miss

Darling"—Hester gestured at Jessica—"is the finest governess to be found. . . ." She dabbed at her eyes. "And so we bring the matter to you, my lord, relying on your fairness and expertise to do what is right for my little dears."

Adele leaned forward and tapped Jessica on the shoulder. "It is awful, is it not, what members of a family will do to each other when money is involved?" she said in French.

"Mr. Danforth cares nothing about the money," Jessica whispered. "He only wants to take his children home."

"So. You defend the man then."

"Yes," Jessica said firmly. "I do."

"My lord," Hester was saying, "I can give the children something Fletcher Danforth cannot: a mother's love."

Jessica clamped a warning hand around Gabriel's wrist as the boy laughed derisively into his sleeve.

"Fletcher Danforth has lived as a prisoner for over five years," Hester continued. She paused as her barrister leaned forward to whisper something in her ear. "He is no more equipped to raise children than—than the savage he is."

The Lord Chancellor looked perplexed. "Savage?"

"Yes." She drew her hands to her bosom. "It is pertinent, is it not, that Mr. Danforth is half Indian?"

Arbiter studied Fletcher. "What say you to this, Mr. Danforth?"

"My sister-in-law is telling the truth . . . on this point." Fletcher suddenly looked taller and fiercer than ever before. Stunned, Jessica leaned forward and clutched the rungs of the bench in front of her.

"My mother was a Mohawk Indian, my lord," Fletcher replied with steadiness and pride.

Jessica expelled her breath in soft, uneven gasps. Finally she understood all Hester's denunciations of her brother-in-law's character, and Fletcher's odd reaction to the drunken Huron at Bartholomew Fair. So. He was an Indian. Staring across the room at him, Jessica no longer saw a smartly clad gentleman. Instead, her imagination transformed him into a half-naked savage moving with feral grace through the mysterious density of a virgin forest. The image both frightened and fascinated her.

Oddly, the Lord Chancellor didn't seem to share Jessica's flight of fancy. The impatient man seemed more concerned with Mrs. Pynchon's comment about providing a proper home. "Do you deny, Mr. Danforth," he asked, "that your children would benefit from a mother's nurturing?"

Fletcher clenched his jaw. "No, my lord, I don't deny it. But Hester Pynchon is hardly the—"

Arbiter glanced at his full docket and raised his gavel.

"Wait." Fletcher's commanding voice stopped the Lord Chancellor from bringing the hearing to an end. The judge frowned at the bold outburst but relented and set his gavel down.

"If I may beg your lordship's indulgence, I'd like to request a brief recess," Fletcher said.

The Pynchons' barrister objected. Arbiter rolled his eyes. "You have exactly one minute, Mr. Danforth."

To Jessica's surprise, Fletcher's eyes found hers. He jerked his head toward the side aisle. After murmuring to the children to keep still, she joined him.

He laid his hand on the oak-paneled wall, close to her face. She felt imprisoned by his stance.

"Jessica," he said urgently, "I need your help."

His use of her given name had an unwelcome effect on her. Feeling suddenly too warm, she forced her gaze to remain steady. "Yes?"

He took a moment to stare down at her. God, she looked sweet and trusting, with her peach-gold curls framing her face and the lace so demure at her collar and cuffs. And those eyes, as wide and guileless as dew-kissed heather . . .

Could he really execute the desperate plan he'd conceived during Hester's testimony? Could he use the scandalous knowledge he had of Jessica Darling to make her—

The gavel rapped sharply. Fletcher had only seconds.

How he wished there were another way to win his children. But he had no time to put his idea to Jessica gently, to woo her into complicity. Fletcher blinked. Woo her? It was not as if she were a well-bred lady, after all. She was a whore. Damnably attractive, beguilingly sweet, but a fallen woman nonetheless. She had been used in worse ways than he intended. The thought hardened his resolve.

"I am going to suggest something to the judge that will make him rule in my favor," he said. "I'm depending on your complete cooperation."

"But what—"

"You'd do well not to question me." Fletcher drew his face into a cold frown so she wouldn't mistake the strength of his determination or think he was bluffing. "You must promise to voice no objection to anything I say. Because if you do—" He broke off, steadying himself for her reaction.

"Mr. Danforth?" she prompted. Well-founded suspicion marred her beautiful face.

"If you fail me, I'll see to it that the Pynchons hear about your association with Madame Severin. You'll never hold a respectable position again."

Jessica's hand flew to her mouth and she stumbled back against his outstretched arm. Her throat worked as she swallowed hard. Her eyes glinted with fury and fear.

"I understand your threat, Mr. Danforth," she finally said coldly. "Far be it from me to deter you from leaving London as soon as possible."

He expelled a sigh. "Then I can count on you?"

"For the children's sake, yes, Mr. Danforth. Not for yours, nor for my own."

Wondering at the strange feeling of guilt gnawing at him, he walked back to the bench. Could he really do this to Jessica, to himself? He almost changed his mind, but then he caught sight of Kitty. His little girl gave him a radiant smile. One tiny finger came up and wiggled in a minute wave. His determination renewed, Fletcher took a deep breath. "I'd like to ask Mrs. Pynchon some questions, my lord."

"Make haste, sir. My patience is nearly at its limit."

Fletcher faced Hester, his face a bland, polite mask. "Mrs. Pynchon, will you please describe for the court your children's governess, Miss Jessica Darling?"

Hester looked at him sharply, as if suspecting a trap. "Miss Darling is intelligent, judicious, and loving with the children. Her personal qualifications are above reproach."

"How has she treated my children?"

"With every bit of patience and understanding she possesses. Miss Darling loves them."

"And what about her—"

"Mr. Danforth!" the Pynchons' barrister barked. "I fail to see the purpose of this line of questioning. We are not here to examine the attributes of Miss Darling, however exemplary. She does not figure in his lordship's decision.''

"But she does, my lord," Fletcher said. "Most highly."

"And why, pray, is that?"

Fletcher looked across the courtroom. His eyes drilled into Jessica's, holding her captive. "Because, my lord," he said slowly, deliberately, eyes still on Jessica, "Miss Darling has accepted my contract of marriage. She is going to be my wife and the mother of my children.''

Shock froze Jessica, numbing her limbs and stealing her breath. Then she shot to her feet, a hundred protests leaping to her lips. But Fletcher's chilling gaze and the cruel, thin line of his mouth reminded her of his threat.

"Simply outrageous, that's my opinion." Maude Dunstan's gasp reached her ears as from a great distance.

"Gabriel, why does Miss Darling look so strange?" Kitty whispered. "Is she sick?"

"Did you hear that, ducks?" Jade murmured. "Ain't he the sly one?"

Jessica turned helplessly to Madame, but her friend only smiled and inclined her head. Feeling sick indeed, Jessica weighed the possibilities. She could call Fletcher's bluff and inform the Lord Chancellor that she had no intention of marrying anyone, but a denial would compel Fletcher to use his lethal weapon against her.

She'd never work respectably again. She'd be out on the streets as before, only this time it would be worse. Because she'd had a taste of security, and it meant the world to her.

Hester Pynchon recovered before Jessica did. She leveled her imperious gaze at the Lord Chancellor. "He lies!" she cried shrilly.

Kitty tugged on Jessica's skirt and whispered, "Miss Darling, are you really going to be my mama? Are you?"

Gabriel's eyes blazed with sudden excitement, but then his face closed. "We have only one mother," he muttered. "And she's dead."

"I *want* you to be my mama," Kitty said stubbornly, clutching her rag baby close. "Esme wants you too." Jessica patted the little girl's hand and said nothing. She'd torn her eyes from Fletcher and was looking at Arbiter.

His thinning eyebrows descended severely. "If this is the case, Mr. Danforth, why didn't you bring it up earlier?"

"I'd hoped you'd rule in my favor based upon my character alone, my lord."

" 'Tis well you spoke, Mr. Danforth, for I doubt I would have favored you without knowing you meant to provide the children with a mother having the impeccable qualities Mrs. Pynchon has described."

"But it's not true," Hester burst out. "Miss Darling would have told me of such an outrageous plan."

Arbiter frowned her into silence. " 'Tis simple enough to test," he declared. He leaned down to confer briefly with the bailiff.

Moments later, feeling like a puppet whose wooden limbs were controlled by Fletcher Danforth, Jessica found herself standing in the box, heard herself mouthing an oath to speak the truth.

The Lord Chancellor asked, "What say you, Miss Darling? Does Mr. Danforth speak the truth? Are you betrothed to him?"

"I . . ." Jessica swallowed a thick knot of tension. The blood pounded in her ears. Surely Fletcher only meant this as a charade to curry favor with the court. After custody was granted, he'd ask no more of her. She looked squarely at the Lord Chancellor. "Yes, my lord."

A murmur of interest rippled from the gallery.

"Very well." At last Arbiter's frown disappeared and his face eased into a smile. "Mr. Danforth, I hereby grant you full custody of—"

"It's a ruse, don't you see?" Hester screeched. "He doesn't mean to marry her. The moment he leaves this court he'll abscond to the colonies with those poor children."

The judge considered for a moment, toying idly with his basket of dried flowers. He seemed to be in a jovial mood now that the hearing was coming to a satisfactory end. "I'll make certain that doesn't happen," he assured Hester. "Miss Darling, Mr. Danforth, would you both approach the bench?"

Fletcher watched Jessica as she moved slowly to his side in front of the Lord Chancellor. She looked pale and shaken, like a condemned prisoner on her way to the gallows. He could feel her trembling as she stood beside him. Damn it, he thought, didn't she realize what he was offering her? His name, his home, a new life in America. By her own admission she was baseborn. Here was a chance at respectability. Then why did she seem so desolate?

The Lord Chancellor murmured to a clerk, who shuffled through a sheaf of papers in a drawer and extracted a printed document. Arbiter scratched his quill across the bottom of the sheet, then handed it along with the quill to Jessica. "Sign here, please," he said, indicating with his finger. Shaking, her eyes blurred with tears, she scrawled her name. Fletcher did likewise, only his eyes were dry and determined.

"Now," said Arbiter with a satisfied air, "in the eyes of the law you are man and wife. Of course, you'll want to have it sanctioned with a church ceremony. . . ."

"Of course, my lord," Fletcher said civilly. "As soon as we reach our home in the colony of New York."

Only Fletcher's strong supporting arm prevented Jessica from collapsing. The haste and absurdity of the act made it seem unreal, as if it were happening to someone else. But it was her signature on the marriage certificate, her fate to be wed to a man she scarcely knew.

Regaining a measure of composure, she pulled away. Perhaps, she thought, her resolve returning, I'm despairing too soon. Surely Fletcher had only staged this farce to win a ruling in his favor. She felt a surge of relief. Of course that was his ploy. Fletcher would release her from this sham marriage the moment they stepped from the courtroom.

But Arbiter's next remark to Fletcher sent that hope plummeting.

"It occurs to me," he said sternly, dusting sand over the parchment, "that this has been a hasty affair. I wouldn't want my work today to be undone. Hence, here are the terms of the custody: Gabriel James Danforth and Katherine Ruth Danforth are permanently remanded into the joint care of you and your wife, Jessica Darling Danforth. Should you and your wife ever seek separate residences, custody shall revert immediately to Charles and Hester Pynchon. Sir Jeffrey Amherst, the royal governor of New York, will be charged with enforcing my conditions. Is that understood?"

"See?" Kitty chirped, her voice rising above the murmurs from the gallery, "she *is* going to be our mama, Gabriel, so there!"

Fletcher's face softened at the sound of his daughter's voice. He turned to the Lord Chancellor. "This is no ruse, my lord. I intend to honor my commitment." His fingers imprisoned Jessica's chin as he tilted her face upward. She nearly collapsed again at the look on his face. His resolution left her helpless; his touch left her breathless.

At the prospect of going all the way to the colonies with this strange, fierce man, a heaviness settled in the pit of her stomach, making her feel sick with a sense of loss. His blackmail had shattered the security she'd worked so hard to achieve. "To think," she whispered scathingly beneath the rising babble of voices, "that I was softened to your plight, that I wanted to help you."

"You have helped," Fletcher said, "and for that I thank you."

Eyeing him distrustfully, Jessica pulled back. Perhaps, she thought wildly, he is just as Mrs. Pynchon painted him: a conniving savage no better than those Mr. Smythe's books described.

Yet despite her fluttering fear and mounting trepidation, Jessica forced herself into a decision. She would not docilely follow Fletcher into a marriage she didn't want and to a land she'd never seen. She would fight to retain her life of secure predictability. And whether or not she won that battle, she would see to it that Fletcher Danforth regretted his high-handed treatment of her.

Chapter 7

"Mrs. Danforth?"

Startled to hear the chambermaid using her unfamiliar new name, Jessica looked up from her perusal of a volume on English civil law. She put the book on the table beside her. It offered no hope, no hope at all. The papers she'd signed before the Lord Chancellor were legal and binding.

She swallowed. "Yes?" Her voice sounded the same. She still occupied the same body, still wore the same somber clothes she'd had on at the hearing that morning. Yet nothing was the same.

Fletcher hadn't allowed her to return to the Pynchons' to collect her things. Instead he'd sent for her trunk and the children's belongings. Now here she sat in a musty-smelling suite of rooms near Gray's Inn, trying not to think about the bedchamber behind the green baize door.

As for Fletcher himself, he seemed eager to leave London. He'd had most of the luggage sent to Falmouth, the port from which they would sail. At the moment he was off arranging the family's passage.

The maid bobbed her head. "The children are asleep, mum, at least the little one is. I expect the boy'll drop off soon enough."

Jessica was thankful that Kitty seemed to be taking the upheaval in stride. The child had solemnly explained to Esme that they had a new mama; she'd peppered Fletcher with questions about their new home.

Gabriel, however, seemed to resent Jessica now as much as he resented his father. He'd sulked and said nothing, but Jessica guessed his thoughts. His heart remained fiercely loyal

114

to his dead mother and he rebelled against anyone who, willingly or not, would take Sybil's place.

Lacing her fingers in front of her starched apron, the maid waited expectantly.

"Thank you . . . er . . ." Jessica's mind worked sluggishly, overburdened with the shock of finding herself married to a stranger and bound for a strange land.

"Alice, mum. Alice Bean." The maid dipped a curtsy.

Unaccustomed to the courtesy, Jessica smiled. "Thank you, Alice. You've been a great help."

"Shall I unpack your things, Mrs. Danforth?"

"No need," came a voice from the doorway. Fletcher's sudden imposing presence brought Jessica to her feet. His face was cold. Not for the first time, she had the impression of a man who kept himself under strict control.

"We'll be leaving in two days," he explained.

"Well." Alice glanced about. "If that'll be all . . ."

Fletcher's expression thawed. "That will be all, miss."

The maid looked from Fletcher to Jessica as if sensing the tension neither bothered to conceal. She scuttled out.

After pouring himself a glass of Madeira at the sideboard, Fletcher turned, bottle in hand. "Join me?"

Jessica refused the wine with a slow shake of her head. She rested her hands on an oak library stand, placing the waist-high piece between them as if to shield herself from him. The open law book on the stand exuded a faint mustiness. Her heart quickened to an unhealthy staccato as she faced his stern, unfathomable countenance. Uncertainty enveloped her. Nowhere in the realm of her experience had she learned the means to deal with a wedding night.

He took a sip of Madeira. "You look," he told her, "as if you expect me to eat you alive."

The smooth-toned remark reached across the room to her, touching nerves laid raw by tension and fatigue. The fact that she was afraid made her angry at herself. The fact that he'd noticed her fear made her angry at him.

Gathering her fury around her, Jessica forced herself to meet his frost-bitten gaze and address his gentle, cruel taunt. "Perhaps you already have, Mr. Danforth," she replied, her voice gratifyingly steady, "in a manner of speaking."

He swirled his drink, then held it up to the lamp to study

its rich color. "Will we, *Mrs.* Danforth, treat the present situation as a comedy of manners?"

"Or better," she shot back, "as a comedy of errors."

One eyebrow lifted on that imperious brow, joining the tumble of jet hair spilling downward. He took a step forward; she instructed her feet to remain rooted to the threadbare carpet. "I'm afraid it's no error, Jessica," he said, his voice curiously apologetic. "You are my wife, and you're coming home with me and my children."

She moved her head slowly back and forth in painful denial. "What right had you?" she asked, then scowled because the question sounded so clumsy, so melodramatic.

For a moment she saw a flicker in his eyes. Guilt? Regret? But the expression was so quickly hidden that she couldn't be sure. "I did only what was necessary," he stated. "My children mean everything to me."

"How noble of you," she said cuttingly, "to shackle yourself to a woman whose moral fiber you doubt."

"I'm afraid we must settle the question of your past," he informed her ruthlessly. "I won't have my children's values tainted."

"Tainted!" Fury raced through her veins. "Mr. Danforth, I have done my utmost to give Kitty and Gabriel all the love and guidance I have to offer."

"Aye," he conceded. "Kitty adores you; that is clear enough, but she must never learn what you have been." He held up a hand to stave off another angry outburst. "Jessica, I do understand that life gave you few choices."

"And you," she shot back, "have managed to narrow those choices to nothing. Nothing!"

"Are you really giving up all that much?" His question probed gently, sending subtle agony twisting through her.

"Only a life I considered perfectly satisfying, a life I spent years preparing for, a life I chose for myself, didn't have thrust on me by the likes of you." She presented her back to him. "America!" she finished with an explosive sigh.

"Your information about America is scant, Jessica, but when we get to New York you'll learn that people there don't stand on past achievements, even dubious ones." He paused, and she heard him swallow a sip of wine. "I can give you things you never dreamed of having: a good name, a fine home staffed with able servants, the status of a lady—''

"I will not live in the world you offer," she said over her shoulder.

"You know nothing of my world."

"And you know nothing of me, if you think to find me bowed down in gratitude for the privilege of being your wife."

Shivering with anger, she settled her hands firmly at her hips and swung back to face him. "Do you think you're such a bloody good prize that I'd willingly give up all I worked for in order to be dragged to the colonies by you?"

He drew a long, unsteady breath. Some of the impassivity left his face, laying open a more human expression. So. She'd struck home. Even a scoundrel like Fletcher Danforth realized the enormity of what he'd done.

"Jessica," he said at length, his voice quiet, "I'm the first to admit I'm no matrimonial prize. I've lived no better than a caged animal for five years; even before that I didn't exactly have my first wife swooning with love for me." He took a hearty swallow of his Madeira, draining the glass and setting it back on the sideboard with an unsteady thunk.

At least, Jessica thought, he didn't have the overblown sense of himself most men seemed to possess. He made her no empty promises and indulged in no deceptive pretenses.

He moved subtly and inexorably forward; then he was standing near and his hands were gripping her, fingers biting into the tense muscles of her upper arms. Surely he felt the shock of her reaction, for she was assaulted by the smell and sight and texture of him. He must have seen the pain his grip dealt her, for his hold relaxed immediately when she flinched. One long-fingered hand climbed to the soft flesh of her neck, curving into the secretive warmth at its nape.

"I know it was not your choice to be wed to me," he said softly, "but you'll want for nothing at Holland Hall."

"What I want," she said, "is my freedom." She tried to ignore the compelling lure of his too-gentle caress.

"My dear, in America you'll be freer than you ever were here in London. No need to wait for the Pynchons to release you on Thursday afternoons or alternate Sundays."

"What about you?" she asked softly. "When will you release me?"

His fingers continued their relentless dance on her flesh, feathering over the nape of her neck, flicking at her burning, pink-misted cheeks. "I cannot risk having my children taken away from me again."

She longed to draw away from his tender torture, but pride kept her still. "Then I prefer being in service," she said. "At least my life has been my own, and would still be if you hadn't blackmailed me."

"Think about it, Jessica. If you stayed in London, you'd be spoon-feeding knowledge and manners to the Pynchon children until they outgrew your care. Then you'd move on to another family, and then another . . . until you collected a wealth of grateful, overprivileged youngsters and a small pension. And then you'd retire, old"—his knuckles brushed her brow—"and alone. . . ." His hand loosed a gold-tinged tendril from her chignon. "Is that what you want?"

She curled her hands into tight fists, feeling an emotion she refused to acknowledge. "It doesn't matter what I want, not anymore," she said in a choked voice. "You've seen to that, Mr. Danforth."

"I'm sorry I wasn't able to give you a choice." The apology sounded as if it had been wrung from unwilling lips. "If you could understand my love for Kitty and Gabriel—"

"I do understand that. But you've shown no respect for *my* wishes." She watched his throat work as he swallowed. Some undisciplined part of her found the working of strong muscle beneath tanned flesh dangerously beguiling.

But the image was shattered when his brows assumed a cynical angle. "I've no doubt you commanded a respectable fee at Severin's," he said, "but can you honestly say any man has ever respected you?"

"Damn you and your foul assumptions, Fletcher Danforth," she exclaimed, struggling in his embrace. "Why do you refuse to believe my ties with Adele are innocent?"

His gentle laughter held a sharp edge of derision. "Because I know you can set a man aflame; I heard it from a duke's own mouth."

"A drunken duke, who had the mistaken notion I'd be willing to satisfy him."

"A lusty duke, who grew impatient with your games. I'm impatient too, Jessica." His hands began a soothing caress over her shoulders. "I've been duped by women in the past," he told her, "but I've learned from my mistakes. You needn't pretend innocence now. You won't find me a cruel husband." With that softly spoken promise he bent and brushed his lips across her brow.

Jessica's heart lurched and her spine stiffened at the gentle, insidious contact. Having had enough of cheap melodrama and battered pride that day, she steeled her will against the impulse to fight him. She'd already humiliated herself once, in London Spa, and her virtuous resistance had landed her on her backside. She would engage in no such comical display tonight. Better to remain indifferent; better to show him he was incapable of moving her.

His hands made a slow descent over her arms and his fingers wrapped neatly around her starched and corseted waist. Jessica fixed her gaze on his cambric shirt, aware that to meet those compelling eyes would be her undoing.

Yet Fletcher Danforth seemed capable of wringing a response from a marble statue. A slight pressure of his hands brought her against him. A second lowering of his head guided his lips to her cheek, sampling her flesh with breathy warmth and then traveling lower still, to her dewy, blush-stained neck. His quiet sigh stirred the tendrils of her hair, baring her skin for the attention of his mouth.

Jessica was sure his sensitive, knowing lips would discover the reaction she fought to conceal. For beneath the light wing beats of his kisses her pulse throbbed wildly.

His hands found hers, long, strong fingers enclosing the tight balls of her fists. "So tense," he murmured into her ear. "Open for me, Jessica." He brought her clenched hand up, holding it between them. "Open, love," he repeated.

Jessica tightened her fist. Fletcher forced it open with a firm pressure she was incapable of resisting. One by one he unfurled her fingers, discovering little half-moon depressions where her nails had bitten into her palms.

"No need to hurt yourself." Ever so gently he brought her hand to his lips and eased the pain with a kiss on each tiny depression. Suffused with a heady feeling of incandescence,

Jessica uttered what she meant to be a murmur of distress, but it sounded more like a yearning plea.

His lips left her palm. His next kiss began like a whisper against her clamped-shut mouth; perhaps he did whisper something, but Jessica couldn't hear the words over the roar of passion-heated blood in her ears. His slow-circling mouth overcame her resistance until she disgraced herself with a telltale shudder.

"Open, Jessica," he said, and this time he wasn't referring to her hands. "Open . . ." His tongue traced the pressed-together line of her lips, spreading a heady nectar over them until Jessica's reason went spinning off to some unknown and undreamed-of realm beyond common sense.

His fingers twined deeply into her hair, sending the net trailing down her back. Peach-gold curls spilled in wanton disarray over her quaking shoulders. His hands framed her face, thumbs massaging her jawline while his mouth and tongue continued to besiege her willpower.

"Jessica," he whispered, "you're beautiful. . . ."

The words penetrated her wall of anger and resentment. Her jaw went slack beneath his circling thumbs and her lips parted. His tongue explored hers in a silken sweep of motion that she felt down to her curling toes.

She sank weakly against him, circling her arms around his firm girth to keep from crumpling. His embrace held a quality she hadn't discerned the last time he'd kissed her. An absurd thought niggled through her passion-drenched mind. Perhaps he did care for her. . . .

As if sensing her acquiescence, Fletcher moved his hands downward. His kiss still held her enthralled as he fitted one arm behind her back and the other behind her knees. In one smooth motion, he swept her up against his chest.

Dazed by the new and alarming heat of desire, Jessica barely noticed his fluid movements as he pushed open the green baize door and carried her to the neatly tailored corner bedstead. Her mouth still locked with his, she felt the yielding of the damask-clad mattress beneath her. Only vaguely did her fogged mind register the spicy scent of dried lavender wafting from the counterpane.

Fletcher Danforth filled her senses. His limbs felt impossibly firm and imminently capable. His mouth tasted of some unnameable masculine sweetness, tinged with the faint musk of Madeira. His scent—that of wild timber and outdoor places—held all reason at bay.

The faint creak of the bedstead reminded her of the grim reality of her situation. Here she was, alone with a man who considered her a whore undeserving of his respect, and she was actually beginning to enjoy his seduction. Grasping at a wisp of rationality, she dragged her eyes open and moved her head to elude his skillful kisses.

"No," she said desperately. "No, please . . ."

He smiled down at her, a wayward black curl straying over his brow. In the shadowy candle glow he looked as wild and dangerous as a . . . The word "savage" came to mind. Even Jade Akura, in the vast experience she delighted in sharing with Jessica, had never demonstrated a knowledge of the habits of American Indians. Oh, God, Jessica thought, does he have some special torture for a recalcitrant wife?

"You want this," he told her, his hand straying down to where her heart was thumping madly against her rib cage. "And what, pray, could be more fitting than a night of love to celebrate our wedding?"

A sudden idea came to her, an idea that might buy her the time she needed to escape him. "I recall no proper wedding," she said urgently. "Surely we cannot consider ourselves truly married until we speak our vows in church."

Sarcasm darkened his eyes. "Your sudden attack of piety rings false, Jessica." He reached for her again, imprisoning her in his arms. "Lovemaking would be a more suitable bond for us than a minister's blessing."

Gathering all her resources, she said, "If you take me now, Mr. Danforth, it will be by force."

Jessica bristled at his derisive chuckle and her mind rebelled against his flippant use of the word "love" to describe what he intended to do to the woman he'd coldly blackmailed into marrying him. She found the strength to twist from his grasp and surge to a sitting position.

He didn't leap upon her in the expected attack. Instead he smiled. "A moment ago you were clutching at me as if you couldn't get close enough," he said. "What brought about this missish change?"

Humiliated by her overly histrionic statement, Jessica

moistened her lips with an unconscious flick of her tongue. Edging toward the foot of the bed, she said, "Mr. Danforth—"

"Fletcher."

"Mr. Danforth," she persisted. "You see, I'm not even comfortable using your given name. We're strangers in many ways. Most brides are given months to prepare for . . ."

"But you need no preparation," he said in a silken whisper. "You've done this many times before."

Too appalled to speak, Jessica tried to flee from the bed. He grasped her arm. "We're not strangers anyway," he told her. "We've known each other for over two months. Most couples have a far shorter acquaintance before they marry."

"We are not most couples!"

"True," he said, grinning.

"I know so little about you. Only today I learned you're not the proper English gentleman you appear. How am I to respond to a man whose mother was a heathen savage?"

His thumb had been stroking her inner arm in lazy circles. Jessica didn't realize how pleasurable the sensation was until he stopped abruptly. He impaled her with his gaze, which changed with frightening speed from hot and languorous to cold and cruel. A quietness stole over him, hardening his candle-lit features. Jessica had learned to recognize quietness as Fletcher's equivalent of screaming rage. Suddenly she wished she could call back her words, wished she hadn't resorted to maligning his heritage.

He removed his hand, still holding her prisoner with the jewel hardness of his eyes. "I see," he said, his voice no longer like liquid silk. He stood up. "So that's what suddenly turned you cold. I never realized your sensibilities would be so offended by intimacy with a savage."

He pivoted on his boot heel and left the room, closing the door with a steadiness that bespoke anger more than slamming would have done. A curious vacuum of loneliness hung in the room.

Staring after him in a fog of dying desire and growing bewilderment, Jessica sighed. Fletcher Danforth's touch had made her hot, but his words had left her cold. She dressed for bed quickly, darting nervous glances at the door, both fearing and desiring his return. Huddling against the wall, she pulled the fragrant linens up to her chin.

Fletcher Danforth was right on one count. She *was* offended by his touch; she did not want intimacy, however compellingly offered. But his assumption that his Indian heritage repelled her was wrong. Her own past and parentage were far more dubious than Fletcher's. At least he knew who both his parents were, while she preferred not to contemplate the man likely to have sired her.

But Fletcher's failure to respect her had nothing to do with the fact that she was a whore's bastard. Instead his disdain stemmed from his mistaken notion that she had worked for Madame Severin.

It occurred to Jessica that the means of convincing him to the contrary were at her disposal. She had only to submit to the feelings he aroused in her. Surely a man like Fletcher would recognize that she was a virgin.

The thought launched a flight of sensual fancy that left her breathless. She imagined his strong brown hands moving over her untried body, bringing to life a deep, hidden part of her. Her senses filled with the memory of his wine-sweet kisses, the firm feel of his heated flesh beneath her fingers. . . . With an effort she subdued the shameful imaginings and vowed she would never give herself to him merely to prove her honesty. There were many reasons for a woman to yield to a man, but that wasn't one of them. Although Fletcher saw her as merely a means to secure his children, Jessica placed a higher value on herself.

She waited, stiff and alert, until the gray tinge of dawn slipped through the half-drawn curtains. Then, still uneasy, she succumbed to a few hours' sleep. Alone.

"Ah, there you are, Danforth," said a pleasant, bell-toned voice. "I never thought to find a newly married man sequestered in my office."

Fletcher offered the barrister his hand. "Good afternoon, Walter." He surveyed his old friend with warm amusement. Walter Whiting had been a barrister for years, yet the man always managed to look as if he'd just tumbled from a hayrick. His rough-spun coat and loose breeches were rumpled.

Mud clung to boots that bore the stitching of numerous resolings. In his hand he held a creel.

"Any luck?" Fletcher asked.

"Not a tad." Whiting grinned. "But you know damned well I go only for the sport. Far more agreeable than sitting in this office waiting for solicitors to come calling with their briefs and fees."

"I'm glad you were present when this solicitor came calling," Fletcher said. "I didn't get a chance to thank you for yesterday."

"The victory was all your doing, lad, and well deserved. Truly, the marriage was a stroke of genius. How'd you know the little governess would go along with you?"

"Let's just say I know her better than most people do."

Whiting removed a tattered billycock hat, baring a shiny pate. His merry, intelligent eyes took in the faded horsehair-stuffed settee against the wall, noting the blanket draped over its back. "Tell me I'm wrong," he said with mock amazement. "Fletcher Danforth, erstwhile rogue of the Inns, has spent his wedding night in a barrister's office?"

Fletcher scowled. "The night and most of the day, too."

"Damn, the girl looked terrified enough when you married her, but I was sure you'd set her at ease. You've a reputation for doing so, you know."

"That was years ago, Walter. And Jessica isn't . . . she's not like the others."

"But she's your wife, man!"

"You know bloody well what the circumstances are. I decided she needed time to get used to the situation." Would Jessica ever get used to the idea that he was an Indian?

"Right kind of you, letting her hold onto her innocence awhile longer." Whiting was not a stupid man. Yet like everyone else, he had no suspicion that Jessica's demure facade was false. Fletcher caught himself wishing that he, too, was ignorant of her past. But then he wouldn't have been able to make her his wife.

"I just wasn't in the mood for a battle," he said.

Walter struck him lightly on the chest. "You've oatmeal mush in that heart of hearts, my friend."

Not mush, Fletcher silently objected, but pride. He simply

didn't want to force himself on Jessica and prove himself the savage she thought he was.

"Perhaps you're wise to wait," Walter mused. "Poor girl's been denied all the pomp of a real church wedding. She'll feel more the wife after a formal ceremony."

Fletcher felt a flash of grim humor. Jessica had used—most unconvincingly—the same argument last night.

"Where is she now?" Whiting asked.

"She's taken the children shopping. I've instructed her to hire some household help as well."

"Shopping?" Whiting grinned. "That'll thaw her prim little heart."

Fletcher shrugged. "Perhaps. But something tells me that with Jessica, it'll take more than husbandly indulgence of the monetary kind."

Whiting scooped a stack of legal briefs off the desk and stuffed them into his creel. "I'm off then," he said.

Fletcher bade him good-bye and remained in the office, feeling at odds with himself. He looked around the room, clinging to the idea that he'd be leaving London soon to resume life with his children . . . and Jessica.

Unbidden, a memory crept into his mind. Thirteen years ago he'd left England with a new wife. The soft luster of Jessica's beauty glowed brighter than Sybil's harsh handsomeness; Jessica's rough past had carved her character, while Sybil's genteel upbringing had left a vapid void. Yet they were alike in too many ways: neither was what she had seemed at first; both were offended by the Mohawk part of Fletcher.

And both marriages had been wrought by convenience, not love.

Shaking his head to scatter the depressing thoughts, Fletcher picked up the blanket and began folding it. Dusty books masked the walls of the barrister's sanctum; papers littered the rickety tables and windowsills. A limp wig hung on the back of a Windsor chair. On the floor sat a round tin box that held Whiting's tonsorial armor.

The window gave out onto an open square refreshed by a burbling fountain. Sunbeams danced in the water and dappled the cobbled surface of the courtyard. Pigeons murmured and strolled beneath the yew trees. Fletcher stood watching the peaceful scene, his mind preoccupied with his new wife.

It was hard to think of Jessica as his wife. The Lord Chancellor had ordered the marriage; the piece of paper they'd signed decreed it was valid. But a legal document didn't give him Jessica's mind and heart. She was instead his unwilling mate, forced into marriage by his desperation.

Perhaps, he reflected, Walter Whiting was right. A church ceremony would solidify the union, would make it more real to them both. Damn, Fletcher thought, angry at himself, why should I bother?

Because, his conscience answered, you are beginning to doubt your right to brand her a whore and manipulate her life.

As if summoned by his conflicting thoughts, Jessica appeared in the courtyard, flanked by the children and trailed by footmen overburdened with parcels.

Jessica spoke briefly to the children and then to the footmen. Kitty skipped to the doorway. Gabriel held the door open for the servants and, except for Jessica, they all went inside.

Alone in the cobbled square, Jessica looked around for a moment, then walked to an iron bench and sat down, setting her fruitwood box beside her. In silent contemplation of the spattering fountain, she touched a hand to the wisps of hair which, as always, had managed to escape her snood.

A stray shaft of sunlight settled over her. Her hair seemed to absorb the golden glow and breathe it back out again, lending her an aura of unspoiled radiance.

His mouth suddenly dry, Fletcher gripped the windowsill. Jessica took paper and scissors from her box and fixed her round-eyed gaze on a robin feeding its young in a yew tree. With great concentration she began to cut.

A few moments later a newcomer appeared, a young barrister in a cotton gown and untied lawn cravat, his tin box held negligently under one arm. He had a wealth of blond hair tied back in a queue. His surprise at seeing a woman at Gray's Inn was obvious as he crossed the cobblestones toward her. His smile was genuine and clarion clear.

Fletcher tried to remember a time when smiling had come that easily to him.

They might have been a young couple courting, the smiling man enraptured by the lovely girl as he admired her art. Jessica spoke to him with friendly ease and Fletcher felt a hot arrow of envy. She was practiced in conversing with strange men and doubtless so used to the effect of her beauty that vanity never tainted her manner.

Jealousy began as a slow, bitter burning sensation in Fletcher's chest. His possessive nature made him want to chase the jaunty barrister off. Why couldn't Jessica look at her own husband the way she was looking at the blond man now, with a ready smile and a total lack of suspicion?

Because you blackmailed her into marrying you, said his niggling conscience.

Fletcher felt suddenly guilty. What right had he to rob Jessica, a beautiful woman and talented artist, of her future? But for his interference, she might one day gain recognition for her art and the attention of a promising gentleman like the one hovering over her right now.

He saw her shake her head in response to something the barrister had said. Reluctantly the man gave her a last grin and disappeared through one of the iron-studded doors.

On legs gone stiff with tension, Fletcher left Whiting's chamber. He rushed down the stairs and emerged into the sunlit yard, boots clicking on the worn cobblestones.

Jessica looked up. For a moment, her face was unguarded and Fletcher thought he saw admiration in her eyes, which pleased him absurdly. The look fled, to be replaced by one of distrust.

"Hello, Jessica," Fletcher said, slightly breathless from hurrying and trying to conceal it.

She inclined her shining head. "Hello."

"Did you manage to find all the things you'll need to take to Holland Hall?"

A satisfied smile lit her face. "Indeed we did. And more."

"I'm glad your outing was productive."

"We'll see how glad you are," she said challengingly, "when the bills arrive."

Fletcher couldn't suppress a wry grin. She couldn't know how little he cared for his wealth and its trappings. He doubted she realized that a single afternoon's shopping trip couldn't make even a small dent in his assets.

"And what about servants? Did you call at the agency for domestics I recommended?"

Jessica grinned. "I engaged two maids and a nurse for Kitty, just as you asked. But I didn't go to your agency."

"No?"

"I have a few connections of my own, Mr. Danforth."

Suspicion stabbed at him, but her eyes, reflecting the sunlight, looked as guileless as gray mourning doves.

"You didn't engage a governess?"

"I'll see to the children's schooling myself."

Fletcher recalled his words the previous night, his statement that he didn't want Kitty and Gabriel tainted by her morals. She hadn't deserved that, he thought ruefully; her conduct with the children had always been impeccable. He'd only lashed out because she refused to see the advantages of being his wife.

She stared at him, her eyes daring him to confront the subject of her past once again. But he was in no mood to argue, not in the middle of the first civil conversation of their marriage. "Very good, Jessica," he said, smiling at her surprised look. "I'm pleased. I'm riding early for Falmouth; the rest of you will follow by coach."

"I've never been outside London before," she said.

"The countryside is much safer than this smoke-fogged city. Still, I've hired outriders to accompany the coach."

He sat beside her and took up the silhouette she'd cut. Shaded by spiny yew leaves, her subject, the mother robin, was poised above her young, who strained toward her, their beaks open.

"Charming," he said with total honesty. He slid a sidelong glance at her. "Could it be, Jessica, that you've a bit of the maternal instinct?"

She faced him squarely. "Mr. Danforth, I've grown to love your children and I believe they need me."

Aye, he thought, it was true. But the feeling that stabbed at him was far from pleasant. He wondered if her lack of reference to him was as pointed as it seemed.

"Jessica." He set down the picture and took her hands in his. She stiffened but didn't pull away. "Where the children are concerned, I have no call to be critical. I appreciate all you're doing."

"I was hardly given a choice, Mr. Danforth."

"My name is Fletcher. Say it, Jessica."

"Another imperative?"

"Please."

"Very well. Fletcher." She glanced down at their entwined hands, his brown and rough, hers pale and dainty. "I resent what you forced me to do in the Lord Chancellor's court, but I want you to know . . . I didn't mean what I said last night, about the Indian part of you."

A gust of warmth rippled through him. "I'm glad," he said softly, running his hands lightly up her arms, "because sometimes I think my Mohawk blood is the best part of me."

Still looking down, she shivered. "You're still as much a stranger to me as you were a few moments ago."

"That will change. We've a long voyage ahead of us, with little to do besides talk"—his fingers were drawn to the soft flesh beneath her chin, his eyes to the gold-spangled sweep of her lowered lashes—"and discover each other. . . ." Hungry for the taste of her lips, he tipped her chin up so that she faced him.

The wary veil of distrust over her eyes put him off as effectively as a slap. "I'm sure I'll find plenty to occupy me, what with the children and the sewing . . . and the new servants," she said quickly.

Frustrated by her reticence, Fletcher dropped his hand. Driven all his life by Mohawk pride and English arrogance, he'd learned to hate failure. Jessica's sensitivity, the unexpected complexity of her character, dared him to do more than simply assert his husbandly rights. He wanted to hold her with a bond stronger than the legal agreement they'd wrought in court.

"I want to know you," he heard himself say.

Her eyes narrowed. "Oh? But you claim to know me so well, Fletcher."

He wished he'd never seen her at Madame Severin's tussling with a besotted nobleman. "I know what you were, not who you are."

"That didn't seem to matter to you when you forced me to swear under oath that I'd agreed to become your wife," she said, her voice soft but bitter. She clapped her box shut and picked it up, standing. "I must see that the children get their supper.'' Her movements caused the picture of the birds to fall to the ground. Heedlessly she trod upon it, marring it with the impression of her heel.

The scent of violets, almost too faint for his senses to grasp, lingered in her wake, then fled on a breath of spring wind. Damn. Her fears played on his guilt, undermining his desire with pangs of conscience. Jessica's perplexing fragility left him more frustrated than would the most artful feminine teasing.

Fletcher expelled his breath with an explosive sigh. He longed for home, where he wouldn't feel like a stranger. Soon, he thought, soon. The mountains and rivers would embrace him; the Mohawk people and his tenants would welcome him. He could lose himself in the all-consuming cycle of planting, nurturing, harvesting. The new task of raising his children beckoned him.

But what about Jessica? Her words tiptoed into his mind: *I will not live in the world you offer.*

He ground his fist into his hand. You will, he told her silently. And not, he finally admitted, simply because he needed to provide a mother for his children.

Despite what she was, Fletcher wanted to show her his America, to make her as much a part of the land as he was.

Why? he asked himself in irritation. Why does her happiness matter?

Because you have broken her dreams, his unmerciful conscience replied.

Fletcher picked up the ruined silhouette and brushed the dirt from it. No more, he decided, would he let himself dwell on her shadowy past, her false innocence. She was his wife. He was duty bound to see to her contentment.

But how? How to convince a frightened, resentful woman to accept him, his home, his children?

Indulge her, his conscience suggested.

And perhaps that was the answer. She insisted that he had no right to lay a husband's claim to her unless she was given a proper wedding.

Starved for a woman by five years of enforced celibacy, his body rebelled at the thought.

Chapter 8

Jessica's eyes roved over the Falmouth wharf area, delighting in its pastel-painted cottages and counting houses, the great hulls of brigs and barkentines towering above the harbor, the robust stevedores sweating as they manned the whip purchases, hoisting cargo. She heard the cacophonous screams of gulls, the shrill whistles of ships' masters, the excited chatter of Kitty, Gabriel, and the new servants who had stepped from the coach behind her. Her nostrils were filled with the unfamiliar tang of the sea, the warm aroma of roasting coffee, the scents of fish and sodden hemp. The flavor of salt air touched her lips like a gossamer kiss. A fresh breeze grazed her face, lifting stray tendrils at the nape of her neck and causing her navy skirts to billow.

"Miss Darling—I mean, *Mama*."

Fondness seeped through Jessica at the sound of Kitty's voice. "What is it, dear?"

"Are we to sail on one of these ships?"

"We are indeed. The coach driver said it's that four-master over there." Jessica pointed. Gabriel shouldered his satchel and surged forward; she clamped a hand on his shoulder. "Not so fast. It may not be time to board yet. Wait here with the others while I go find your father."

Gabriel seemed on the verge of a major sulk, so she added placatingly, "I'd feel much better knowing Kitty was safe with you." He brightened immediately.

Jessica searched the wharves with nervous eyes. Two days she and Fletcher had been apart. Two days during which she had wondered frantically what Fletcher's reaction would be to her choice of household help.

131

"Come on, Gabe," said Jade Akura with a gleam in her eye, "we ladies need your protection. I'll show you a card game called *manille*. Right popular with sailors, it is, and a way to win a crown or two."

Gabriel's grin reinforced Jessica's conviction that she had every right to bring along maids of her choosing. Surely it was too late for Fletcher to object now.

Adele joined Jessica as she strolled toward the ship. *"Tiens,* we've a moment to talk at last. The coach ride left us little privacy to say the things that need to be said."

Jessica stiffened. "You're assuming I have something to say on the matter of my husband."

"Bien sûr. Are you not the slightest bit . . . moved . . . to find yourself the wife of such an interesting man?"

"Don't you see, Adele? Fletcher Danforth cares nothing for me. He married me only to win guardianship of his children. He's avoided me ever since." Most probably, she admitted to herself, because she had turned aside his attentions. Just as she intended to do today and every day until Fletcher realized exactly how resentful she felt about the cavalier way he'd rearranged her life.

"But you seemed agreeable enough in court."

Jessica drew a dark strength from the anger surging through her. "Marriage—with any man, let alone Fletcher Danforth—was the last thing I wanted."

"It is done, *copine.* You must resolve to make the best of it." Adele gripped her fichu as a sea breeze snatched at it. "And it is not so very bad, eh?"

Annoyed at Adele's inflated opinion of Fletcher, Jessica scowled. "He blackmailed me, if you must know the truth. He formed the misbegotten assumption that I *worked* for you and he threatened to tell the Pynchons as much. I'd have been dismissed and all my training would have come to naught."

To Jessica's chagrin, Adele laughed. "I should like, then, to have seen his face when he discovered his mistake on your wedding night."

Jessica looked away. "There was no wedding night." Her frown deepened at Adele's shocked expression. "Yes, he spared me, but not because he was being noble. I . . . made him angry."

"So he still thinks you are a fallen woman?"

"Yes. He will listen to no explanation to the contrary."

"Then I shall set him straight myself."

"No!" Jessica's loud objection startled them both. "The matter is between Fletcher and me," she added.

"As you wish." Adele set her lips into a familiar Gallic pout. *"Dommage.* I do so want to like him."

"Why?" Jessica asked. "Why do you want to like him?"

"Because our fates are in his hands, *copine."* She shook her head. "We can only hope your *barbare* from America is more honorable than my Spanish pirates."

"Does it shock you?" Jessica asked her. "Is it so horrible that he's half Indian?"

Adele chuckled. "I find it . . . interesting."

"Can it excuse his behavior toward me?"

"He was desperate, Jessica, and he loves his children."

"So desperate he forced me into this marriage without the slightest consideration for my feelings." Despair clawed at her. "I'm trapped, Adele." Impatiently she thrust aside her feeling of helplessness. "But Fletcher is wrong if he thinks he can continue to run roughshod over me. My husband he may be, but he'll soon learn I've a will of my own."

The Frenchwoman regarded her sharply. "Have you told Mr. Danforth about me and the girls?"

Jessica hesitated. Fletcher would be mortified to learn that his wife and children would be served by former ladies of the evening. She envisioned his deadly quiet fury.

A slow smile spread across her face, a smile of ill-gotten amusement. Hiring Adele, Jade, and Nan was the expression of a small but significant rebellion, the first of many she intended to inflict on Fletcher.

"Adele," she said, savoring the thought, "my husband will be positively beside himself when he sees Jade and Nan."

"I leave you to it then, *copine.* Go and find your husband." Adele went back to join the others, shaking her head and muttering under her breath.

Jessica spied Fletcher some distance down the quay next to a berthed ship, leaning an elbow on a battered crate, cocked hat dangling from his fingers, the wind ruffling his hair. She held back, unwilling to face him just yet. She needed a few moments to still the sudden slamming of her heart against her rib cage.

From just a moment's study, she realized Fletcher had left London behind like a man shrugging off a cumbersome burden. He looked relaxed, almost happy. The salt air lent a dash of ruddiness to his tanned face, making him more maddeningly handsome than ever. She swore it was resentment that made her insides quake, but she'd never known resentment to feel so heady.

Fletcher was speaking with a slovenly individual notable only for his sheer size. A head of spiky russet hair poked a good six inches higher than Fletcher's; his belly jutted conspicuously in front of him. Although the man dwarfed Fletcher in size, he didn't seem a likely match in intellect. Studying the large, whey-colored face, Jessica wondered what her husband was doing with this simpleton.

Like garners like, she thought uncharitably as the two men burst into sudden laughter. Then, as if feeling her gaze, Fletcher looked directly at her. Embarrassed at being caught staring, Jessica flushed.

Fletcher invited her to his side with a grin and a sweep of his hat. Reluctantly she picked her way around a jumble of barrels and bundles, scattering a small flock of gulls with her rustling skirts.

Then Fletcher was reaching for her. Almost without thinking she placed her hand in his and was surprised at how perfectly natural it felt to be hand in hand with the stranger who was her husband.

"Jessica," he said, smiling, "I'd like you to meet Roelof van Twiller, master of the *Shadow Hawk*. Roelof, my wife, Jessica."

The beefy face opened into a broad smile, revealing long yellow teeth and an unexpected gleam of merriment in his hazel eyes. "Blast me, but you're a pretty little thing."

Unused to such talk, Jessica bristled.

Van Twiller chuckled. "And square-rigged too," he added quickly. "Pleased to meet you, ma'am." His voice had a musical lilt and a tenor pitch discordant with his massive size. "Looks like I'm to be bearing you to your home port," the giant added.

Jessica's eyes climbed beyond the smiling face to the rail atop the ship's hull. "*You* are going to sail this ship?" she squeaked. As soon as the words were out she realized how rude she sounded. "Oh dear, that is . . ."

Laughter issued from van Twiller, clarion bright with amusement. "I'm a big dolt of a fellow, ain't I? But I've a sense for the things that count in sailing a ship."

"You should know better than to judge someone on first impressions," Fletcher said, not nearly as amused as van Twiller. "You'll be in the very best of hands."

"Of course," Jessica said hastily. "You must come and meet the children, Mr. van Twiller." She'd intended to relish Fletcher's reaction to the help she'd hired, but suddenly she wanted a buffer for his anger.

Van Twiller shook his great, spiky head. "Later, ma'am. I've things to do if we're to sail with the tide." His bow was awkward, his smile genuine as he clapped Fletcher on the back. "Damme, Mr. Danforth, I thought we'd be bringin' the *other* one along, kickin' and yowlin' like a wet cat. This one's a bloomin' angel compared to her."

Fletcher shouted with a rare thunderclap of laughter. "Lord, Roelof, you do know how to turn a phrase," he exclaimed. "Go to it then." His laughter ebbed to a gentle chuckle as the giant ambled away, shouting orders and curses to the sweating men on the quay. He mounted the gangway and his manner seemed to change. Suddenly the huge, lumbering man became a master of authority.

"Hatches secured?" she heard him demand.

"Aye, sir, and battened tidy!"

"Breakwaters built up?"

"Aye."

"Bear a hand there! Gear clear for running? Main and mizzen yards trimmed? Foreyards braced?"

Every staccato query was smartly answered. Jessica conceded her error in judgment with a sheepish smile at Fletcher. "I stand corrected," she said magnanimously.

"No harm done. Van Twiller likes you."

She was seized by curiosity about the master's reference to Fletcher's first wife. The image of a wet, screeching cat startled her. What sort of woman had Sybil Danforth been?

Fletcher gave her no time to ponder. "I trust you had a pleasant trip from London," he murmured.

Jessica thought of the days she'd spent cramped in the

musty-smelling coach with two lively children, two talkative former courtesans, and the ascerbic and self-satisfied Adele. Fatigue and poor tavern fare had settled in her bones and rumpled her clothing beyond repair.

"Quite pleasant, thank you," she replied, unwilling to give him the satisfaction of hearing her complain.

"Fine. Now, where are my children and where are the three paragons you've hired to join us?"

Jessica caught her lower lip in her teeth. Hiring Adele, Jade, and Nan had been an act of petty defiance against the man who had taken over her life. She wanted her friends with her, that was true, but now that he was about to discover what she had done, she began to doubt her wisdom.

She marshalled her courage. No act of revenge was complete until the victim felt its sting. "I'm sure you'll be quite . . . impressed . . . by them," she said sweetly.

The maids and the children waited beneath a canvas awning. Jessica knew the moment Fletcher recognized the women. He stopped walking and his fingers bit into her elbow. The air around him seemed to cool by several degrees.

"What the devil are *they* doing here?" he demanded.

Jessica swallowed. "I should think it's obvious," she said, enunciating her words as if speaking to an idiot. "Adele is reading Voltaire, Nan is trying to explain to Kitty why the little girl must not peek beneath her eyepatch, and it appears Jade is teaching Gabriel a card game."

"Jessica, I trusted you to engage *decent* household help for this family."

His voice was too quiet, too controlled. Nervously she imagined the rage simmering beneath the smooth, calm surface.

"And so I have," she told him with more composure than she felt. "Despite your opinion of those women, they are kind and loyal. I trust them completely."

"Trust," he repeated, scowling. "The term's as loose as their virtue."

"Didn't they care for Kitty and Gabriel well enough at Bartholomew Fair?" she challenged. "And what was it you were saying about not judging people by first impressions?"

"Touché," he said with a ghost of a smile. "I didn't realize I'd be dining on my own words for luncheon." But his voice was still cold when he added, "What do they know of serving a family?"

"A good deal more than your average sniveling, uneducated maid," she retorted. "Madame gave me a home when I had none; the least I can do is offer her the same now that she has lost everything." There, she thought, eyeing his softening features with satisfaction. He's wavering. "Jade and Nan can make a new start in the colonies," she added. "I believe it was you who pointed that out to me."

"Converting fallen women is a job better left to missionaries."

"I hardly expected three days ago that I would be a married lady in charge of selecting maids."

The acid tone of her voice reminded Fletcher of her bitterness toward him. He let out his breath with a hiss. Of course she was bitter. "It's too late to find other help now," he said gruffly. "But if you don't see to their behavior, I'll ship them straight home."

"You won't be disappointed," Jessica promised brightly. "However, you'd best get rid of that scowl on your face. You'll frighten them all the way back to London with it."

The scowl remained until Kitty spied him. "Papa!" she called, scrambling from Nan's ample lap. Fletcher's heart turned to the oatmeal mush Walter Whiting had referred to a few days before. "Hello, little love," he said, scooping her up. "Are you ready to go to America?"

Kitty looked down at her doll. "Esme is afraid of that big boat," she told Fletcher gravely.

He hugged her close. "You just tell Esme that everything is going to be fine. A ship is just a great, floating house. The *Shadow Hawk* is in a special book called the *Lloyd's Register;* it has the highest rating for safety."

Seeing that the little girl was unimpressed by the coveted rating, Fletcher took a different tack. "The crew tells me the ship's cat had a litter of kittens. You and Esme can play with them."

Kitty gave a squeal of delight. "Did you hear that, Mama?" she piped. "Kittens! Auntie Pynchon always said she didn't like pets. . . ." The little girl danced away, suddenly eager to go aboard.

Fletcher's heart lurched to hear his daughter claim Jessica

as mother. The title seemed so natural, so appropriate, that he felt an unexpected wave of affection for the woman he'd once thought of as no more than an available means to a necessary end. He turned to Jessica and saw her giving Gabriel a firm prod. The boy shuffled forward.

Gabriel looked magnificent, his cheeks reddened by the salt air and his eyes shining with fascination as they drank in the scene on the wharf. But his handsome face became a guarded mask in response to Fletcher's friendly smile. " 'Lo, sir," he said truculently, kicking at an oyster shell near his feet.

"Would you like to go aboard the *Shadow Hawk*, son?"

The boy shrugged. "I guess so."

Fletcher waved to a group of sailors. "Here's Mr. Frick, the boatswain. He'll show you around." He watched, smiling, as Ebenezer Frick ambled up the gangway, Gabriel scampering behind, lugging his satchel.

Kitty tugged on Fletcher's hand. "Come, Papa! See who we've brought with us." She began pulling him in the direction of Jessica's friends. Fletcher paused to send his wife a dubious look, then followed his daughter.

To their credit, the women had gone to some trouble to dress respectably. Adele Severin was regal and refined in a traveling gown of black superfine, a caleche on her head and kid gloves covering her hands. Nan Featherstone looked little short of comical in a green muslin dress which strained at the seams. The civility of a mobcap did nothing to detract from the oddity of her black eye patch. Jade Akura was as exotically beautiful in a plain gold gown as she would have been in a courtesan's *robe de chambre*. Her smile as she stepped forward was as brazen as ever.

"Mornin', sir," she said in the cockney tones that were so at odds with her delicate beauty. "Damme, I ain't been under the canvas since I was, oh, like of an age with your little girl there. Nay . . . come t' think on it, I was with that Neapolitan bloke on 'is . . . never mind. Ain't been on the high seas since I come all the way from the Japans with a load of jade icons."

"I see." Fletcher guessed that Jade Akura had fared better over the years than those jade icons.

Nan dimpled in several unlikely places as she greeted him.

"Ain't never seen the outside of London meself," she said. With her good eye she cast a wary look at the *Shadow Hawk*. "Took your missus some bit of talkin' to con me into comin' along, that it did."

"Oh?" Fletcher sent Jessica a stern look. "And how, pray, did my wife manage to convince you?"

Nan folded her pudgy hands over her middle. "Well, sir, Jess done appealed to me soft ol' heart, she did."

Fletcher raised one eyebrow. "Did she, now?"

Nan bobbed her head, saffron curls spilling from under the cap. "Said ye'd be lost without me. Nice of ye to ask for me personal like, sir. Warms the cockles of me heart."

Feeling Jessica's nervous eyes on him, Fletcher hid a smile. "It was rather nice of me, wasn't it?"

"Aye, sir." Nan's eye darted to the side. " 'Scuse me, but the little girl's wandering a mite too close to the water's edge for my likin'. Come on, Jade."

Fletcher turned to watch Nan galloping away with more speed than he would have believed possible. Jade followed, and in moments Kitty was couched in safety between the two women.

"You see, m'sieur," Adele said in her silken voice, "you have nothing to fear in bringing Jade and Nan along. I am certain they will suit."

"That remains to be seen," Fletcher said darkly.

"You won't find them pilfering your silver, I assure you. For ten years Nan Featherstone has kept my keys for me. I shall take full responsibility for their actions."

Jade's voice rose in a sudden vivid oath as the hem of her dress caught on a rusty barrel hoop.

"A pity you can't take responsibility for their speech, madame," Fletcher said wryly.

"Hmph. Gabriel has undoubtedly heard worse at Harrow. And as for Kitty . . . I shall do what I can, monsieur."

Fletcher couldn't help the stab of respect he felt for this intrepid, snowy-haired French woman. She couldn't be younger than sixty, yet here she was embarking on an adventure even some men feared.

He glanced at Jessica. She was watching Adele with a mixture of pride and affection. Nearby, Jade and Kitty were repeating their disappearing shilling trick.

Fletcher clenched his jaw. Three months ago if anyone had told him he'd be returning home wed to a former courtesan and accompanied by three other ladies of the night, he would have thought it a bad joke.

The important thing, he reasoned, was that he was bringing his children to Holland Hall at last. Marrying Jessica and importing her colorful friends was a small enough price to pay. But what other tricks did his unwilling wife have in store for him?

The women and Kitty were in their snug cabin at the stern. Jessica had spared only a brief nervous glance at the stateroom she was to share with Fletcher, then decided to stay on deck to watch the fascinating process of getting the big square-rigger underway.

Gabriel had announced his intention to bunk in the foredeck with the sailors. At this moment he stood at the forecastle head near the capstan to watch the weighing of the anchor. Jessica saw him gazing wistfully at the boys stationed aloft to overhaul the running gear while the sails were set. She had no doubt that Gabriel would soon attempt the dangerous climb through the rigging.

The crew, she noticed, was a sturdy assortment of some twenty men, tan of face, wearing simple garb, unerringly diligent in their preparations to make sail. At last Fletcher came aboard with the last of the *Shadow Hawk*'s many debarkation papers. From her vantage point near the helm, she watched his fleeting but keen assessment of the ship.

Roelof van Twiller lumbered forward, giving Fletcher a salute. "All is ready, sir," he boomed.

Fletcher glanced over the decks once more. His gaze alighted on Jessica for the blink of an eye—but it was long enough to raise a blush in her cheeks.

"He's a keen one," said the boatswain from behind her.

"Is he, Mr. Frick?" Jessica was wearying of the men's almost slavish admiration of her husband.

"Oh, aye," the sailor replied. "The barque's three hundred feet long and drawing twenty-four feet of water, but Mr. Danforth can spot the smallest detail out of order."

Apparently all was as it should be. Fletcher strode across the deck to Jessica's side. Van Twiller called, "Heave short!"

and the crew leapt into motion. Jessica heard a grinding sound as the anchor, worked from the capstan, was drawn up.

Breathlessly she tilted her head back to watch as the sails were loosed. There was drama in the sudden appearance of canvas, and majesty in the shape of the sails as the wind puffed its first breath into them. After a few more staccato orders from van Twiller, the ship was free of its ground tackle and began to move, pivoting first until she was headed west into the sun. Once the ship was canting nicely to her course, the anchor was secured to the cathead.

"We're properly underway, Mrs. Danforth," Fletcher said.

She chafed at the title but, ignoring it, commented, "I didn't feel much of a breeze, yet it seems we are."

Fletcher took her hand and, before she could snatch it away, touched his tongue to the tip of her finger and held it to the wind. "Sailors say as much wind as can be felt on the weather side of a moistened finger will suffice."

Alarmed by the sudden shimmer of excitement she experienced, she lowered her hand, wishing she could dive down one of the many hatchways and hide from the curious stares of the crewmen.

Fletcher brushed one flaming cheek with his finger. "You mustn't blame the men," he said gently. "To them, we look like newlyweds, like lovers. I see no reason to shatter their illusions."

"And I," she countered, "see no reason to subject myself to ship's gossip." She glared at him, certain he would point out that, for a ruined woman, she seemed overly preoccupied with her reputation.

But Fletcher said nothing, only sketched a bow and moved away toward the chart room. Jessica remained near the helm, looking astern to see the shores of England falling away.

She was leaving behind everything she'd ever known. Much of her past she wanted to forget—fifteen years of wanting and not having, of fearing and not showing it. But the five years since then had been much better—years of learning and striving to learn more, years of security, stability . . . and predictability.

Yet, curiously, Jessica felt no tug of melancholy. For however much she might resent Fletcher Danforth, she was

setting off with her three dearest friends and two children she
was coming to love with a ferocity that surprised her.

As for Fletcher himself . . .

A fresh breeze plucked insolently at her curls, sending them
flying from her net.

Determinedly Jessica tucked the curls away. She was his
wife in name only. She intended to keep things that way for
as long as possible, because to yield to him would be to
surrender the only part of herself she still owned.

Following supper in the galley, the binnacle lamps and
sidelights were ignited. The master placed flares handy in the
chart house to signal passing ships. Kitty had been put to bed
by her three self-appointed nurses; Jessica could hear the
women taking turns crooning to the little girl. Gabriel bedded
down with the sailors and was no doubt having his ears filled
with improbable yarns and bawdy ballads.

Lingering in the shadows of the main deck, Jessica idly
snipped a silhouette of the bowsprit. Webbed by rigging and
shaped by the royal yard and topgallant sails, the subject was
new and challenging. Jessica often used her art to acquaint
herself with new things, new people. Already she felt more
at ease on the ship. Unfortunately, the method hadn't worked
with her husband. She had at least a half-dozen portraits of
him in her work box, but none of them had brought her any
closer to understanding how she felt about him.

Hogs grunted in their sty beneath the forecastle head and
chickens cackled in their hutches aft. Jessica hadn't seen
Fletcher since the evening meal, but a lamp burning in the
chart house led her to guess that he was with van Twiller,
perhaps plotting their course.

Frowning at her work, Jessica gave a disgruntled sigh and
crumpled the tissue she'd been cutting. The uncertain light
of the lanterns and a rising moon proved inadequate for another attempt. She put her things away and, unable to think
of an excuse to postpone retiring, went to the stateroom. The
few crewmen she passed nodded in deference, although she
could hear their low, masculine chuckles. Lord, she thought
in irritation, did they have nothing better to do than speculate
about their employer and his new wife?

A handsome lamp with a frosted chimney burned in the

stateroom. Jessica stood looking around the beautifully appointed cabin, feeling the luxury of a gold and crimson Turkish carpet beneath her feet and the gentle rocking of the ship under full sail.

A bolted-down table supported an assortment of charts and brass instruments. The metal angle of a sextant and the casing of a chronometer gleamed brightly. The table was also laid with a pewter bottle, a glazed earthenware bowl, a bronze chafing dish, and a wooden-lidded jug. Jessica had the sudden impression that Fletcher was more than a mere passenger on this ship. He was keenly interested in every aspect of the enterprise, from cargo stowage to sailing. Somehow, the awareness didn't surprise her.

She found her belongings neatly folded in an iron-maple chest in the corner. Nan had obviously been at work here, stowing smallclothes and petticoats and filling the basin like any well-trained lady's maid.

Jessica extracted a cream-colored night rayle and shook it out, looking askance at the low-scooped neckline. The garment was a gift from Jade, who had once declared it too plain for her customers' tastes. But after Jessica put it on and glanced down, she felt anything but plain. The sheer fabric revealed far too many details of her anatomy. Her breasts mounded high above the neckline, and the hem was slashed in the front, baring her legs.

Hearing footsteps, Jessica snatched the India cotton coverlet from the bed and clutched it around herself like an oversized shawl. When Fletcher stepped into the stateroom, dismay washed over her. She was ashamed of the picture she made—shrinking, trembling, speechless—and helpless to do anything about it. Just then the ship listed gently and she swayed.

His oddly appealing half-smile did nothing to set her at ease. "Dear me," he said, "you really must put the women to work on some new clothing. I won't have my wife swaddling herself in bedclothes for want of a proper gown."

Jessica chewed her lip. "I do have . . . a serviceable night rayle."

Frowning slightly, though still smiling, Fletcher crossed to her and pried her fingers from the coverlet, letting it drop to the floor between them. She heard the soft hiss of his quick-drawn breath as he studied her, his warm gaze seeking places no man's eye had ever touched.

"It does," he said slowly, "serve you well." He reached for her, closed his hands around her upper arms and held her away from him, still staring, staring. . . .

"Oh, God," Jessica said, her heart pounding. "Must you. . . ?"

He smiled down at her, not unkindly. "Must I what?"

"Must you take such liberties with me?" Lord, she thought, a bad player in a melodrama couldn't have said it worse.

"Ah, liberties, I remember," he said, growing cold. "You've never given yourself away for free before."

Anger caused her to forget modesty. Drawing away, she snapped, "Damn you, I've never given myself to a man at all!"

An unexpected smile teased the corners of his mouth. "I spoke out of turn, Jessica, and I'm sorry. I'll not dwell on your past any longer." He took a step closer. "Besides, we'll know each other soon enough."

She recoiled at the suggestiveness of his comment. He was, of course, referring to the fact that he intended to test her claim in a way no words could refute. "You know," she said, edging away, "I really should check on Kitty—"

He snared her wrist and held it, rubbing his thumb along her leaping pulse. "But she's in the best of hands, is she not? Or have you lost faith in your hired help already?"

"But—"

A knock sounded at the door; Jessica went weak at the timely reprieve. Fletcher answered the knock, spoke briefly to Roelof van Twiller, and scratched a quill across some forgotten ship's document.

" 'Night, sir," the master said. "And may I say, sir, it's right good to have you aboard your own ship again."

"Good night, Roelof."

Fletcher turned back; Jessica stared at him with a mixture of awe and disbelief. *"Your* ship?"

"Who did you think owned the *Shadow Hawk?"*

She couldn't imagine anything as massive as this ship belonging to any one person. There was more, much more, to Fletcher than she had ever suspected. She'd thought him an

English gentleman and colonial farmer; now she discovered he was half Indian and a shipowner. What else was he hiding?

"You might have told me," she said peevishly.

"You might have asked," he countered. "But never mind the ship. Come here, Jessica."

She stood rooted, dismayed that he intended to resume his seduction. He shrugged and crossed to stand in front of her. "I'm a reasonable man, Jessica. I'll meet you halfway . . . in most things."

"Reasonable?" she asked. "Tell me, where is the reason in what you've done to me? Would a reasonable man force an unwilling woman into marriage and then drag her halfway across the globe?"

"I married you to win custody of Kitty and Gabriel, but my reasons for wanting you have nothing to do with the children."

The hot mist of a blush climbed from her throat to her cheeks. He reached for her, frowning slightly when he discovered the stiff reluctance of her body.

"You really are too demure. Don't tell me you sleep with your hair bound." His fingers found all her hairpins, plucking them until her net fell away and curls tumbled wildly over her shoulders.

He chuckled softly. "In case you haven't realized it yet, Mrs. Danforth, I'm enamored of your hair."

Self-conscious, she ducked her head. How could any man find favor with her unruly mass of curls?

His gaze swept downward. "And I confess to becoming fascinated with the rest of you."

Jessica was too numbed by mortification to resist him. When he led her to the bunk, she didn't protest. When his hands pressed gently on her shoulders, she sat down, half yearning for his embrace, half fearing it.

But Fletcher didn't gather her in his arms. He merely took a plate-backed hairbrush from the laver, turned her to the side, and began brushing her hair.

The long, gentle strokes soothed her frayed nerves. Jessica felt herself relaxing, caught in the spell of his tender gesture. She tingled from scalp to waist as the brush furrowed through her curls. If this was a prelude to lovemaking, she didn't find it so disagreeable after all. And yet his actions seemed so proprietary that she rebelled.

"You needn't act the lady's maid," she said.

"But you are so adept at acting the lady," he replied calmly. His fingers lifted the locks from the nape of her neck and his lips brushed lightly over her flesh.

Jessica didn't feel adept at anything with him around. She couldn't think, could barely talk. She knew an insult lurked in his wry observation, but she could think of no riposte. Her brain was sawdust; her body was molten honey. Irritably she moved away and swiveled around to face him.

"Please stop," she said. "You make me uncomfortable."

"That's mild enough compared to how you make *me* feel."

He gathered her close and kissed her, catching her gasp in his warm, moist mouth. "But I'm feeling better, Jessica," he said against her lips. "Much, much better."

Heat roared through her veins and alarm bells rang in her head. Fletcher was her lawful husband, they were alone on the high seas in his lamp-lit stateroom and, worst of all, her wayward body urged her to submit to him.

She went slack in his embrace, as troubled by the hot, heady sensations coursing through her as she was by her indefensible predicament. It occurred to her to ask him to treat her gently, but she dismissed the idea. He thought her experienced in the ways of men, and perhaps she was because of all she'd learned from her mother. But she was unprepared for the things he wanted of her. He'd not treat her like the virgin she was, with kind words and gentle touches. Instead he seemed determined to arouse every wanton part of her.

His hands moved into the soft mass of her hair and his mouth sipped from hers, drinking away her resistance, encouraging a response. He pressed her downward so that they were both reclining, thighs touching.

A series of quick thoughts and hazy images flashed through her mind in the space of a heartbeat: her mother, silhouetted against the hanging blanket that divided their garret, a dark male form looming over her. Jessica shuddered. Soon Fletcher would claim her body for his own. Would there be pain? Or would he realize his mistake before he hurt her?

But it was not the pain she feared so much as the power Fletcher would have over her once the marriage was consummated. She already belonged to him under the law; if he took the last vestige of her private self, she'd have nothing left of the identity she'd carved for herself.

Tears came from her hopelessness, trickling hot and shameful from her tightly shut eyes.

She felt Fletcher pull away. Opening her eyes, she found him studying her with a deep, probing stare. He dropped his hands from her shoulders as if touching her had suddenly become unbearable.

"My God," he whispered, sounding half angry, half astounded, "you're afraid."

Miserably she turned her face toward the wall, seeking comfort in the cool scent of the lemon-bleached bedclothes. "Of course I'm afraid. My whole life has been turned upside down and you expect me to behave as if I'd been properly courted and properly wed, as if this"—she waved a hand, indicating the cabin—"were no more than a pleasure boat on the Thames. I . . . yes. I am afraid."

He swore under his breath. The bed creaked as he left her side. She heard his footsteps thudding on the carpet and the sound of his opening a sea chest, rifling through its contents. By the time she dared a glance in his direction, he was abed— in a net hammock suspended between two vertical posts.

Too astonished to appreciate her relief, Jessica sat up. "You—you're sleeping there?"

"Would you mind putting out the lamp?" His voice was hard with baffled anger.

Jessica stared at him. "I don't understand."

"Then let me explain," he replied, so softly that she knew he was furious. "I'm not such a savage that I'd take you by force."

So that was it, she thought. She hadn't realized her insult about his heritage had cut so deeply. She hadn't meant it to. "I thought you understood that I'm sorry for what I said about you being a savage," she told him. "Truly, Fletcher, that aspect of you does not frighten me."

"Then why the hell are you so afraid?" He sat up and leaned forward, his hammock swaying, concern shadowing his brow. "Good Lord, Jessica, have you been mistreated by a client? Is that why you're fearful of men?"

Bitter laughter welled up in her. "No, Fletcher," she

stated. "I don't suppose you'd believe I've never been in a position to be mistreated in that way."

He scowled at her. "I don't know what the devil to believe about you. Now put out the light."

Numbly Jessica reached for the lamp and drowned the wick. Moonlight slanted subtly in through the diamond-shaped windows of the stateroom, picking out his rumpled shape whose rigid posture told her he was anything but sleepy.

"Fletcher?"

Silence.

Jessica bit her lip, then began again. "Fletcher . . . thank you."

His breath came out in an impatient hiss. "Don't thank me. I'm mad to allow myself be taken in by you, but I'll leave you to yourself . . . though not forever. You are my wife; my name is not just some title you wear like those demure gowns of yours. It's what you are, like it or not, and one day you'll learn what that means."

She lay listening to the slap of the sea against the hull, staring into moon-shadowed darkness and wondering why he'd granted her this reprieve. Why, in the heat of his desire, had a tear or two stopped him cold?

His mercurial changes of mood confused Jessica. One moment he was hard with fury, giving her a tongue lashing over Jade and Nan, and the next he was soft as pudding, taking time to reassure his daughter about the voyage. He could be domineering while issuing orders to the crew, generous while overlooking a cabin boy's small mistakes. He was endearingly kind to Kitty; he was cautiously affectionate with Gabriel. He was indulgent; he was restrictive.

But one aspect of Fletcher's character remained constant. In all her husband did, he was masterful. Whether arguing a case in court or supervising the loading of cargo, he was always in control.

Despite his acquiescence tonight, Jessica suspected he would attempt to assert a similar authority over her. With a grim smile, she vowed to resist the man who had torn her from her life of quiet security.

But how? she wondered helplessly. Fletcher was a puzzle whose picture hadn't been revealed to her. He wasn't a simple colonial farmer but a man of unimaginable wealth. He wasn't what she'd wanted from life, but he was her husband. She had no idea what that meant for her. She didn't know how to be a wife to such a man.

She didn't know how to be a wife at all.

Chapter 9

Jessica, Fletcher soon learned, knew little of wifely ways. She stayed abed long after he was up and working in the chart house or reckoning his accounts. She was often late to table, unaware that the evening meal would not start without her. She was the last to notice a missing button or frayed cuff on one of Fletcher's shirtsleeves but the first to disagree with him on some matter concerning the children. She was more likely to be sprawled on the floor playing at jackstones with Kitty than she was instructing the girl in needlework. She treated the women she'd hired into her service like old and trusted friends. Yet oddly, Fletcher found her ignorance of marital conventions endearing.

Expelling a disgruntled sigh, he put aside the ledger he'd been writing in, his eyes drawn to a stack of silhouettes on the corner of the table. Jessica's scissors had been busy; the stateroom was littered with the portraits, the floor sprinkled with tiny snippets of black paper.

He began idly flipping through the pile. There was Gabriel in the crow's nest, peering through a spyglass; Jacques, the skinny cook, dolefully contemplating a fresh-caught codfish held at arm's length; Jade and Nan standing on deck, their heads inclined as if in deep conversation.

And—unexpectedly—Fletcher found a picture of himself standing at the bow, one foot braced on the capstan as he looked out to sea. He stared at the portrait, studying the artful angles and clever curves that looked so simple, yet were so complex.

To Jessica's credit, she had a considerable talent for imbuing her subjects with emotion. To Fletcher's discomfort, he saw that the emotion she'd given him was anger. The figure in the portrait appeared brooding, troubled. Perhaps it was the honesty of the depiction that hurt. God, he thought bleakly, she knows me far better than I know her.

Fletcher was well aware that he *did* brood, that he *was* troubled. Bringing his children home was a victory, to be sure, but all would not be well until they were truly a family. Kitty was young enough to accept the turn of events. But Gabriel showed no signs of softening. The boy hung on the fringes of the family, preferring to mingle with the crew and learn their ways. And Jessica . . .

She seemed grateful that Fletcher, at considerable cost to his composure, kept himself from her bed. His nights were far from restful; lusty visions of his reticent wife left him in a fevered sweat. As the days passed, he often caught himself staring at her, moved beyond all good sense by the glint of the sun on her hair or the glimpse of a bare foot peeping from her skirts as she sat on deck.

Strangely, he was most attracted to her when she was at her most defiant. He suspected it was because he preferred her as his intrepid, reluctant bride rather than as the frightened girl she had been that first night on shipboard.

Scowling, Fletcher rubbed the back of his neck. Passing night after night in the hammock, he'd developed a constant crick in his neck. But that discomfort seemed negligible compared with the physical torture of knowing Jessica lay nearby, sleep soft and voluptuous, blissfully unaware of his thwarted desire.

Exasperated with the turn his thoughts had taken, he set aside the silhouettes and left the stateroom. On deck, Grady the sailmaker was at work, oblivious to the repeated stabs of the big needle into his leatherlike palms. Nan and Adele reclined in canvas seats, doing fancywork, their dainty sewing a curious foil to Grady's industrious jabbing.

The women paused to smile and wave. Bemused, he waved back, reflecting that he'd never had servants treat him with such easy familiarity. But then, he'd never had servants like Nan Featherstone and Adele Severin before.

Gabriel stood at the forecastle head, tending the jib sheets under the watchful eye of Roelof van Twiller. Barefoot and in knee breeches, the boy sported the windburnt face and tousled hair of an experienced sailor. Fletcher felt a surge of pride at his son's quick adaptation to life under sail. Gabriel gave him the barest of nods, then turned back to his chore.

Fletcher felt a familiar sting at the slight, but then Kitty came tumbling from a hatchway, her arms full of kittens. Her smile warmed him like sunshine. "See what I've got!"

He stooped to admire her two kittens, which bore the child's clumsy embrace with laudable patience. "You look pretty today, sweetheart," he said. "Is that a new dress?"

She nodded. "Jade just finished it this morning."

Fletcher studied the dress. Jade Akura had a fine talent with the needle and a keen eye for style. Perhaps bringing her along wasn't such a foolhardy idea after all.

"Jade's doing one for Mama now," Kitty explained. She wrinkled her nose. "But it's not nearly as pretty as mine."

Fletcher wondered what she meant. Jessica had expended a great deal of money on fabrics; he'd assumed she'd purchased something lavish and lovely for herself.

One of the kittens squirmed free and Kitty scampered after it. Curious, Fletcher strolled to the maids' cabin. Through the slightly opened door he saw Jessica standing on a crate. Jade was kneeling beside her, cursing around a mouthful of pins as she took up the hem of the new dress.

"Damme, Jess, you'll have the look of a Quaker woman in this toggery."

Fletcher studied the garment. Was it indeed a new dress? In truth he couldn't tell. The drab, high-necked gown looked exactly like every other Jessica owned.

Annoyed, he compressed his lips. This was obviously another of Jessica's little rebellions. She meant to shame him by dressing like a common servant.

Pivoting, he strode down the deck, bellowing orders.

Some time later he pushed open the door of the women's cabin. With a lordly air he stepped aside to admit a parade of sailors, staggering beneath hemp-bound wooden cartons.

Jessica gasped, whirling in a rustle of gray bombazine. Pins dropped from Jade's open mouth.

"Good day, Jessica," Fletcher said curtly. "Jade."

Jessica clutched the raw edges of her unsewn bodice, trying to conceal herself. "Fletcher, what are you doing?"

The sailors set the crates down and left. Fletcher extracted a knife from his boot and began cutting through the ropes. "I'm doing what you were supposed to have done in London," he said over his shoulder. "Finding some decent fabric for your clothes." He pried open a crate.

"But I already have—oh!" Jessica stared as he unfurled a shimmering length of sea green velvet and tossed it to Jade.

"See what you can do with that," he said.

Jade grinned, her brown eyes gleaming with admiration. "Now, that's more like it," she declared, running her hands over the supple folds of fabric.

Fletcher yanked several more bolts from the crate. The brocaded silks, printed cottons, and rich satins had been meant for trade and would have fetched an extravagant sum in New York, but Fletcher had chosen a more satisfying destination for them: his wife's shapely body.

Jessica, who had been staring mutely at the luxurious cloth, stepped down from the box and raised her chin to a mutinous angle. "I don't agree with your choices."

He straightened, eyeing the coarse weave of her half-finished dress. "You spent a small fortune shopping in London. What the devil did you buy, anyway?"

"Things for the children. Books, ink, paper . . . I told you that, Fletcher."

"How in heaven's name did you wind up with nothing better for yourself than those drab rags?" He gestured in annoyance at her dress.

"I'm used to dressing this way. I'm comfortable in these clothes."

He stared pointedly at a wicked-looking bone stay peeping from her unfinished bodice. "You look about as comfortable as a frigid spinster on a sweltering May Day."

At that she bristled in indignation. "Get out, Fletcher. I won't have you dictating what I'll wear."

He could see the stiff, high neck of the dress chafing her tender throat. He smiled in grim triumph. "You're my wife, Jessica," he told her. "I won't get out and I won't have you dressing like a scullery maid."

"I tried to tell her, sir," Jade said, rubbing a swatch of silk between her thumb and forefinger.

"I'll dress as I bloody well please," Jessica snapped. She took a step forward, catching her foot in the unhemmed edge.

Her sudden lurch yanked the bodice out of her clutching hands. The unsewn dress rippled downward, pooling at her feet and leaving her in nothing but stays, shift, and petticoats. She gasped and clasped her hands around her.

Fletcher couldn't suppress a grin as he went to her, placed his hands on her upper arms, and lifted her away from the dress. Then he put Jessica down and gathered up the offending garment.

"I'll see if Grady can use some of this in repairing canvas," he announced. He looked at Jade, who sat grinning delightedly amid the various fabrics he'd put in her charge. "You seem an able mantua maker, Jade," he said. "Surely you can devise a more . . . fashionable cut of garment for my wife."

Jade sent him a challenging look. "Don't bullyrag yourself, Mr. Danforth . . . I'll do justice to your cloth." She picked up the mound of sea green velvet. "This warrants Madame's opinion. I'll see what she has to say before I set me scissors to it." She slipped from the room.

Jessica, who had hastily donned her other dress, planted herself before Fletcher. Her face was flushed the color of a dawn sky and curls danced around her face. Fletcher had never known anger to look so well on a woman.

"I won't dress as your whore," she stated.

"You are not my whore," he shot back.

"No? You seem to delight in branding me one."

"Jessica," he said, reaching to button the long row of fastenings as a placating gesture, "I've grown weary of that argument. I want nothing more than to put it behind us." His fingers climbed her bodice from waist to throat. Her body felt warm and her hair smelled faintly of violets.

She drew an unsteady breath. "Why must you constantly foist your standards on me, Fletcher? Does my manner of dress matter so much to you?"

Everything about you matters to me. The unexpected thought gentled his voice. "Please understand. You think us provincial in the colonies; you think us devoid of culture. But at Holland Hall there are certain . . . standards to be upheld. I've been away for five years, but I hope to rejoin the community of Albany in grand style, by hosting balls and keeping holidays as well as any English family."

Giving voice to the eventuality ignited a dream in Fletcher. Pride swelled within him as he imagined himself appearing in his grand hallway with Jessica on his arm.

"A woman as beautiful as you deserves beautiful things." His hand lingered at her throat as he fastened the last button.

Jessica seemed jarred by the compliment. She looked around as if to see whether Fletcher were speaking of someone else. Good lord, he thought, was she really so unsure of herself? He took her chin between his thumb and forefinger and tilted her face up to his. Mist-colored eyes regarded him uncertainly.

"Wear those fabrics for me," he said gently. "Please."

"You say that as a request, but I know you mean it as an order."

Frustrated, he longed to shake her and tell her it bloody well was an order. But the bleakness swimming in her eyes made him soften. "Think of the children then," he said, drawing on her most tender sentiments. "They need a mother who dresses according to her station."

"That's ridiculous," she said. "I doubt my clothing matters one whit to Kitty and Gabriel."

"But it will, Jessica. One day it will. I know."

"You know," she repeated mockingly. "Will you add expertise in women's fashions to your long list of accomplishments?"

Cut by her sarcastic tone, he dropped her hands. "My mother never abandoned her Mohawk doeskins and leather-wrapped braids," he admitted. "She was ever a source of amusement for my English playmates." Fletcher had never shared the memory with anyone before. He glanced hesitantly at Jessica, bracing himself for another scathing riposte.

She said nothing at first, only stared at him oddly. Then she laid her hand on his arm. "All right." The agreement was preceded by a soft sigh. "I'll dress as you see fit."

Unaware of what he was doing until his lips tasted the warm satin of her brow, Fletcher pulled her close. Feeling the beginnings of resistance, he let her go and stooped, gathering up a length of peach-colored silk. "This might do for a wedding gown."

"A w . . . wedding gown?"

He grinned at her wide-eyed incredulity. "Aye, you heard me. You'll have a proper wedding at Holland Hall."

"Really, Fletcher, I don't think—"

He bent to speak in her ear. "Isn't that what you're waiting for? God, it's what I've been waiting for."

She swallowed. "It was one thing to agree to a marriage of convenience in court," she said, "but it would be wrong to speak vows neither of us mean in a church."

"You had no such qualms about hypocrisy on our wedding night."

"But that was because . . ." Color flared in her cheeks and she looked down.

"Because you saw it as a means to avoid consummating the marriage," he finished grimly. She refused to look at him and he knew he was right. Yet instead of anger, he felt a twinge of tenderness.

"Jessica," he said, "the people at Holland Hall are our servants and tenants; they'd never forgive us if we didn't allow them to share our celebration. They expect it."

"And what do you expect, Fletcher?" she asked in her low, throaty voice.

"I think you know."

She looked desolate, with her head bowed and her shoulders slumped. "I see."

Fletcher took her hands. "It's more than that, Jessica. You say you've spent years preparing to be a lady. I'm offering you a chance to live the life you've trained for."

Her large, misty eyes searched his. She drew a long, shuddering breath. "Very well, Fletcher," she said at length. "You'll have your wedding. I will mouth the vows some consider sacred; I'll accept the blessing of your servants and tenants; I'll be a mother to your children." Her eyes shone bright with defiance. "But I will never forget that you gave me no choice."

Within three weeks Jessica had the beginnings of a wardrobe that would have done any London woman of fashion proud. Jade's clever hands and unerring eye more than did justice to the luxuriant fabrics Fletcher had provided. Jessica knew the gowns looked well on her; she had only to see the warm, appreciative light in her husband's eyes as he studied her from across the decks or the dining table. She discovered features of herself she'd never paid attention to before: the graceful curve of her neck, the gentle flaring of her hips. She liked the feel of the fabrics: the down-soft velvets, the whisperlike silks, the cool, smooth satins.

Yet despite her fetching new clothes, and probably because of their argument about the wedding, Fletcher avoided her. He never retired until she was asleep; he always rose before she'd awakened. He was by turns tender, uncertain, tolerant, and angry. She felt little closer to him now than the morning they'd embarked for America.

Within three weeks, Kitty seemed to think of the *Shadow Hawk* as her home. The girl adapted to the daily routine with the ease only the very young possess. When not being spoiled by Adele, the child enjoyed setting up housekeeping under an upended ship's boat with her rag baby and the kittens. But Jessica noticed, from time to time, a pucker of worry on the child's brow, as if Kitty somehow sensed the tension of the adults.

Within three weeks, Gabriel had become as capable as the other ship's boys. He responded smartly to the boatswain's commands, hauling away at clews and buntlines like a seasoned tar. He thrived on the danger-tinged tasks of seamanship and spared little time for his usual pranks. But Jessica noticed how Gabriel's eyes sometimes followed his father, eyes full of pain and questions the boy refused to ask.

Jessica hoped to see a reconciliation between them. Fletcher tried; he invited closeness with anecdotes about Gabriel's boyhood; he sought his son's opinion on matters concerning his business. Still Gabriel hid behind his wall of resentment. The ship, Jessica reflected, with its close quarters and unending work schedule, was hardly the place for father and son to resolve their differences.

For all aboard the *Shadow Hawk,* the voyage seemed to be a time of waiting . . . and for dreaming. Life under sail had a rhythm all its own: the regularity of the three watches, the cadence of the sea mounding against the hull, the harmony of the winds. Jacques, the cook, baked bread twice weekly and served up meals in the galley. Each morning, van Twiller dispensed lime juice as required by law to prevent scurvy. Even the cats found their scraps saturated with the stuff.

The barque bounded along "with a bone in her teeth," as the seamen liked to say, referring to the hull cutting through the water. Their path was west-southwest, passing Ile d'Ouessant and the Bay of Biscay. Van Twiller stayed clear of land, however; land was more dangerous than the sea.

Jessica concurred, though not for the same reasons. Every day brought her closer to a bond that was impossible to escape.

"Try that passage again, Gabriel," Jessica said. "I know you can do better."

The boy shifted restlessly at the galley table, his gaze sliding to the diamond-shaped portal, which framed a cloudless sky and the distant billows of the sea. "I don't see why I have to learn Latin," he said sulkily. "What good is construing Virgil once we're in America? Will I recite Ovid while splitting logs?"

Kitty, who sat nearby, giggled at his tone. Jessica pursed his lips. "Your father says America has some very fine colleges. He wants you well prepared."

"I'll only be sent down, just as I was in Harrow."

"See that you aren't." She indicated the book he was holding. "Now read. If you get it right, I'll dismiss you for the day."

Gabriel read in a disinterested monotone. Kitty burst into gales of laughter, doubling over and hugging her rag baby. "Esme, did you hear that? Gabriel sounds funny."

Jessica bit the inside of her cheek, trying her best not to share Kitty's mirth. "Kitty, hush," she said sternly. "Gabriel, that wasn't quite right. Again, please."

Scowling, he repeated the passage. Giggling, Kitty mimicked him. Gabriel slammed the book shut and surged to his feet. Kitty dove for Jessica's skirts, burying her face in the heavy, fawn-colored velvet.

"Kitty," Jessica said reprovingly, "it wasn't nice of you to mock Gabriel. You will apologize at once."

Sobered, the little girl looked up at her red-faced brother. "Esme and I are sorry, Gabriel," she said dutifully.

The boy gave an ungracious snort. "You and that infernal doll can go fin up to the sharks!"

Kitty's face paled. Before Jessica could scold the boy for

frightening his sister, Fletcher strode into the galley. He clamped his hand on Gabriel's shoulder. The boy tried to wrench away, but Fletcher held him fast.

"You've no call to speak to your sister so." Fletcher's eyes flicked to Jessica. She recoiled at the coldness there. He turned back to his son. "Apologize to your sister."

Aware that Fletcher hadn't heard what had precipitated Gabriel's outburst, Jessica put Kitty aside. "Fletcher, please. Gabriel *was* rude, but Kitty—"

Ignoring her, he said to Gabriel, "You're not leaving this room until you ask your sister's forgiveness."

"No," Gabriel said softly.

"What did you say?"

"No!" Gabriel lifted his foot and brought it down with all his might on Fletcher's. Then he lunged for the door; Fletcher grabbed his arm and hauled him back.

"I've endured your rudeness long enough," Fletcher said, and in that moment Jessica knew Gabriel's deliberate slights had cut Fletcher even deeper than she'd guessed. Still, in this case Gabriel was justified.

"Will you please," she said slowly, "give the boy a chance to explain?"

Gabriel glared at her. "I don't need you to take up for me," he retorted, wrenching his arm from Fletcher's grasp.

Even Kitty seemed to sense the taut, quiet rage emanating from her father. "It's all right, Papa. I was teasing Gabriel about his Latin." She gave him her most appealing round-eyed look. "Papa, you promised to teach me cratch cradle." She began tugging him away from the galley. *"Please,* Papa . . ."

Fletcher looked from Kitty's imploring face to Gabriel's stubborn one, then leveled a glacial stare at Jessica. She flung an equally cold look back at him, along with a mute promise of retribution.

She let out her breath as the little girl led her father from the room. Kitty spoiled the effect of her magnanimity by turning at the last moment and sticking her tongue out at Gabriel. Jessica saw the boy stiffen, but Gabriel said nothing, only stared in furious silence at the now-empty doorway.

"I think," she said quietly, picking up the Latin grammar, "that we are finished with lessons for today."

Gabriel seemed not to have heard. "I hate him," the boy said slowly, almost to himself.

Jessica longed to reach out to Gabriel, to soothe that handsome, hurting face. But she knew he'd pull away from her. "Gabriel, he's trying very hard . . . but you're making it difficult by behaving badly and shunning him." The boy sneered but she continued. "He made a mistake today, I'll admit; he judged you before he learned what happened. But he's not perfect, Gabriel. He's human and fallible . . . and worthy of your love and respect."

Gabriel shot her a keen look. "*You* don't love him and you're his wife."

"He's agreed to open his home to me and my friends. I shall try to make the best of it and I suggest you do too."

"Jessica," Adele said, neatening her white hair beneath her black leghorn hat, "such a thing cannot be kept from me. I know you too well."

The breeze picked at Jessica's curls and ruffled the tissue she was cutting. The silhouette of the ship's cat perched on Ebenezer Frick's shoulder didn't please her. Nor did the topic of their conversation. Adele read her like a book, had guessed that she and Fletcher still didn't share a bed. "Why must you always be so . . . so correct?"

The French woman looked smug and tucked her lap robe more securely around her. "Bear hide," she muttered under her breath. "Who can credit it?" Her expression turned sympathetic. "Talk to me, *copine.*"

Jessica didn't respond to the endearment. At that moment Fletcher emerged from the chart room, his fearnought cape flapping in the Atlantic breeze. He paused to speak to Mr. Frick. The sun shot blue highlights into his wind-tossed hair. He looked fit and handsome; an air of authority clung to him like costly cologne.

Unconsciously, Jessica reached for another piece of paper and her scissors began sculpting Fletcher's image. But, as always, her art failed to capture his elusive vitality.

Adele watched with a canny eye. "He defies your skill yet, Jessica."

She slid a glance at Fletcher. "Yes. He's a challenging subject."

"And a challenging man."

Jessica pressed her lips together. "Perhaps so."

"You cannot create his image on paper unless you invite him into your heart."

"Then I'm wasting my time, Adele." Several feet away, Fletcher finished his conversation with Mr. Frick and went back into the chart house. She cut in chagrined silence for a moment, then Adele spoke again. "Why do you not share a bed with your husband?"

Jessica's breath caught in her throat. From anyone else, the intimate question would have been unseemly. But this was Adele, who had been both mother and mentor these five years past.

In her hands the scissors hesitated, then bit into the paper again. "I'm surprised you would ask that, Adele. 'Twas you who once told me it was an act of love. And love has nothing to do with my arrangement with Fletcher. Without that bond, that commitment, it becomes a bloodless, businesslike transaction."

Adele was quiet for so long that Jessica set aside her cutting and glanced up. The woman's bright, intelligent eyes held a look of profound sympathy. Gently Adele took the scissors and toyed with them in her stiff, arthritic hands.

"You know, *copine,*" she said, "I taught you well in many things, but in one area I have failed you."

"Adele, no—"

"*Tais-toi,* do not interrupt," Adele said sharply. "I am an old woman and I wish to reminisce. If you listen you might learn something." She glanced down at the silver stork scissors, her gnarled hands no longer capable of wielding them. "Long ago I promised I would tell you about these."

Jessica blushed. "As I recall, I was trying to steal them from you."

Adele drew her lips together and made a clucking sound with her tongue. "You were a brash little *voleuse*. I came this close to turning you out." She measured a minute space with her thumb and forefinger.

Jessica smiled at the recollection.

"*Alors,*" Adele said, looking back at the scissors. "My parents discovered in me a modest talent for the art of cutting silhouettes. These scissors were a gift for my fifteenth birthday. That, and a sailing excursion.''

Jessica understood the sudden deep sadness on Adele's handsome face. She knew the story of the pirate attack on the sloop off Normandy. Adele's parents had been killed.

Aching with sympathy for the young girl Adele had been, she took the scissors back and set them aside. ''You don't have to speak of it,'' she said.

''The years have muted the pain, *copine,* but not the memory. I only want to tell you that I may have done you a disservice in allowing you to think ill of men. I learned cruelty from my Spanish captors and greed from my London patrons. But such is not the way of all men. My father loved my mother. I recall a certain . . . passion between them.''

Jessica looked out to sea, her eyes tracing the silvered undersides of the clouds on the horizon. ''Perhaps your parents were happy. But perhaps, too, they were a rarity. I lived with the Pynchons for over a year and never once observed an instance of genuine affection or deep feeling.''

''The Pynchons.'' Adele gave a Gallic snort. ''I cannot believe you would make such a comparison. They are shallow, passionless people and you and Fletcher . . . are not.''

Jessica moved restlessly beneath Adele's discerning stare. ''He was unhappy with his first wife; that much I've guessed. Why should this new marriage be any different?''

''Because of you, *copine.* Because of you. You are a fine person and worthy of a man's love.''

Jessica thought of her ruined plans, her shattered sense of security, and resentment welled in her. ''I don't want his love even if he were willing to give it. I want only to be free of him.''

''One day you might discover, *copine,* that there is more freedom and happiness to be had in a loving relationship than a lifetime of independence.''

Jessica squinted at the sculpted billows of the clouds. Was it true? she wondered. Willingly or not, she'd find out soon enough.

Fletcher was surprised to find Jessica awake when he entered the stateroom to retire. She stood turned to the window, her finger idly tracing a path in the dew on the pane. Her lavender combing gown draped from shoulder to floor. A loose spill of peach-gold curls fell over the fabric, catching glints from a candle lantern.

To his disappointment, her pensive attitude made her seem distant, although he longed to be closer to her. In another setting she might have been a goddess, endowed with unearthly powers and otherworldly wisdom.

He grimaced at the fanciful thought. How many men before him has seen her look thus? Had they been as foolishly stirred by her as he was?

The face she turned to him was quietly beautiful, contemplative . . . and troubled—the face of a fallen angel.

"You're up late," Fletcher said.

She wiped her finger on a fold in her gown. "I wanted to talk to you . . . about Gabriel."

Fletcher felt both pleased and frustrated. Part of him had hoped that his wife, so fetchingly dressed, would wish to speak of more personal matters. But another part of him was relieved. He *did* want to talk about this morning's incident.

"He had his reasons for being angry at Kitty," Jessica said. "He'd been working on his Latin and she mocked him."

"I didn't hear that part." Feeling suddenly tired, Fletcher rubbed his forehead. "Fathering used to come so easily to me."

Her look of sympathy warmed his heart. "Every parent is bound to make mistakes," she said, a half smile curving her lips into a bow. "I've done that so many times in my teaching. I once blamed George for hiding the key to the buttery and later found the infernal thing in my own apron pocket."

"And yet"—his eyes roved over her lavender-clad form—"you've managed to shed your hair shirt."

She flushed. "I thought George would never forgive me. But then I discovered a phrase that went a long way toward mending fences."

"Oh?" He stepped closer, drawn to her warmth, her honesty. "And what was that?"

" 'I'm sorry, I was wrong.' "

Fletcher drew in his breath. He could attach any number of meanings to her statement. How many times in his life might he have said those words? How many times would an apology—simple, straightforward, unqualified—have righted a wrong?

"I've learned that children can be very forgiving, Fletcher." She used his given name quite naturally now. Was it possible his wife was lowering the shield of her indifference, becoming more accepting of their situation?

"I'll do as you say," he said. "But there is little of the child left in Gabriel."

"I know."

"He's kept his distance all through this voyage."

"Perhaps that is best. For now. Gabriel is still adjusting. You'll have all the time in the world to repair your relationship once we reach Holland Hall."

Fletcher suddenly found himself reaching for her, drawing her soft form against him. She gasped but didn't pull away. Looking down into her face, he said, "Jessica . . . what of our relationship?"

She swayed against him, her thighs pressed to his, her cheek against his chest. Instantly his body flared to life; but unexpectedly, the feeling became complicated by something more than simple desire.

Jessica lifted her eyes to his. "I can't answer that—"

He stopped her speech with a gentle finger to her lips. "The answer in your eyes is enough. Perhaps at last you're aware that there are worse fates than moving to the colonies. Do you realize that, for the first time, you've voiced the fact that we're going to Holland Hall?"

Her smile was rueful. "I thought that did not need saying."

He brushed a tightly wound curl from her temple. Apprehension flared in her eyes; then she looked away.

Fletcher felt a sudden urge to shake her, but he stopped himself. Doubtless she had been used by coarser men than he; surely her stiff-necked spirit was immune to mishandling. Roughness was not the way to banish her fear and win her favor.

"Jessica . . ." He brought his lips close to hers, a whisper away. The kiss he gave her was tender and full of longing; the kiss she returned was tentative and full of promise. All the weeks of wanting her and denying himself fell away as Fletcher filled his senses with the purity of her scent, the dewy freshness he tasted on her lips. She was warm, pliant, sharing herself with a generosity of spirit that, finally, bespoke willingness, not surrender.

Driven by passion honed to a keen edge, he felt himself losing control. He yearned to toss away his scruples and bury himself in the velvet petals of her femininity. . . . but he'd failed with Sybil, made mistakes he didn't intend to repeat with Jessica. She was drawing him toward an intimacy he suddenly wanted even more than the brief satisfaction of lust. He held her lightly, moved his mouth over hers with unhurried gentleness. She sighed softly against his lips.

Fletcher felt an unfamiliar stab of affection for the stubborn, wise, and infuriating woman in his arms. When Sybil had left him to the redcoats, he thought he'd never feel anything but contempt for a woman again. Yet the tenderness trickling through his body nourished a part of himself he'd long considered dead.

Bewildered by the onslaught of new sensations, he broke the kiss to gaze at her. She stared back, her lips gleaming and swollen from his kiss, her eyes alight with some emotion he didn't recognize.

"What is it, love?" he whispered.

"Do all husbands kiss their wives like that?"

He chuckled in spite of himself. In some ways she was so naive. "Were you trying to conjure a picture of Hester and Charles locked in a passionate embrace?"

Shyly she fingered his stock. "I can't believe Mr. Pynchon would be able to kiss that long without sneezing. He is so fond of his snuff."

Fletcher warmed even more to her. "It's a gift, Jessica, to be able to give and receive pleasure." How absurd the words must sound to a woman who had probably never given herself freely to any man. He searched her misty heather eyes for a glint of derision, but all he saw was sweet, quizzical confusion, and perhaps an invitation too. . . .

He bent to kiss her again.

"Papa! Mama!" Kitty's thin, piteous wail reached them from the companionway. *Damn!* Fletcher's face flashed with anger and frustration. Then a wry smile pulled at the corners of his mouth.

"I'd almost forgotten," he said, "that being a parent is not always unrelieved joy."

"Papa!" the child called again. The sorrowful sound sent Fletcher and Jessica hurrying to the door, their tentative intimacy forgotten in the face of Kitty's panic.

An uncertain predawn light slid dimly through the windows of the stateroom when Jessica heard Fletcher enter. She sat up in bed, moving gently to avoid disturbing the sleeping child beside her. A marmalade-colored kitten stirred from its nest in the blankets, blinked, then resumed its purring slumber.

One look at Fletcher's haggard, distracted face told her his search for the missing doll had not been successful. One look at Kitty's tear-stained, pale cheeks told her the news wouldn't be received well by the little girl.

"What could have happened to Esme?" Jessica whispered.

"Damned if I know," he replied in quiet frustration. "Did you manage to get Kitty to say when she last had her?"

"She swears she took Esme to bed with her as she always does." Jessica soothed the child's brow. "She never forgets."

He scratched his head and swore again.

"Fletcher, she's heartbroken. It took me—and the cats—three hours to get her to sleep. Did you look everywhere?"

He gave her a sardonic smile and she realized the foolishness of her question. For most of the night she'd sat up listening to Fletcher's bellowed orders, to the running feet of a crew suddenly less concerned with manning the ship than with finding a well-worn rag baby.

Jessica had pictured Fletcher literally tearing the ship apart from stem to stern in search of the doll. It was one of the more endearing images she had of him. "Never mind," she said, absently stroking a kitten. "I know you tried, Fletcher."

He laid his hand alongside her cheek. "I'd say you had the harder task. You had to comfort Kitty."

His touch felt warm and oddly tender. She smiled. "I think simple exhaustion did more for her than any reassurances."

"Thank you all the same."

She watched him, felt his hand linger on her cheek, remembered what had happened that night. And knew he was thinking of the same thing. What would have happened between them if Kitty hadn't appeared?

She wondered if he could feel the heat of her blush as she recalled kissing him. She searched among the feelings sifting through her but found nothing as tangible as regret. Slowly, unaccountably, she was beginning to soften toward her husband. Could this unorthodox arrangement work after all? Perhaps, bonded by their mutual concern for the children, they might become friends or . . .

"You were lovely last night," he told her quietly. "And you were right about Gabriel. I'll speak to him today."

"Yes," she said, forcing away a sudden wistful thought. "Yes, he'll appreciate that."

A tiny sob issued from the bedclothes. "Esme . . ."

Jessica slipped her arms around Kitty, cradling the sleep-warm child against her breast. "Hush, darling. Everyone is still looking for her."

Kitty opened her round, wet eyes. "What if she went overboard? What if she's gone fin up to the sharks?"

Fletcher rumpled her sable curls. "I'll find her, poppet." A large tear had gathered on her nose; he brushed it away. "But if you don't get some sleep you'll be too grumpy to play with her. A smile for luck?" he asked. "Please?"

The little red lips trembled at the corners. Fletcher bent and kissed his daughter, gave Jessica a smile of his own, and left the room.

He found Gabriel in the seamen's quarters of the forecastle head, which had been ransacked during the night as all hands not directly occupied in sailing the ship had searched through the cabin looking for the doll.

Gabriel was practicing knots, his face a sullen mask. He kept his eyes fastened on the rope.

Picking up another length of rope, Fletcher lowered himself onto one of the bunks. Deftly he worked the line into a sheet-bend knot. Gabriel ignored him.

"Ever try this one?" Fletcher asked conversationally. He wove another knot. "It's called a clove hitch; useful for its holding power." Gabriel watched for a moment, shrugged, then looked away. Fletcher ached to touch his son, to smooth the lock of hair from the boy's brow. "Gabriel, look at me."

He obeyed, but with a cold insolence that made Fletcher long to slap him and embrace him all at once. "I was wrong yesterday when I upbraided you. I'm sorry, son."

Studying Gabriel's deep blue eyes, Fletcher discerned a tiny flicker of something familiar, something he'd once seen in a seven-year-old boy who had loved him. But the flash was so quickly gone Fletcher thought he had imagined it.

Just then Orin van Twiller, a deckhand and Roelof's son, bounded into the cabin. Spying Fletcher, he licked his hand and plastered a spiky lock of red hair in place. "Mr. Danforth, I didn't know you'd be in here. I just come to tell Gabe we've sighted land."

Gabriel was on his feet immediately, but Orin lingered. "We're still after the little girl's doll, sir," the stocky boy added. "But Lord a'mighty, there's no place left to look." Orin's eyes moved dolefully around the cabin. His gaze lit on a small leather satchel partially concealed beneath a bunk. "Lord a'mighty! How'd that escape us?"

Orin moved toward the satchel. Gabriel was quicker; he planted himself in front of the big fellow. "That's mine, Orin," he said in a grim voice.

"But we're s'posed to look everywhere."

Watching a guilty, guarded look creep over Gabriel's face, Fletcher felt sick. He kept his smile bland as he said, "Orin, go above. Gabriel and I will be up shortly."

Scratching his head, the youth left. Gabriel faced his father, eyes hard and jaw firm.

"Do you know where Kitty's doll is?" Fletcher asked.

Gabriel thrust up his chin. In a flash, Fletcher had a vision of Sybil. God, he thought. He's Sybil's son too.

"I don't see why everyone is in an uproar over that stupid doll anyway."

"To you it's a stupid doll," Fletcher agreed. "But to Kitty that rag baby means comfort and security. You used to have an old Indian blanket yourself." With pain, Fletcher recalled the last time he'd seen that blanket—clutched in Gabriel's hands the night of Fletcher's arrest.

The boy's blue eyes grew colder. "Mother threw it overboard when we were sailing for England. It was just another filthy memento of my Indian heritage."

Fletcher winced. He could hear Sybil's voice in that comment—Sybil's hate-filled, scathing voice. "How did you feel about that, son?"

"I didn't care."

"I won't argue about that now. Your sister's beside herself. And I think you know where the doll is."

Gabriel betrayed himself a second time by glancing ever so briefly at the satchel.

Hating what he had to do, Fletcher reached for it. Ignoring Gabriel's angry curse, he tore the bag open and retrieved the doll. He faced Gabriel, trying to still the pain that tore through him. Stealing the doll was a minor act, a petty theft, yet it was symbolic of a greater conflict. Gabriel was hurting and his turmoil had manifested itself in cruelty to his sister. Fletcher ached for the boy, but he knew better than to gloss over what Gabriel had done.

"This time," Fletcher said evenly, "you *will* apologize to Kitty."

"No!" Gabriel's face was stained a deep, remorseless red.

Fletcher went to the door. "You won't be allowed to leave this cabin until you speak to Kitty. I hope you decide to do so, because landfall is an agreeable sight. A true sailing man wouldn't let his pride keep him from it."

His chin ducked low, his eyes veiled, the boy trudged out into the gangway.

Sides streaked and sails pressed for landing, the *Shadow Hawk* bounded into New York Harbor. The anchor hung in readiness at the cathead.

"Down helm!" van Twiller bellowed across the cleared decks. The ship heeled. "Let go!" the master ordered, and the anchor fell with a great rattle of cable.

As sailors ran aloft to bind the sails into harbor stow, Fletcher's eyes sought the land. From their anchorage at Ellison's Dock, he could see the steep slope of the Hudson waterfront, the rearing spire of Trinity Church, the brick-and-marble houses set broadside to the streets. To the left lay the green expanse of King's Farm, bordered by a ropewalk and stretching to the northern reaches of the settled part of Manhattan Island.

Fletcher's disappointment over Gabriel was washed away by a sense of accomplishment. Five months ago he'd embarked from this harbor with one purpose in mind. And, despite numerous and unexpected obstacles, he had achieved that purpose. He'd brought his family home.

He turned to see how they were greeting America.

Leaning on the rail, Adele looked stately and grave. Jade looked cocky and confident; Nan sagged against her, not bothering to conceal her relief at the sight of dry land.

Fletcher's gaze moved to Gabriel. The boy's insolent pride had been shaken, but he'd managed to tender a decent apology to his sister. Now his face held a strained look of suppressed eagerness.

Clutching her doll, Kitty moved into the folds of Madame's gown. The little girl's brighter-than-sunshine smile was back in place.

At last Fletcher's eyes found Jessica. Of all the company he was bringing to this new land, he found he was most concerned with his wife's reaction. Deep inside himself he had discovered a need to make her a part of the land and his family . . . and himself.

Her face betrayed nothing. Looking as impassive as a figurehead, she gazed at the houses of the West Ward.

Fletcher crossed to her side. He took her gloved hand in his and squeezed. "Almost home, Mrs. Danforth," he said.

Chapter 10

A lateen-rigged sloop and a Dutch-built schooner, both belonging to Fletcher Danforth, were being laden at the broad mouth of North, or Hudson's, River. Eager to escape the accusing looks of the sailors who'd forfeited their sleep searching for Esme, Gabriel wandered down the quay.

The brick weigh houses and rickety warehouses didn't interest him, nor did the colorful array of laborers, merchants, traders, and hawkers wandering through the unpaved, pig-infested streets. These were people of a country Gabriel had no desire to be a part of, people whose single-minded industry seemed strange in contrast to the rigid society of London. Stuffing his hands into his pockets, he ambled toward a large block-and-tackle hoisting machine, which was surrounded by tall hogsheads.

The sound of a familiar throaty laugh filtered through the screeching of gulls and the haggling of hucksters. Gabriel peered around a hogshead and spied Jade Akura and Nan Featherstone seated on the ground, casting dice.

His interest piqued, he paused to watch them. Jade and Nan were as unlike as pastry and bread. Jade was petite and exotically beautiful. Nan was large and pleasantly plain. Jade had a sharp wit and a sharper tongue; Nan had a gentle nature and a facility with kind words.

But this morning, Gabriel noticed, the two women exhibited a commonality that transcended their outward differences. Both were well and truly, deeply and definitely drunk.

Pleased to have found something mildly diverting, he approached. Broad, lopsided smiles greeted him. At least *they* didn't hold him in contempt for what he'd done to Kitty.

"Come join us, Gabe," Jade invited, waving a clay bumper of gin, "if you've got a penny or two to wager."

"Aye, Jade's playin' an honest game today," Nan said. "I made her keep her cogged dice in her pocket."

Grinning, Gabriel joined them and promptly won the entire meager pot with a few throws.

"Damme, if that don't tear it," Jade said, her words slurred as she took another pull at the gin. Her dark eyes smiled at Gabriel. "You've done us in, lad."

He frowned. The day still loomed long and lusterless before him. "That I have," he conceded.

Nan hiccupped gently and wrested the earthenware bottle from Jade. "He's a right jolly shooter, is our Gabe," she chortled. She drank deeply, wiped her mouth on a corner of her shawl, and groped in her tightly-packed bodice. "Plum out of coppers, I am. How about you, Jade?"

After a similar search of her own garments, Jade said, "Beggared. You've pinched me out of a week's wages, Gabe."

"Then win your coin back," he said with a grin.

Nan shook her head. "What for, lad? Ain't no need for coppers where we're agoin', or so says Mr. Frick."

Gabriel's grin wavered. Nan Featherstone couldn't know how right she was. If his dim memory served, Holland Hall was far from any center of commerce. Still, the alternative to gaming with Jade and Nan was a day of loitering, of Jessica's relentless optimism, of his father's constant, overbearing presence, of Kitty's silent, hurt looks.

"One more toss," he said, summoning the wheedling grin he'd often used to sway meek parlor maids and offended schoolmasters.

They shook their heads in unison. "We've no coin left to wager." Jade was trying to snare the bottle from Nan.

"A forfeit then," he said with sudden inspiration.

Nan chortled, relinquishing the large vessel. "Tell me, you little wiseacre, what we've got that you want."

Gabriel's eyes gleamed. "I'll have a pull on that bottle. I had a taste of claret once, but never gin."

"Oh no, you don't," Nan said, squinting at him with her good eye. "Mother Geneva ain't for the likes of you."

"Now wait a minute there, Nanny," Jade said, her interest growing. "One punt and we've got our wages back."

"*If* we win."

Jade smiled sweetly. "No problem."

Gabriel admired her guile. Had she not imbibed so much gin, she might have succeeded in substituting her cogged dice for the legitimate cubes. But drunkenness had made her clumsy; he noticed the switch. Deftly he switched them back.

Moments later he was gloating over his win and cradling the big earthenware bottle in his hands.

"All right, you've proved your prowess with the dice," Jade said, laughing. "No need to show us what you can do with the gin. Give us back the bottle, ducks."

He easily eluded her reach. Grinning, he scrambled to the top of the rope-shrouded block, just inches beyond their reach. He raised the bottle in mock salute and took a hearty pull.

A good portion of gin landed in his stomach before its bite seared his tongue. On his second swallow a lightning bolt shot down his throat and detonated in his belly.

His eyes widened and watered. His mouth burned and blistered. His stomach roiled and rebelled.

Gabriel felt himself go completely still on the outside, but his insides were churning and burning. He tried to focus on the women below, to hear what they were yammering about, but to no avail. They appeared as fuzzy shapes and their voices sounded like penny trumpets.

The gin he'd imbibed was clamoring to get back up; his boyish pride kept it down. When at last Gabriel conquered his mutinous stomach, he felt a dark, woozy triumph. Now he became aware of Jade and Nan reaching for him.

He clutched the bottle and climbed higher, sitting in a slinglike web of rope. Out of reach of their grasping hands and rapidly sobering admonitions, he set himself to the task of consuming the rest of the gin.

"Ho, there," Jade said. "That's about enough, Gabe." He heard her clearly now; concern edged her voice.

"Not by half," Gabriel taunted, taking a sip.

"What'll we do?" Nan asked worriedly, wringing her chubby hands. Her good eye winked up at him. "Come down, now, ducks; you've had your fun," she wheedled.

Gabriel laughed, swung his legs, and pulled a face.

Jade's temper flared. "Get the hell down from there, you little bas—"

"Mind your tongue," Nan interjected.

"—mother's son," Jade finished.

Mother. Knife sharp, the word cut through his foggy brain. "Mother," he muttered, and the word tasted more bitter than the gin. His mother had belittled him for five years; then she'd committed the ultimate atrocity of bleeding to death while he watched. Grimly he hoisted the bottle with an elegant sweep of his hand.

"A toast," he cried, then frowned, considering. "To my dear, departed mother, whose kindness and understanding will ever live in my heart." He forced a smile to hide the venom behind the remark and forced more gin down his throat.

"Don't much like the sound of that," Nan murmured.

Gabriel ignored her. "And to my father," he added, "and his glowing reputation as a half-breed and a felon." His tongue felt thick as he uttered the slurred insult.

To quell the resentment welling up in him, he took another swig. "A last tribute," he proclaimed grandly, nearly tumbling from his rope seat. "To Nan and Jade, the ladies who helped me forget it all." With that, he tipped back the jug and held it aloft until the last drop had settled in his belly.

"God bli' me," Jade said worriedly, "the lad's done sucked nigh on half a gill of Mother Geneva!"

Nan bit her lip. "Drunk as a sailor on shore leave."

Feeling giddy and fuzzy and numb, Gabriel pulled himself up to stand on the block. He swayed, waving the empty bottle before letting it fall to the stone surface of the wharf. The earthenware jug made a satisfying crash.

Gabriel lurched; the cobbles rippled like ocean swells. Odd how the distance didn't seem so great anymore. Through the gin-thickened fog shrouding his mind he became aware of a new presence below, a new voice.

"What in *hell* is going on here?"

Gabriel stiffened. Even in his befuddled state of mind he recognized the quiet tones of repressed anger in his father's words. His grip weakened on the ropes.

For a moment Gabriel's vision cleared. Briefly he saw his

father's livid face fill with concern. Briefly he saw a coil of rope on the cobbled surface of the wharf rise up to meet him. And then he saw nothing at all.

Gabriel became aware of his surroundings by degrees, as if he were groping in the dark for something of unknown size and shape. He smelled the sourness of gin and sickness and knew his game with Jade and Nan had ended in disaster. He felt the coolness of a clean sheet beneath his cheek, felt a gentle rocking, and knew he was abed and afloat. He heard footsteps, then a curse uttered softly by a male voice. Bile churned in his stomach. Oh, God, his father was nearby.

Gabriel lay still, his eyes closed and his mind spinning. He was reluctant to face his father's anger, to face his own misery. Oh, God, he'd really done it now.

Through whorls of dizziness he became aware of a variety of aches and bruises, not the least of which was lodged like an andiron in his head. Adrift on a sea of pain, he felt a sudden shameful yearning to reach out to his father.

A door opened. The pacing halted. Gabriel thrust his childish need aside.

"Well?" His father whispered the query.

"I've spoken to Jade and Nan." That was Jessica. And that was her hand, coming to rest on his forehead. Gabriel resisted a strong impulse to jerk away, to escape the cool touch of the woman who seemed to want, despite his rude resistance, to be a mother to him.

"And?" Fletcher's voice was tense and anger laden.

"They're sorry, Fletcher. They never meant Gabriel to get hold of their gin. It all started as a harmless wager, but he snatched the bottle and climbed out of reach."

"And of course," came the sarcastic reply, "they were too deep in their cups to stop him."

"Something like that." Jessica sounded regretful, conciliatory. "They've promised never to—"

"What's bred in the bone can't be promised away," his father said darkly. "Damn, Jessica, they're born dissolutes. They've been earning a living on their backs for so long they don't know how decent people behave."

Gabriel gave a mental frown. On their backs? He was familiar with the phrase, but how did it apply to Jade and Nan? Unless . . .

"Stop it," Jessica whispered. "I cannot defend what they did, but I won't have you maligning my friends."

"I made a serious mistake in allowing them to come with us, Jessica. I should have realized you can't pull women from a brothel and —"

"You pulled *me* from a brothel," she shot back acidly.

Gabriel nearly stopped breathing. A brothel? He was confused. And fascinated.

"You're different," Fletcher said. "You've managed to live down your past, not drag it around with you like so much baggage."

"Different, am I?" The quality of Jessica's voice changed almost imperceptibly. Gabriel heard, to his uneasy surprise, a trace of the London wharves in her words. "I'm not so bloody different. I've learned to speak like a lady, but I stand by those who don't hide behind affectations."

"You would," he said scathingly. "For a moment I nearly forgot. You were just like them, only a more refined version."

Gabriel choked back a gasp of astonishment. *Jessica? Like Jade and Nan?* Perhaps the gin still distorted his senses. Or had he truly heard his father declare that Jade, Nan, and Jessica were whores?

"Believe what you will," she snapped.

"I'm shipping them back to England," Fletcher said. "I'll book passage in the morning."

"Damn you." Jessica's voice sounded taut, strained. "You'll do no such thing."

"I won't have two gin-soaked whores looking after my children."

"Then you won't have me either," Jessica stated. "If you send Jade and Nan away, I'll go too."

"My God." Fletcher's voice was rough with quiet fury. "You'd do that, wouldn't you? You'd allow my children to be forfeit for the sake of your loyalty to those two strumpets."

"They stay, or I go."

A long, tense silence spun out. Gabriel fought to keep his breathing even. If he stirred now, they would know he'd heard what they'd surely never meant for his ears. It was not protectiveness or sentiment that kept him still; nothing so noble as that. It was spite that made him lie limp and seemingly unconscious until at last Fletcher said, "Very well. They can come to Holland Hall. But if anything like this happens again I won't do them the courtesy of paying their return passage. They can earn it . . . on their backs."

"You've seen the last of gin and dice," Jessica said, no longer sounding angry. "I, too, care about your son. In fact, I think he should be punished for what he's done."

Gabriel tensed. Fletcher swore. "I was too hard on him for what he did to Kitty and look what it drove him to."

"He's old enough to take responsibility for his actions."

"I'll decide what's best for my son," Fletcher said. He must have realized how sharp the remark sounded, for his voice gentled. "Jessica, you've known I am Mohawk, but you still don't know what that means. The Mohawk way with children is far different from the English way. Mohawk parents aren't stoic taskmasters who ply a cane at the slightest infraction."

"The infraction was not slight."

Gabriel pulled his mind from whorehouses long enough to make a bitter observation. Mama had always insisted on severe punishments and now Jessica seemed to be changing from gentle governess to harsh stepmother.

"Am I? Damn it, Gabriel's a product of five years of English discipline and it's obviously not been successful. The Mohawk have a much saner view, I think. Their lot is hard enough without the added severity of punishment."

"You're making a mistake, Fletcher."

"It won't be the first time then, will it? I never should have allowed you to bring Jade and Nan with us."

"I suppose you're having second thoughts about me as well, Fletcher." Her footsteps receded with angry haste.

Gabriel forgot his aching head and bruised limbs. For now he knew the dark secret of Jessica's past. A secret he intended to keep . . . until he decided what to do with it.

Through the murk shrouding his mind he saw himself on the stair landing that night five years ago, clutching his blanket and wailing for Papa. He'd screamed until his mother slapped him into silence. And Papa hadn't come back.

Perhaps here was a way to pay his father back for abandoning him.

The next day Jessica was still smarting from her argument with Fletcher, but fate had given her a reprieve from facing his disapproval on a daily basis. The skipper of the sloop that was to take them up the Hudson had fallen ill, so Fletcher was obliged to captain the vessel himself, leaving Jessica and the women to follow on the slower schooner. Protesting that he'd recovered from the bruises inflicted by his fall and the sickness imparted by the gin, Gabriel insisted on sailing ahead with the men.

As Jessica stood at the rail of the schooner watching the sloop scudding northward on the broad, placid Hudson River, she gave a sigh of relief and tried not to think what lay at her journey's end. Pushing thoughts of her disturbing husband aside, she spent her days studying the dense wilderness around her.

The bustle of New York harbor rapidly gave way to forests so thick and vast that Jessica had the sensation of looking at a fantastical painting rather than a real landscape. Mountains and morass, creeks and coppices, rose up in V formation on either side of the river. Gauzy curtains of fog shrouded the indigo hills and tinged the air with a vague, mystical haze.

Jessica spent hours alone in reflection, contemplating the strange, wild, and empty place that was to be her home. Rocky cliffs projected over the river like the pointed angles of bastions. Their sheer limestone faces intensified and echoed every sound: Kitty's singing, the crewmen's laughter, the calls of catbirds, the sudden leap and heavy splash of a sturgeon.

One night as the moon set and the fog rose, Richard Schoonhaven, the skipper, came to announce that the *River Hawk* would make Holland Hall by morning.

Fireflies darted in a glowing frenzy. A light finger of apprehension touched Jessica. Tomorrow would bring her first view of her new home.

Adele proceeded down the dock with her usual self-possession. Equally undaunted, Jade swaggered after her, followed by Nan. But Kitty seemed to share Jessica's trepidation. The child clung to her hand and stared round-eyed down the length of the dock, which seemed to lead only to a thick wood with a narrow dirt path issuing from it.

Good Lord, Jessica thought, am I to live in an uninhabited wilderness?

A figure was coming down the leaf-hooded path. She watched, her heart in her mouth, as the raven-haired man approached with long-limbed strides. Only five days had separated them, but she had the uncomfortable sensation of watching a stranger. Fletcher's color was high and vigorous, his smile broad and easy. His usual air of assurance seemed magnified in the wild setting. Jessica quickly realized she was seeing a man who had come home at last.

Just as quickly, Kitty seemed to forget her hesitation. "Papa!" she squealed, tearing her hand from Jessica's grip and pushing past the women. The little girl catapulted herself into his outstretched arms. Laughing, he lifted her high in the air and swung her around. Surrounded by silver-leafed trees and dappled by morning sunshine, father and daughter made a picture of familial contentment that caused a knot of emotion to form in Jessica's throat.

The idea that she had had, however reluctantly, a hand in bringing them together made her feel absurdly noble. With a lighter heart and quick steps, she began walking toward them.

Fletcher set Kitty on the ground, a smile lingering on his lips and merriment dancing in his eyes. With heart-pounding relief, Jessica saw him nod amiably at Adele, Jade, and Nan. So. He had forgiven the episode with the gin.

Then he turned to her, still smiling. "Hello, Jessica. Kitty and Esme tell me you had a pleasant voyage."

Her smile was subdued. "The landscape is beautiful, in a wild, forbidding way."

"No doubt your clever fingers have chronicled it all in silhouette. You'll come to love the mountains and forests," he assured her. His hand reached for hers and cradled it firmly. "Shall we go up to the house? They're all anxious to greet you."

Apparently the homecoming had banished his anger over the quarrel. As he led her along, Jessica tried not to show her hesitation. The idea of meeting servants and tenants was daunting when her entire social experience consisted of afternoons with Hester Pynchon's visitors.

As if sensing her thoughts, Fletcher squeezed her hand. "Just give them that smile of yours, my dear, and you'll soon have them eating out of your hand."

She darted a quick glance at him. He spoke cordially enough, but her distrustful ears heard an undercurrent of mockery in his voice.

Kitty skipped up the path ahead of them; Adele, Jade, and Nan walked behind her. The leaf-hooded track ended abruptly at the edge of a broad, close-clipped lawn.

Jessica stopped, her eyes moving up the sloping yard to the house. "Sweet, merciful heavens," she breathed, staring.

The house crowned a gentle hill, sprawling across the green expanse in gleaming, lime-washed splendor. A wide flight of steps led to a fern-decked porch framed by soaring white columns. Dormer windows with sun-lit balconies marched along the upper stories. Rose trellises, heavy with new blossoms, softened the stark lines of the house.

Jessica fixed her eyes on the ground floor, then looked upward, silently counting.

Fletcher must have guessed what she was doing from the movement of her lips. He leaned down and said, "Four stories, and all as solid as Blue Mountain granite."

She shook her head, pointing. "Five."

He grinned. "The cupola on top is merely an ornament, although I passed many a rainy day there when I was a boy."

"Papa," Kitty piped, dancing excitedly, "is this the house where I was born?"

His smile grew soft with fondness and he ruffled her curls. "You were born in Albany, poppet, but you lived here as a baby. Holland Hall is my birthplace . . . almost."

Kitty raced up the lawn, suddenly full of confidence as if the knowledge gave her a sense of belonging.

"Almost?" Jessica asked, frowning.

He nodded. "My mother returned to her people to bear me. She never quite trusted English doctors."

Jessica stared at him, intrigued anew by the story. He was a product of both English gentility and Indian savagery. In spite of herself, she decided that the divergent heritages were united in Fletcher in an irrefutably attractive way.

"Come," he said, stirring her from a thought so warm that she blushed, "let's go inside."

She held back, remembering something he'd told her in London: *My home does have a few modern amenities.* "You might have prepared me for this," she said, eyeing the intimidating grandeur of the house.

"Would it have changed your opinion of me?"

"If you're asking whether I would have been more willing to uproot myself for the sake of living in a mansion, the answer is no."

Annoyance flickered in his eyes, but he said nothing, only took her hand again and led her into the house.

In the opulent, wood-paneled entrance hall, she caught a brief glimpse of a two-tiered chandelier, a winding dark oak staircase, and a grand balustrade above.

A murmuring group of servants turned to them en masse and fell silent. Fletcher's hand was firm on Jessica's elbow as he propelled her forward. "Your new mistress," he said formally. "I'm sure you'll all make her feel welcome."

The friendliness of their smiles in no way masked their curious stares. Jessica had the distinct feeling she was being measured against the former mistress of Holland Hall.

She summoned polite greetings for the sturdy housekeeper, Hilda, and the elderly cook, Mercy. Jasper van Cleef, Fletcher's agent, smiled beneath a drooping gray moustache; his clerk, Mr. Elphinstone, fussily groomed and efficient looking, bowed stiffly. Houseboys and footmen, clerks and parlor maids, all paid their respects.

Kitty's entrance spared Jessica their lengthy scrutiny. The child edged inside the door, surveyed the people gathered there with big, unblinking eyes and a bigger smile, then said, "I'm Katherine Ruth Danforth. Does anyone remember me?"

"Ach, the lamb," Hilda said, her florid face suddenly wreathed in smiles. "Only Mercy, Jasper, and I remain from before. I remember you, darling, but you were just a baby when I last held you." Her starched apron rustled as she bent to enfold Kitty in her arms. Within moments, Hilda and Mercy were vying for the little girl's favor, admiring Esme and the marmalade kitten from the *Shadow Hawk*, and arguing over who would have the privilege of taking Kitty to the kitchen for a treat of cake and buttermilk.

Jessica looked at Fletcher and saw pride and indulgence in his eyes as Kitty was led away.

Silence fell like a sudden chill when Adele, Jade, and Nan arrived. Adele glided to the center of the room with all the stately grace of a ship under full sail. "Yes," she said, smiling graciously. "Yes, I think I shall be quite comfortable living here."

Jade followed, her smile brazen, her beauty instantly the focus of the unabashed admiration of the male servants and the source of affronted frowns of the females. Behind her, Nan arrived and surveyed the entrance hall and the company with a friendly grin.

"Well, now," Jade said, "ain't that the tops. You've all come to meet us."

Jessica thought she detected the tiniest glint of amusement in Fletcher's blue eyes. "Adele Severin is joining us as Kitty's nurse," he explained. "Jade Akura will serve as dressmaker and Nan Featherstone will be my wife's maid."

Relief soothed Jessica's taut nerves. Even Adele appeared impressed by Fletcher's tact. With a diplomat's smoothness he had forestalled resentment of the established household help, allayed Jessica's fears that he was still angry about the gin, and defined respectable and fitting roles for the three newcomers.

Obviously relieved that their positions were secure, the staff fell to presenting themselves and asking innumerable questions. Adele inspired a comfortable deference, Jade an avid fascination, and Nan an air of familiar jollity.

Before she quite realized what she was doing, Jessica found herself reaching for Fletcher's hand, tucking her own inside it and giving it a squeeze. He glanced down at her, his gaze lacking its usual faint contempt.

He pulled her away from the milling company and bent low to whisper in her ear, "Courage, love. That hurdle's been cleared." He touched his lips to her brow.

Heat shimmered to her cheeks as she drew back to stare at him. Once again he looked like a smiling, dangerous stranger. A savage . . . She tried to force the unbidden thought from her mind, telling herself Fletcher was a gentleman farmer, as unthreatening as spring rain. But the slight coppery tint of his skin over high, sharp cheekbones gave him the look of a haughty warrior; the burningly blue eyes communicated a potent, thinly veiled desire.

"Yes," she whispered unsteadily. "Yes, it has."

Still smiling, he brushed aside the lace of her fichu, baring the flushed ridge of her collarbone. The light caress of his finger as he traced that delicate line belied the heated, repressed tension she sensed in him. In spite of herself, Jessica felt a deep, warm curl of anticipation.

"Now we can get our wedding underway. And the wedding night," he added, moving his finger to her jawline, then outlining the bow of her lower lip. "I've been patient long enough."

Chapter 11

Two weeks later Jessica stood in her rose and mint green bedroom, contemplating the door to Fletcher's huge, sparse chamber. She shivered, although the air wafting in through the French window was warm and sweet with the scent of roses and freshly clipped grass. After today that door, the last barrier separating her from Fletcher Danforth, would no longer stand between them. After this wedding she didn't want and couldn't escape, they would truly be man and wife.

"Tiens, you have a wedding to attend, not a funeral."

Startled, Jessica turned to Adele. She managed a shaky smile. "Am I truly that obvious?"

"No, but I know you well." Adele bent and inhaled the fragrance of a bowl of violets. "You are afraid."

Jessica lifted the hem of her combing jacket and studied the beading on her satin slippers, another item Fletcher had pulled from the hold of the *Shadow Hawk*. He was free enough with gifts but still shared little of himself. "I hardly know the man, Adele."

She drew her lips together and made a sound of disapproval. "You have been avoiding him."

Jessica nodded absently and went to the window. She brushed aside a gossamer veil of curtains and stepped out onto the balcony. The rolling grounds of the manor seemed about to burst with summer bounty. Amid a profusion of blue-topped grape hyacinth, mountain laurel, and maidenhair fern, stood a careful arrangement of stone benches and wrought-iron chairs clustered around a modest wooden dais.

The tenants of the estate were beginning to arrive from their fields and cottages; people from the town of Albany had stepped from their yachts and come up from the dock to form a colorful crowd in the garden. The women gossiped; the men smoked. Idly Jessica wondered if she might find a friend among them . . . but the notion fled when Fletcher appeared, walking to the dais with the minister.

As always, he looked like a stranger, harshly handsome, swathed in mystery. The idea that her destiny lay with him was unsettling . . . and curiously exciting.

He spoke with the minister at some length, then crossed back to the house with long, easy strides. Jessica supposed he'd planned the ceremony as dispassionately as he planned all other aspects of her life. Annoyance pricked at her. He might have sought her opinion on some small matter, if only for the sake of appearing to care about her wishes.

"Why?" Adele called from the bedroom, stirring her from her disquieting musings. "Why have you and Fletcher been avoiding each other?"

Jessica continued to gaze from the balcony. The manor reminded her, oddly, of Fletcher. The woods were distant and wild, rugged and forbidding, yet in part the land had been softened into cultivation by patient hands. Spiny cockspur hawthorne hedged an apple orchard; a rubble-built wall of bluestone rocks enclosed Mercy's kitchen garden. Like Fletcher, the land was hard and unyielding . . . except where someone had lavished a good deal of care.

"*Alors,* will you stand there woolgathering while your guests wait, or would you like to talk about it?"

Jessica stepped back into the room. "It's true," she admitted. "We have been avoiding each other."

Her eyes strayed to the door again. Night after night she'd lain sleepless, staring at the crack of golden light beneath that door, knowing he was up too. She pictured him sitting at his massive Goddard desk, laboring over ledgers stuffed with trading certificates and bills of lading. From time to time she'd hear the quiet clink of crystal, the splash of whiskey in a glass. The later the hour, the more frequent the sound.

Yet he was always up at dawn, tearing across fields and tenant farms on his blooded stallion, overseeing crops, helping to dig a foundation for a new granary, driving a team in front of the stoneboat laden with rocks for mending fences. Jessica shivered thinking of him, sun bronzed and sweating as he worked the land. Only sunset or rainstorms brought him home, and then only to gulp a quick meal and disappear again behind a mountain of correspondence.

He seemed determined to drive himself to exhaustion each day and Jessica could only guess why. Maybe Fletcher was trying to rebuild those lost years and spending his seemingly limitless supply of energy to do so. Then again, it might not be the land at all. Fletcher's frantic actions might be an effort to repress that volatile passion that always seethed just beneath his surface. Whenever he was near, she felt its hot, tangible presence and knew his patience was burning away.

"*Tiens,*" Adele said, again startling Jessica from her disquieting thoughts, "Mr. Elphinstone helps with the paperwork, Mr. van Cleef with the farming. I would think you'd try to spend more time with Fletcher."

"I've not been so idle myself," Jessica replied defensively. "It took me fully a week to learn where all the linen closets are, *and* the bakehouse, *and* the smokehouse, *and* the conservatory. . . . Nor have I neglected the children's lessons. With that, and Jade's interminable fittings, I've had little time to spare."

"Hmph." Adele tossed her head, setting her cloud of snow white hair bobbing.

Jessica darted a nervous glance at the dark oak door. "I daresay that will change shortly."

Adele's look was sage and sympathetic. "So. That is what has been bothering you." The gnarled hands reached out; Jessica walked into Adele's embrace. The scent of lavender water, Adele's favorite, enveloped her.

"*Pauvre petite,* I keep forgetting you are a bride and still innocent of a man's touch."

"I'm afraid my upbringing disqualifies me as an innocent."

"Then I will not bore you with tedious explanations. Still, it is one thing to know what a man can do to your body and yet another to know what he can do to your heart."

Jessica swallowed and felt burning tears behind her eyes. "Perhaps that's what I fear the most."

"Fletcher is a good man; belowstairs they gossip that he has not always been so brooding and unapproachable. His wrongful arrest and imprisonment and his first wife's betrayal have changed him." Adele held Jessica at arm's length. "I have been thinking of placing my savings in his hands."

Startled, Jessica looked at her sharply. Adele was always so careful with her money. "You would trust Fletcher with your pension?"

"But of course. He has plans to build a paper mill and I would like to invest in it."

"But what about the Duke of Claremont? He has overseen your affairs for years."

"And quiet successfully. For all that His Grace is an eccentric and a sot, he has a fine sense for business and money. But I am getting too old for his cautious, conservative investments." Adele stared, chagrined, at her crippled hands. "I meant to write him, but my hands are so useless these days. I haven't sewn a stitch since the voyage, and I can scarcely hold a pen. After the wedding, when we are more settled, I'd like you to post a letter to the duke informing him of my decision."

"Of course, Adele. But are you certain?"

"Fletcher expects a profit margin of one hundred twenty percent on the paper he will produce. He showed me the prospectus he's drawn up."

"There. You know more about him than I do."

"I know him well enough to believe my pension will flourish in his care." Adele gave Jessica an encouraging smile. "I also know he will treat you decently."

"You forget he believes me to be a whore," Jessica reminded her bitterly, pulling away.

Adele glanced at herself in the cheval glass and tucked a white curl back into place. "I have not forgotten. Nor have I forgotten you've forbidden me to speak to him of it."

"The problem is between Fletcher and me."

"Then the two of you will resolve it." Adele cocked her head as sounds issued from the hall. "That will be Jade and Nan," she said, "come to help with your toilette. I must go find my little charge now." Briefly she rested her cheek against Jessica's; then she pulled away, blinking against the rare sheen of tears that had formed unbidden. "Who would have thought my little *voleuse* from Billiter Lane would end up a colonial lady?" she mused.

"It wasn't at all what we'd planned," Jessica whispered.

Adele gave her a last squeeze. "Be happy, Jessica. You have a talent for giving of yourself. Use it well."

Jessica turned away, drew a deep breath, and went to open the door. Adele glided serenely away; Jade and Nan bustled inside.

"Damme, Jess," Jade said in agitation, "why didn't you send for us sooner? They're all out there waitin'." She shook out the gown and petticoats as Nan began brushing Jessica's hair with vigorous strokes.

Beset by a sudden assault of nerves, Jessica scowled irritably. "Let them wait," she replied. "Do you think they've anything better to do?"

" 'Tis not the guests I'm worried about," Nan murmured, "but Mr. Danforth. He's been up since dawn, bellowin' orders every which way."

So, thought Jessica with dark satisfaction, perhaps he wasn't as self-possessed as she'd supposed.

Fletcher stood at the dais in the garden, facing the wedding guests and trying to conceal his growing consternation. Everyone, from the royal governor to the youngest stable boy, was assembled and waiting. Kitty had made her solo promenade across the lawn, strewing flower petals while a string quartet played a dulcet melody.

Jessica should have followed, stepping through the ballroom doors to join him, but she had not come.

For a wild moment, he imagined she'd fled. Quickly he squelched the notion; the thick wilderness around the manor was all but impenetrable even to a seasoned woodsman.

Drawing a taut rein on is doubts, he surveyed the congregation. Kitty was sitting beside Adele, her slippered feet kicking to and fro beneath the hem of her yellow frock. Under the bench, the marmalade kitten batted at the strings of her sash. Seeing her father's eyes on her, Kitty waggled her finger at him, then blew him a kiss. Fletcher's tension gave way to a powerful surge of love for his daughter.

Then he looked at Gabriel, who sat at Adele's right, not bothering to conceal a yawn of boredom. Something inside Fletcher grew chill. He and Gabriel were little closer than they had been two weeks ago. The boy was given to long silences, preferring his books and solitude to his father's company. Fletcher longed to get this wedding behind him, to dispense with the ceremony and bid the guests good-bye, so that he could give more time to his family. Jessica's conspicuous absence, however, hinted that she lacked his eagerness.

He glanced at Sir Jeffrey Amherst and Sir William Johnson, who sat in the front row. The former was the royal governor; the latter had been Superintendent of Indian Affairs. Together the pair represented most of the political power in the colony.

Fletcher had no desire to use his wedding as a vehicle for garnering official favor, but Amherst's presence was warranted by the Lord Chancellor's edict, whereas Will Johnson, so esteemed by the Mohawk that they made him a sachem, was an old friend of Fletcher's.

Molly Brant, Will's Mohawk mistress, caught Fletcher's eye. Her face remained impassive, but her eyes smiled at him. Fletcher garnered similar looks from the other Mohawks present: Kayanere, Great Knife, and Great Knife's daughter, Kateri. Unbidden, a thought tiptoed into Fletcher's mind: If Indians had been present at his first marriage, Sybil would have gone into a dead faint. How would Jessica react to the men's greased scalp locks, to Kateri's beaded dress and moccasins?

The midday sun glared down at the garden and he felt the crispness leaving his cheviot wool coat and buff knee breeches. The aroma of honeysuckle and ripening apples smelled overly sweet, almost oppressive. The quartet played its limited repertoire yet another time. And still Jessica did not appear.

The guests were beginning to murmur and look toward the house. Fletcher aimed a scowl at Jade and Nan, who were sitting toward the back. They looked at each other and both shrugged.

"Perhaps you should send someone for the bride." Reverend Fairfax's quiet suggestion penetrated Fletcher's growing anger.

"Yes," he said. "Yes, you're quite right." He considered going himself, then thought better of it. His present mood might chase his reluctant bride away for good.

But as he was trying to catch Adele's eye, he saw the verandah door open. Jessica stepped out.

Something must have shown in his face, for the entire congregation turned as one and released a heartfelt collective sigh.

Fletcher, too, nearly succumbed to a similar display of sentiment as he watched her approach. That Jessica was a pretty woman had been apparent to him from the start. But today, clad in a gown of shimmering peach, her hair flowing over her shoulders in a mass of loose curls, she surpassed every dream that had haunted his restless nights.

More than the magnificent dress and the sunshot spill of curls, it was Jessica's face and demeanor that arrested his eye and stilled his heart. She wore a look of innocence like a halo.

Damn, Fletcher thought, annoyed at his susceptibility, the heat must be getting to me. He forced himself to remember that beneath that sweet exterior Jessica was a practiced whore. Sybil, too, had been beautiful on her wedding day.

But Fletcher hadn't felt this way about Sybil. He hadn't experienced this pounding eagerness—this surge of desire to take her in his arms, explore that magnificent body, and bring a sparkle of passion to those deep, mist gray eyes.

Jessica's promenade ended at the dais. Her expression was startled, round eyed, and uncertain. Fletcher fancied she might bolt at any moment. And he found himself praying to a God he rarely acknowledged that she wouldn't.

His hand closed around hers. The gesture seemed to calm her and he allowed himself a silent sigh of relief. At close range she was even more enchanting. The beadwork of her stomacher sparkled in the sunshine, but not as brightly as her eyes.

"Ready, love?" he asked.

"Yes." Her breathy whisper and the slight trembling of her hand stirred an unexpected tenderness in Fletcher.

The preacher opened his missal. "Shall we begin?"

"In a moment," Fletcher said. He motioned to Kayanere, who shuffled forward, oblivious of the distrustful stares of the English people.

The preacher frowned. "Mr. Danforth, this is—"

Fletcher held up a hand. "I know. You'll have your ceremony in a moment. But I am a Mohawk as well as an Enlishman. I intend to be married in the eyes of my mother's people as well as in the eyes of my father's.'' After years of having to hide his heritage, he now wanted to proclaim it to the world.

The preacher heaved a long-suffering sigh and stepped back to allow Kayanere to stand before the couple. The Mohawk prayer was brief and sincere in its simplicity. The elderly shaman called upon the gods for a blessing and bestowed his own good wishes.

Fletcher glanced at Jessica, half dreading her reaction. Sybil would have been revolted by the idea of an Indian ritual, but Jessica stood firmly at his side, watching Kayanere with a mixture of curiosity and admiration. Although she could not understand the words, she seemed to find no threat in the shaman's prayers.

When Fletcher handed her the ceremonial deer's foot, decorated with ribbons and beads, she accepted it without hesitation, only eyeing him quizzically.

''A symbol,'' he told her, ''of my promise to provide for you.''

Her sudden smile sent his heart slamming against his rib cage. Her murmured thanks washed over him like a soothing balm. Clasping her hands around the deer's foot, he smiled down at her and wondered how a woman with her past could seem so guileless and giving.

Kayanere finished speaking, added his handclasp to theirs, and then moved aside. From the corner of his eye, Fletcher saw the shaman ineffectually trying to strike a flint to light his pipe. He suppressed a grin. As far as Kayanere was concerned, the ceremony was over.

The Anglican preacher began reading smugly from his missal, his distaste for the Mohawk prayers evident in his haughty elocution. Irritated, Fletcher turned his attention to Jessica. She'd removed her hands from his and was toying with the beads on the deer's foot.

''You're a Mohawk's bride now, as well as an Englishman's wife,'' he whispered. ''And it's about time.''

She lowered her eyes, the gold-tipped lashes sweeping cheeks gone pale. Her teeth worried her lower lip and her hands tightened convulsively around the deer's foot.

Fletcher was angered by her sudden withdrawal. He wanted to take her by the shoulders, shake her, and demand why.

Why is it so hard to give yourself to a husband . . . when you've sold yourself to so many other men before?

Instead he responded to the minister's prompting: "I vow to love, honor, and cherish thee, and to thee I plight my troth."

Jessica stared up at him, mesmerized by the subtle contempt in his expression and the richness of his voice. She wanted to fling his gift in his face, to rail: Why do you persist in doubting me? Have I not done all you've asked?

Instead she answered the promise: "I vow to love, honor, and obey thee, and to thee I plight my troth."

As they exchanged rings and the minister read the concluding words of the ceremony, rebellion welled in Jessica. She narrowed her eyes and whispered, "A church wedding doesn't make me your wife."

To her dismay, he smiled devilishly. "Be assured, love," he murmured before bending to kiss her, "I'll make you my wife."

Late afternoon sunlight filtered into the ballroom. A colorful assortment of farmers, townspeople, dignitaries, and Indians were gathered there to wish the couple well. Toasts had been drunk, each more outlandish than the one before, and a huge dinner had been served.

Jessica was dancing with her husband. Feeling awkward, she was grateful for his smooth, practiced steps. He guided her with a masterful touch, communicating with the slightest pressure of his hand on the small of her back or a brief nod of his head.

He communicated with her in another way as well, with hands that strayed subtly to her neck, her ears, the pulse at her wrist. In his eyes and in his touch she read the message: It was time she grew accustomed to his caresses.

Somewhere deep inside her, she *was* responding to him. When his long brown fingers brushed against her throat, she felt a warm and breathless yearning that left her dizzy and confused, uncertain of how to act on her feelings.

He squeezed her hand and she felt the unfamiliar pressure of the ring on her finger. They were married now, in the eyes of the church as well as the law, and tonight the last barrier between them would be breeched. Her cheeks heated.

His lazy smile disturbed her. "What are you thinking?" she asked, hoping to catch him off guard.

"I'm thinking you blush prettily," he murmured.

The crimson color in her face burned hotter. The quartet's sweet, liquid minuet sounded fainter, replaced by a roar of alarm in her ears. She ducked her head.

"Damn," he said, "don't look away. A blushing bride is every man's dream."

She kept her eyes averted. "Could we stop now?" she asked. "I'm thirsty."

The tremble in her voice must have betrayed her nervousness, for Fletcher softened and looked annoyed at himself rather than at her. "Of course. I'll get you some cider."

A few minutes later she was seated in a window recess, sipping the cool drink he'd brought her. Fletcher remained standing, one arm braced against the wall. His hand strayed downward, brushing a wayward curl from her temple.

Her cider cup clattered in its saucer. She felt vulnerable, exposed. Yet his closeness, his scent, the hand that lingered in the curls at her temple aroused a compelling sense of wanton warmth.

Grasping at a neutral topic, she said, "Everyone has been so kind to me today."

"You handled all their questions gracefully."

"You sound surprised."

"No, Jessica. You're a graceful woman. You turned aside Margaret Fairfax's comment on the brevity of our courtship as if it were no more than a remark about the weather."

Probing the crowd, her eyes found the plump, pink-draped form of Mrs. Fairfax on the other side of the dance floor. Jessica couldn't suppress a smile as she recalled her conversation with the minister's wife. She knew the type well, had met several of them in the Pynchons' drawing room. Questions cloaked by false concern, barbs hidden within the folds of backhanded compliments . . . she was familiar with the techniques. "To be fair," she said, "her curiosity is natural. She seems harmless enough."

Fletcher's chuckle was soft and knowing. "You disliked her on sight."

"I mean to cultivate her friendship."

"You're welcome to try. But tread carefully around Mrs. Fairfax; she's not as harmless as she looks."

Jessica was certain he'd made the warning out of concern for his own reputation, but she tucked the information away in a corner of her mind, because she didn't want her new life to start steeped in scandal.

Mentally dismissing the minister's wife, she spied the royal governor basking in the attention of a knot of bewigged gentlemen. "Tell me about Sir Jeffrey Amherst."

Fletcher's lip curled. "He considers himself the hero of the war against the French and believes his triumph hasn't been sufficiently appreciated by the Crown."

"You dislike him," Jessica said, adopting the same tone he had used earlier in referring to Mrs. Fairfax.

"I dislike the way he's abused his Indian allies."

"How is that, Fletcher?"

"He disfavors making treaties with them. His inclinations seem to run more in the direction of . . . extermination."

She looked over his shoulder at the arrogant, unattractive governor. "Surely not," she breathed.

"At one time he contrived to introduce smallpox into some of the disaffected tribes."

Appalled, Jessica gasped. "But that's inhuman."

"Like most Englishmen, Amherst doesn't consider Indians human."

"Then why do you allow him here?"

"Because of my agreement with the Lord Chancellor."

Jessica nodded. "I'd forgotten how much you're willing to endure for the sake of your children." He must have heard the quiet indictment of her tone, for he looked at her sharply. Aware that the ballroom was no place to renew their conflict, she nodded at Sir William, who was dancing with Molly Brant. "What of him, Fletcher? He seems very familiar with the Indians."

"We call him Warrahiyagey. He-Who-Does-Much."

Jessica noted Fletcher's pointed use of the word "we."

"So," she said, "are you an Englishman like Sir Jeffrey or an Indian like Kay—Kayanere?" She flushed, stumbling over her words.

"I live like an Englishman, but I know the way of the Mohawk as well. My people, I think you'll find, are not a tribe of naive natives but a nation of proud warriors." His gaze was probing, as if he were trying to gauge her reaction.

"I'm not Sybil," she assured him, suddenly determined to keep the distinction between herself and his first wife very clear. "Your manipulation of me is objectionable, but your background is not."

Something flashed in his eyes. Guilt? Regret?

"Go play the host, Fletcher," came a booming voice. "You've monopolized this beautiful lady long enough."

Jessica looked up at Sir William Johnson, a big man with an easy smile and dancing eyes. "May I?" he asked Fletcher, but he was already reaching for her hand.

"Do you really mean to wait for my permission?" Fletcher asked, grinning. He took Jessica's cider cup. "That's hardly your style, Will."

Laughter rumbled from Sir William. "I'm a crude man and too old to stand on manners," he declared. "I've just gotten a lecture from our esteemed governor because of that very flaw." He saw Fletcher's mouth grow thin with contempt and shook his head. "Don't go leaping to my defense, Danforth. Amherst is bothered by a lot of private concerns."

Fletcher cocked an eyebrow. "Oh?"

Will nodded. "His estates in England are going to ruin and his wife's been committed to a madhouse." They looked at Amherst, who was smiling ingratiatingly at Mr. Guyver, a timber factor from Albany. " 'Tis no wonder his favors are so easily bought," Will concluded.

Jessica saw a bright flash in Fletcher's eyes, as if an idea were forming. But Will led her away and she forgot the governor. Will danced less skillfully than Fletcher but made up for his lack of grace with an open, friendly smile—a smile she needed.

"This must be a happy day for you, Jessica. You'll allow me to call you by your given name, won't you?"

"Of course . . . Will." She smiled up at him, having an unexpected liking for this jovial man. She'd heard he was vastly wealthy, was master of a tenantry of Highlanders numbering over one hundred families who produced flour by the shipload to trade in the West Indies. Yet the friendly Irishman possessed an inborn geniality and outgiving nature that inspired ease rather than intimidation.

"I confess I was surprised when I received Fletcher's urgent summons to his wedding," Will said. "Hadn't realized Sybil had passed away. No one heard much about his first wife after she—" He broke off, looking annoyed at himself. "Ah, Molly'd have my tongue for that. I should know better than to speak of a man's first wife with his present one."

Jessica laughed at his comical, self-effacing expression, pretending she didn't feel threatened by the mention of Sybil. In truth she did. According to Mrs. Fairfax, Sybil had been lovely and ladylike . . . and wellborn. Something Jessica could never be, whatever else she was.

Determined to hide her self-doubt, she laughed again, more loudly. "I forgive you, Will. You'd be far less interesting without your loose tongue."

Hearing a musical burst of female laughter, Fletcher surveyed the dance floor. With an uncomfortable feeling of mingled annoyance and amusement, he saw her still swirling around, laughing up at her partner. Will had always gotten what he wanted, be it a grant of land or an Indian concubine. At the moment the man seemed intent on winning over Jessica.

Feeling foolish at the envy stabbing at him, Fletcher shook his head. Will was perhaps fifty and, while the years had been good to his big, athletic frame, he was no longer youthful. Still, he had to trouble coaxing smiles and laughter from Jessica.

Lord, Fletcher thought, he'd never had such a way with women. His own looks and wealth had won him his share of female attention, but he'd never had the gift of banter and ease of manner that Jessica was enjoying at the moment. Unbidden, memories of Sybil arose. Passionless in the bedchamber and overly concerned with appearances, she'd been difficult even in the early years of their marriage. But had he been any better? He'd put a grand roof over her head, he'd clothed her in silks and lavished her with jewels, but had he ever truly given of himself?

Looking down at his hands, Fletcher wondered at the turn his thoughts had taken. Since when had making his wife happy become so important to him? He needed Jessica, yes, but as mother to his children, not as the mate of his soul. She'd been a whore, she'd lived a lie, but she was more than that. She was a beautiful woman, a talented artist, and she had dreams and desires of her own.

His eyes found Jessica again. Well, so did he.

"You've married her in grand style, monsieur. I should think now that the courtship is over, you would relax."

Fletcher swung around, sloshing cider from his cup. Calmly, Adele Severin took a napkin from a salver on the table and dried his fingers.

"Thank you," Fletcher said stiffly. The woman's gaze measured him, probing like a surgeon's knife. "I suppose," he said, "you look so triumphant because, after procuring Jessica for London gentlemen, you've finally procured her for a husband."

Adele was too practiced at diplomacy to betray her fury to the wedding guests, but Fletcher detected a bolt of outrage in those jet eyes. "You are a fool, Fletcher Danforth," she told him quietly. "You don't deserve Jessica."

"Whether or not I do doesn't matter. She's my wife now."

"More's the pity for her."

"Damn you. Damn you for a hypocrite, Adele. You are the one who led Jessica into ruin. Do you feel no shame in that?"

"I could say much about where I've led the girl," she snapped, "but I will not. I'll leave it to you to discover how wrong you are about her." Raising her chin to a regal tilt, Adele sailed away. Dressed like a duchess, her head crowned by that nimbus of snowy hair, she walked into the midst of the wedding guests as if to the manor born.

Fletcher felt his anger die. Resolutely he turned his eyes and mind back to Jessica. She'd finished her dance with Will and had gone out on the verandah with him, where they were now conversing with Molly Brant, Kayanere, and Great Knife.

Curious about Jessica's reaction to his Mohawk brethren, Fletcher joined them. He expected to find her tongue-tied and fearful, as most whites were with Indians; instead, she seemed animated and interested. Her head was cocked charmingly to one side, a spill of peach-gold curls adorning one shoulder, and she was . . . Fletcher paused and stared. She was fashioning a silhouette of the elderly shaman.

"Shadow Hawk has spoken of your talent," Kayanere was saying.

"Shadow Hawk?" Jessica's brow quirked prettily.

"It is my Mohawk name," Fletcher explained, coming to her side.

She paused in her cutting and looked taken aback. Guilt, as familiar and unpleasant as a rash, crept over him. He'd shared so little of himself with his wife.

Preparing to go back to her cutting, Jessica studied Kayanere with the measuring look Fletcher recognized. The old man stared back, watching her hands. Some minutes later she presented the shaman with his portrait.

Fletcher told himself he should be accustomed to the depth of Jessica's talent by now, that the impact of her art should have lessened with time. But when he saw her depiction of Kayanere, a proud profile true to the last detail of an eagle feather in his headband, he gasped with as much fascination as the others.

Kayanere held the picture in unsteady hands, his eyes bright with emotion, his smile soft with warmth. "I will give this to Sawatis, my youngest grandson. He has been sick and it will cheer him. Jessica, I thank you."

"You are most welcome," she said graciously. She seemed touched by his gratitude, his admiration. Fletcher wondered at the fact that a woman he'd pulled from a brothel could inspire such pride in him.

Within minutes, portraits of Great Knife, Molly Brant, and Will Johnson appeared.

"By God," Will Johnson declared, " 'tis a grand talent you have, Jessica." He slid a sidelong glance at Fletcher. "If you ever tire of your great brute of a husband, I'd be pleased to welcome you to Johnson Hall, up on the Mohawk. We've a potash works, a carding mill, a free school, and a gristmill, but certainly no resident artist. I've been meaning to have a crest fashioned for my growing family. . . ."

A pleased flush stained her cheeks. She looked as demure as any innocent bride as she said, "Thank you, Mr. Johnson, but Holland Hall is my home now."

Fletcher had to work to keep his jaw from dropping. It was the statement of a loyal wife, delivered as if she had not fought him every inch of the way to the colonies. Could she indeed overcome her past and . . . He recalled her promise after the wedding vows. Suspicion crowded out his elation. Surely she spoke only for the benefit of the guests.

Childish laughter interrupted his thoughts. Kitty was racing across the lawn to them, her arms full of flowers. She smiled from behind wispy blooms of purple larkspur and bright bursts of marigolds. "Hello!" she said. Then, suddenly finding herself the object of half a dozen fond stares, she ducked her face behind the bouquet again.

"My daughter Kitty," Fletcher said, brushing his hand over her sun-warmed hair. Patiently, he recited the names of the guests. The little girl shed her shyness as she dipped in a curtsy to each. She seemed especially intrigued by Kayanere, who regarded her with solemn admiration. Impulsively, she plucked a marigold and held it out to him.

"Papa says you're my great-grandfather."

Taking the flower, Kayanere said in Mohawk, "A pretty girl-child, generous of heart."

Kitty giggled. "You talk funny."

Indulgent as all Mohawk were with children, Kayanere smiled. "I speak the language of my people. We are your people also, *Katsi'saro:roks.*"

Fletcher chuckled at Kitty's blank look. "Kayanere has given you a Mohawk name. It means Gathering Flowers."

Kitty mumbled a garbled version of the name; laughter erupted from the Mohawks. "I'm going to fetch Esme so he can give her a name too." Another curtsy and she darted away.

Great Knife's daughter arrived, streaking across the lawn from the direction of the river. For most children the age of thirteen was an awkward precipice between girlhood and womanhood. But Kateri bore herself with grace and her laughter trilled with a blend of mischief and merriment.

"The English boy is after me," she said to Great Knife. "I challenged him to a foot race and he's angry because I won."

Catching Jessica's quizzical look, Fletcher translated for her. To his surprise, she grinned. "So. Gabriel has met his match and she's outrun him."

At that moment Gabriel appeared, his stock askew and his frock coat missing. His face was red, his eyes an angry blue.

"I hear you've been racing Kateri." Fletcher spoke lightly, hoping to dispel his son's temper.

"She cheated," Gabriel declared crossly. "She took a short cut through the woods."

"Choosing the shortest path isn't cheating, it's merely logic," Jessica said. She spoke earnestly to Gabriel; she never talked down to the boy, but Fletcher recognized a glint of humor in her mist-gray eyes.

"Women," he said to Gabriel, rolling his eyes in mock disgust. "They're forever explaining their misdeeds away by invoking logic."

For a moment their gazes locked and Fletcher felt a sudden and welcome sense of kinship with his son. He'd seen that look before, on the face of a seven-year-old boy who delighted in sharing private jokes with his father. But just as quickly the expression in Gabriel's eyes changed to one of accusation.

"She cheats like any Indian," he said and, not bothering to witness the impact of his insult, marched off.

The indulgent head shakes and murmured laughter wouldn't have pleased Gabriel. The Mohawk admired displays of temper in their children, regarded tantrums as a valuable show of aggressiveness.

"And what," Great Knife asked Kayanere, "will you call that one?"

The old man's eyes danced with merriment. He uttered a long string of syllables.

"Burning Sapling," Fletcher translated for Jessica and grinned. He couldn't have thought of a more apt title for his son if he'd tried.

Jessica nodded appreciatively. Then she lowered her eyes. "I wonder what the Mohawk would call me?"

"You already have a title," he said, tipping her face up to his. "You are Mrs. Fletcher Danforth.

Moonlight spilled over the river landing, picking out the shapes of departing yachts. Standing at Fletcher's side, Jessica lifted her arm to wave farewell to the wedding guests. Then, together, they turned and walked back toward the house.

Primroses, opening their ghostly yellow petals to the night, exuded a faint and pleasing fragrance. Above the flapping of sails and the whir of sheets being worked, the night birds called. Fireflies darted randomly, flickering pinpoints of light in the moon-shadowed darkness.

Laughter issued from the drawing room, followed by murmurs of conversation. Sir William and Molly Brant were staying the night, as were Fletcher's Mohawk friends. The Indians, Great Knife in particular, had struck up an unlikely friendship with Jade and Nan. Jessica paused to watch Nan handing a cup of Madeira to Great Knife, who looked as if he'd already had quite enough.

"It's late." Fletcher's voice startled her.

"Yes," she agreed. "I should check on the children."

He laid his hand on her arm. "Adele took them upstairs hours ago."

"I see." Jessica's nerves tingled with an odd sense of anticipation. "Then I'll just see if anyone in the drawing room needs—"

The pressure of his hand increased. "Jessica."

His tone made her go still, except for the pounding of her heart. "Yes?"

"You've fulfilled your duties to our guests." He pulled her around to face him. His hand climbed to her shoulder, found the secret warmth beneath the curling hair at her nape. "A wife's duty awaits you now."

Chapter 12

Jessica had thought herself prepared for the moment she was to face her husband in the bedchamber. She'd gone over the scenario in her mind, had clung to Adele's assurances and her own second-hand knowledge. She knew what would happen—physically. She couldn't remember a time when she had not known; the curtain separating her from her mother in their garret room had been too thin to shield Jessica from the reality of animal grunts, a big gin belly, grasping hands. . . .

And yet, standing in Fletcher's candle-lit room and waiting for him to return from some errand at the boathouse, she finally realized that one important element was missing from her preparation. What was about to happen was more than a simple matter of coupling, a feat accomplished by the lowest of beasts. What she'd failed to recognize was that it was a matter of the head and the heart as well as of the body.

Feeling her courage waver, she summoned up an image of Fletcher. He wasn't like the men who had used her mother. He couldn't be. His straight, strong body and hard, handsome features, coupled with his compelling, driven personality, made him unique. She remembered the sensual promise of his kisses and suddenly her fear was gone. Because buried under her stubborn resentment lay a truth she was finally willing to acknowledge: she desired him, in all the ways a bride could desire her new husband. She wanted to feel his body close, his lips on hers. She wanted to share his secrets, his dreams, his life.

But that could only happen if Fletcher wanted those same things, and she knew he didn't. He thought her a whore; he'd used her to bring his children home.

Unnerved again, Jessica began to pace the unfamiliar room. Like Fletcher himself, it was forthright and unpretentious, the epitome of a gentleman's retreat. The furniture was of dark oak; Jessica supposed that a woman more discerning than she could have marked the pieces as Chippendale or Goddard. She saw only that the bed, desk, table, and chairs were handsome, simple in line and polished to a dull gleam. The bed and windows were draped in a stiff fabric printed with a geometric design.

The curious absence of personal items unsettled her until she reminded herself that Fletcher hadn't used the room in five years. The only luxury he had indulged in was the eiderdown coverlet on the tester bed, which looked deep enough to drown in.

Eager to draw her attention from the bed, Jessica studied the pleasing arrangement of Delft tiles around the fireplace. According to old Jasper van Cleef, Fletcher's father had been an admirer of Dutch innovation, their penchant for neatness and utility. Holland Hall was a monument to that style.

She wondered how much of Sybil Danforth lingered in the decor. Fletcher's first wife had lived here for eight years, after all. Had she commissioned the elegant drapes, the skating scene over the mantel? Jessica's eyes darted back to the bed. Had Fletcher made love to Sybil there?

Her fears came rushing back. *She* was his wife now. In just a short time his claim over her would be absolute.

Shivering despite the scented warmth of the June evening, she fussed at the laces of her night rayle, which Jade had fashioned for this occasion. Tonight Jessica had declined Nan's help with her toilette. She admitted, though only to herself, that she needed time alone to compose herself and fight down the anxiety lingering in her mind.

Moving restively, she opened the French windows and stepped out onto the balcony. The play of moonlight over the lawn and river comforted her. Fletcher loved this land with a passion she was beginning to comprehend, to share.

All would be well, she said to the night breeze and the winking fireflies. All would be well. Because whatever Fletcher thought of her, whatever mysteries surrounded him, she knew that within him resided a core of decency that would keep him from knowingly hurting her. At least she prayed so.

Returning from the boathouse, Fletcher noticed a glimmer and a stirring in one of the second-story windows, where old roses twined up a sturdy trellis to the railed balcony.

Captivated, he stopped. Jessica stood in an aura of orange and gold backlighting, staring dreamily out across the lawn. An incandescent glow hovered around her, silhouetting a form so flawlessly feminine that Fletcher's mouth went dry. Heat jolted through him, settling uncomfortably in his loins.

Unaware of his presence, Jessica leaned over the rail and plucked a rose, then lifted it to her face.

Lord, he thought, resuming his progress toward the house, physical beauty was a capricious virtue that it would favor a woman like Jessica. Her loveliness taunted and haunted him, inspiring hot desire for the woman she was and cold disdain for the courtesan she used to be. His strides lengthened and quickened with impatience.

He knew the moment she spied him. The rose dropped from her fingers and landed in the grass beneath the balcony. From her sudden stiffness and the way she gripped the balustrade, he sensed that she was fighting the urge to flee. But she stood rooted. She lifted her hand in a tentative salute.

Suddenly and inexplicably seized by a whim, Fletcher picked up the rose she'd dropped, tucked it into his waistcoat pocket, and gripped the trellis. Fully aware of the absurdity of his gesture, he climbed upward, reaching the balustrade in moments. Unable to suppress a grin at his own foolishness, he vaulted over the rail.

With an exaggerated bow, he held the rose out to her. "I believe you dropped this, milady."

Wide-eyed, a smile hovering on her lips, Jessica took the flower. "You might have fallen," she said.

He shrugged. "I made good use of the trellises when I was a lad. A fine way to escape a dancing lesson or a visit from the parson."

"Well, you're a grown man now and should make use of a perfectly sturdy stairwell."

"I thought you'd be impressed. Earlier today you told Gabriel there was nothing wrong with choosing the shortest distance between two points.'' He took her hand and led her inside. ''And this is the shortest distance to the bedroom.''

Sending him a nervous look, Jessica laid the rose on the table near a bowl of fruit, then stood watching him like one trying to puzzle out a problem. Behind her a candle flared, illuminating for an instant the ripe shape of her body through the gown.

Filled with a yearning so intense that he nearly shook with it, Fletcher pulled her into his arms. The clean scent of violets and Jessica swirled around him, permeating his senses. His body's reaction was immediate, untamable. Desire gathered heavily in his center and radiated outward, touching every straining nerve. His manhood pressed into her, a frank message of lust.

Jessica's reaction was equally swift. She went rigid and gasped sharply. He looked down to see her cheeks stained a bright, mortified pink. Her laugh sounded tremulous and forced. ''You move so quickly,'' she said, discreetly trying to pull away. ''You startled me.''

With an unbidden stab of sympathy, Fletcher loosened his hold. She whirled away, her eyes unnaturally bright. ''I've been looking around your room,'' she said quickly. ''So many fine things . . . but there's little of you here.''

Impatience sent his sympathy spiraling away. He pulled her back into his arms. ''There's as much of me in this room as you'll need tonight, Jessica.'' He began leading her toward the bed.

She glanced wildly at the crystal bowl on the table, its facets winking in the glow of a pair of beeswax tapers.

''Are—are you hungry, Fletcher? Sir Jeffrey gave us a gift of fruit from Georgia—plums, pears, peaches. . . .''

Fletcher scowled and shook his head slowly. ''I have a different sort of appetite tonight, my dear.''

He threaded his fingers into her hair, luxuriating in its gossamer softness and springtime fragrance. His lips found a warm, downy spot near her temple. ''But were I to liken you to a fruit, I'd say you were a peach. Soft, ripe . . .'' He kissed her gently on the mouth. ''. . . and unbearably sweet . . .'' His tongue found the soft openness of her lips, communicating a potent desire with a clarity she could not fail to understand.

He was stunned, though not surprised, by the force of his need. He longed to gather her scent and her softness around him like a veil, to bury himself in her sweet warmth and soothe, at long last, the ache that had been building since the day he first spied her, playing like a child in the Pynchons' entrance hall. It mattered little that she gave him no encouragement, that she remained stiff in his arms; the barreling power of his passion was inducement enough.

His hands began a slow exploration of her lush form. His fingers discovered delicious curves and valleys while his tongue savored the beguiling moistness of her mouth. Filling his hand with the yielding shape of her breast, aware of a tremor eddying through her, he felt his control slipping. Too long, he thought, his thumb bringing her nipple to life. *It's been too damned long.*

His fingers were less than steady as he found the fastenings of her gown. Between the kisses he rained over her face, his breath came in short, staccato gulps.

"Fletcher." She called his name pleadingly, a whisper against his neck.

He gazed down at her, expecting for no good reason to see an answering desire in her face. But what he saw instead turned his heated blood to rivers of ice. Uncertainty haunted the swirling mists of her eyes and sapped her cheeks of color.

Fletcher swore under his breath and drew back with rough abruptness. That familiar look had kept him at bay for weeks. He'd been patient; he'd let her hide behind pretenses of propriety. But not anymore. He gripped her shoulders. "What game are you playing now, Jessica?"

She flinched at his harsh touch. "I—it's no game, Fletcher."

"I've given you a proper church wedding, even solemnized our union in the Mohawk way. What more do you want from me?"

"I've asked for my freedom, and you won't give me that."

He caressed her pale cheek with his finger. "Then what *do* you want, Jessica? Jewels for your pretty throat, a greater household allowance . . . ?" He let his voice trail off, because he knew better than that. Still, he was desperate to find a reason for her reluctance, any reason to keep from feeling the burn of rejection once again.

She wrenched away and folded her hands across her bosom. Color began to seep back into her face—not the soft, rosy tint of desire, but bright red flags of anger. "I want nothing of the sort. I haven't tried to resist you tonight."

"That missish look on your face, my dear, is resistance enough. You've managed to put me off for a good while with your little pretenses, but it won't work now."

"I am not pretending."

He moved toward her again; she took a step back. Frustrated, he ground his teeth. "Yet you shrink from me."

Her eyes narrowed. "Why should I welcome the touch of a man who thinks me no better than a whore?"

Clenching his fists, he pushed away the hurt her words aroused with a fresh surge of rage. "What would you have me think of you? I know what you were. What sort of woman would tend children by day, then entertain men at night?"

She caught her lower lip with her teeth, but not before he saw her chin tremble. "I did no such thing."

"You sound as if you really believe what you're saying. As if you expect me to believe it."

Sadness mingled with the anger in her eyes in a uniquely appealing way. "Just what is it you want of me, Fletcher? I'm quite capable of carrying out your commands, but you must first put them into words." Her breasts rose and fell quickly and her eyes glittered a challenge.

Frustrated passion obliterated the last shreds of his patience. "All right—you want commands? Then take off that gown," he said. "Now."

Her defiance vanished. Chin ducked low, she clutched at the neck of her gown.

"You asked me what I wanted," he reminded her. "Need I make myself any plainer?"

She swallowed. "C . . . could we put out the candles?" she asked, her voice a curious mixture of anxiety, pleading, and stubbornness."

"No, by God," he snapped. "I would see the bill of goods I bargained for."

To his utter dismay, her eyes filled with tears. "Fletcher, don't do this to me . . . to us. I've tried to tell you, I'm not—"

"Your pretense of being a wounded virgin has grown

stale,'' he stated. ''And it doesn't become you. I want the woman you are in my bed, not the innocent you would have me believe.''

She dashed the tears from her cheeks with a savage swipe of her hand. ''You want a whore in your bed?'' she said loudly. ''Very well, Fletcher Danforth, make me your whore!'' She tore the gown from her body like petals being plucked from a flower.

Gaping at her, he barely heard her bitter words. Here at last was the woman she'd kept hidden from him all these weeks. Her gesture was as welcome as it was unexpected. At last she offered herself to him, with defiance rather than submission, heated anger rather than icy indifference.

His blood pounding, his senses reeling, his body wracked by bright dagger thrusts of desire, he lifted her against him and carried her to the bed, then watched as the thick eiderdown billows engulfed the lush splendor of her body. ''It's a wife I want, Jessica,'' he told her gruffly, shedding his clothes.

Her face lay in shadows and he was glad of that, glad because she was so damned adept at making him believe the uncertainty in her eyes was genuine, that the protests she voiced were real. Bracing himself above her, he added, ''This is how a marriage was meant to begin, darling.''

He wove his fingers into the springy silk of her hair and lowered his mouth to hers. Her breasts rose and fell beneath his chest, their taut peaks scorching his skin. He burned for her with a wild, primitive passion that made a mockery of his self-control and turned his skepticism to something shockingly akin to worship.

His hands left her hair and moved downward, finding her flesh warm, impossibly smooth, the satin of an angel's robe. Her beauty put him in mind of forest nymphs or the elusive *thak-lani* of Mohawk legend. And yet she was real, vital and feminine, and she was his at last.

The weeks of waiting had aroused a need so powerful that his throat constricted, his chest tightened. He was like a youth again, with a youth's undisciplined impulses. Although aware that Jessica lay still and silent, that she could not possibly share his fierce yearning, he could wait no longer.

''There will be other times when I'm more attentive to your

needs," he promised. With fevered urgency his mouth moved over her face, her neck, her breasts. "The second time and the third . . ." He poised above her, hovering, burning, staring into her beautiful, shadowed face. "Because, you see, I want you so very much, my love. . . ." His words trailed off as he gently parted her legs and sank down. Her body resisted his invasion and he nearly bellowed with frustration. Instead he asked through gritted teeth: "Is this another of your whore's tricks, Jessica?"

"I don't know what you mean."

Her faint whisper tore at his heart, but his potent lust forbade him to listen. "Then I'll show you," he said, curling his tongue into her ear. He came to her once again, only this time he was not so gentle. Her tight, velvet moistness was so unexpected that he gasped with pleasure.

"Fletcher . . . it hurts."

He heard Jessica's words through the exultant roar of blood in his ears. Only when he moved more deeply into her did he fully understand.

"Oh, God, no."

He knew now what he'd done, knew shame and regret, and tried to pull away. But the demands of his body overrode all logic and caution.

"Jessica . . ." he choked, "forgive me . . ." In the space of a heartbeat, his misbegotten assumptions about her were shattered. Summoning all the tenderness he possessed, he fought the rampant urgency of his body and slowed his frantic pace. Moving to her side, he lowered his head to kiss her eyelids, her cheeks, the curve of her neck. A sigh slipped from her and he caught it with his mouth, while his hand wandered down the length of her torso, circling her breasts, mapping the curves of her stomach and thighs. His palm cupped the warm nest of her womanhood, bruised by his unthinking urgency.

She tensed and he murmured endearments against her lips, stroking, kissing, until he felt her relax. "Oh, darling," he said, moving slowly over her, "I didn't know . . . I won't hurt you again." He lowered himself gently, almost trembling, until her feminine warmth wrapped him in splendor.

His control wavered. He thought he would burst. Innocent, immobile, she lay still and for that he was thankful, because the slightest movement would tear down his resistance and rob him of the chance to pleasure her. But suddenly her hips lifted toward him in an instinctive movement.

Fletcher tried not to breathe, but when she spoke his name and arched her back, he gave himself up to the long, hard thrusts his tortured body clamored for.

Between shimmering bursts of pleasure he heard her moan softly and felt her clutch at him, as if she, too, shared the exultant sensations coursing through him. He opened his eyes and saw that hers were wide with wonder.

He buried his face in her fragrant hair, feeling relief but at the same time reaching a new level of self-contempt that made every low thought he'd ever had about himself seem like a compliment in comparison. If guilt were a liquid element, Fletcher reflected grimly, he'd be a drowning man right now.

Slowly, reluctantly, he lifted himself from her. He stared at her lovely body so intently that she flushed and burrowed beneath the eiderdown. But not before he'd seen the evidence of his offense; not before he'd seen a trace of her virgin's blood.

Jessica gazed in silence at her husband. He gazed back, his eyes dark with pain and confusion. Very gently, he placed his hand on her cheek.

"How do you feel, my love?"

She swallowed. Her body tingled with sensations she could not yet name. She had felt as if she were teetering on a precipice, desperate to plunge over. But far too quickly he had left her there, bewildered, bewitched, and yearning for something she didn't understand.

Fletcher was looking at her, waiting for an answer. She glanced away. "I . . . It was everything I thought it would be."

"I was too rough," he confessed. "If I'd accepted your word . . ."

"You don't have to explain, Fletcher," she said. *I liked what you did to me.* "You found me in an indefensible situation; anyone would have jumped to the same conclusion."

He expelled his breath in a long, unsteady sigh. His eyes probed her face. "Who are you?" he said in an aching whisper. "What are you?"

"Only what you've made me, Fletcher," she answered.

As if suddenly mortified by her nearness, he leapt from the bed. He shoved his legs into his breeches and went to stand at the open window, his bare torso limned by moonlight. Jessica wanted to call him back, to let his power enfold and surround her again until she understood the feelings he'd ignited in her. Yet unable to read his mood, she turned her face into the eiderdown, inhaling the scent of their bodies and wondering why that fragrance made her feel so unaccountably restless.

A long silence thrummed between them. His shoulders tensed and he breathed in shallow gasps. At last, as if he could stand it no more, he spun around. "For God's sake, Jessica, you should have fought me!"

"I didn't want to fight you anymore," she admitted quietly. And it was true. She'd wanted him to take the decision away from her, to make her accept the fact that she longed for his lovemaking.

Raking his fingers through his hair, he asked, "Why don't you have done with it now? You're more than entitled to all the recriminations I know you would like to heap on me."

Once, she'd envisioned triumph after this night, waving the proof of her virginity in his face like a banner of truth. Yet she found no dark pleasure in proving him wrong, because their conflict had become far more complex. Because somewhere within the hurt and the doubt existed a strange core of mutual concern.

"There was a time," she said softly, "when I would have taken great satisfaction in doing just that, Fletcher. But now . . . I see no need to antagonize each other further."

He leaned heavily against the window frame and gazed into the night. "You're too damned reasonable."

He felt guilty, she realized, and rightfully so. Yet she didn't want apologies. She wanted him to come back to her and revive the warm, wonderful sensations she'd begun to feel after that first, fleeting pain. But his withdrawal left her feeling too unsure to ask for that.

Sighing, she sat up in bed, tucked the coverlet around her, and stared hard at her husband. Fletcher had made her a woman tonight, for all that he seemed to despise that fact. Perhaps now she would learn the facets he kept hidden from her.

Although her eyes probed deeply, she still couldn't fathom the man. Despite what they'd shared, despite all the emotions she felt, he remained a brooding figure, cool and distant, like a shadow on the moon.

Her sudden sob of despair brought Fletcher rushing to the bed. He brushed a curl from her cheek.

"Are you in pain, Jessica? Shall I send for Nan, or—"

"No, I'm not in pain," she choked.

"Then why are you crying?"

She stared at him through misty, tear-drenched eyes. "I thought, after tonight, that I would know you, Fletcher. But you are still a stranger to me."

Chapter 13

Jessica awoke to the faint fragrance of masculine warmth—Fletcher's essence. She tried to decide how she felt about awakening in his bed, but the effort made her head throb. She moved her leg in a tentative search and realized she was alone. Opening her eyes, she blinked at the late morning sunshine.

The movement of her leg resurrected an ache that brought tears to her eyes. Tears of regret, because her hopes for a harmonious union with Fletcher had been shrouded by the shadows of their wedding night.

Crushing the coverlet to her face to muffle her bitter sobs and absorb her hot tears, she wept. She'd learned to sublimate raw emotion as a child, yet now, she told herself, she had a right to cry. But only for a moment. She drew rein on her sorrow and checked her tears.

She hadn't the strength to impose a similar discipline on her thoughts. She recalled the night before with stark clarity: her apprehension and resolve to achieve harmony, Fletcher's dramatic entrance over the balcony, the sweet nectar of his kisses, and then the heated exchange that had prompted her to . . .

Oh, God. She burrowed deeper beneath the eiderdown. Had she really flung her bedgown off like the common slut he thought she was? Had they really said such hurtful things to each other?

Yes; she remembered every bitter word, every scathing glance, the rough urgency of his touch.

She recalled Fletcher's voice afterward, soothing yet gruff with regret as he admitted he'd been wrong about her. Now she felt a yawning emptiness that no apology could fill. He hadn't given her a chance to explore the man he was, to discover the secrets of his body as well as her own.

The last clear picture she saw before tumbling into exhausted, tear-induced sleep was of Fletcher sitting on the edge of the bed, fingers furrowed into his hair, head bowed and shoulders slumped as if he'd been saddled with an insupportable weight.

Was that what she had become to him? Only yesterday he'd considered her a whore to be tolerated for the sake of his children; did he now see her as an unwanted burden?

The door to the dressing room opened. Jessica turned away, feigning sleep. A cowardly act, she admitted, but she wasn't ready to face her husband, not yet. Not with her cheeks stained with tears, her body wracked by unfamiliar aches, and her mind whirling with confusion.

She tried not to tense as she heard Fletcher approach the bed. His footsteps hesitated and she imagined him standing there, impeccably dressed for the day, his face harshly handsome. She prayed he couldn't see her trembling.

He smoothed a wisp of hair from her temple, his touch so unexpectedly gentle that Jessica nearly betrayed herself by collapsing against him and weeping yet again.

Tingling from his tender caress, she held still, aching all over, inside and out. She didn't know how things stood between them, but that was a question she would ponder later, when the wounds weren't so raw.

Fletcher's footsteps receded. She heard the door open and close, and a wavering sigh escaped her.

His horse was lathered to a high chestnut sheen by the time Fletcher reached the northern boundary of his manor. His troubles, he conceded, angling his mount toward the river, were too deep to escape by racing over hills and through forests. But emotion, not logic, ruled him today. It was natural to move away from something painful and being near Jessica brought pain. She had made him see himself for what he was: arrogant, self-serving, unreasonable . . . a product of the dark savagery of male pride.

The landscape filled his vision: soaring mountains and pathless woodlands silently penetrated by the wide, dark ribbon of the Hudson. Images of Jessica filled his mind: old images, yet new because last night had changed everything. He saw her differently now, as she had been at their first meeting: a laughing, fresh-faced girl chasing beads across a marble floor. He remembered being struck by her honesty then, her straightforward manner, her beauty.

How quickly his admiration had turned to cynicism. How ready he'd been to read ulterior motives into her actions.

Why hadn't he believed that first impression? Why had he thought the worst when he discovered her association with Adele? He had doubted Jessica when he should have been doubting himself. He'd condemned her for sins she hadn't committed; now he condemned himself for treating an innocent woman like a trollop.

Self-contempt ripped at his heart. He'd failed Jessica, failed to listen to her instead of crediting the rantings of a besotted duke. A spiral of agony climbed from his gut to his throat. Fletcher turned his horse northward. He wasn't ready to return to Jessica, not yet. He hoped to approach her with a clear mind and a concrete plan, because he couldn't simply use her now. He'd been so arrogant to think himself admirable for offering his name and his home to a woman he hadn't let himself consider worthy.

As he had often done in boyhood, he sought the company of his mother's people. The Mohawk had a gift for listening without judging, for advising without preaching. And Fletcher needed that now.

He rode along the riverbank, ducking beneath the branches of chestnut and water-beech trees. Kayanere and his party had left Holland Hall at dawn, characteristically neglecting to bid their host good-bye. Fletcher knew better than to feel slighted; a Mohawk never said good-bye.

He spied Great Knife, Kayanere, and Kateri a short distance upriver. The two men sat at opposite ends of an elm-bark canoe, stirring the water with their paddles; the girl sat between them. A longing welled up in Fletcher, a longing for a simple life that could never be his.

Were he fully an Indian, he, too, would possess a Mohawk's placid conception of his ordained place in the world. Were he fully an Englishman, he'd have the sense of self-righteousness to deny his mistakes, secure in the knowledge that he was lord and master of his manor, that his actions and decisions were beyond question.

But he was neither; he was a product of Mohawk forbearance and English arrogance. He possessed an Indian's conscience and an Englishman's sense of duty. The dichotomy made self-forgiveness impossible.

Fletcher hailed the travelers in their own tongue. Great Knife brought the canoe to the bank and held the craft steady while Kateri and Kayanere climbed out. The girl drifted over to a patch of elderberry bushes, gathering twigs for beading.

Fletcher helped his grandfather mount the bank. "Did you find the supplies I left in the kitchen?"

Kayanere nodded. "I will share your gifts of cloth and silver with the clan."

Fletcher grinned. His grandfather had no conception of the value of the gifts. A white man would be dazzled by the amount of silver and the quality of the cloth, but not a Mohawk. To Kayanere, thrift and avarice were equally contemptible. He took only what he needed, then cheerfully shared the surplus.

The shaman squatted on a warm rock and took out his pipe and pouch. Tamping a wad of tobacco into the calumet, he said, "I do not care for the shiny oval in which I could see my face. What have I to gain by gazing at this?" Scowling, he jabbed a finger at his wizened face.

Fletcher laughed. "Give it to Kateri then. She has far more reason for vanity than you, Grandfather." He caught the girl's eye and winked, and she sent him a merry smile.

He watched Kayanere trying to light his pipe. After observing a good many fruitless sparks, Fletcher took the tinder, flint, and charred linen from the old man and performed the task. Kayanere grunted his thanks and sat back on his heels, regarding Fletcher through a mist of smoke. "So, Shadow Hawk, has she driven you from the nest already?"

A shaft of pain buried itself in his gut. "As a boy, I shared all my joys and secrets with you, Grandfather. Now I come to you as a man, to share my pain and regret."

Great Knife finished securing the canoe. Chewing on a piece of white bread from Mercy's kitchen, he eyed Fletcher. "Shadow Hawk bears no scars from the wedding night, yet here he is, leagues away from his new wife when they should be sharing a hearth.''

Fletcher took no offense at the probing stares. He trusted these men, knew he could speak in confidence. Though both were widowers, they'd each been married for years. Surely in that time they'd learned how to redress a wrong against a wife.

"Jessica and I are . . . in discord," he said simply. "And the fault is mine."

Kayanere shook his head. "You have decided this after just one night?"

"I maligned her, you see. Misjudged her." Fletcher laid out the story for his friends, sparing himself not at all. He spoke candidly of his disdain for what he had thought Jessica was; he was generous in describing her restraint in not flinging recriminations at him—a restraint he didn't deserve.

Kayanere and Great Knife looked at each other, then back at Fletcher. The older man tapped his pipe against the rock, then scattered the ashes with a nut-brown, callused finger. "Why did you not take her at her word, Shadow Hawk?"

Fletcher let a silence spin out, listening to the hiss of the wind in the leaves and the lapping of the water at the bank. Unlike the English, the Mohawk didn't feel compelled to fill every lull in a conversation with inanities. They were more contemplative and given to moments of introspection.

He plucked a strand of sword grass and drew it slowly through his fingers. He searched Kayanere's face, studying the lines around his eyes, seeking wisdom in their depths.

"Sybil taught me to take no woman at her word," he said dully. "That bitter lesson was my justification for using Jessica."

"Now you have learned she is a good woman," Kayanere said.

"I think I always knew that here." Fletcher pointed at his head, then brought his hand to his heart. "But this part of me did not listen. I *wanted* to find some flaw in Jessica, some reason to excuse what I did to her in the English court. Since the time I discovered her entertaining a duke in a house where gentlemen pay for such privileges, I clung to that evidence like a mountain cat to a spring fawn. I believed ill of her so I wouldn't have to think ill of myself."

"A poor way to measure yourself, my friend," Great Knife murmured. "And not like you at all. Do you not remember what you once were, before the English seized you? Because of you, the clan was able to fend off the French—by our own strength, not the strength of English soldiers. You gave your people a gift more valuable than any trading truck; you gave us independence. Such a man need not doubt his worth."

"Five years of enforced labor at Fort Orange can make a man doubt whether the sun will rise at dawn." Fletcher wound the blade of grass around his finger and inhaled its pungent fragrance. "Besides, my actions on behalf of my people have little to do with my attributes as a husband and father."

"They have everything to do with it, Shadow Hawk," Kayanere said. "The Englishmen's treatment has embittered you, but that man—the man who loves life and cherishes his family—still exists. You have only to find him within yourself."

"Even if I could, that wouldn't change what I did to Jessica."

"True. So you must decide what you will do about her."

Fletcher fixed Kayanere with a cynical glance. "Do you have any suggestions?"

Kayanere shrugged. "Give her a child," he said offhandedly. "That is how I always placated my women. A baby is the greatest apology of all."

Fletcher couldn't help grinning. "You must have offended your wives many times then, for the village of Canajoharie is overrun by your 'apologies.' "

His smile disappeared as his thoughts returned to Jessica. Could he do as his grandfather said, bring another human life into the circle of pain he had made of his family? He may have already done so. His heart leapt with a feeling too achingly bittersweet to bear. Quickly he thrust it aside.

"That is not the answer. I cannot bind Jessica to me with another child." He turned to Great Knife. "What of you, my friend? When we were boys you showed me how to coax a squirrel into taking a hickory nut from my hand. Have you a means for coaxing a woman to trust me?"

Great Knife's face remained serious. "Had I that gift,

brother, I would have stayed at Holland Hall, feeding Jade and Nan from my hand.''

Fletcher laughed. ''Both of them, Great Knife?''

The brave smiled sheepishly. ''You know me, Shadow Hawk. I am a man of . . . varied appetites. Jade is favored with beauty and alacrity; Nan, with bounty and humor.''

''And they both saw fit to favor *you* with their attention,'' Kayanere said, snorting.

''You're too old to covet my good fortune,'' Great Knife taunted. ''Neither woman seemed adept at lighting your pipe; I don't know what else you would need them for.'' Kayanere muttered something about Great Knife's mother and her sensitivity to the mating call of a moose. Great Knife plucked a spear of grass and aimed it at the old man, but he was laughing.

Then he turned back to Fletcher. ''I am sorry, my friend. We spend our time jesting and I have not answered your question.''

He stretched out his legs and toyed with his deerhide belt. ''I have had three wives in my lodge, all as different as snowflakes. But they were alike in one way. They gave me their hearts when I gave them what they wanted.''

Fletcher tossed the blade of grass away and leaned back on one elbow, staring out across the wide, placid river. A sturgeon leapt and splashed against the surface. A wild goose rose from the reeds at the water's edge, beating its wings against the summer sky.

''Sybil could be bought off with pearls and perfume like an Algonquin with cheap rum,'' Fletcher mused. ''But not Jessica. She isn't overfond of baubles.'' He remembered her startled reaction to the bosom bottle he'd given her at Bartholomew Fair. She hadn't trusted the sentiment behind that gift and he couldn't blame her.

''What does she want?'' Great Knife asked.

''Her freedom.''

''But you can't offer her that,'' Kayanere said. ''The English court says you must keep her.''

Frustrated, Fletcher let his mind wander. ''When I was a child not much older than Kitty, I caught a marten in the bakehouse. My mother cautioned me to set it free, but I insisted on keeping it.'' He swallowed painfully. ''The marten died in the cage I fashioned.''

''Your Jessica will not die,'' Kayanere said softly.

''Nor will she ever be happy,'' Fletcher replied. He blew out his breath and let his mind meander again, hoping it would lead to an answer.

''A pity,'' Great Knife said contemptuously, ''that your life must be ruled from across the sea and enforced by one so low as Jeffrey Amherst.''

Fletcher remembered what Will Johnson had said about the royal governor the day before: *'Tis no wonder his favor can be so easily bought.*

The thought barreled into his mind with the shattering force of a cannonball. Amherst was needy and greedy enough to accept Fletcher's bribe, to turn his back on the Lord Chancellor's edict.

The idea settled like a cold stone in Fletcher's gut. Bribe the governor? Give up Jessica? His heart recoiled at the notion, because Jessica had found a way deep inside him, a place that would wither and die if he lost her.

But what about her? his conscience asked. Won't she wither and die if you keep her caged?

Fletcher dragged his will to a reluctant decision. He'd been selfish long enough and his selfishness had made Jessica an innocent victim. It would take a few months, perhaps, for the furor over the marriage to die down and for him to arrive at an agreement with Amherst. Then Jessica could return quietly to England as she longed to do and the children would remain safe at Holland Hall.

It was perfect. For in giving Jessica her freedom, he'd be punishing himself. Sending her home meant he could not risk getting her with child. Denying himself the unearthly delight of making love to her was a greater penance than any wrathful Mohawk god could assign.

His pride rebelled at the plan, demanded that he redeem himself in the bedchamber by showing Jessica the pleasures of physical love. But his conscience forbade such self-indulgence. ''I have the answer,'' he told his friends grimly, and explained his plan.

''You'll give up your wife?'' Great Knife asked.

"Aye. And a small fortune too. I'll see to it she is able to live well in England."

"What if you make a child together?" Kayanere asked.

Fletcher's fist clenched. "We won't."

Kayanere gaped and Fletcher read the thoughts etched on his grandfather's face. Although the clan was headed by matriarchs, Mohawk women were trained from girlhood to practice industry, cooperation, and self-effacement.

"Bringing pleasure to the marriage bed is a woman's duty ordained by the gods, a duty to be embraced with eagerness," the old man said.

"I, too, have a duty. I owe Jessica freedom . . . from the marriage bed and from my life."

"If you are certain that is what she wants, Shadow Hawk," Kayanere said slowly.

I will not live in the world you offer. He recalled Jessica's words with cold clarity. "I'm certain," he said bitterly. "It's what she's wanted all along."

A call from upriver brought them to their feet. A canoe glided around a bend, bearing south.

"It's Billy," Kateri called, running to the riverbank.

Billy Wolf was Great Knife's eldest son, a thickset youth of fifteen summers. Bringing his canoe ashore, he greeted them with uncharacteristic seriousness. His congratulations on Fletcher's marriage seemed distracted.

"Ill news," he muttered, absently giving Kateri's braid an affectionate tug. He turned to Kayanere, laying a hand on the old man's shoulder. "Your grandson, Sawatis, has died."

Kayanere's shoulders sagged and a ragged sigh escaped him. Fletcher felt a painful wrench of sympathy as he watched his grandfather's face go pale, the lines deepening into furrows of grief. Fletcher moved toward him, but Kayanere waved his hand and turned away, not ready to share a grief so new.

"We must go," Great Knife said, reaching for Kateri's hand.

"Wait," Billy Wolf said. "Sawatis had a rash. The rash of the smallpox."

Great Knife hissed as if burned. "The white man's scourge. . . . Have others fallen ill?"

Billy nodded. "Sabra's baby and Old Hunter. I am safe,

Father, as are you and Kayanere; we've survived the disease and the gods keep us from being touched by it again.''

Great Knife's eyes found Kateri, who had been listening gravely to Billy's report. The girl gave a cry and stumbled back. "What will you do with me, Father?"

Great Knife considered for a moment. "Billy can take you to Johnson Hall. You will be cared for there."

Kateri went into his arms and sobbed against his chest. "But I don't want to leave you. Warraghiyagey and Molly Brant are strangers to me. Please, Father."

Great Knife gazed helplessly over her head at Fletcher. "I cannot risk bringing her back to our village."

Fletcher stepped forward, taking Kateri gently by the shoulders and bringing her around to face him. He went down on one knee so that his eyes were on a level with hers. Staring into the brown, tear-drenched depths, he said, "Kateri, your father only wants to protect you. But you need not go to Johnson Hall. You may come home with me."

She rubbed her doeskin sleeve across her face and looked back at Great Knife. "If I may not return to the village, then I would rather go with Shadow Hawk."

"I will take her there myself," Billy said, motioning toward his canoe.

"It is done then." Great Knife looked relieved. "Thank you, Shadow Hawk." They clasped hands briefly. Fletcher felt a surge of satisfaction. For years he'd had to deny his ties to the Mohawk, but now he had a chance to openly embrace one of his mother's people.

"I'll bring more things—medicine, blankets," he said; then he turned to Kayanere. The shaman was once again trying to light his pipe with sad, ineffectual strokes, his mute grief more poignant than screams of mourning. Gently Fletcher took the flint and steel.

"The light has dropped from the sky," he said softly, echoing a phrase of Mohawk mourning. "But you, Grandfather, you must lift up the light and replace it in the heavens."

Kayanere shook his head. "I've borne many sadnesses, Shadow Hawk. I no longer have the strength." His voice sounded thin and reedy, as frail as the delicate old bones of his body.

Fletcher felt a wave of love and sadness for his grandfather, for all his people. The English scourge, smallpox, made a mockery of the Indians' values of peace and harmony, intruded upon their lives like the white man himself. Fletcher grieved for the forests his father's people had razed, the land they'd fenced off . . . and he grieved for his young cousin, Sawatis.

"I will follow you to Canajoharie," Fletcher said. "Billy and I will be but a few hours behind you."

Kayanere trudged to the canoes. Kateri dried her tears, bade her father good-bye, and followed Billy to his canoe.

Fletcher rode homeward bearing a different burden than he'd carried away. He'd taken responsibility for yet another person, another life.

And although his heart reared in denial, he had gained a means to redress the wrong he'd committed against Jessica. He allowed himself only one minor indulgence. He wouldn't tell her, not right away. He told himself it was to spare her disappointment if by chance Amherst proved unwilling. But a dark, selfish part of him wanted to pretend, if only for a short time, that she would stay with him.

Trying to put aside her turmoil over the events of the night before, Jessica strode across the yard toward the springhouse.

"You have no mercy for an old woman's frail constitution," Adele complained, puffing slightly as she followed.

"You're neither old nor frail," Jessica said teasingly. "You only demand the privileges of one who is."

The lightness of her tone belied her mood and she looked away to hide her face. Adele, more easily than anyone else, would guess her state of mind, would guess the hurt Jessica had been battling all day by throwing herself into frenzied activity. Biting her lip, she continued toward the springhouse, Adele trailing behind her. Beneath the small straw and clay building, an icy stream trilled a clear, liquid melody.

Her face drawn taut with concern and impatience, Adele caught Jessica's arm. With her other hand she adjusted her bonnet. *"Tiens,* Jessica, would you kindly tell me why you insist on performing a servant's errand? You are mistress here, after all."

Jessica's smile felt strained. "Precisely. I've my guests'

comfort in mind. The Johnsons are likely to stay a few more days. Mercy thought to fix a ham for supper. . . .''

"*Nom de Dieu,* then let Mercy fetch the ham!"

"She's busy. Today is baking day."

"You have been busy also. Busy avoiding me. You've heard the children's lessons, played an interminable game of piquet with Gabriel, bade good-bye to that dreadful Jeffrey Amherst, reckoned accounts with Mr. Elphinstone. . . .''

"These things must be done, Adele." Hearing the quavering note in her voice, Jessica changed the subject. "I wonder if we've enough rashers in the pantry for tomorrow's breakfast. . . ." Her voice trailed off as she tried to devise yet more tasks so that she wouldn't have time to think.

Adele folded her arms. "I've better things to do than to follow you around like a mongrel," she snapped.

Jessica expelled a lingering sigh. "I'm sorry, Adele. I have been avoiding you because I knew I would have to talk about last night."

"You do not have to, *copine*. But I think you need to."

'It's not fair to burden you with my problems."

Adele's nostrils narrowed in an imperious sniff, though her eyes were soft with sympathy. "You've chosen an odd time to conclude that our friendship cannot bear the weight of your troubles. You had no such qualms five years ago."

She pulled Jessica over to a patch of grass beneath a spreading hickory tree. A chipmunk scampered away as they sat down in the shaded grass.

"Your wedding night was not a success," Adele stated.

"How can you be so sure?" Alarmed, Jessica stiffened. "Have you spoken to Fletcher?"

"No. I did not have to."

Jessica sank onto her elbows. "Oh, Lord. Then everyone knows." Feeling miserable, she imagined the banter belowstairs, the gossip among the guests.

"Do not concern yourself with the opinions of others," Adele said. "Surely you did not expect to be magically transported on your first night together. Such is the stuff of fairy stories, not of real life."

"But is it so wrong to expect . . . intimacy, communication? Fletcher gave me neither."

Adele's lips thinned. "Was he cruel to you?"

"We quarreled. He never believed I was not a whore, Adele. Not until . . . he encountered irrefutable proof."

"I pity the man," Adele mused. "Self-loathing is a terrible thing for a man to face."

"Self-loathing? No, Adele, not Fletcher. He is not a man to despise himself. Especially since the failure was mine."

"How can you say that, Jessica?"

"Because I know it to be true." Jessica yanked a fistful of grass up by the roots, remembering Fletcher's ardor and her own lack of response. She tossed the grass away. "Good Lord, Adele, I lay there like a dry stick, then wept like a ninny."

"Fletcher expected to find you practiced in lovemaking. Obviously he did not exert himself to show you pleasure."

"But afterward . . . he seemed so angry."

"At himself, *copine*. Think of it. Fletcher blackmailed you; he forced you to come to the colonies only to find that you were not what he believed you to be. *He* was wrong, Jessica, not you. And now he must live with himself."

"And with me." Jessica flopped onto her back on the grass, staring up at pieces of the sky through a canopy of shag bark hickory branches and leaves. "What shall I do, Adele?"

"Decide what it is you want. Then do what you must."

The sweet scent of apples wafted from the orchards. Jessica focused on a passing cloud. "I used to want to avoid him. But now . . ." She let her voice trail off and a subtle warmth crept over her body, a warmth that had nothing to do with the midday sun but everything to do with the turn her thoughts had taken. She remembered Fletcher's touch, the heat of his caresses and the fire of his kisses. Even after their bitter words had driven the tenderness from his touch, his passion had burned away her fears. But he couldn't have known that. Ignorant of his needs and confused by her own, she hadn't given him a clue as to her feelings.

Wincing at the memory, she spoke more to herself than to Adele. "He's no longer simply the man who wed me against my will. He is infinitely more complex, like a figure surrounded by ever-changing shadows, too elusive to capture. I cannot fathom him."

"Yet you wish to, *copine*."

"Yes. Yes, I do. I want to know him, to help him with his children and with Holland Hall. I want to be Fletcher's wife in every way possible." She closed her eyes and formed an idyllic image of herself and Fletcher, working together, caring for their children, loving each other as man and wife.

She heard Adele's satisfied grunt, heard her friend move away. After a few moments had passed Jessica sat up to see Adele emerge from the springhouse. She was hefting a large bundle wrapped in cheesecloth.

Jessica scrambled to her feet. "What are you doing?"

"I am taking Mercy her ham."

"I can do that, Adele."

"*Bien sûr.* But you have something more important to do." Adele looked past Jessica at a rise of land beyond the orchards to the north. "You must tell your husband what you have decided."

Jessica whirled around. Stunned by the picture Fletcher made, she caught her breath. Bending low over the stallion's neck, thighs gripping the chestnut sides, he absorbed his mount's supple strides. With the sunlight bringing blue highlights to his midnight hair, he looked as untamed and elemental as the forest-clad mountains rising above the river.

Desire poured through Jessica, leaving her shaken yet feeling strangely powerful with a sense of purpose. This morning Fletcher had left a weeping, helpless girl in his bed. He would come home to find a woman in her place, a woman determined to learn about all the feelings only hinted at the night before.

"Yes," she said decisively, marching toward the stables, "I most definitely have a few things to say to my husband."

Chapter 14

Jessica paused uncertainly in the stable yard, waiting for Fletcher to emerge from the stone and shingle building. As she began pacing, the earthy smells of clay and horses surrounded her; sunshine chased her shadow. Her nerves jangled as she tried to frame a conversation. It was one thing to devise a plan, yet another to confront Fletcher.

She reached to tuck a few straying curls into her net.

"Don't."

Startled, she turned. With a smile, Fletcher approached and drew her hand from her snood. "I'd hoped to see the last of these dreadful nets," he told her. "Do you mind terribly?" Without awaiting her consent, he found the pins. Her thick mass of curls tumbled free.

Fletcher immediately regretted his impulse. Less than an hour ago he'd decided to send Jessica back to London, yet here he was behaving like the husband he desperately wanted to be. Against all expectations, she was smiling as if she were pleased to see him. She really was too reasonable, just as he'd accused her of being. His plan for her, he admitted with a jolt of pain, would be damned hard to carry out. How long would it take to buy off the governor and send her home? Three months? Six? Every minute was going to be torture. He tried to school his features into a facade of indifference. Her warm smile made the attempt impossible.

"It doesn't seem to matter whether I mind or not," she replied cheerfully, tossing her curls and wishing Fletcher were so easy to please in other things. She drew a deep breath. "Fletcher, I—"

"—have something to tell you." They spoke at the same

time, stared at each other, then laughed. Jessica felt silly, but wistful too. They'd shared so few moments like this. Too few.

A smile teased the corners of Fletcher's mouth as he laid his hand on her shoulder. His thumb explored the hollow of her throat. "You know," he said, "your laughter sounds like sunshine."

"But sunshine is silent," she said stupidly.

"Only to those who don't listen."

"Fletcher, the things you say sometimes—"

"I rarely say things I don't mean." His smile faded. Jasper van Cleef emerged from the stables, his arms full of supplies for the Indians. "Let's find a place to talk."

Tucking her hand in the crook of his arm, he led her to a curved stone bench in the garden. Ivory honeysuckle, alive with bees, tumbled over the wall behind them.

Jessica regarded him from the corner of her eye. His manner, as usual, mystified her. He was by turns lighthearted and moody, reaching out one moment to tease her about her hair and then drawing away. He was probably thinking about last night, probably wondering what to do about his dry stick of a wife. She wanted to reassure him, to tell him that tonight would be different. . . .

"I must go away for awhile, Jessica."

Her heart took a sickening plummet. His announcement should not have surprised her, nor should it have sent her spiraling into disappointment. But it did both. Was he already so bored and disappointed with her that he'd seek solace elsewhere? She drew a deep breath and expelled it slowly. "I see."

"Do you, Jessica? Are you not even curious about where I'm going, how long I'll be gone?"

"I . . . of course, Fletcher."

"I'm going to Canajoharie, Kayanere's village. His youngest grandson has died."

Jessica immediately felt guilty. Thank heaven she'd waited for an explanation instead of leaping into recriminations. She stared at him, recognizing a look of profound sadness in his eyes. She placed her hands over his. "Your cousin?"

He nodded. "I saw Sawatis in Canajoharie just before I left for England. He was about three, building a fort in the dirt out of sticks. . . ." Fletcher pulled his hands away and ground his fist into his palm. "He was a beautiful boy and he was so damned proud of that fort. . . ."

The ragged pain in his voice made Jessica's heart wrench. "I'm so sorry," she said awkwardly, knowing how inadequate the words were. "Would you like me to come with you?"

He looked surprised, almost pleased. But he shook his head. "A canoe trip upriver is difficult. And you'd feel out of place in the village."

"I've felt out of place since the moment I boarded the *Shadow Hawk*." Suddenly it was important to convince him she should make the trip. "Please, Fletcher, I'd like to see your other life, meet the people who mean so much to you."

"No. The children need you."

"Rather more than you do." The words tumbled from her lips without forethought.

"I can't afford to let myself need you," he muttered, then his voice turned light. "I'm a big boy now. Besides, Kateri will be staying while I return to the village."

With fondness, Jessica recalled the pretty Mohawk girl. "I shall make her feel welcome," she promised, and Fletcher rewarded her with a smile.

"You'll probably have her reading Shakespeare by the time I get back." He grew serious. "The smallpox killed Sawatis, and others as well. Do you know what that is?"

She nodded slowly. "The disease haunted Billiter Lane. Somehow I escaped the fever and the awful lesions and the agony . . . but I remember many who didn't."

Fletcher caught her hands in his and for a dizzy moment she thought she recognized a spark of affection in his eyes. "Kateri will remain here until the smallpox has run its course." His eyes darkened. "The illness was unknown to the Mohawk . . . until the white man brought it along with his trading truck and firewater."

Jessica felt his bitterness and then fear stung her. "What of you, Fletcher? You could catch the smallpox too."

"I'm immune. My father had me inoculated when I was a boy." He smiled at her blank look. "It's a way of introducing a resistance into the blood. Dr. Boylston of Massachusetts has used the method for years."

"Then we must have our children in . . . inoculated as

well.'' He looked at her strangely and she wondered if she'd said something wrong. ''Don't you like the idea, Fletcher?''

''I like it very much.'' He stood up and drew her to her feet. ''Do you realize,'' he said, ''that you just referred to Kitty and Gabriel as *our* children?''

She felt suddenly shy. ''I'm beginning to think of them as my own.''

''I'm not sure that's such a good idea.''

She dropped her eyes to a patch of sunlight on the ground. ''I didn't mean to seem presumptuous, Fletcher. I understand that I can never take Sybil's place.''

''You can't.''

Her head jerked up.

His mouth softened and his eyes warmed as his hands tightened on hers. Certain he would kiss her, certain that she wanted him to, Jessica tingled with anticipation. She breathed in, caught a hint of his familiar earthy fragrance. Her eyes fastened on his mouth and something inside her turned warm and watery.

His hands came up to her shoulders, thumbs skimming the heated flesh exposed by the neckline of her gown. His eyes, warm and steady, searched her face.

''Jessica . . . about last night . . . I'm sorry. I was wrong.'' A smile tugged at the corners of his mouth. ''You see, I learned something from you.'' The smile faded and pain flashed in his eyes. ''Damn, how could I have been so mistaken about you?''

''For the very same reasons I gave up trying to defend myself. What you saw that night at Madame's would have incriminated a saint.''

His eyes hardened and his fingers tensed on her shoulders. ''You needn't do this, you know. You needn't provide excuses for my behavior.''

''Fletcher, I think we should put this behind us.''

A look of surprise crossed his features; then he seemed to grapple with some emotion she didn't recognize. Yearning? Affection? Before she could put a name to that curious, appealing look, his expression turned quickly to a mild, impersonal smile. ''I'd best go down to the landing,'' he said, his voice cool and distant. ''Kateri and her brother Billy will be arriving soon.''

A chill wind swept over her. How easily he was able to put her aside. But she shouldn't be surprised; what did he feel for her, after all, except guilt?

He began walking, then stopped and looked back. "You'll bring the children to welcome Kateri and see me off?"

"Of course," she said, and started for the house.

"Jessica?"

She stopped. "Yes?"

"What was it you had to say to me?"

Turning, she gazed at him for a long, tense moment. He was going away; what good would it do to tell him now that she wanted to be a wife in every sense of the word?

She made her smile as bloodless as his own. "It's not important, Fletcher," she said quietly. "Not now."

The Hudson lapped quietly at the pilings beneath the dock. Annoyed at himself, Fletcher paced the planks.

Why didn't you tell her? his conscience asked.

I must be sure Amherst can be bought before I raise her hopes.

Liar. The governor's not known to suffer from sudden attacks of integrity.

She was so damned pleased to see me.

She would have been even more pleased by your decision.

But I don't want to send her away.

You're a selfish man.

Just let me be selfish a little while longer.

The illusion would be shattered soon enough. Scowling, Fletcher made quick perusal of the supplies Jasper had delivered to the dock: flour and coffee and medicines, blankets, a purse of silver coins. Fletcher brought no personal belongings; while in the village he would dress as a Mohawk, would speak their tongue, would mourn their dead as a brother.

He scanned the river for the canoe. He was eager to be underway, to hear the Mohawk chant of welcome and even the solemn strains of the mourning prayers.

And yet he felt the pull of home . . . and her. Never in his life had he been so divided between what he wanted and what he knew was right, between what he felt in his heart and what reason told him.

Still, perhaps the separation would prove useful. Even now desire stung his loins; yearning defied his conviction.

Finding her in the stable yard smiling, wanting to talk, had been a boon he didn't deserve. She'd seemed nervous, yes, but not bitter. That fact eased his conscience, but it also ignited his passion and the determination to make amends. He remembered how she'd been last night, naked, defiant, frightened, vulnerable . . . unutterably lovely. If only he had it to do over again, he'd prove himself worthy of her innocence, her untried passion. . . . But he wouldn't give himself that chance. Squinting up at the afternoon sun, he set his jaw and renewed his vow to keep his marriage chaste until he could send her back to England. She was desirable, but she wasn't for him. Damn it, why hadn't he recognized that fact in London?

A shout from the river yanked his attention away from the turmoil inside him. Billy Wolf guided the canoe to the dock; Fletcher helped Kateri alight. "Welcome back," he said. He gave her shoulder a squeeze. "You'll like it here, Kateri; you'll have many stories to tell when you return to the village."

"Thank you," she said in soft, hesitant English. Looking brave and sad, she left the dock, wandered along the bank, and squatted down amid the reeds where a snapping turtle sunned itself on a rock.

The breeze shifted slightly, bringing the warm scent of fresh bread from the bakehouse. Billy closed his eyes and inhaled, a dreamy smile on his face. "Does Mercy still tend your hearth, Shadow Hawk?" he asked.

Fletcher laughed. "Go ahead, Billy." The youth strode eagerly toward the bakehouse. He nearly collided with Kitty, who came hurtling down the path from the yard, her lacy petticoats gathered in one hand and her rag baby in the other. She sketched a brief curtsy, then resumed her headlong pace. Bending, Fletcher caught her in his arms.

"Mama says you're going away. Is that boy taking you away, Papa?"

Fletcher placed his fingers beneath her quivering chin. "Yes, but only for a few days. I must be with Kayanere."

Her lower lip poked out. "I don't want you to go."

"I wish I could stay, little one, but Kayanere is very sad right now, and he needs me."

"Oh. I wouldn't want great-grandfather to be sad."

"Anyway, you won't have time to miss me," Fletcher said. "Kateri's come back."

Kitty's face brightened when she spied the Indian girl. "Esme and I like Kateri, Papa."

"I think she's found a snapping turtle, sweetheart. Why don't you and Esme go see?" Kitty scampered off. His gaze lingered on the girls. Shy smiles and glances signalling the beginning of a new friendship, soon gave way to rapid, animated conversation.

"They seem so happy, but what can they possibly be talking about?"

Fletcher turned to see Jessica standing before him, smiling, her hands clasped demurely in the folds of her daffodil gown. She'd left her hair loose, a peach-gold halo framing a wistfully lovely face. Damn, he thought guiltily, the very air around her practically breathed innocence. His body yearned for her; his will summoned the strength to resist.

"Happiness," he said wryly, "is a simple matter to the very young."

Her smile wilted. "What an odd thing to say, Fletcher."

"I take it you have a different opinion."

"Of course. Happiness can be had by anyone who reaches for it."

"Sometimes the contentment of one person is costly to another," he said. "Is Gabriel coming?"

"I couldn't find him. But Jasper's still look—" A new smile blossomed on her face. "Here he is now."

Gabriel was running toward the landing with long, loose strides. For a moment the years fell away and Fletcher saw his son as a little boy again, untouched by the prejudices Sybil had instilled in him. A rare childish exuberance lit Gabriel's blue eyes; he seemed on the verge of smiling.

Slowing to a walk, the boy put out his hand. "Look what I've found," he said. The rock he held had been cracked open like an egg to reveal a mass of pointed purple crystals.

"You've rediscovered your rock collection." Fletcher spoke casually, concealing the wild hope that leapt in his heart. The collection was a part of the past they'd shared as father and son, a past Fletcher longed to recapture.

"It's lovely, Gabriel," Jessica said, running her fingers over the crystals. "Where did you find it?"

"Pa . . . we used to collect them high in the hills." He turned to Fletcher. "I've forgotten the way to the quarry. Do you think you could take me there this afternoon?"

Fletcher's heart plummeted. Gabriel's overture came just when Fletcher could least spare the time.

"I'd be happy to take you, son," he said carefully, "just as soon as I return from Kayanere's village."

Gabriel stared down at the canoe as if realizing its significance for the first time. His eyes grew as sharp and cold as mountain crystal. His almost-smiling mouth tautened into a bitter line. "You're leaving to be with those Indians again?" he asked, his voice brittle with accusation.

Jessica made a small sound of dismay. Fletcher reached for Gabriel's shoulder; the boy jerked away. "I have to, Gabriel," he said in frustration. "They're my family too. . . ."

The explanation died on Fletcher's lips as Kitty's laughter drifted up from the reedy bank. She was dancing a merry circle around Kateri, who had caught the snapping turtle.

Gabriel stared at Kateri with a look that blazed hatred and resentment. "What's *she* doing here?" he demanded.

"She's staying awhile, Gabriel," Fletcher told him evenly. "There's smallpox in the village and—"

Gabriel didn't wait to hear the rest. Flinging the geode at Fletcher's feet, he whirled and fled, pounding along the riverbank until the woods swallowed his fleeing form.

"He still has so much to learn," Jessica said. Her hand fluttered to his arm, her thumb rubbing the ridges of muscles gone taut with tension. But her sympathy couldn't soothe him, not now. He drew away, swearing with quiet savagery.

"You'll have time, Fletcher. The quarry will still be there when you come back."

"Don't you see, Jessica? That was just an excuse. He came here offering me a chance to be his father again and I disappointed him."

"I'll speak to him," she said. "Surely when he learns why you have to go, he'll understand."

"No. He's hurting; he'll think with his heart and not his head. His only reality is that I'm leaving him."

She took his hands in hers, her touch firm this time, almost stubborn. "You'll make things right with Gabriel when you get back," she said with conviction. "I know you will."

I mean to make things right with you too. Yet, once again, he couldn't bring himself to say the words. "Would that I had your faith in me," he muttered, staring at her small hands and wondering why her grip felt so strong.

"I know Gabriel loves you. And needs you."

"An interesting observation," Fletcher said dryly. "But you're wrong. For the past five years Gabriel's been taught to hate me, to despise my heritage as well as his own."

"He just doesn't know how to ask for affection, Fletcher. He's much like you in that. Although you hide it, I suspect there is something inside you that begs to be healed."

Her statement took him by surprise. Staring down at her, he saw a woman who, against all logic, seemed to care for him. The sweet honesty of her expression warmed a place in him that had long been cold.

Without thinking, he caught her against him, burying his face in the tightly curled silk of her hair. Desire flared instantly. Remembering her pain the previous night, remembering his vow to set her free, he started to pull away.

But he could not relinquish her, not yet. Her gilt-fringed eyes held an imploring look; her lips were moist and slightly parted. Tenderness crept through him and gave him the strength to do what must be done.

"Jessica," he whispered, "I want you to know that what happened last night won't happen again. I've decided—"

"No!" The word burst from her lips and a blush leapt to her cheeks. "I—I don't want to talk about last night," she said, faltering. "Not now. Too much has happened and you have to go." She smiled tremulously. "We'll speak of it when you return. After we've both had a chance to think."

Fletcher had done all the thinking he needed to do. Yet the words still stuck in this throat unuttered, as they had been all day. And there they would remain, because he was so selfish and she was so beautiful.

"Aye, later," he murmured, bending to her lips. "But for now . . ."

His kiss was fierce with desperation and longing. She responded, not with a courtesan's indifference, nor with a maiden's clumsiness, but with the ardor of a passionate woman.

She moved her mouth beneath his until his blood sang in his ears. When at last he released her, she was smiling.

His chest felt tight.

"You're making it damned hard for me to leave," he muttered. And she was making it harder for him to keep to his unspoken promise.

Billy Wolf arrived, a fresh-baked loaf under each arm and a look of satisfaction on his face. Fletcher made hasty introductions, trying not to smile as the thunderstruck youth nearly stumbled off the edge of the dock.

"Kateri said you'd brought a wife from across the water," Billy said, speaking in Mohawk, "but I did not expect a princess."

Fletcher looked at Jessica, with her misty heather eyes and sunny curls and clever hands folded against her apron. "Nor did I, Billy," he said. "Nor did I."

Perched high in the crook of a horse-chestnut tree, Gabriel nearly choked with disgust. His father had never treated his real mother that way, clasping her against him as if he never wanted to let go.

Gabriel ground his fists into his eyes, pushing back the tears. He was the only one who cared that his mother had died. He was the only one who lay awake at night, afraid to sleep because it meant seeing her again, seeing that angry sweep of her hand, seeing her life bleeding away.

Her death meant only one thing to Papa. It meant he was free to marry Jessica Darling.

And what was worse, everyone seemed to love Jessica: Kitty, Hilda, Mercy . . . Gabriel was sick of hearing them laugh at her stories, praise her art, call her mistress as if Mama had never existed.

But they'd think differently if they knew the truth about Jessica and those cheap women. He wondered what the servants and tenants and townspeople would say if they learned Jessica had been pulled from a London whorehouse.

He scowled at the dock. His father lingered with Jessica, his head bent at an intimate angle. Kitty and Kateri sat nearby, laughing at the turtle they'd caught. Papa and the Indian stranger launched the canoe while the others waved farewell. To Gabriel, they looked like a happy family. A family that didn't include him.

As he watched the canoe gliding away, he felt a twist of pain. Papa was leaving again. He told himself it didn't matter. He'd gotten along without his father for the past five years.

But the pain refused to go away. Gabriel was hurting and he wanted to hurt back. He'd borne the burden of his father's tainted blood, borne schoolboys' taunts and his mother's temper. And yet Fletcher expected his son to welcome him back with open arms, to excuse his absences, to accept a sneaky Mohawk girl like Kateri.

A dark decision took root in Gabriel's mind. When Papa returned home, he might not find things as harmonious as he'd left them. And then he'd notice his son.

The trill of bird song and the smell of old roses filled the sultry air of high summer. Adele sat napping on the verandah, a book propped, forgotten, in her lap. Smothering giggles at their jokes, Kitty and Kateri were watching Hilda feed her doves. Molly Brant plaited Nan's saffron hair, showing Jade how to weave beaded leather into the braids.

Sighing, Jessica put the final touches on a silhouette of Molly. As usual, Gabriel was nowhere to be seen. She ached for the boy; he'd been stonily silent and strangely secretive even since Fletcher's departure three days earlier.

"Done," she murmured and handed the portrait to Will Johnson, who sat beside her in the grass.

He grinned appreciatively. "She's a beauty, is my Molly. It's uncanny, Jessica, the way you can capture a person in shadow."

"Molly's an easy subject, Will. Her honest nature is written in her profile."

"Remarkable," he said. "Are all faces so easy to read?"

Jessica glanced down, veiling her eyes with her lashes before admitting, "Not all, Will."

He opened the lid of her fruitwood box. Before she could protest, he took out a stack of finished silhouettes, all of the same subject. Fletcher, from every angle and in every setting and mood she had seen him: in the park at New Wells, standing at the bowsprit of the *Shadow Hawk,* talking with Kayanere, accepting a posy from Kitty. . . . Over the weeks she'd captured him dozens of times. Unsuccessfully.

With embarrassment, Jessica saw Will studying a cutting she'd done, after her wedding night, of Fletcher standing at the window in the pale predawn light. She'd captured the stark lines of his sinewed shoulders, the poignant angle of his head, the tenseness of his features. That portrait was closest to her heart, for it came closest to expressing her confusion and fascination with her husband.

"I assume I'm holding the exception in my hand," Will said.

Jessica felt bleak. "No matter how many times I depict him, I simply cannot discover the man beneath."

His ruddy face full of concern, Will put the portraits away. "Perhaps it's because Fletcher is so adept at hiding his feelings. He's a man of many layers, fathoms deep. You'll only know that part of him he wants you to know."

"And if I want to know more. . . ?"

"You'll have to find out by other means." Leaning back on one elbow, he drew a silver flask from his boot and took a generous swallow.

"By asking an old and trusted friend? An Irishman with a taste for whiskey and a loose tongue?"

He quickly capped the flask. "I'd best go see if Molly's packed for the trip to Johnson Hall."

Jessica stayed him with a hand on his arm. "Nonsense, Will, you know Jade and Nan helped her pack this morning."

"But—"

She leveled the points of her scissors at his chest. "Talk, Mr. Johnson."

" 'Tis long in the telling."

"We've hours before you're set to depart."

"Ah, very well, I can always say I yielded under threat of bodily harm. What is it you wish to know about Fletcher?"

"Everything. You may started at the beginning."

Will leaned back on his elbows and studied the summer sky. "Fletcher is much like his mother. She was a Mohawk princess, torn between her love for an Englishman and her devotion to her clan. Fletcher attended English schools, but he also learned Mohawk ways. And he is the best of both, Jessica. The very best.''

"But his dual heritage troubles him.''

"For good reason. He was fifteen when his mother died and his father sent him to England.''

A knot of sympathy formed in Jessica's throat. She knew what it was like to be fifteen and motherless. She knew how desperate that could make a person.

"The one thing he despised above all others was prejudice; the one thing he feared was failure. He fought his way through school, devoted himself to proving a Mohawk could be as clever as an Englishman, as skillful in warfare, as cunning in matters of law and government. And when he couldn't make his point through logic, he made it with his fists.''

"Just as Gabriel does,'' Jessica murmured.

Will sent her a penetrating stare. "But the boy's still young enough to change. Fletcher wasn't.'' Will looked down at his hands. "I daresay he was in no state of mind to take a wife at the age of twenty, but he made short work of marrying Sybil because he was in a hurry to leave England and because he was enchanted by her beauty.''

"She was beautiful?'' Jessica forced herself to ask.

"Aye, in a brittle, bloodless sort of way. And treacherous as hell, but Fletcher didn't learn that until later. We were embroiled in a bitter war with the French and their Algonquin allies. Secretly, Fletcher took it upon himself to see to the Mohawks' defense, because the Royal Americans were never wont to put themselves at risk for Indians. The arrangement worked well . . . until Sybil discovered the truth. She gave evidence against Fletcher.''

"But why, Will? Why would she betray her own husband?''

"I suppose she felt betrayed herself. She was mortified to find out about Fletcher's Indian blood, a taint she felt he'd passed on to their children. Before he was hauled off to Fort Orange, Sybil promised she'd never let him see Kitty and Gabriel again.''

Jessica wondered how it was possible to feel such hatred for a dead woman, and yet she did. Sybil was gone, but her bitter legacy lived on in the form of Fletcher's scars and Gabriel's resentment.

"Will," she said, "thank you for telling me."

He took a final swig from his flask and put it away. "I knew Fletcher never would." Grinning, he added, "You can repay me one day. I'm thinking of commissioning a family crest from you."

"I'll have one for you next time you visit," she promised.

"Or better yet, you could bring it to me. It's but a day's ride; the trail's so clear a greenhorn could make it."

Jessica nodded absently; thoughts of Fletcher lingered in her mind. Suffused with sadness for all his pain, she hugged her knees to her chest and stared out across the yard. Although sunlight touched the misty mountaintops, the area beyond was indistinct. Somewhere far away Fletcher was with his mother's people, mourning their dead.

Like the land that was so much a part of him, he was shrouded in mystery, cloaked in shadows. Would he ever share himself with her? What, she wondered, was he thinking now?

Chapter 15

Fletcher was thinking of Jessica. Although he grieved for all the Mohawk had lost to the smallpox, there was a place in his heart that now belonged solely to his wife. He'd maligned her; she'd defied him. He'd misused her; she'd confused him.

Somewhere along the way she'd gotten under his skin. She gave him no peace. He saw her eyes in the rising smoke of the council fires, heard her laughter in the melody of the shimmering leaves, felt her touch in the caress of the summer breeze.

He supposed his fascination had taken root from the first. They had been on some uncharted course, moving inevitably toward an indefinable destination. He felt something he didn't understand and couldn't trust, not a grandiose passion but more of a steadily deepening devotion. He felt as if he'd been wounded by some unseen foe, yet didn't realize it until he'd begun to heal.

In the past he'd tried to choke off his feelings, strangling sentiment in a clench of anger, feeding resentment with disapproval. But how could he resent Jessica now? Only yesterday a shipment of blankets and food had arrived from Holland Hall—a gift from his wife to people she'd never met, yet still seemed to care about. She was like a flower that refused to die for want of nourishment. Somewhere within her burned a spark of strength and patience that would not be doused, not by his anger, his disapproval, his silence.

He spent a few moments deluding himself about their dilemma. He imagined he could assuage her pain and his guilt

241

by heaping gifts and promises on her, by erasing his roughness with tenderness.

I will not live in the world you offer.

Her words scudded into his mind like a dark cloud, and he
knew she'd never be happy so long as she was his wife. He
had to set her free and he had to do it soon, because imagining life without her was getting harder every day.

Kayanere joined him as he sat brooding by the fire. "Sabra
will recover," the old man said.

Fletcher closed his eyes and took a deep breath. "The gods
be thanked for that. Are there any other infected ones?"

A brown-spotted hand traced a sunburst pattern in the dirt.
"Yes, Shadow Hawk. The scourge will not run its course
until the harvest is near. The manitous revealed that to me in
a dream."

Fletcher wanted to cry out at the injustice his people suffered from a disease brought by the white man. But he only
nodded. A shaman's dreams were not to be scoffed at.

"You must go now, Shadow Hawk," Kayanere said, raising his eyes to the palisades at the river's edge.

"Not yet, Grandfather, I—"

"You have helped me through my grief; your medicine and
blankets have helped our people through sickness. Now there
are others who need you."

Fletcher didn't have to ask who Kayanere meant. In one
way or another, the people at Holland Hall commanded his
responsibility. He glanced up at the afternoon sun. "I will
leave today."

Kayanere grunted and took out his pipe. "Great Knife will
go with you."

"I will be glad for his company. Grandfather . . ." Gently
Fletcher helped the old man light his pipe. "Will you let me
send Dr. Wharton from Albany? He has a medicine that will
prevent the smallpox."

Kayanere drew himself up proudly. "Too many in the clan
distrust the white man's cures. They will not accept your Dr.
Wharton." The old, deep eyes surveyed the compound.

Fletcher clenched his jaw. Kayanere was no doubt remembering times fifty years past, when the Mohawks' fate was
not so intimately entwined with the caprices of their British
overlords.

"There are some things even you cannot change," Kayanere said. "Your white brothers' insanity in plowing up our
hunting grounds and fencing off parcels of the Great Spirit's
divine gift cannot be cured on a battleground or across the
council fire."

Fletcher felt a throb of sadness and guilt. The avaricious,
thoughtless actions of land-hungry newcomers struck at the
heart of the Mohawk. The Great Spirit had never intended
the precious gift of land to be merchandise. "I feel," he said
darkly, "that I have violated the clan by occupying Holland
Hall."

"No, Shadow Hawk, you have been judicious in your occupation. You hold the tract in trust for your children. That
is the way it should be."

Fletcher watched a pair of women slicing fresh sturgeon
and setting the strips to dry in the sun. Others worked wearily
among the milling shoats and skinny dogs. With so many
dead and dying, royal princesses were reduced to washing
down horses and tending the sick. Strain etched worry lines
on their unsmiling faces. Some yards distant, a young brave
was quarreling with a visiting Seneca; the argument promised
to deteriorate into physical violence.

Fletcher felt a welling of sad affection. The Mohawk, the
true lords of the forest, had been brought down by their English aggressors who had the audacity to call themselves allies. Now, dispossessed by the British and divided by clan
rivalries, the Mohawk were in danger of losing their identity
as a people or disappearing completely.

"If the clans of the Iroquois would band together,"
Fletcher said, "you could preserve your land."

"Perhaps so, Shadow Hawk. Fighting amongst ourselves
saps our ability to restrain the white advance."

"Aye, Grandfather. At your knee I learned the legend of
the weak single stick's inferiority to the strong bundle."

Kayanere nodded grimly. "It is a shame our brothers will
not heed that lesson."

"Our existence as a people must be preserved," Fletcher
said, his fist striking the ground. "I'll see to it myself if need
be." He took a deep breath. Once again, he'd committed
himself to the Mohawks' cause. It was well, he decided, that
he was sending Jessica back to London. His first wife's be-

trayal had cost him five years of his life, his children's es-
teem, and estrangement from the Indians. If Jessica ever did
likewise . . . his heart lurched painfully in his chest. The cost
to his soul would be even higher.

Kayanere cleared his throat. "You bear too much already.
Were you ten men, you could not answer the needs of all
those who depend on you."

"But I must try, Grandfather. Running Wolf was able to
treat with the redcoats, but then they killed him and now
there is no one else."

The specter of the events to come in the months ahead
darkened his mood like an untimely shadow. Fletcher bade
his grandfather farewell and trudged down to the river landing where Great Knife was waiting. Now that he'd made up
his mind to free Jessica, he could concentrate on the Indian
problem, for it would fill the lonely hours without her.

Jessica stood at the dock by the riverside, trying to contain
her excitement at seeing Fletcher again. She'd had five days
to nourish her hopes, five nights to lift her expectations. Her
determination to fulfill her marriage and forge the residents
of Holland Hall into a family would soon become reality.
The healing would start where the hurt had been sharpest,
she decided. In Fletcher's bedchamber.

From the corner of her eye, she saw Kateri leap, laughing,
into Great Knife's arms. To Jessica's surprise, Jade and Nan
arrived to welcome the brave. Great Knife was ushered to the
house by an unlikely bevy of women.

Jessica's attention fastened on Fletcher as he emerged from
the boathouse. Suddenly filled with uncertainty, she caught
her breath. He wore the breechclout and hunting vest of a
Mohawk, which gave her a beguiling view of long, lean
thighs, muscled shoulders, a sweat-glistened chest. *Shadow
Hawk,* she thought. But for the uncompromising blue of his
eyes and the absence of a scalp lock, he looked as Indian as
Great Knife. The costume accentuated his masculine form in
a way that conventional clothing never could; days of river
travel had burnished his skin to a deep coppery hue.

The unfamiliar costume with its beads and fringe fascinated her. Strange, primitive sensations eddied through her,
making her feel wild and wanton. She yearned to touch that

sweat-slick flesh, to breathe in the fragrance that always reminded her of a night forest, to explore his lean, long-limbed body and learn every facet of the exotic man who was her husband. Some day, she vowed, they would be close enough for her to admit to all the feelings he evoked in her. Some day, she decided, suppressing a mischievous smile, she might even confess to Fletcher what the sight of his bare legs did to her.

She stood waiting for him, a smile on her face and hope in her heart. He reached the end of the dock, then hesitated, staring at her, the look in his eyes unfathomable. Shadows stalked the sunlight around him, lending an air of intriguing mystery to his face.

A knot of tension gathered in her throat. She swallowed it and stepped forward, holding her hands out to him.

"Hello, Fletcher. I'm glad you're home." She grimaced at her awkward greeting. Glad, she thought, was hardly the word for the seething clamor of emotions suddenly streaking through her.

Fletcher searched the misty depths of her eyes, trying to control his reaction to seeing her again. The breechclout could hardly disguise the sudden rigid leap of his manhood. Damn— how he ached for her. He wanted to wrap her against him, take that lower lip she was worrying with her small, white teeth, and . . .

"Is Kayanere all right?" she inquired.

He hesitated for the briefest moment, a heartbeat, then took her hands. She tipped her face up, expecting a kiss of greeting, hoping it would be as ardent as the one he'd given her on leaving. An odd, slumberous look crept into his eyes as he bent toward her. But something seemed to awaken within him and he released her.

"My grandfather has borne many sorrows and died a little with each one. But he remains strong." He spoke tenderly, his love for the old man so obvious that Jessica felt the burn of tears in her eyes.

"Is the disease very bad?" she asked softly.

His face hardened. "Aye. Especially for the very young, the very old, the very weak."

She laid her hand on his arm. "Can we do anything to help?"

He let out his breath in a long, weary sigh. "I'll do as much as the clan will allow. I've sent for Dr. Wharton of Albany to inoculate the children." He fixed his gaze on her hand, staring so long that, chagrined, she let go.

"Where are the children, by the way?" he asked, his eyes skimming the yard.

Inwardly she recoiled and looked away, hiding her hurt. It was only natural he would ask after the children, she told herself logically. Gabriel had certainly given him enough to worry about during his absence. Still, couldn't Fletcher have spared more than a moment to greet his wife?

"Kitty is having her nap with Adele," she said dully. "Gabriel went off at midday and I haven't seen him since."

"I'll go find him. He might have gone to the quarry."

Willing herself not to be angry at his abrupt departure, Jessica laced her fingers together. "I'd best see to this evening's meal," she said to his retreating back. When he did not respond, her anger defied all control. She called his name sharply.

He turned, a slight frown furrowing his brow. "Yes?" For a long, tension-heavy moment he stared at her, his gaze burning a path over her body from head to toe. His eyes reminded her of storm-churned water; he seemed to be warring within himself.

Before Jessica realized what was happening, he closed the distance between them with two long strides and grasped her shoulders, hauling her against him. His arms captured her waist as his mouth claimed hers in a long, scorching kiss. Dazed by desire, she moved her hands over his bare upper arms, feeling the sheen of sweat on his skin and the ripple of muscles beneath. His tongue darted into her mouth, then retreated, and his muscles tensed. He ended the kiss and stared down at her. She let her hands linger on his arms.

"Damn," he said in a low voice, "you almost make me think you're happy to see me."

"Of course I am," she said, inhaling the scent of woodlands and sunshine and sweat that clung to him. "Isn't every wife happy to see her husband after a long absence?"

A veil of shadow dropped over his face and he stepped away. He looked confused, as if he hadn't expected her words.

He reached out, cupped her chin in his hand, and searched her face. "I'd best see to Gabriel," he said and walked away.

They stood on the verandah at dusk, watching each other while trying not to appear to be doing so. Jessica had spent most of the day thinking about the way Fletcher had kissed her and mentally preparing for the night ahead. Her body hungered for his touch and her spirit yearned for his closeness.

But for the moment, another problem loomed ahead of them. The supper hour was approaching and Gabriel was nowhere to be found. Jessica knew Fletcher was worried; he'd searched for hours and hadn't found a trace of his son.

"He's gone off like this every day," she said, trying to sound reassuring. "He always returns by dark."

"I left him in your care," Fletcher snapped, his voice so sharp that she winced. "How could you have let him run off?"

"You know as well as I do that I can't force Gabriel to my will," she flung back. "Nor can you force him to yours."

His face froze and he looked so guilty she was almost sorry she'd spoken out. She realized her anger was as much for Gabriel as for what Fletcher had said. The boy thought nothing of disappearing for hours on end; he cared not at all about the worry he caused.

"I'm going to organize a search party," Fletcher said, and turned on his heel. He was halfway down the stairs when Kateri emerged from the gardens. She was twirling a hoop made of wild grapevine while humming tunelessly to herself.

Spying Fletcher, she gave him a sunny smile and greeted him in Mohawk. They spoke for a few moments in rapid, aspirated tones. Then Fletcher nodded and the girl ran off, heading into the forest beyond the tenant farms.

He looked up at Jessica. "She says she can find him."

"She probably can," Jessica said. "She outwits Gabriel every chance she gets. It infuriates him."

He smiled, but concern still lingered in his eyes. "How has he been, Jessica?"

Impossible, she thought. Rude, defiant . . . almost vindictive at times. But she wasn't about to reveal the truth to Fletcher. His relationship to Gabriel was too fragile to bear yet another rift. "He's been . . . distant. I'm afraid he hasn't accepted your reason for leaving."

He swallowed. "He can't get past the idea that I left him again. I wonder if he'll ever trust me."

Jessica stepped forward and touched his sleeve. "He spent five years under Sybil's influence, forming his opinion of you. Those years can't be undone quickly."

A long sigh escaped him. "Damn Sybil," he muttered.

Jessica remembered Will's story, remembered that Sybil had betrayed Fletcher. Her husband, she reflected, had wounds that might never heal. She wanted to ask him about Sybil, to share his pain and anger, but fear of a rebuff held her back. The time was wrong; he was preoccupied with Gabriel and still a stranger to her in many ways.

They stood in silence on the verandah, awaiting Kateri's return. Fireflies darted about the gardens, sparking points of light in the evening shadows. A murmur of laughter drifted up from the yard.

Jessica exchanged a glance with Fletcher. "Jade and Nan seemed pleased at seeing Great Knife again," she commented.

His face relaxed into a smile. "Great Knife loves women. Apparently his appeal isn't limited to Mohawks."

"He is quite charming."

Fletcher looked at her sharply. "He's a fool where women are concerned. A blind fool. His heart's been broken a hundred times, yet he keeps coming back for more."

She held his gaze. "While you, I take it, know better."

"I do. But I learned the hard way, Jessica."

The sound of Kateri's chattering interrupted them. A derisive snort told Jessica the girl had found Gabriel.

"I have much to say to the boy," Fletcher murmured. "Pray God he'll listen."

I have a few things to say to Gabriel too, Jessica thought, about the right way to treat the people who care about him.

But she knew she'd not have the chance, not tonight. Tonight belonged to Fletcher.

Chapter 16

Standing next to his bed, Fletcher scowled at the eider-down coverlet. Comfort, he decided, was a state of mind. He'd been far more at ease in Canajoharie, on a hard bed of deerskins. Here in his immaculate chamber, he was burningly aware of Jessica's presence in the next room.

Unable to relax, he moved to the open window. The roses on the trellis were fading now, their petals dropping to reveal rose hips. Distracted by an unbidden memory of Jessica, her beautiful face buried in a blossom, he scowled.

He'd meant to spend the evening pondering his dilemma over Gabriel. The boy had been even more withdrawn than usual, unwilling to talk to his father and, curiously, unable to meet Jessica's eyes. Fletcher admitted that he, too, had trouble facing that mist-soft gaze, that sweet, smiling mouth . . . but for a far different reason than the boy's.

After a few moments he abandoned his frustrated plans to deal with his son and concentrated instead on his plans for Jessica. He crossed the room and seated himself at his desk.

A stack of correspondence littered the desk; letters to wool and wheat factors, people he hadn't done business with in nearly six years. He moved the letters aside and made a mental note to have Elphinstone send them on the next packet from Albany.

Dipping his quill into the inkhorn, he scratched a salutation to Jeffrey Amherst. And found himself at a complete loss. The situation was awkward enough in his own mind; how in hell did one explain to an official of the Crown that he needed to rid himself of his wife? A wife the Lord Chancellor had insisted he take. A wife who, despite Fletcher's armor of indifference, had discovered a secret back door to his heart.

He frowned, remembering how she'd nearly made him lose control that afternoon. Her radiant smile and outstretched arms had made a mockery of his resolve to keep his distance. Her welcoming embrace and generous kiss awakened an ache deep within him that went beyond simple desire. The feelings Jessica stirred in his were maddeningly complex, impossible to ignore.

Fletcher decided to dispense with a lengthy explanation to Sir Jeffrey. The royal governor's curiosity was not nearly as strong as his greed. For the right sum, Amherst would ask no questions. Fletcher penned a straightforward note, certain that the amount he hinted at would suffice. Feeling grim and empty, he began to scrawl his signature.

A soft tapping at the door caused him to smudge the ink. Damn, he thought, am I that edgy? He wrenched open the door and saw no one. Only when the tapping resumed did he realize the sound came from another source—the door separating his room from Jessica's.

Stiff legged and scowling, he answered her knock. Smiling tentatively, she said in her low, throaty voice, "May I come in?" Taking his silent gape as an invitation, she stepped into the room.

Fletcher was unable to stifle a quick-drawn breath. His vision filled with her: a waterfall of curls tumbling down her back; a lithe, womanly body concealed by her thin robe; eyes glowing with . . . with what? Innocence? Invitation? Obviously he had no idea of the danger she courted by placing herself so near him.

She looked up at him, cocking her head to one side. Bright locks of peach-gold hair dropped onto her shoulder. That smile plucked at the threads of his composure; he felt a sheen of sweat spring to his brow. She moistened her lips.

"I hadn't meant to be so long. Kitty simply refused to settle down until I'd read her a half dozen fairy tales."

"I thought Madame did that." Fletcher heard himself speaking in an ordinary, conversational fashion. He was amazed that he could actually sound coherent, that he could conceal the desire that suddenly gripped him in a stranglehold.

"Kitty's usually content to listen to Adele, but tonight she confessed finding LaFontaine's fables tiresome. . . ."

Fletcher felt as if he had a small bale of cotton wool in his mouth. He knew Jessica meant to sound blithe and chatty, but he could tell she was nervous. She spoke quickly; her smile trembled and her beautiful, clever hands clutched, white-knuckled, at the folds of her robe.

Damn, he thought, as she launched into a droll account of Kateri's first experience sleeping in a bed, I should have told her my decision before I left. I could have spared her days of distress. . . .

"Fletcher?" She gave him a soft, quizzical look.

"Yes?"

"I asked you a question. You seem so distant."

That's because I'm trying my damnedest to keep my hands off you, my love. "Sorry," he said gruffly.

"I asked if I was . . . interrupting anything."

"I just finished a letter to Jeffrey Amherst."

"I see. Then you weren't expecting me."

"Actually, no."

"Would you like me to leave?"

"No!" The vehemence of his denial surprised and dismayed him. The sudden blossoming of her smile disarmed and confused him. Jessica, he thought in a moment of wild, absurd hope, was behaving as if she actually wanted to be here. "Er, that is," he added hastily, "I'm glad you came, for I think I should tell you why I was writing to Sir Jeffrey. You'll welcome the news, Jessica." But he couldn't swallow past the knot of yearning in his throat.

Her gold-tipped lashes lifted, revealing eyes that brimmed with artless allure. "You look tired," she said, reaching up to brush aside a lock of hair from his brow.

His resolve splintered into bright shards of longing. He drew her against him, placed his lips very close to hers. All thoughts of Amherst fled in a sudden swirl of desire. What had seemed such a simple matter when he'd pondered it in Canajoharie suddenly became an unconquerable task.

"As a matter of fact," he told her, "I feel very much awake at the moment." He caught her surprised gasp in his open mouth, filling himself with the sweet taste of her. Her gentle response drove reason and resolve to a far-off corner of his mind.

He crushed her against him. As her hands crept up his arms and wound around his neck, he felt great knots of tension leaving him, soothed away by her touch. He suddenly felt light, as if her arms alone held him earthbound.

"I'm not sleepy either," she confessed with a sigh.

Beyond all control, he gathered her close and carried her to the bed. The eiderdown billowed around her and candle glow bathed her face in soft, golden tones. The throb of desire in Fletcher sharpened to a pang of passion. He turned away, yanking off his waistcoat in quick, jerky motions.

When he turned back, Jessica wore nothing but a smile, her robe discarded at the foot of the bed. Gazing up at him, she somehow managed to look both timid and brave.

Fletcher's eyes burned over her, taking in every lush curve and enticing hollow of her lovely form. Burnished curls spilled over her pale breasts. One leg was drawn up shyly, shielding the womanly part of her. Arousal stormed through Fletcher as he discarded his shirt, boots, and breeches.

Looking at Jessica, he saw her reaching for him, and the gesture drove him beyond caution. He came to her swiftly, before he had time to think, covering her body with his and raining long, wet, devouring kisses over her. Then he was inside her and time fell away as he heard her surprised gasp of pleasure and felt the subtle velvet pulse of her release.

He drove into her one last time, joining her, his sounds of ecstasy mingling with hers until, replete, he buried his face in the damp, fragrant warmth of her neck.

Long moments later he felt her stir beneath him and moved away. She stared at him with soft, lustrous eyes, a tiny smile hovering on her lips. Her body glowed pink and gold, flushed with ardor.

A fresh, savage gust of passion seized him and he reached for her, gliding his hand over the heated silk of her belly. He longed to bury himself in her again, to spill his love into her welcoming body.

"Now," she said, snuggling against him with a satisfied purr, "if you'd like to tell me about Sir Jeffrey . . ."

He stopped in midmotion. Her voice reached through a

heavy fog of desire, conjuring up an image of that lissome form swollen with the fruit of his seed.

"Oh, my God," he said unsteadily. He snatched up her robe and draped it around her. "Put it on." His voice was hoarse with mortification at what he'd done. He left the bed and rammed his legs into his breeches.

Jessica pushed herself up onto her elbows, staring at him as if he'd suddenly lost his wits. "What is wrong, Fletcher?"

"Just put the robe on and go back to your room."

Looking reluctant and confused, she obeyed. But by the time she had tied the sash at her waist, he could see she was angry. She planted herself in front of him. "I demand an explanation. You just made love to me and now you suddenly can't seem to tolerate my presence. It just doesn't seem . . . natural."

His frustrated body roared in agreement. "I cannot risk getting you with child."

"Why not?" she snapped. "Do you not find me worthy to bear your child?"

He shook his head, amazed that she'd hit so far from the mark. "Don't be absurd. I tried to tell you the reason when you first walked into this room, but you have an uncanny talent for distraction. I'm sending you home. That's what my letter to Sir Jeffrey is about."

Her expression was soft, inquiring, uncomprehending. "Home? But . . . Holland Hall is my home, Fletcher."

There was a time when he would have given his soul to hear those words from her. But not now. Not now that he'd decided to put selfish needs aside. He stepped closer, tipped her chin up, and studied her face. "No, Jessica. Bringing you to Holland Hall was a mistake; I know that at last. I'm sending you back to London. I'll provide for you for the rest of your life. Of course, all this cannot be arranged right away. There are negotiations to be made. . . ."

The stricken look on her face gave him pause. "Damn it, Jessica, I'm only asking a few more months, half a year at most. I thought perhaps around Christmas. . . ."

Her eyes were large and disbelieving. "*Why,* Fletcher?"

"Because we're going to have to buy our way around the Lord Chancellor's edict and that takes time."

She shook her head slowly, looking dazed, as if he'd hit

her. "That's not what I meant. Why are you sending me away?"

"Because I wronged you. On false pretenses, I dragged you from a life you loved. I know I cannot redress . . . everything, but I shall try to make things as easy as possible for you."

"I must remain your wife," she said firmly. "You could lose the children again if you do not keep to your vow."

"Jeffrey Amherst will be more than willing to modify the terms of my custody . . . for a price."

She stepped away from him, throat working as she swallowed. "You mean to buy yourself free of me and ship me back to London."

"It's your freedom I'm buying, Jessica. Isn't that all you've wanted from me since the day we married?"

"I . . . I did argue for it at one time. But that was before I committed myself to . . . this family."

Despite his pain, he could not resist touching the rumpled silk of her hair. "You've a generous nature. I learned that too late. I'll see that you want for nothing once you reach London."

"I'm your wife. You cannot buy yourself free of that."

"The circumstances of our marriage are so unusual as to allow for an annulment. I'll see you suffer no shame; such things can be handled discreetly." Unable to stop himself, he leaned down and brushed his lips over her brow, steeling his nerves against a new stirring of desire and despair. "I give you back your life, Jessica, with all attendant apologies. The security of London, the freedom to practice your art and do as you please . . . even your name. You'll be Jessica Darling once again." A small, sad smile hovered on his lips. "I always thought the name suited you."

"But who will take care of Kitty and Gabriel?" She sounded almost desperate.

"I'll not deny they've grown to depend on you, but ultimately they are my responsibility."

A spark of anger leapt to life in the misty pools of her eyes. "I accepted responsibility for the children when I became your wife. It is not a commitment to be blithely relinquished simply because you've grown tired of me."

He was stunned that she could so misunderstand him, misinterpret his motives. He clutched her shoulders, drew her close, stared into her angry face. Lord, but she was lovely.

"Tired of you?" he echoed incredulously. "Do you really believe that is the case?"

"Why else would you be so set on casting me out of your house, out of your life?"

"Because I owe you your freedom. I thought, I truly believed, I had wed a whore masquerading as a lady. When I learned how wrong I was, I could only come to one decision. To send you home." He tried to ignore the softness of her flesh beneath his hands, the enticing fragrance emanating from her.

She looked as if she didn't believe him. And Fletcher knew he'd given her cause never to trust anything he said. "I give you my word, Jessica," he said. "As soon as it can be arranged, I'm sending you back to London."

"No." She spoke so softly, he barely heard her. Her denial had the caressing quality of a lover's whisper. But the glitter in her eyes spoke fury more eloquently than words.

"Isn't that what you want, to be free of me?"

"What I want," she replied, still quiet, still controlled, "is to be free of your infernal, highhanded, presumptuous attitude." Her voice gathered volume as she plunged on, her words darting arrows of hurt into old scars. She began to pace, her robe flowing in wispy billows around her. "Ever since you walked into my life, Fletcher Danforth, you have directed things. Your blackmail gave me no choice but to obey your overbearing mandates. For the past several months, my life has not been my own. And now once again you seek to dictate where I'll go and how I'll live. I'll not stand for it!"

He couldn't believe his ears. "My God. You're arguing against your own freedom."

"Freedom! How can you call it freedom? I don't recall ever having a say in the matter." Her hands flew up in a wrathful gesture, her sleeves flapping like the wings of an angel. An avenging angel. "You are the most arrogant, selfish—"

"Selfish! Damn it, Jessica, this may well be the most *un*selfish thing I've ever done." He planted himself in front of her, halting her pacing. "You can have your old life back."

He swallowed hard, tearing his eyes from the enticing sight of her heaving breasts, her flushed face. "And until it can be arranged, it will be a chaste marriage." Hell, he thought, how much more unselfish can I be than that?

"Don't do this, Fletcher," she said, sounding now more fearful than angry. "Don't make this mistake."

He clenched his fists at his sides, resisting the urge to touch her again, to take her back to bed. "I've already made too many mistakes," he said. "Now I'm trying to make things right."

"You truly believe what you are doing is right, that I can stop caring for . . . your children because you command it."

"Damn it, Jessica, what by all that's holy do you want from me?"

She started to speak, then caught her lower lip in her teeth. She took a deep breath. "What I want," she said, "has never mattered to you. You've never listened to me."

He longed to gather her against him and kiss away that wounded look. It came to him that this promised to be the longest six months of his life. "I think you should return to your own bed now."

"Yes. By now I'm used to doing as you command." She backed away, looking hurt and confused, not at all relieved and grateful as he'd thought she would be.

Fletcher felt drained as he watched her disappear behind the door. A vacuum of silence hung in the room. The clock struck ten, shattering the stillness, almost making him jump out of his skin.

Cursing, he seized a decanter of brandy from the sideboard and poured a full measure into a glass. Taking a generous swallow, he cursed himself in the name of every Mohawk deity and Christian saint his passion-drugged mind could dredge up. The liquor scorched a path down his throat.

You lost control, friend, his conscience taunted.

But she came to me, damn it.

Because she thought you expected it of her. You used to delight in reminding her about wifely duties.

She wanted me. I could see it in her eyes, feel it in her response. I made her happy tonight, I know it.

You hedged your experience against her innocence. She

fell victim to sensations you roused in her body, not in her heart. That kind of happiness doesn't last.

I know, damn it, I know!

By the time the clock signaled the half hour, the decanter was empty.

"Mr. Danforth?" Each knock was a hammer blow to Fletcher's throbbing head. "Mr. Danforth, I'm sorry to disturb you, but the mail packet from Albany has arrived and the skipper won't wait."

"Come." Fletcher rasped out the command and dragged a pillow over his aching head to blot out Mr. Elphinstone's footsteps.

"Sorry, sir," the clerk said, "but who knows when the packet will be back? You did say your letters were of some urgency. . . . I'll just get them from the desk. . . ."

Fletcher barely heard the clerk's muffled monologue; his mind was thick with the fog of too much brandy and too little sleep.

". . . your wife's letters too," Elphinstone was saying. "My, but she is well connected, isn't she, sir? To have a correspondence with the duke of Claremont—"

Claremont? Recognition tickled at Fletcher's awareness, then bored unmercifully into his mind. "What the devil are you talking about, Elphinstone?" he demanded hoarsely, squinting at the clerk.

Elphinstone reddened. "I didn't mean to be indiscreet, sir; I was just commenting on your wife's correspondence with—"

"—the duke of Claremont," Fletcher finished dully.

Still prating on about impatient Dutch skippers, Mr. Elphinstone shut the door. Fletcher winced.

He lay back and smiled grimly into the dark softness of the pillow. Clever, Jessica, he mused. She'd almost been a victim of Claremont's lechery, but never had it occurred to him that she might have some other connection with the duke. How long, he wondered, had she been writing to him, and about what? Perhaps she'd been in contact with him from the start, prevailing upon his influence to gain her release from this marriage.

Well, he thought, dragging the pillow from his face to

squint at the mocking brightness of the morning sun, then
what in God's name does the woman want from me?

Jessica wanted desperately to understand Fletcher's rejection of her. As she lay alone in her bed, she tried to sort
through the rage and hurt and uncertainty that had kept her
muscles knotted with tension and her pillow damp with tears
through half the night.

She focused on one emotion at a time, afraid that to suc-
cumb to all of them at once would be her undoing. The anger
was easiest to deal with. Outrage brought her surging from
the bed and propelled her to the washstand, where she bathed
her flushed face and swollen eyes with violet water from the
Delft porcelain bowl.

How dare he make such a presumptuous decision without
consulting her? she thought between splashes.

She daubed her face dry with a towel and glanced in the
mirror over the dressing table. The sight was daunting. The
night rayle she'd so carefully selected in order to please
Fletcher hung in damp and wrinkled disarray. Her hair, which
she'd left loose because she thought he liked it that way, was
a nest of tangled curls. Her eyes, red rimmed and puffy,
suddenly dimmed as her anger subsided.

Listlessly she took up an onyx-handled brush and dragged
it through her hair, feeling a pain so profound that her eyes
began to swim with new tears. She had gone to his room last
night thinking he needed a wife's comfort. His swift, ardent
lovemaking had filled her with awe and ecstasy. She'd allowed herself to hope that physical intimacy would transform
their sham of a marriage into a living, breathing relationship,
one that would provide the foundation for a strong, vital,
happy family.

His caresses had left her body aglow with the luster of
fulfillment, but his callous plan had left her heart still empty
of his love.

She finished brushing her hair and rang to summon Nan.
As she waited, confusion and uncertainty riddled her. When
had winning a man's love and forging a family become so
important to her? She'd never consciously wanted a husband
and children; her ambition in life had been to live in unen-
cumbered independence and unbreachable security.

But somewhere, somehow, her goals had changed. The life she'd so painstakingly carved out in London now seemed empty and dull and selfish since she'd experienced the satisfaction of having a family of her own to care about.

An ironic smile twisted her mouth. Fletcher had dragged her, kicking and screaming, into this situation. She'd fought him every step of the way, never realizing he was offering her a fulfillment she now knew she could not live without.

And now that he'd given it to her, he wanted to take it away.

Later that day Jessica sat in the drawing room, nervously stroking Kitty's hair. Across the room, Great Knife was speaking to Jade and Nan in low tones; for once the brave wasn't behaving in his usual lusty fashion. Kateri and Gabriel scowled at each other across a chessboard, the girl growing impatient as Gabriel demonstrated the correct way to move a rook. Looking tense and preoccupied, Fletcher sat in an armchair opposite Adele and Dr. Wharton, the physician he'd summoned from Albany.

The doctor set down his teacup and reached for his black leather satchel. The movement caused all heads in the drawing room to turn.

Jessica looked quickly at Fletcher, studying his grim, haggard face. She derived little satisfaction from the idea that his night hadn't been any more restful than hers. He glanced up; their eyes locked and held. A silent message passed between them. The present situation was more important and more immediate than their own turmoil. For now, mutual concern for the children linked them and the bond was strong enough to hold their conflict at bay. For a time.

"I'd like to explain the procedure, if I may," the doctor said, positioning himself in front of the tile-bordered fireplace. "Understanding will help take some of the fear out of it."

"No," Jessica said, her arms tightening around Kitty. "Dr. Wharton, I really think—"

"I can stay and listen." Kitty turned her large, luminous eyes to Jessica. "Papa said this in—in—"

"Inoculation," Gabriel supplied in a bored voice. Nonchalantly he captured one of Kateri's pawns.

"Papa said it will keep us from getting sick, and so we must all do it," Kitty finished.

Fletcher looked ready to burst with pride at his daughter's brave words. But Jessica, holding the child close, could feel her trembling. She gave Kitty's shoulders a reassuring squeeze.

"Dr. Wharton," she said, "why don't you explain to Esme? Then we'll all understand." With grave obedience Kitty held the rag baby out to him.

The doctor smiled, accepting the doll. "A fine idea," he said. He took Esme and sat her on his knee. To Jessica's delight, he treated the doll like a real child.

"Now, young lady," he said, addressing Esme, "inoculation is a new way to prevent the smallpox. Did you know that several years ago it prevented an epidemic in Boston?" In a pleasant, matter-of-fact tone, he explained that kinepox would be introduced into the blood by means of a thread treated with the agent. Jessica felt Kitty stiffen as the doctor pointed out that a deep cut would have to be made in the arm.

For a moment, silence settled over the parlor.

"By damn and by dash," Jade burst out, "I'd rather take me chances with the smallpox." Obstinately she folded her arms across her chest, her almond-shaped eyes snapping.

"You will let the white doctor treat you," Great Knife said in a quiet, firm voice. Jade opened her mouth to protest, but the brave's upheld hand silenced her. "I have lost too many to the smallpox," he said softly.

Amazed, Jessica saw Jade's beautiful face melt into a soft smile. To everyone's surprise, the piquant, argumentative woman was brought into submission by the gentle smile of a Mohawk brave. With a grunt of satisfaction, Great Knife smoothed back his forelock and faced the doctor. "We are ready. And do not howl with the pain," he cautioned Jade. "A Mohawk woman endures in silence."

Great Knife took a handful of broken reeds from the pouch at his waist. Together, he and Fletcher distracted the children with a Mohawk game of wagers, extracting outrageous forfeits from each other.

The doctor motioned the women to a chair by the window. Obviously determined not to be outdone by their Indian rivals, Jade and Nan took the treatment with a minimum of fuss. Adele followed, her reaction no more than a haughty sniff. Jessica felt her cheeks pale at the bite of the knife in her own arm. Feeling Fletcher's eyes on her, she forced a smile. "That wasn't so awful," she said, feeling blood seep into her bandage. "Come, children. You're all so much braver than I; you'll hardly feel it."

Kitty gasped and Gabriel stiffened. Kateri, who apparently had understood the operation through Dr. Wharton's gestures, stepped forward. Her face impassive, she sat in the ladder-back chair in front of the doctor and calmly turned up the sleeve of her doeskin dress.

Jessica glanced at Gabriel in time to see an expression of relief across his features, but the look was quickly replaced by glowering resentment. The boy started forward, determined to be the first.

Fletcher halted him, gently putting a hand to his shoulder. "Your turn will come soon enough, son," he said softly. Gabriel wrenched away but said nothing; apparently he felt he'd satisfied honor by making the gesture.

Jessica held Kitty close. When the doctor wielded his thin-bladed knife, she turned the child's face toward her, trying to shield Kitty's eyes.

Kateri, she saw with admiration, was magnificent. The girl sat ramrod straight, her face betraying nothing as the knife sank into her flesh and the treated thread was moved back and forth through the wound. A sudden pallor and tightly clenched fists were her only reaction.

Nan moved forward to bandage the wound, managing to sound sympathetic even as she unleashed a fluent stream of profanities.

"I think," Jessica said softly, "that Kitty should be next. We may not find a more opportune time."

They all turned to look at her. Slowly heads began to nod. Kitty had fainted dead away.

After Adele had borne the child away, Gabriel stalked across the room, his head held high, his pale face rigidly controlled. He was determined to bear the operation as bravely as Kateri had.

But Gabriel had a serious disadvantage, Jessica realized

with a jolt of concern. Not so very long ago, the boy had
watched his mother bleed to death of a wound to the arm.

Her eyes flicked to Fletcher. He was staring at Gabriel with
a look of such heartbreaking worry that she knew he was
thinking the same thing. Gabriel might not realize it consciously, but deep inside he surely would. Fletcher followed
the boy to the chair, and stood in front of it, rigid with tension.

Gabriel slid a glance at Kateri; her calmness seemed to
renew his determination. He yanked back his sleeve, baring
his arm for the doctor.

"You needn't look, lad," Fletcher murmured.

Gabriel flung him a defiant glare. "I'm not afraid." He
held his arm steady. The blade bit into his flesh, sinking to
the bone. The thread sawed through the wound, causing an
eruption of blood to slide down the boy's arm.

All semblance of stoicism left Gabriel. His eyes grew wild
and agonized. "Papa!" he screamed and pitched himself into
Fletcher's arms.

Jessica watched, her heart in her mouth, as father and son
embraced for the first time since she'd known them. She agonized for Gabriel but felt a rush of gratitude as well. If this
were the first break in the boy's armor of insolence, it was
well worth the pain.

But Gabriel checked himself quickly. He hauled back,
twisting away from Fletcher's arms. Jerking the bandage away
from Nan, he blotted the wound. Fury and resentment replaced distress and dependence.

"I hope you're satisfied," he spat, backing away from
Fletcher. "I hope you're bloody well satisfied!"

Hearing the low tone of Jessica's voice and the chiming of
Kitty's music box, Fletcher paused at the door to the nursery.
He looked in to see Jessica sitting on the edge of Kitty's bed,
absently stroking the marmalade cat.

Jessica looked up and gave him a soft, winsome smile that
nearly melted his heart. The events of the afternoon hadn't
solved their dilemma, but concern for the children had formed
a bond between them. She beckoned him into the room and
put a finger to her lips to caution him to be quiet.

He touched one of Kitty's sable curls. "How is she?"

"Well enough. I daresay she'll nap the day away. The others?"

"All fine. Thank God it's over." Fletcher glanced at the bulge beneath her sleeve. "What about you, Jessica?"

Her smile was tinged with irony. "I'll survive. I've suffered worse wounds."

"Have you?" He was suddenly seized by a desire to know more about her, more about the person she had been before he'd entered her life. It was idiotic, he told himself, to want to grow close to a woman he had every intention of severing from his life, but he couldn't help himself. "Tell me about it."

She shook her head and moved her hand restlessly over the cat's fur. "I was not what one would call an overprotected child," she said matter-of-factly. "When I was seven, I broke my arm in a scuffle. My right arm. Adele thinks that is the reason I favor my left hand."

"What sort of scuffle was it?"

Her mist-colored eyes hardened. "I'd picked a gentleman's pocket," she said, "and he caught me. I was lucky to escape with no more than a broken arm."

He wondered if she knew how desolate the memory made her sound. She eyed him challengingly. "Does that shock you, Fletcher, to know I was a thief?"

He drew a long, steadying breath. An image of a bedraggled child with peach-gold curls flashed through his mind. His heart lurched; she'd undoubtedly been a victim of the worst kind—a victim of the indifference of poverty. Her confession shocked him, yes, but not in the way she supposed. Rather than disapproval, he felt a throb of sadness for a neglected little girl. He was amazed at the poised, beautiful woman that poor, thieving child had become.

"If you hope to win my disapproval, you'll be disappointed to know that I feel only sympathy, Jessica," he said. Damn, he thought, his words sounded so impersonal. He wanted nothing more than to gather her into his arms and offer compassion to the wounded child she had been.

But he had no business comforting her; she didn't need him. His only duty now was to unshackle her from this marriage.

She looked at him for a long moment, as if trying to decide

just what he meant. Then she shrugged and bent to tuck the coverlet around Kitty.

"You protested my plan because of the children, didn't you?" he murmured, touching a curl at her temple.

She drew away, as if his closeness were offensive. "I'd certainly be a fool to want to stay because of you, wouldn't I, Fletcher?"

Chapter 17

Late summer blazed over the acres of Holland Hall, cloaking the green hills in a mantle of leaf, bud, and blossom. Jessica gazed up at a sky so blue her eyes ached from looking at it. The scent of roses hung heavy in the air, mingling with pungent odors from Mercy's kitchen garden. The distant fields were thick with corn and oats and rippling grass.

Outside, all was growing and thriving, but inside Jessica something was withering and dying. Her hopes of harmony with Fletcher and peace in the family had plummeted to a dismal low.

Every day further distanced him from her. He seemed indifferent to the point of contempt, replying curtly to her questions, interested only when she spoke of the children. When they were together she sensed he was hovering on the edge of control, as if he shared her desire but always reeled back. She wanted him, but not just to soothe the ache of her body's longing. If she thought physical intimacy would lead to closeness, she might have humbled herself and taken back the bitter words she'd spoken on the day of the inoculation, but their lingering estrangement told her it was impossible.

She had developed the habit of taking solitary walks, carrying her workbox with her in case a particular scene lent itself to her art. The box was now filled with scenes of daily life at Holland Hall: a tenant farmer tilling his fields, children playing at the riverbank, the orange cat perched on the well sweep, a boat down at the dock being laden with goods.

Although reluctant to admit it, Jessica realized what she was doing. She was cataloguing images from this life she'd grown to love so that she would have something to remember when Fletcher sent her away. Like a mother cat counting her kittens, Jessica sought out the children and her friends.

She reached the garden wall that sheltered Hilda's dovecote and paused to watch the old woman putting out trays of grain for the birds. Hilda smiled and raised her hand in greeting, then held out a little gray dove. "Go on, *mevrouw*, he's quite tame," she said, addressing Jessica as mistress in her native Dutch.

Jessica extended her finger and Hilda perched the dove there. "Why, he feels so light," Jessica remarked, stroking the bird's silky underbelly with one knuckle.

"The master used to play here when he was a boy," Hilda said, gently taking the bird and replacing it in the dovecote. Her eyes grew soft and wistful. "He spent hours finger training the birds." The housekeeper eyed Jessica from beneath her starched cap. "He wasn't always . . . as he is now, *mevrouw*. The house used to fairly ring with his laughter." Hilda shook her head. "He's changed, that he has, and no mistake. What man could survive a wife's betrayal and five years in prison without some changes? And now that infernal boy . . . Gabriel used to worship his papa, and rightly so." Hilda shook her head again and muttered, "Och, listen to me. 'Tis not my place to prate about such things." She brushed the kernels of grain from her apron and started back toward the house. "Enjoy your walk, *mevrouw*."

Pondering Hilda's words, Jessica wandered away from the dovecote. It was hard to imagine a lighthearted Fletcher shouting with laughter, embracing life. She could understand all too well why he was no longer that way. Yes, Sybil's betrayal had embittered him, prison had broken him, and Gabriel's hatred had wounded him. But Hilda had, either out of kindness or out of ignorance, neglected to mention another reason for his brooding nature.

Fletcher's marriage to a woman he did not love and would not keep had to be largely responsible for his current too-quiet mood. Silence in Fletcher was like a signal flare illuminating his anger. And he'd been very silent these past four weeks.

Trills of laughter drew her to a glade by the river, the cheerful sound lifting her spirits a little. Moving aside a thick curtain of willow branches, she saw Jade, Nan, and Great

Knife on the bank. Great Knife seemed in no hurry to return to Canajoharie. He'd rather lamely explained that he wanted Kateri to learn English, but Jessica knew it was just a ploy to allow him to pursue his own interest in Jade and Nan.

He'd just landed a good-sized sturgeon and was menacing Jade with the fish. She shrank back in mock horror while Nan shook with laughter.

"Blimey, Jess," Jade called out, "don't just stand there; stop this devil. He'll have me stinkin' of fish!"

Jessica smiled, aware that Jade was enjoying the jest.

"Hm," Great Knife said, tossing the fish into a creel woven of willow branches. "A good Mohawk woman does not shrink from the food a brave brings to her hearth." He lay down, nestling his head in Nan's ample lap.

Jessica peered into the full creel. "I daresay Mercy won't shrink from it."

Great Knife studied her through half-closed eyes. "Hm," he said again, "she cooks all the flavor away. Mohawk women like their sturgeon dried by the sun."

"And English women like their peace and quiet, dearie," Nan retorted. "Hush, Great Knife, and go to sleep. It's time for your afternoon nap."

"Hm," he said one last time, "your tongue is becoming as sharp as Jade's." But he dutifully closed his eyes. Nan leaned down and whispered something in his ear. His eyes flew open; he extricated himself from her lap and stood up. Whispering in Jessica's ear, he repeated Nan's comment. "What does this mean?" he asked innocently.

Jessica burst out laughing and blushed. She clutched her box and backed away. "It means," she said, "that Jade and Nan think very highly of your . . . manly attributes."

Great Knife's face split into a grin of pride and pleasure and he settled back into Nan's generous lap.

Jessica was still chuckling as she left them, her heart lighter because happiness did exist at Holland Hall, even if it did not touch her. As she walked toward the orchard, she pondered the relationship between Jade, Nan, and Great Knife. He seemed equally enamored of both women, and neither suffered for lack of his attention.

But what would become of Jade and Nan if Fletcher was determined to send them all back to London? Jessica couldn't bear the thought of her friends being forced to take up their degrading way of life once again. She knew Jade and Nan would rebel at the idea. She must convince Fletcher to allow them to stay at Holland Hall. They belonged here, even if she did not.

For the second time during her promenade, Jessica heard laughter. Looking over the orchard wall, she spied the children. Kateri and Kitty were giggling at Gabriel as he tried to turn a grapevine hoop with a stick. His face determined, he tried again and again to right the hoop. Kateri sidled over and soon had it spinning a wobbly path. Jessica tensed, expecting Gabriel to lash out. When he took the stick from Kateri, Jessica thought he would break it.

But he didn't. He chased the rolling hoop with obvious delight and called something over his shoulder, something that sounded suspiciously like "thank you."

Pleased, Jessica waved at them and moved on. Of all the people to find the chink in the armor of Gabriel's aloofness, Kateri was the least likely. Yet the girl was nearly always in his company, undeterred by his rude rebuffs. Her sunny disposition could not be dimmed by Gabriel's animosity.

Jessica was glad someone had taken Gabriel in hand. She herself had tried, but even as the boy warmed to Kateri, his resentment toward Jessica grew. She understood, even if it hurt. Sybil Danforth was less than a year dead and Gabriel still clung fiercely to her memory. He would not betray that loyalty by accepting Jessica.

As she left the orchard, the acrid smell of charcoal smoke and the ear-splitting sound of clanging metal greeted her. Seeing the squat wood and stone forge barn, she paused. The straw and clay chimney belched a plume of smoke.

Georgie Watts, the blacksmith at Holland Hall, was recovering from a severely burned hand. He should have been abed, not laboring at the forge. Concerned that he could injure himself again by returning to his tasks too soon, Jessica headed for the forge barn.

But when she reached the smithy and looked through the open door, she could not speak at all; she could only gape in slack-jawed astonishment and breathless wonder.

Shirtless and pouring sweat, Fletcher was half turned from her. He bent before the forge, drawing out a nail rod with strong, rhythmic strokes of the hammer. The charcoal fire cast him in orange light and coppery shadows, carving contours and picking out highlights in the surging sinews of his body. His skin glowed with exertion and glistened with sweat; inky locks of hair clung to his brow and neck.

His beauty was one of motion as well as form. The hammer came up in an arc, then descended with a metallic peal. Power pulsated through his rippling muscles as he shaped the nail rod with swift grace.

Jessica let her breath out in a great whoosh, realizing only then that she had been holding it. Shaken, she leaned against the door frame staring at her husband in a way she'd never done before.

Feeling warm and liquid inside, she clutched the fruitwood box to her chest. Still unaware of her rapt attention, Fletcher paused to pump the bellows, then returned to the andiron. Only after long moments had passed did Jessica manage to move, to think. Dizzily she considered using her art to preserve the magnificent symmetry of Fletcher at work. Rendering his image might help her understand what she was feeling, might help the fear of wanting him so dreadfully and hedge the pain of losing him so senselessly.

A foolish notion, she decided, setting down her box. No amount of skill could ever depict the graceful, shadowy figure at the forge. His bare arms and shoulders simply did not lend themselves to paper. She longed to feel those arms around her, to run her hands over him and bury her fingers in his damp hair.

Her artist's eye saw the beauty of his masculine form; her woman's heart felt it. She'd thought she wanted to capture him in shadow but now admitted that what she really desired was to capture his heart.

Still disturbed by the ripples of warmth lapping at her senses, but no longer afraid of what she was feeling, she sighed and gave herself up to the simple joy of watching him. He chiseled the rod into nail lengths, then turned and saw her for the first time.

Perhaps it was only the flickering light, but for a moment Jessica fancied she saw a spark of pleasure in his eyes. Then the light changed and his face hardened into a polite, indifferent mask. Her gaze drifted to the taut, bunching muscles of his upper torso. She caught herself and forced her eyes away.

"Did you need something?" he said.

The cool inquiry made her feel awkward and she flushed. Yes, she thought. "No," she said, "I was out walking and heard noises."

Fletcher snatched up his shirt and started to pull it over his head.

Leave it off, Jessica mused wickedly. Nakedness becomes you. Her flush deepened and she said, "I was afraid Georgie was trying to work too soon after his injury."

Fletcher's head emerged from the neckline of the shirt. He regarded her curiously, the glow from the charcoal fire dancing in his eyes. "You knew about Georgie's accident?"

"Of course. Isn't that part of my role here?"

His gaze sharpened. Slowly he rolled back his shirtsleeves. "I suppose I'm surprised by your concern."

"I care about everyone at Holland Hall." *Even you*.

He turned away, snapping the nails off in a nail header and then tossing them into a bucket of water to cool.

"Isn't it unusual," Jessica asked as steam hissed from the bucket, "for you to do the work of a common laborer?"

He shrugged his massive shoulders. "I'm not one to shrink from any work that needs to be done."

"No," she quietly agreed, "no, you're not, are you?"

He picked up the bucket of nails. "I'd best get these to Jasper. The workmen need them for the new granary."

Impulsively she laid her hand on his forearm, finding it slick with sweat and beguilingly warm and hard. She froze, gripped by a sudden, intense stab of yearning. Fletcher felt something too; she heard it in his quick-drawn breath. A feeling pulsated between them—potent and powerful, eluding the dictates of rational will. Jessica's fingers tightened on his arm; she wanted to explore the rest of him, to see if he felt that good all over.

Slowly her eyes climbed to his face. His expression was not so cold now. But then his mouth tautened and he jerked his arm away. "I must go," he said gruffly.

"Perhaps . . . I could go with you."

He shook his head. Jessica knew her hurt must show, because he set the pail down and gently placed his hands on her shoulders. "Perhaps another time, Jessica."

There was nothing gentle about the reaction boiling up in her. " 'Another time, Jessica,' " she mimicked hotly. "And when might that be? Another month? Two? Just when do you intend to face the fact that I am your wife and expect to be treated as such?"

His grip tightened. "Exactly what sort of treatment do you mean, Jessica?" he shot back. "Shall I play the smitten husband, ply you with gifts, cast roses at your feet?"

She swallowed, willing back the tears that welled in her eyes. "The favor of your company occasionally wouldn't be so unreasonable."

For a moment his lips softened and his eyelids slid downward. She knew the expression; he always looked like that just as he was about to kiss her. She waited, breathless, for the touch of his lips.

But his lips didn't merely touch her; they ravished her mouth in a long, powerful, desperate kiss that fanned her desire to a hot glow. A primitive growl tore from his throat and Jessica found herself wrapped in his embrace and backed against the forge-warmed wall of the barn. With a tremor of shock she realized he was going to take her here, now. Her thoughts must have shown on her face, for he slackened his hold, eased back, and said, "If you want me to stop, say it now or . . ."

She knew what he'd left unsaid, that he'd have her with or without her consent. The dark, sensual promise in his eyes beckoned her. "Don't stop," she whispered.

His mouth made a hot, ravishing journey over her cheek to her neck, where his tongue moved in liquid circles that left her dizzy with arousal. Passion sizzled down her spine as she felt him raise the hem of her gown, felt her lawn drawers drift to the floor, an easy victim of his skilled touch.

His lips took hers in a lavish, fiery kiss that made her so hungry she stood on tiptoe, straining to taste him more fully. Then she felt herself being lifted up until her feet left the floor. He caught her startled gasp with his lips and murmured against her mouth, "Does this make you uncomfortable?"

In truth the realization that they needn't confine their lovemaking to a bed with curtains drawn made her wild, blazing with need. She shook her head.

With gentle and unexpected grace he guided her legs around his hips and then they were joined and white-hot streaks of pleasure seared her every nerve. She felt Fletcher stiffen, heard him rasp out her name, and then shudders rippled through them both.

For several heavy, drawn-out moments they clung together, both dazed by the explosive sexual power that linked them no matter how deeply their hearts were in discord.

Fletcher was the first to move away. Gently he set her down, straightened her clothes and then his own, and very tenderly daubed her brow and neck with her fichu.

She leaned against the wall, waiting for him to speak, certain he'd no longer deny his need for closeness.

A hot, tortured look blazed in his eyes. "Now do you understand why I keep my distance?" he whispered.

She stared at him in disbelief. "You're afraid, aren't you?"

"If I fear anything, it's getting you with child."

"Oh, that again," she snapped, feeling the wistful luster of afterlove subside, to be replaced by biting anger. "For a moment I forgot that I've ceased to be of use to you."

"Damn it, Jessica, you're twisting things all around. Do you deny that you want to return to London, to be free to live your own life?"

"I—"

"I know about Claremont, that you've been in correspondence with him."

Confused, Jessica frowned. Then she remembered; at Adele's request she'd penned a letter asking Claremont to forward a draft so Adele could invest in Fletcher's paper mill.

Hurt and angry, she lifted her chin and decided not to give Fletcher the satisfaction of a perfectly reasonable explanation. She was feeling perfectly *un*reasonable at the moment, because he'd pushed her too far.

Suddenly she wanted to be away from him, away from the oppressive heat of passion and the icy chill of rejection.

"You've meddled quite enough in my affairs, Fletcher, and I bloody well wish you'd stop."

She didn't wait to watch the barb bury itself, because to discover that she'd hurt him would make her want to take back her words. Turning, she picked up her workbox and ran from the forge barn.

Fletcher settled into the deep copper bathing tub, scrubbing away the smoke of the forge, the sweat of hard work, and the lingering, violet-sweet essence of Jessica. As he scoured his hair with lye soap, a rueful smile twisted his lips. He wished it were that simple to cleanse himself of his feelings for his wife.

Once again he'd broken his vow to keep the marriage chaste; once again he'd let passion overcome reason. The combined assault of Jessica's sensual charm and his own frustrated desire threatened to turn his resolve to dust. Clenching his eyes shut, he saw Jessica in the forge barn, regarding him with those huge misty eyes and the smile that made mincemeat of his willpower.

His loins ached at the thought of her beauty and the memory of how she tasted and smelled.

He decided to work harder at keeping his distance, keeping his promise, even if it meant masking his feelings with indifference. Not even for Jessica could he play the part of the attentive husband. Not with the platonic way of life he himself had dictated. Chance meetings like the one today must not be allowed. It was dangerous to find himself alone with her. She made it too damned easy for him to lose control, to give in to selfish impulses.

He dragged himself from the tub and dressed for the evening meal. Having renewed his resolve to leave Jessica alone, he felt ready to turn his mind to other problems.

Gabriel's attitude had worsened in the past month. Fletcher struggled to recapture his ease at being a father, but the years had changed him, hardened him, strangled his sensitivity, made him a stranger to the idea of a loving family.

Likewise, the years had changed Gabriel from a sunny, agreeable child into a bitter, morose twelve-year-old.

Fletcher went to look for Gabriel. He found his son in the conservatory. Unnoticed by the boy, Fletcher paused in the doorway.

Surrounded by plants and bathed in evening sunlight, Gabriel sat amid a litter of wood and string and cloth, painstakingly measuring off a thin length of white-ash wood. His brow was puckered in concentration; the tip of his tongue peeped between his lips as he worked.

Fletcher cleared his throat and fixed an inquiring smile on his face. "What are you doing, son?"

Gabriel's head snapped up. The unguarded look left his face. He glanced away and muttered, "Building a kite."

Approaching slowly as he would a skittish colt, Fletcher moved into the conservatory, bending beneath a long frond of a fern. "There's always a good breeze from the river for kite flying. I used to do a lot of it when I was your age." He grinned in self-deprecation and lied, "My kites were never much good." In truth he'd forced himself to excel at all he did, even at so mundane a task as making a kite. It was all part of proving to the world that a boy of mixed heritage was as worthy as an Englishman, as skillful as a Mohawk.

Gabriel's intrigued expression pleased Fletcher. "You weren't good at kite building?"

Fletcher held out his hands, still grinning. "All thumbs, I'm afraid."

Gabriel stared ruefully at the mess of paper and string. "I've been working all afternoon and I still can't get it right."

Moving closer, Fletcher took off his frock coat and hunkered down beside Gabriel. "Maybe if we work together we'll be able to come up with a passable craft."

Gabriel sent him a skeptical look. "I can do it myself."

"I'd like to help you, son." If they could build a kite together, they could build a bridge.

"Oh, very well," Gabriel said with a nonchalant shrug. He pushed a crude sketch at Fletcher. "That's my design."

It was exceedingly poor, Fletcher saw with dismay. Hadn't the masters at Harrow taught the boy anything? Hadn't Sybil urged him to cultivate the skills of drawing and design? "Looks adequate," he said carefully, "but you may have mismeasured this strut." He picked up the measuring rule and scowled at it. "This is what's to blame. The markings are too faded to read. I'm sure you meant to extend the strut to here."

Gabriel glanced at him sharply, then snatched the rule and pencil. "You're right, Pa—sir. I knew it should be longer." Quickly he corrected the design.

Fletcher made certain that every change appeared to be

Gabriel's idea. When the light began to dim, he rang for a servant to bring a candle. It was nearly dark by the time they finished. The result was a roughly made but perfectly adequate kite. Gabriel held it up proudly. Fletcher could see he was trying not to smile. Then the boy gave up the battle and grinned broadly, his expression so heartbreakingly familiar that Fletcher's eyes stung.

Carefully he took the kite from his son to admire the workmanship. The paper was wrinkled, the glue blotted in places. "An altogether worthy bit of work," he pronounced.

Gabriel's eyes shone. "I'm going to fly it tomorrow. Pa . . Papa, would you like to watch me?"

"By all means," Fletcher replied with elaborate casualness. He almost grabbed Gabriel and hauled him into an embrace; instead he tucked a finger beneath his own stock, loosening it. "Damned hot in here," he remarked.

Gabriel nodded. "Hellish." He seemed boyishly pleased to be practicing the manly art of cursing.

"Why didn't you work in Jasper's shop, son? It's better ventilated and you'd have had all his tools."

Gabriel frowned. "I wanted to work where *she* wouldn't come pestering me."

" 'She?' "

The boy's eyes darkened. "That damned infernal redskin girl you brought here," he bit out.

Dismayed by Gabriel's sudden change of mood but instantly ready to defend Great Knife's daughter, Fletcher said, "She has a name, Gabriel. I'd appreciate it if you'd remember she's the daughter of my good friend."

"She's a filthy savage and nothing but trouble," the boy said hotly. "Fancies herself so much better than I when she's about as lowborn as a mayfly."

Fletcher felt a huge tearing sensation deep inside. Consciously or not, Gabriel had dictated the terms of his affection. And the terms were too high. As Sybil's had been. Not even for his son would Fletcher deny his ties to his kin. "Gabriel," he said quietly, "the Mohawk are your people as well as mine. I cannot let you malign them."

"I don't need your lectures. Mama told me all about your lies and your cheating, and your traitor's ties to those savages." The boy lunged forward. "Give me back my kite!"

As he wrested the kite from Fletcher, the cloth tore. A stick snapped. The pieces drifted to the floor. Silence reigned as father and son stared at the mangled remains of the kite they'd built.

Gabriel was breathing hard. "It's broken," he said.

Fletcher touched his shoulder. "We'll fix it, son."

"You've ruined it." Gabriel's voice dropped to a scathing whisper as he backed away. "You always ruin everything!" He darted out of the conservatory.

Fletcher followed, calling his son's name. But with a sick feeling in his stomach, he already knew the effort was futile. Like the kite, the fragile trust they'd built had been destroyed by Gabriel's resentment and his own insistence on defending his people.

Intent on talking to Gabriel, Fletcher barely noticed Jessica as she approached him in the corridor. She spoke his name, said something about supper being served, but Fletcher didn't wait to hear the rest. Pray God, he thought, the argument's not as irreparable as the damned kite.

Filled with concern at what she'd overheard, Jessica stared after her husband. She'd come to fetch them to supper and had found them in turmoil.

She stepped into the conservatory and dropped to her knees beside the broken kite. Her heart rose to her throat. *You ruined it,* Gabriel had said in an accusing whisper. *You always ruin everything.*

She ached for Fletcher, feeling his pain, wanting to help. As she gathered up the torn cloth and broken sticks, she wished she could show him how to love the boy again.

But that was impossible, she realized with sudden clarity. Fletcher was a man divided in his loyalties and he'd let that turmoil come between him and his son. He'd forgotten what it was like to love unconditionally.

Jessica gave an unsteady laugh. That, she finally admitted, was the key. After the explosive scene in the forge barn she was convinced he needed her body. Now she knew he needed her love as well in order to love again.

And Jessica found, to her giddy amazement, that she loved her husband quite powerfully.

Chapter 18

Jade and Nan were constantly in the company of Great Knife. For two days Jessica waited for a chance to speak to them privately about the matter that had obsessed her since that afternoon in the forge barn. Then Jade fell ill of chicken pox and was confined to bed, giving Jessica the perfect opportunity.

In those two days her goal had taken on a subtle change. At first she'd merely wanted to entice Fletcher, to take her place as his wife, to prove to him that he was wrong in wanting to send her away. But after discovering the extent of his need—a need he doubtless didn't even know he possessed—she no longer wanted to take from him. She wanted to give . . . as a woman.

Holding a cup of medicine, she entered Jade's cluttered little room. Nan's saffron-colored head was bent over the patient as she plumped the pillows.

"Now, don't you be scratchin' at them sores," Nan admonished, "or you'll be scarrin' that pretty face."

"Blimey, Nanny, I never felt such a damned unholy itch," Jade complained. "Leastways not above the neck!"

Nan moved away and Jessica saw Jade scowling, her lovely face blooming with chicken pox. "If you've come to wail over me," she snapped at Jessica, "don't bother."

Jessica smiled cheerfully. "You look miserable."

"I bloody well am miserable," Jade retorted, glaring disgustedly at the sores freckling her arms. "I thought I'd seen me share of the pox in London."

"But them was the French pox, dearie," Nan explained with a sage look. "This here's your *honest* variety. Hmm.

Can't think why you didn't get it over with when you was a
tad.''

"Folks didn't get *honest* pox where I grew up," Jade
grumbled. She clenched her fists to avoid scratching.

Jessica handed her the cup. "Kateri made this for you."

Jade took the medicine and sniffed it. "What'd she do, find
a tar pit somewheres?"

"It's willow-bark tea, to bring down your fever."

Jade shrugged. "Can't be no worse than rotgut gin." She
took a deep breath and drained the cup. After a few moments
of outraged spluttering, she found her voice and emitted an
articulate stream of profanities.

"I think she liked it," Nan said, winking her good eye.

"I'll give Kateri your compliments, Jade."

"Remind me to ask Great Knife to teach me the Mohawk
word for—"

"Now, dearie," Nan said, "don't get all in a dither. The
girl means well enough." She pushed an embroidery hoop
toward Jade. "Here, see to your stitchin'. Might keep your
hands off those sores."

Afraid she might lose her nerve, Jessica forced herself to
broach the subject she had come about. "Why don't we talk
about something else?" she asked, plopping down on the
bed. When Nan joined her, she was reminded of Thursday
afternoons at Madame's when she'd cut caricatures and listened to the girls' bawdy talk.

"Anything to take me mind of this accursed itching."

Feeling awkward, Jessica flushed. "Shall we talk about
. . . men?" They looked astounded. Jessica understood; back
in London she was always the last to show interest in males,
other than to frown uncomprehendingly at Jade's jokes.

"Might you," Nan said slowly, "be referrin' to one man
in partic'lar, hmm?"

Jessica stared down at her hands. She nodded briefly.

"So that's the way of it," Jade said. "You ain't happy in
'is bed." She darted her needle into the fabric.

"That's just it," Jessica told her with sudden, pain-filled
candor. "I'm not *in* his bed . . . not as often as I'd like to
be."

"Good God a'mighty," Jade breathed, drawing a long

stitch. "No wonder the man stalks around the place like a leashed tomcat durin' the full o' the moon."

Nan nodded vigorously, then adjusted her eyepatch. "What's wrong with the buck?"

"That's just it, Nanny, he ain't hardly buckin' nobody! An' he ought to be." Jade's needle stabbed savagely at the design she was sewing.

Ordinarily Jessica found their frank talk amusing, but not when the subject was her husband. He was volatile, vulnerable, intriguing . . . but never laughable.

"There is nothing wrong with Fletcher," she said. "At least not . . . in that way. He's made love to me, but each time it's been . . . hurried, frantic, and we quarrel afterwards. Is there something wrong with me that he won't give me the time to let me love him?"

"You?" Nan's good eye widened. "Ain't a bleedin' thing wrong with you, dearie. Pretty as a picture an' sweet as a maid. All bred up like a real lady, thanks to Madame. I'm surprised the man can keep his hands off you."

"Most of the time he seems to have no problem with that," Jessica said bitterly.

"It ain't his hands we're speakin' of," Jade stated.

Jessica drew a long, unsteady breath. "Madame did teach me the ways of a lady, but not those of a wife. There are ways I want to touch him, but . . ." She blushed, unable to continue.

Jade's dark eyes gleamed. "Ah, so that's what you're askin' us. How to heat things up in the bedchamber, eh?" She settled back against her pillows, looking wise and sleek as a cat, despite the small sores dotting her face. "Well, Jess, you've come to the right place."

"Aye," Nan agreed. "Heat things up, my arse. We'll tell you how to scorch the damned bedclothes!"

Jessica felt her stomach flutter with a mixture of amusement and trepidation. "I want more than just physical intimacy. I want to learn how to love him."

Jade and Nan exchanged a long stare. "She's got it bad," Nan breathed.

"Real bad," Jade agreed.

"Is it so terrible that I've begun to care about my husband?"

Nan's smile gaped wide. "I think it's grand, dearie."

Jade nodded. "I know you've thought all your life that men is ragtag an' bobtail. Reckon I was of the same mind."

"Me too," Nan added. "Then a bloke comes along who ain't like any other bloke you've ever met. He just don't fit in with what you think you know. So you fight it."

Jade scratched idly at her cheek; Nan slapped her hand away. "But then you accept it, Jess, an' see what you're about." Nonchalantly, Jade went back to her stitching.

Jessica looked at them, amazed at the precision with which they'd summed up her turmoil. A sudden flash of insight made her grin. "It sounds as though you're speaking as much for yourselves as for me. It wouldn't have anything to do with a certain handsome Mohawk brave, would it?"

To her everlasting astonishment, she saw the two women blush. Jade Akura and Nan Featherstone, who had scoffed at sentiment, made sport of men, and performed outrageous carnal acts in the interest of turning a profit, now flushed scarlet at the mere mention of Great Knife.

"I think," Jessica said slowly, "that we're all suffering from the same affliction."

"Aye, an' ain't it glorious."

They giggled like schoolgirls, muddling the bedclothes and mangling Jade's stitchery. Jessica gasped for breath as another thought struck her. "You're *both* in love with him."

Jade and Nan nodded triumphantly.

"But won't that make things rather . . . complicated?"

The two women shared a knowing look. "No, just the opposite," Nan stated. "Great Knife ain't your ordinary bloke and we ain't ordinary females bound to convention. He has something to give each of us, something no other man has, and we're content to share, ain't we, Jade?"

Jade nodded. "Nan and me, we couldn't do without each other, not for any man." She leaned toward Jessica, her face suddenly serious. "I got to tell you something, Jess, that you might not have thought on."

"What is that?"

Jade stared down at her sewing and traced her finger over the design of an eagle, a design meant for Great Knife. "Once you love someone, you ain't safe from anything."

Jessica bit her lip. What Jade said was all too true. "At

one time," she said slowly, "that would have scared me. I wanted safety, security. But not anymore. Now I want Fletcher, even if it means getting hurt."

Nan gave a grunt of approval.

"Fine," Jade announced, suddenly brisk and businesslike. She set aside her embroidery frame and faced Jessica. "So. He ain't been comin' to your bed. You'll just have to brazen your way into his."

"I don't know how." Wincing at painful memories, she twisted her hands in her lap. "The things he makes me feel always come as such a shock. Each time we've made love, I've felt as if the whole world were just beginning to open up to me, but I feel so damned awkward."

Nan patted her shoulder. "That's because you were confused, dearie. But you're not anymore, are you?" Nan's kind, earnest face took on a lovely glow and suddenly Jessica recognized the beauty Great Knife had incisively attributed to the plump, one-eyed woman.

"No, I'm not," she said shakily. "At first I was afraid; I spent days wondering how it came to be and I can't say when I started to love him. Now it seems as if I've always loved him."

"So there's your answer," Jade stated. "You see, Jess, lovin' ain't all just a matter of body parts. It's a feeling in your heart. That makes all the difference."

"Not to Fletcher. I can't simply walk up to him tomorrow and say, 'Excuse me, but I believe I've fallen in love with you, so would you please start taking me to bed?'" She gripped Nan's hands, feeling helpless and foolish and slightly off balance. "I need some practical advice. I want to *show* him how I feel."

"Practical matters then," Nan said. "Kiss him first. That's always a good place to start. How're you at kissin'?"

Jessica recalled the feel of Fletcher's lips on hers, that first unexpected embrace in New Wells that had sent her sprawling on her backside, the hungry, desperate kisses they'd shared in the forge barn. . . .

"I think," she said, "that I've mastered kissing."

Jade and Nan exchanged a glance. "You have, have you? Well, what about . . ." Jade leaned forward and whispered in Jessica's ear.

Jessica felt hot color seep into her cheeks. Drawing back, she regarded Jade with wide, incredulous eyes. "You want me to kiss him *where?*"

A saddlebag in hand and the morning sun at his back, Fletcher stood gazing down at the people who owned his heart. They were all gathered at the river's edge. Gabriel slouched with his shoulder propped against a tree, the customary sullen look on his face. Kitty squatted on the ground, watching Kateri with open-mouthed wonder. Moving closer, Fletcher saw that the Indian girl was fashioning a ball from a sturgeon's gullet. Adele Severin stood nearby, watching with considerably less fascination than Kitty.

Jade, Nan, and Great Knife sat chatting on the dock. Jade's face, healing from the chicken pox, was tilted to the sun. Nan was drawing a comb through Great Knife's scalp lock.

Fletcher gave his attention to Jessica last, because she confused him the most. In the past few days her manner toward him had undergone a subtle and disturbing change. Perhaps frustration had colored his perception, but he detected a new air about his wife. An air of seductiveness. A seemingly inadvertent touch as he held her chair for her at supper, a sidewise glance emanating from beneath the dark gold skirts of her lashes, an offhand comment that could be interpreted in more than one way.

It was as if Jessica had discovered within herself a wellspring of feminine charm and she'd chosen to turn it full force on him.

Why? Fletcher wondered wildly, clutching the straps of his saddlebag. Didn't she know what those "accidental" brushes, those cryptic comments did to him? Of course, he decided, stopping in his tracks. Of course she knew. It must be her means of vengeance against the man who had disrupted her life. Her methods were very effective, he thought with rueful admiration.

Yet at the moment Jessica looked like anything but a vengeful woman. Wearing a pink India calico gown, her hair caught in matching ribbons, she was demurely sweet and earnest as she made some comment to Gabriel. The boy said nothing, only snorted and turned away.

Fletcher felt a pang of sympathy as he saw his wife's face

crumple in dismay. At least, he thought grimly, we are on equal ground with Gabriel; neither of us can reach him.

He felt a stab of respect as Jessica turned back to the others, a brave, bright smile fixed on her beautiful face. She was nothing if not tenacious. He started walking again.

Jessica bent forward to watch Kateri work, affording him an unexpected and thoroughly disconcerting view of her cleavage. Her breasts mounded over the top of her bodice in a way that made his blood sing and his hands itch to fill themselves with her soft, feminine flesh.

Tearing his eyes from the sight and his mind from the notion, Fletcher approached the group and greeted everyone. Then he turned to Gabriel, who was busily tracing a pattern of arrows in the dirt with the toe of his shoe.

"I thought we could go up to the quarry, son," Fletcher said. He lifted the saddlebag. "Mercy has fixed up a dinner, so we can spend all day if we like."

Gabriel didn't look up. He stiffened the slightest bit and hunched his shoulders, and Fletcher's hopes wavered.

"What a lovely idea," Jessica exclaimed, clasping her hands. Briskly she said, "Run along and get into your riding boots, Gabriel, and I'll send word to the stables to have your horse brought 'round."

Fletcher caught her eye for a moment, silently thanking her for the effort.

Gabriel flung his head up. "I'm going riding," he snapped, "but not with *him*. Jasper's expecting me for a jumping lesson."

"I'm sure he won't object to a change of plans," Jessica said, too quickly.

"There won't be any change." Gabriel stuffed his hands in his pockets and sauntered toward the stables.

"I'll go." Kitty's bright, piping voice drove away the heaviness in Fletcher's heart. "Esme and I have never been to the quarry."

"It's a long ride, sweetheart," he explained. "You and Esme would get very tired and saddle weary."

"What's saddle weary, Papa?"

He grinned and gave her backside a gentle swat. "It afflicts you right there."

"Oh! Never mind. I wouldn't want that!"

"I'll tell you what. Why don't you and I walk up to the orchard and we'll have our dinner there?"

Kitty was too young to pretend interest. "I've already been to the orchard, dozens of times. Kateri said she'd take me berry picking while we wait for our ball to dry out. If it's all the same to you, Papa, I'd rather go with her."

He chucked her fondly under the chin. "Of course, sweetheart." Slinging the pack casually over his shoulder, he started back toward the house, forcing his mind to the business he'd planned to neglect in favor of being with Gabriel. The uncritical stacks of letters and ledgers on his desk might take his mind off the hurt . . . for a while.

From the corner of his eye he saw Jade and Nan gesturing frantically in his direction. But by the time he turned back they were merely sitting, elaborately nonchalant, beside Great Knife. Shrugging, Fletcher continued walking.

He hadn't taken three steps when his name, spoken softly in Jessica's melodious voice, brought him to a halt. He swung around to find her staring up at him, her eyes a wide, misty gray, her bosom lifting with quick, shallow breaths.

Heat surged to his loins, tautening his voice. "Yes?"

"Take me, Fletcher."

His mouth went dry as he gazed at her. In his present state of mind, he found her choice of words maddeningly ironic. "To the quarry, you mean?"

"I . . . yes, of course. What else would I mean?" Her lips parted in an intriguing smile.

"I haven't time," he told her curtly. The thought of an afternoon alone with her was too much for his faltering restraint to bear.

"That's not so, Fletcher," she chided. "You specifically made time for an outing. I'm sorry Gabriel didn't go, but there's no sense in wasting Mercy's dinner."

"Jessica—"

"I would like to see the quarry."

"You don't ride. And it's too far to walk."

"I'll ride pillion behind you."

"Why are you being so persistent, Jessica?"

"Why are you being so obstinate, Fletcher?"

Before he quite realized what was happening, she was tugging at his sleeve, pulling him toward the stables, behaving for all the world like an eager, playful little girl. Except that she looked nothing like a little girl.

Neither did she feel like one once she was seated on the pillion behind him. Her breasts were soft against his back, her arms firm around his waist as he rode out of the yard. When he urged his horse to a canter, her hands gripped his middle in a way that nearly made him lose control.

"Jessica." He spoke her name from between clenched teeth. "Must you clutch at me like that?"

Her laughter sounded nervous. "I've never been on horseback before."

"You haven't?" he asked, surprised. "Even Kitty is learning to handle her pony. I sat my own horse at the age of four."

"You were fortunate to have the means," Jessica murmured at his back. "My childhood steed consisted of a crating plank set atop two upended dustbins."

Fletcher lashed himself with a few well-chosen silent curses. How inexcusably insensitive of him. "I didn't think," he said and patted her hand. "I tend to forget you weren't always as you are now."

Her small hand captured his and clung. "And how is that, Fletcher? How am I now?"

"You're a lady," he admitted, gently extracting his hand from hers. "Right down to these pretty little fingernails. And I'll see you get your own horse," he added, then scowled. He ought to know better than to bind her even more closely to him with gifts and promises.

He turned his horse up a mountain track, suddenly less reluctant to spend the day with her despite his depressing thoughts. In truth the outing would cost him little . . . except in terms of his self-restraint.

"There's our path," he said, pointing up the mountain. "We'll have to ride several miles."

Jessica felt giddy with delight. Jade and Nan had insisted that Fletcher's indifference was only a facade. He could have refused her today, but he hadn't. She was pleased about that. After two days of lively, frank discussion with Jade and Nan, she was eager to try her skills.

Not caring that she was probably ruining her petticoats by riding astride, Jessica enjoyed the feel of the horse moving beneath her. And she loved being close to Fletcher, the firm feel of his body beneath her hands and his wonderful masculine, woodland scent.

Excitement rippled through her as she pondered the hours to come. No one would interrupt them, not the bustling, overefficient Mr. Elphinstone, nor Jasper van Cleef, nor any of the tenant farmers and Indians who seemed to look upon Fletcher as an authority on farming, husbandry, medicine, even in settling gambling disputes and trading agreements. Jessica intended to make use of every moment.

To pass the time, she asked Fletcher about the landscape. Soon she could identify the whirring sound of a wild pigeon, the spicy scent of a giant hemlock, the shimmering underleaf of a silver maple. The thrusting profile of the mountains, burnished by the strong morning sun, formed a rugged, compelling picture. Jessica equated that picture with Fletcher. Like the mountains, her husband possessed a hard, unapproachable magnificence, a soul that seemed impenetrable.

But as the sure-footed horse climbed a rocky, winding trail, she began to see the mountains in a new light. From a distance they looked cold and lifeless; up close the terrain wore the shy, tender blossoms of the wild stonecrop and vibrated with breezes and bird song. The mountains embraced them in autumn finery. Jessica's hopes lifted.

The trail narrowed and became rockier. They reached a tiny glade beside a rushing spring. Fletcher drew the horse to a stop, dismounted, and helped Jessica down. She wanted to linger in the steady clasp of his hands at her waist, but he quickly dropped his arms and turned away.

"The trail gets steeper," he said. "We'll have to walk from here, if you're still interested in seeing the quarry."

"Of course I'm still interested," she said, grinning. "You may think me a lady, and I do thank you for that, but please do not equate me with vaporous parlor matrons like Mrs. Fairfax."

He looked as if he might smile. He didn't, although humor danced in his eyes. "I don't think I'm likely to make that mistake." He tethered his horse and unbuckled the saddle-bag, then led the way up the overgrown path.

Soon enough, Jessica realized why they'd had to leave the horse behind. Brambles tore at her skirts and rubble cut into her feet. But she followed Fletcher doggedly, concentrating so hard on keeping her balance that she barely noticed that the swish of the spring had risen to a roar.

She was reaching down to pluck a twig from her hem when Fletcher took her hand. She raised her eyes, first to his face and then to the splendor behind him. Her hem dropped, forgotten, from her fingers.

"We're here," Fletcher said. "Was it worth the price of some new lace for your dress?"

She gazed at the cascade spilling from a high cliff, plunging into a turquoise pool. "Yes," she breathed, stepping closer to the quarry pond. "Oh, yes."

"I used to come here often with Gabriel. It was . . . special to us."

Jessica's heart ached for them both. "He'll come back here with you. But today . . . I'm glad you chose to share it with me."

His mouth lifted in the beginning of a smile. "You didn't leave me much choice."

Laughing, she whirled around, her skin cooled by a rush of mountain air. "Fletcher, why have you never brought me here before? It's so beautiful."

He looked nonplussed. "To be honest, I didn't think it would hold any interest for you. I always thought London-bred ladies preferred more domestic settings."

"I thought," she said, "we'd settled the matter of my breeding—or lack of it."

For the first time in longer than she cared to admit, he smiled at her. A real smile, from the heart, unconstrained by his usual cool politeness. Instead of icy blue, the color of his eyes recalled the brilliance of a jay's wing—something warm and alive, something that could be touched.

Unthinkingly she reached for his hand. "Aren't you going to show me around?" She hadn't forgotten her purpose in coming here but was remembering Jade's advice: "Don't just pounce on the bloke, for Chrissake. You lead up to it, gradual like."

Feeling the sculpted firmness of Fletcher's hand cradling hers, Jessica finally admitted that she was ready for more. Much more.

He led her in the direction of the waterfall, supporting her as she stepped over a large upthrust of rock. "The Dutch settlers started quarrying blue limestone from here over a century ago," he said, raising his voice over the roar of the cascading waters. "They used to roll the boulders down the mountain. That's how the trail was carved."

Jessica looked back, imagining one of these huge rocks zigzagging at breakneck speed down the mountain.

"The Dutch church in Albany is built of these stones," Fletcher said. "No one quarries here any longer."

"I'm glad." She inhaled the fresh smell of tumbling water. "This place is lovely just as it is."

They continued picking their way over huge, slanting expanses of rock. The effort of clambering over the uneven terrain brought a sheen of sweat to Jessica's brow. She could feel her curls tightening against her neck. The sun glared unrelentingly, sending heat down on her unprotected head.

They had almost reached the waterfall when her foot encountered a sharp edge. The rock cut through the thin leather sole of her shoe and into the bottom of her foot.

Dull pain seeped up her leg. "Bloody hell!" She grasped Fletcher's arm and turned her foot up to inspect the damage, but the layers of her skirts kept getting in the way. She opened her mouth again, another curse ready to spill from her, when Fletcher deftly swept her up and seated her on a broad, flat rock.

She began sorting through her skirts and petticoats. Gently Fletcher pushed aside her hands. "Let me see."

She obeyed; his face was drawn with concern and his touch was gentle. He removed her shoe, holding it up and scowling at the gash in the sole.

"I knew I shouldn't have brought you here today."

"That's nonsense," she retorted. "It's the fault of inferior leather, not your lack of judg—oh!" She bit her lip as he slid her skirts upward and moved his hands along her leg to find the top of her stocking. A swirl of delicious feelings eddied through her as he disengaged the stocking from its buttons and slowly rolled it down her leg. She glanced at Fletcher, certain she'd find an answering passion in his eyes.

But he kept his gaze downcast, his face impassive as he deposited the wisp of white silk on the rock beside her.

"Stocking's ruined too," he said and took her foot be-

tween his hands. Tenderly he touched the cut with one finger.
"I'll have to carry you back to the horse."

Jessica winced, but not from the pain. "You'll do no such
thing, Fletcher Danforth!" She wrenched her foot from his
hands and upended it in her lap, heedless of her unladylike
pose. "It's naught but a scratch," she declared indignantly.
"I did not climb all the way to this quarry only to turn straight
back around."

He grinned at her, pleased that she treated her injury so
lightly. "You'd make a good Mohawk woman," he remarked, trying to tear his eyes from the enticing sight of her
bare leg.

"Would I?" Her eyes sparkled and a smile teased her lips.

Trying to ignore the powerful surge of desire welling up
inside him, Fletcher cleared his throat. "Yes," he said, keeping his tone light. "Mohawk women are rather matter-of-fact
about physical discomfort. How do you feel?"

Jessica stared at him. Her lids lowered languidly over the
misty gray of her eyes. She caught a handful of curls at the
nape of her neck and lifted the silky mass, her torso swiveling
to give him a mind-numbing view of her bosom. An artist's
model could not have contrived a more seductive pose.

"Hot," she said. "I feel hot."

Stunned by her reply and not trusting himself to speak, to
move, Fletcher could only gape at her. Jessica's lips turned
up in a smile and slowly, still smiling, she removed her other
shoe and stocking.

"I didn't realize," Fletcher said in a raspy voice, "that
you'd hurt your other foot as well."

"My other foot is fine. But I said I was hot, and I intend
to do something about it." Leaping up, she walked, limping
a little to spare her injured foot, down to the edge of the
sloping, flat rock and sat down again, hiking up her skirts to
dangle her feet in the water. A soft, liquid sigh escaped her
as she swung her legs slowly through the crystal water. Her
lashes dropped blissfully over her smiling eyes.

She had, Fletcher thought wildly, the shapeliest legs he'd
ever seen. When she braced her hands behind her and let her
head drop back, tilting her face to the sun, a mad urge seized
him. He wanted to bend over her, to touch his lips to her satiny

throat, to taste the dewy sweetness of her skin. But he wanted more than that, he . . .

She opened her eyes a tiny bit. "Will you join me? The water feels delicious."

Fletcher drew a long, ragged breath, then yanked off his boots and stockings. What he needed was to plunge his aching body into the icy, spring-fed depths. Instead, he sat a judicious distance away and let the water lap at his feet. His eyes were drawn to her bare feet and then up her legs until his entire being emptied of everything but her. He didn't understand her and he didn't understand himself when he was around her. Something inside him cried out for her. The urge was not merely of the flesh; he felt another, deeper need that physical intimacy could only begin to answer.

With an effort he tore his gaze from her slowly swaying legs. He lay back against the sunwarmed rock, closed his eyes, and pondered the irony of his situation. Here he was alone with a beautiful woman who happened to be his wife, yet he could not have her. It was a fitting punishment for his arrogance in the Lord Chancellor's court.

He heard her move away from him and was sure then that she did not want to be there. Immediately lonely for her, he opened his eyes and turned. A gust of relief escaped him. She had only gone to a patch of grass nearby. She gave him a sunny smile and bent to pick a wild sorrel blossom, lifting it to her face to inhale its scent.

Fletcher lost himself in the pleasure of watching her and flayed himself with the torture of wanting her. Yet she seemed blithely unaware of his conflict. She hummed a vague melody and filled her hands with flowers.

Mesmerized by her artlessly seductive movements, the way the wind stirred her curls, the winsome smile curving her lips, he was able to forget the turmoil his life was in. For this time-frozen moment his world consisted solely of autumn sunshine and mountain breezes and a pretty girl picking flowers. Lost in the pleasant deception that all was well with the world, Fletcher leaned back against the rock and closed his eyes again, because dreaming was safer.

A few moments passed; then he realized he could no longer hear her humming. He sat up and squinted, his eyes dazzled by shards of sunlight glinting off the water.

Jessica had drifted away from him; her flower gathering had led her to the foot of the cascade. By the time he shot to his feet, she was inching toward the plunging torrent on a narrow outcrop of the rock face.

A curse exploded from his lips as he sprinted toward her. Dread pounded through him at the thought of losing her beneath the surging waterfall. When he saw her disappear behind the curtain of water, terror blossomed in his breast and turned his blood to ice.

But as he drew nearer, he saw that she was in little danger of falling into the swirling foam. The ledge was a wide, accommodating shelf. Weak and shaking with relief, Fletcher paused.

She stood directly under the cascade, her face misted by droplets and her gown drenched. He called her name, but she seemed not to hear over the roar of rushing water. Instead she blithely occupied herself in tossing her flowers, one by one, into the cascade.

Fletcher's heart still pounded, no longer with dread but with desire. Her gown was soaked through, revealing the curves of a pagan goddess, a wood sprite. A creature not of this world but of another, saner place. A place where the practice of casting wildflowers into a waterfall was considered a worthy occupation . . . a place with room for him.

As he walked toward her along the ledge, he thought, this beautiful, strange, complex, unpredictable creature is my wife. His blood sang, mocking his careful plan to send her back to London where she belonged. *She belongs here,* said a quiet, insistent voice in his head. *With you.*

She dropped the last of her flowers into the water and turned to him, her damp face bright with exhilaration. "Isn't it grand, Fletcher? We're inside a waterfall!" Her eyes shone like sun-sparkled gemstones, reflecting the clear, dancing water. "Can there be anything more wonderful than that?"

You, he thought immediately. *You are more wonderful than that.* He closed the distance between them and caught her against him in a sudden, fierce embrace.

The water crashed down around them, but he no longer heard it. Icy droplets soaked him, but he didn't feel them. His only awareness was of the warm, wet woman in his arms. A thought surged up from his heart. Jessica had become precious to him. Swiftly, before reason had a chance to intrude upon the madness of the moment, he lowered his mouth to hers.

She tasted of spring water and dewy freshness. Her cool lips soon warmed against his. She returned his kiss eagerly, twining her arms around his neck and fingering the damp locks at the back of his neck.

He thought he already knew what it was like to kiss Jessica. But this was different; this kiss was freely given and throbbing with new emotion. He could feel her response in the way her mouth opened beneath his, in the soft yielding of her curves against his straining, rigid form. Fletcher held her for long, breathless moments, until he nearly shook with wanting her. At last his passion-fogged brain made him aware that she was shaking too.

He lifted his head to gaze at her, half expecting to see fear in her eyes. Instead she was smiling, her face misted by moisture, her lips swollen by the ardor of his mouth.

"I'm a little c-cold," she told him ruefully.

"Did you expect a hot spring?" he asked, a wry smile on his lips. He led her back along the rock shelf, then put his hands about her waist and lifted her down to the dry grass. "Would you mind terribly," he asked with exaggerated formality, "explaining what you were doing venturing beneath a cataract?"

"I wanted to f-feel it," she said, her smile still bright, her eyes still shining.

He frowned at her, puzzled by her appealing manner and tantalized by the charms her sodden gown revealed.

Her smile wilted. "You're angry."

He brushed a damp tendril from her cheek. "No, Jessica," he said quietly, "I'm not angry." And yet a part of him was livid. Just when he'd begun to think it was possible to live without her, she was tiptoeing back into his heart.

"You are angry. I know you are. You always become quiet when you're angry."

He was not so surprised that she was correct, only that she'd noticed. She knows me, he thought. Better than anyone else. How had that happened? "You might have fallen," he said, effectively snuffing out a sudden spark of affection.

"Nonsense. The ledge is quite wide enough."

"Why? What possessed you?"

"I'm London born and bred, Fletcher. I've never seen anything like this before. I wanted to experience it, t-to be a part
of it." She shivered violently, rubbing her arms.

His eyes were captured by her slender arms, her trembling
lips. "No doubt you'll pay for the experience by catching
cold."

"It didn't feel so very cold," she confessed. "But now . . ."
Her voice failed her as she began to shiver anew.

Concern pushed into Fletcher's mind. A decidedly bluish
cast colored her lips and suddenly she looked unutterably
frail and vulnerable.

"My horse would probably balk at wet riders. It'll take
hours to dry all those layers of clothing." He sent her a long,
unsmiling look. "You'll have to take off your dress," he finished dully.

Her trembling stilled as she stared at him, then began anew,
more violently. "Yes," she said, "I s-suppose you're right."
With unsteady fingers she reached behind her and plucked
ineffectually at the fastenings.

"Turn around," he muttered impatiently. She obeyed and
he applied his fingers to the annoyingly intricate row of buttons and frogs. He concentrated on the operation, trying to
ignore the idea that he was in the act of undressing a woman
he'd sworn to resist. He trained his eyes on the tiny marcasite
buttons in order to avoid looking at her damp, tangled curls,
her narrow back pinched into stays, the sweet, fragrant flesh
beneath her shift. By the time he'd finished, he was trembling.

"Thank you," she murmured. Swiveling, she pulled her
arms out of the sleeves. Her bodice fell forward; then the
gown collapsed at her feet in a puddle of India calico.

"Oh, dear," she said, gazing down at her tightly laced
stays. "I'm wet to the skin."

"Turn," Fletcher said tautly. He knew he sounded gruff
but didn't trust himself to say more. He'd disrobed his wife
a thousand times in his dreams. But dreams allowed him to
tread where conscience forbade him to go. His fingers were
clumsy with the laces. For interminable moments he fumbled
with points and eyelets.

"Why do you bind yourself into this infernal contraption?'' he demanded. ''You hardly need it to slim your waist.''

Soft laughter sailed over her shoulder. ''It's for my posture, Fletcher.''

''There's not a blessed thing wrong with your posture.'' At last the stiff-boned stays fell away.

She whirled around, a sigh of relief exploding from her lips. His heart stilled as he regarded the wet shift the stays had concealed. Pressure from the boning had molded the garment to her form. He found himself staring dumbly at her breasts, the tips puckered tight and straining against the filmy translucence of the fabric.

''That's ever so much better,'' Jessica said, plucking at the wet ribbons of her under petticoat. This joined the other clothing on the ground, and at last she stood in only her shift. A self-conscious blush stained her cheeks as she bent to gather her wet clothing. Fletcher thought she'd do more than blush were she aware of the way he was looking at her backside.

She carried her clothes to a gorse bush and spread them on its thorny branches to dry in the sun. That done, she turned and grinned.

''You're wet too, Fletcher.''

Within a few moments, she'd managed to tease and cajole and browbeat him out of his waistcoat and shirt, but he balked at removing more. One glimpse of his passion-wracked body in its present condition was sure to send her screaming into the woods.

''Oh, look!'' Jessica exclaimed as she finished draping his shirt over a bush. ''Grapes!'' Reaching up, she plucked a dark purple cluster from a vine. ''Are they edible?''

''Yes,'' he said, ''but only . . .'' Amused, he paused to watch her pop one in her mouth and bite down. She deserved no less for the anguish she was wreaking on his body. ''. . . after the first frost,'' he finished innocently.

Her features crumpled into a grimace and her eyes began to water as she spat out the sour grape. ''Beast,'' she called and ran to the water's edge to rinse the taste from her mouth. ''You should have stopped me from eating it.''

Fletcher chuckled. ''But you're ever so much quicker than I,'' he rejoined. Reaching for her hand, he helped her up.

They ate in a shady patch of grass some distance from the

water. Or rather, Jessica ate and Fletcher watched. He'd thought that dinner would divert his thoughts from her, but his appetite was not the sort to be sated by food.

His wife, he thought wryly, had no such problem. She ate her cold roasted chicken, hoop cheese, and strawberries with the same dainty elegance with which she did all things. Wiping her hands and mouth on a napkin, she looked up at him.

"Delicious," she announced, beaming. "But our clothes are nowhere near dry." She edged over and seated herself close to him. She smelled of wind and water.

"You've barely touched your food, Fletcher," she scolded good-naturedly. She made a sweeping gesture over the flat stone they were using as their table. "Aren't you hungry?"

Ravenous, he thought grimly. He shook his head.

"Do try the strawberries," she persisted. "Kitty and Kateri spent hours gathering them." Without waiting for his consent, she pressed one to his lips.

Fletcher bit into it, too burningly aware of her nearness, her fingers at his lips, to taste its sweetness. One of those small, clever fingers caught a droplet of juice which she took into her own mouth. The sight nearly drove him wild.

"Now," she said, very softly, still very close to him, "we've explored the quarry, we've eaten our dinner, and our clothes are still not dry."

She put another strawberry to her lips, sucking thoughtfully. "What else shall we do to pass the time?"

Chapter 19

Jessica felt the rumble of a low groan from Fletcher's throat as he hauled her against him. Her heart gave an exultant leap. His sudden loss of restraint and his bone-crunching embrace told her that she'd won his passion at last. Deep inside she knew passion wouldn't be enough. But it would be a start. How else could she get close enough to convince him that they belonged together?

Eyes shining, she turned her face up to his, felt his warm, strawberry-sweet breath just before he kissed her. His lips pressed hard, sending sparkles of desire shimmering through her, burning a path to her core.

His tongue rimmed her lips, softened them, then searched her starved and sensitive inner mouth. Bursting with ardor, she clasped him tightly.

She'd known the powerful magic of his kisses since that first time in London. But this moment was different. She felt it in his yearning touch and in her own joyous response. She no longer fought him and knew he no longer fought her. Locked in a fierce embrace in this sun-spangled patch of heaven, they left behind the shadows of strain and discord.

As she gave herself up to his embrace, a far-off corner of her mind tried to recall Jade's discourse on the intricacies of kissing. But Jessica didn't need instruction now; she had only to follow where passion and emotion led her.

She curved her hands up his arms, fitting his brawny shoulders into her palms before moving them to his back. Night after night she'd dreamed of touching him like this, of exploring the muscular sinews of his body with her eager hands. Now reality turned her dreams to the palest of shadows. Her imagination could never have conjured such vitality, such warmth, such masculine magnificence.

Fletcher's hands, like hers, would not be still. His fingers delved into the damp mass of curls at the nape of her neck, warming it and making the rest of her ache for his touch. His hand wandered down her back in slow, soothing circles, but Jessica felt anything but soothed.

She pressed closer and slid her tongue into his mouth. He stiffened and she feared he would pull away, but instead he strengthened his hold on her and allowed her to explore his mouth at leisure. He tasted of the berry she had fed him, sweet and warm and impossibly delicious. His breathing quickened and she felt giddy with the knowledge that her kisses were as potent as his own.

The cascade thundered over the rocks, adding its roar to the pounding of blood in her ears. Jessica strained closer to her husband. The gentle pressure of his hand on her shoulder sent her reclining onto the soft grass. The tender blades tickled her bare arms and legs and gave off a wild, herbal aroma.

Fletcher loomed above her, his handsome face and wind-blown hair framed by blue sky and sunlight. His eyes, low lidded and dark with passion, stared intently down at her. His mouth, she saw with a pang of delight, bore evidence of her kisses. His lips were moist and looked softer somehow. And he was smiling.

"I'll never survive if that's the way you feed me," he told her.

Jessica placed her hands on his chest and moved them slowly upward, tracing the lines of his collarbones and then circling his neck. "You hardly have the look of a starving man."

"Then I'm a better imposter than I thought," he replied, lowering his mouth to hers, plunging his tongue into her mouth.

Desire thrummed through her as she took his full weight. Her breasts strained against him, teased to a sweet ache by the pressure of his hard chest. Another kind of hardness branded her lawn-clad thigh, sending a shaft of pure excitement to the deepest part of her.

His kiss burned hotter as he pressed closer, his hands roving her tense, eager body. His knuckles brushed her breast and she caught her breath, bringing her knee up to his thigh in a fluid, caressing motion.

Fletcher drew back. His smile was gone. His eyes burned like two bright flames.

Dismay suffused her. She recognized that torn, distracted look.

"Jessica." His breathing was ragged, labored. "Jessica, I must not . . . What if we make a child?"

Battling frustration and despair, she knew she must act before he reasoned himself out of the fulfillment they both craved. With an unsteady hand she reached for the tiny buttons of her lawn shift and undid them one by one. "Would that be so terrible?"

She could tell he was trying to keep his eyes away from her shift. Then his gaze flicked downward and she saw his conviction waver. Encouraged, she continued plucking at the seemingly endless row of buttons, all the while rubbing her bare foot slowly up and down the length of his calf.

"A child would bind you to me for all time," he said, his voice a hoarse, strained whisper.

She continued unbuttoning her shift. "Must you always think in terms of eventualities? Truly, I sometimes think you've planned the very day and hour of your own death."

"Do I inspire such morbid thoughts in you?"

"What you inspire in me, Fletcher Danforth," she said, sitting forward to shrug out of her shift, "is anything but morbid. And a lady would never speak of it."

Triumph filled her as she watched his reaction to her nakedness. His eyes blazed, his mouth gaped as he stared at her. Jessica faced him proudly, as a wife certain of her husband's need and determined to awaken his affection.

"You've changed," he whispered. Frustrated fingers furrowed a path through his hair. "I just don't understand you. All day I've felt as if I were moving through a fantasy world. When I saw you standing under the waterfall, for a moment I didn't even believe you were real."

"But I am real. I'm no longer the shy, clumsy girl stumbling over beads in the Pynchons' entrance hall." She fixed a bold gaze on his wavering hand. "Touch me, Fletcher. *Please.*"

His hand—poignantly, humanly unsteady—crept down her

bare shoulder to cover her breast. A shower of sparks radiated from the pleasure point. Jessica arched toward him, filling his palm with her softness. Their lips met again for a brief, stirring moment.

And then his mouth left hers, trailing down her throat, over her bosom. She threaded her fingers into his hair. A gasp burst from her lips as his teeth and tongue performed an intricate and lovely dance upon her flesh.

His hands, no longer hesitant, scorched the length of her bare torso and singed the sensitive flesh of her thighs. His tender, probing touch tore his name from her throat. She threw back her head, certain that any moment something would burst inside her.

Through a warm mist of desire, she discovered a need to share what she was feeling. Jade and Nan had given her the means; her love for him gave her the heart.

Trembling, she set her hands into motion. His stomach muscles tautened as she undid the buttons of his breeches.

Before, she'd averted her eyes from his body, confused and fearful, her head filled with her mother's bitter words about men and the ribald insults of Madame's girls. Now, with her heart full of love and her mind open to passion, she looked freely upon her husband.

"You are beautiful, Fletcher."

His eyes widened in surprise; then he smiled. "Somehow I think those words should have come from me, directed at you."

"You'd never say such a trite thing." Her hands traveled downward, over his middle. "Your compliments are much more inspired, like the time you told me my laughter was like sunshine. But I meant what I said. You *are* beautiful."

"I've a body like any man," he said gruffly. The coppery tint of his face darkened a shade.

"Good heavens, Fletcher, did I make you blush?"

He ducked his head, but not before an errant shaft of sunlight fell across his face, illuminating the redness of his cheeks.

"You *are* blushing," Jessica said in astonishment.

"It's not every day a man hears such pretty words from his wife," he grumbled, nuzzling her throat as if to distract her.

"Did—didn't Sybil ever admire you in this way?" Her hand continued straying downward.

"The only thing Sybil ever admired about me was my banking ledgers."

"Oh." Her tongue darted out to moisten her lips. "I've never seen your banking ledgers, so I've no basis for comparison."

"You are a witch, Jessica," he said, suddenly pressing her back onto the ground. The smell of bruised grass mingled with his own masculine scent. "And you talk too much. If you admire me so much as you claim, why don't you show me?"

Jessica did. Summoning up all the love in her heart and all the practical advice Jade and Nan had planted in her head, she set about proving her feelings. Not with words, but with the tender, evocative language of her hands and heart and mouth.

The isolated setting and the joy singing inside her set her free from all restraint. She found it impossible to be shy and maidenly in this idyllic place, with this idyllic man. She loved every part of him, every hollow and swell of his form, every scar and every sinew.

And Fletcher, looking slightly dazed, returned her lovemaking in kind, stroking, probing until she nearly wept for wanting him. At last he loomed against the sky again, bracing himself above her.

But something made him hesitate. "Are you sure, Jessica?" he whispered. "Are you very, very sure?"

His damned misguided conscience again. "You talk too much," she murmured and brought her lips up to his. With an unconstrained groan he sank down, filling her with a heat that burned hotter and brighter than the afternoon sun.

Jessica lost herself in the incandescence of their passion. She arched against him, reaching for a closeness she'd longed for all her life but had only recently recognized.

He raised himself up and she clutched at him, suddenly fearful that he would leave her as he had the other times when he'd so quickly doused their passion with his cold scheme to send her away. As if he understood, Fletcher smiled and tenderly kissed the corner of her mouth.

"Put you legs around me, darling," he said. "That way I can't escape."

"Of course," she replied, frowning in sudden concentration. "I should have remembered that. . . ."

He looked confused. But when she complied, his gaze turned to one of pure, intense rapture, and he set the rhythm of their love into motion. Like the water racing over rocks, emotion sped through her.

Stifling a cry of delight, Jessica buried her face in the side of his neck. Then, realizing there was no one within miles to hear, she unleashed her sounds of ecstasy, listening to the echoes of her own pleasure as the mountains sent her voice tumbling back. She felt herself being lifted higher than the trees, higher than the mountaintops, and then she was soaring, soaring toward completion with the man she loved so fiercely that tears gathered in her eyes.

Fletcher whispered her name with tender urgency. He gave deeply of himself, pouring his heat into her with a force that took her breath away.

The rhythm crested, slowed, stopped. Jessica drifted back to earth, replete and glowing with fulfillment. She found herself suddenly draped by six feet of warm, satisfied man.

For long, sultry moments they lay still. Jessica felt overcome; her heart flared like dry tinder in a forest of wildfire. They were closer than they had ever been before. He'd fulfilled her, whispered a hundred endearments, and she finally dared to hope he'd given her a new part of himself, the part she wanted the most. His love.

His love? Was she expecting too much too soon? Five years of bitterness couldn't be wiped away in a single afternoon. But it was a start. She lay listening to the roar of the cascade and the trill of bird song—and the sound of her husband's rapid breathing. Fletcher made a move to draw away.

She held him fast with her legs and arms, just as he'd instructed her to do. "Stay," she whispered, tracing his ear with her tongue. She tightened her clasp. "I won't let you pull away from me this time, Fletcher." When he rolled to one side she followed, straddling him.

"You're a tenacious witch," he said, reaching for her breasts.

She leaned down, her mouth lingering over his. "Precisely,'' she murmured. Then she moved so that her breasts brushed his lips. His tongue roughened each peak in turn and sent renewed heat crackling through her.

"Jessica," he muttered, "I'm afraid I can't . . . that is, I need a few minutes to—"

"Nonsense, you're perfectly fit."

"Yes, but I can't simply revive myself at your request."

"I request nothing," she said, rubbing sensuously against him. "I insist." She executed a move that would have done Jade Akura proud.

"My God," he said, his eyes kindling as he stirred restively. "Where the hell did you learn that?"

But she knew he didn't really want an answer, not now, not when her clever movements had revived his passion. A slower pace drew out their loving until pleasure was honed to the sharp edge of pain. Straining limbs and halting breaths melted together in ecstasy.

Afterward Jessica was the one to move away, pulling on her shift and settling herself in the grass beside him. She nestled her head in the curve of his arm. He leaned down and inhaled the fragrance of her sun-warmed hair as she languished in his musky scent.

"Jessica." His hands parted the shift and glided over her body until her nerves hummed. Amazed, she sensed that he wanted to make love again. With even greater astonishment, she realized that she wanted to wait. She would never tire of his kisses and caresses, but her love was so new, her senses so raw that she needed time to lie close to him and mull over her feelings. And yet his hands were insistent.

"Oh, Fletcher," she said, "I don't think—"

"Pass the strawberries, Jessica." He chuckled and drew on his breeches as she moved away.

"Devil," she said happily, reaching for the earthenware crock. "Here's your due." She plunked the container down on his chest and fished out a strawberry.

Possessed of a new-found confidence and her own brand of devilment, she teased his lips with the berry, only to snatch it away and place it in her own mouth. He took it back, but not with his hand. The juice spurted between their mouths.

"Ouch!" she said suddenly as her elbow encountered something hard. She sat up, rubbing the bruise.

Fletcher rose and pried the rock from the ground. "For you, my lady," he said with elaborate gallantry. He placed the stone in her palm. "You've found a treasure."

"Charming," she murmured with a wry smile. "Is this all I get for my trouble?"

He shook his head and made a clucking sound with his tongue. "So quick to judge," he chided, taking the rock from her before she could fling it away. "Things are not always what they seem on the surface. Look what you're refusing."

He moved away and, raising his hand high, brought the stone crashing down on the flat rock that had been their dinner table.

The stone in his hand broke open, revealing a sparkling wealth of amethyst jewels.

"Oh," Jessica breathed, picking up a winking fragment. "Mountain crystal, just like Gabriel's."

"You can have it for your very own," Fletcher said, closing her fingers around it.

They stared at each other deeply, feeling their bond strengthening. "I'll keep it always," she said, placing it carefully at her side.

But Fletcher snatched it back. "Not until I get what I want from you, young lady."

Jessica decided that if he asked her to harness the stars, she would sprout night wings. "Very well. What is your price?"

"I want some answers. I want to know why you've been acting so seductive lately, and where you learned all those damnably clever tricks."

Jessica shook her hair forward to hide her blush. It was one thing to seduce him, yet another to admit to having planned it. "I don't know what you mean."

In that instant, a butterfly landed on Fletcher's knee, paused briefly, and then tumbled away in a flurry of black and gold.

"How pretty," she exclaimed, seizing the convenient distraction. "Why, it must be a *papillon d'amour*. I've heard they are often found in the company of ardent lovers." Pleased with her new knowledge of lovers' lore, she grinned and settled back on her heels.

Fletcher threw back his head and hooted with laughter.

Jessica scowled at him. "Is that so terribly funny?"

His shouts of mirth subsided to chuckles and he gave her back her crystal stone. "It's all yours now, darling. You've answered my question."

"I certainly did not. 'Tis a woman's secret."

"Not any more." Humor still danced in his eyes. "You've had some lessons from Jade Akura and most probably the artful Nan Featherstone too."

Dismayed and embarrassed, she flushed furiously. "How can you be so sure?"

"Because, my sweet," he said, gently pushing her shift down and exposing her breasts, "only a seasoned courtesan would refer to crab lice as 'butterflies of love.' "

She drew her hand back, threatening to pitch the stone at him, but he caught her wrist, cast her shift aside, and brought her fiercely against him. Desire crackled anew. Their humor dissolved. Their bodies fused into one being, one rhythm, one soul.

Gabriel sat on the stone fence of the stable yard, idly paging through a volume of essays. He tilted the book to catch the last rays of the setting sun. But this evening no book could hold his interest. For today he'd accomplished a feat he'd longed to master since he was old enough to sit a horse. Under Jasper's tutelage, he'd managed a series of jumps that would put even a Mohawk horseman to shame.

With boyish magnanimity Gabriel had decided to perform his feat for Papa. It was about time Papa noticed him for something other than his misbehavior. Putting the book aside, Gabriel turned his face to the setting sun and conjured up the scenario in his mind. He'd sail over the hurdles while Papa watched in awe and pride. Papa would gasp with pleasure and would be waiting with outstretched arms and fatherly pride when Gabriel dismounted. Gabriel just might allow him one brief, manly embrace. He blinked and his smile disappeared. One thing was missing. Mama.

"What are you doing, Burning Sapling?"

Kateri's voice, her newly acquired and curiously precise English, startled Gabriel. He scowled. "You know I don't like it when you call me that."

The girl shrugged and smiled brightly. Gabriel looked

away. He also didn't like it when she smiled like that. Her eyes got all shiny like dew on a ripe chestnut and her mouth took on a shape that could almost be mistaken as pretty.

"What are you doing?" she repeated, swinging herself up to sit on the wall.

She always smelled like wintergreen; he suspected it had to do with those rinses Jade was always putting on the girl's hair. He edged away from the unnerving scent and kept his eyes carefully averted from the smooth, tawny skin of her bare arm. He didn't mind her unladylike habit of wearing frocks without sleeves, but the thin, crescent-shaped scar from her inoculation bothered him. He hated any reminder of his loss of control that day.

Kateri picked up his book. "Tell me about this, Bur—Gabriel."

He expelled a long-suffering sigh and took the book from her, turned it, and handed it back. "You were holding it upside down. The words don't mean anything unless you hold it the proper way."

"Oh. Thank you for showing me the proper way."

Gabriel stared down at his hands. Kateri's English was still rudimentary, but she'd quickly mastered the feminine art of mockery.

"You may tell me about the story now," she prompted.

"You're always asking me about reading and books. Why are you so interested in them?"

"I cannot help it, Gabriel. I see you looking at these—these leaves and the leaves speak to you."

"That's the way civilized men preserve their thoughts."

She was either too naive or too generous to rise to the insult. "It is like catching and taming a wild hawk, is it not?"

Gabriel shrugged. "I suppose so."

"I want to know what thoughts are on these leaves."

"Then you should learn to read. It's not so awfully hard, even for an . . ." He let his voice trail off, suddenly aware that he didn't want to hurt her. More and more lately he'd been sensitive to her feelings and he didn't know why.

"My father does not care about reading. He would rather I learn to tend a hearth."

"Jessica would teach you if you asked." Gabriel grimaced. "She's so concerned with pleasing everyone."

"Could *you* teach me, Gabriel?"

He glanced at her sharply, then just as quickly looked away from that appealing expression on her face. "No."

"Oh. I did not know you were not able."

"Of course I'm able!"

"Good. Then let us go and you can teach me right now."

"But I—"

"You said you were able. Are you afraid I will find out you are wrong?"

"No! That's ridiculous, Kateri. I can teach you as well as anyone."

"Thank you, Gabriel." Kateri jumped down from the fence. "Let us go. Now."

He wasn't sure how, but he'd just been maneuvered into instructing Kateri in her letters. It might not, he decided, but such an unpleasant diversion at that.

"Not now," he said, repressing a grin at her eagerness. "I have to wait here for my father."

"Oh." Kateri folded her sunbrowned arms on the fence. "Where has he gone?"

Gabriel shrugged.

"Perhaps he went to the quarry. It's where he wanted you to go this morning."

Her voice was so soft; he was sure he only imagined the note of accusation that colored her words. He'd felt guilty about refusing his father's invitation, but Papa would forgive him when he saw what Gabriel had accomplished today.

"He didn't go to the quarry," he stated with certainty. "He'd never go there without me." Although he pretended to have forgotten, Gabriel remembered every happy moment he'd spent there with his father in earlier years, before everything changed. The quarry was their special place. It belonged not to one or the other, but to both of them. For Fletcher to go there without Gabriel would be like violating a trust.

Letting his mind slip back to those easy, happy hours, he looked in the direction of the quarry. Where the mountains softened to foothills, a horse and rider appeared and began descending a tree-lined rise. The dying sun burnished the mount's coat to deep copper.

Forgetting Kateri and the commitment she'd wheedled out of him, Gabriel began walking toward the rider. Papa's hair was windblown and unkempt; he wore no waistcoat or frock-coat. The sleeves and tails of his shirt billowed in the evening breeze. He must have had a hard day, Gabriel decided. He squinted into the orange and pink sun. Yet Papa seemed to be smiling.

The horse emerged from the shadows and angled down toward the stable yard.

Gabriel froze in his tracks. His heart leapt to his throat, then plunged sickeningly to the bottom of his belly. He knew now why Papa was smiling.

She was with him. Arms draped around his middle, cheek cradled against his back, and bare legs dangling carelessly over the horse's flanks, Jessica rode pillion behind him.

Gabriel swallowed, taking in great, painful gulps of air. Jessica's hair was a gleaming tousle of curls and her face was a picture of dreamy contentment.

She was the first to spy him. The hand she raised in greeting was not empty. The slanting sunlight sent a sparkle shooting into Gabriel's eyes.

Jessica might as well have shot a bright arrow through his heart. Because she was holding a piece of mountain crystal, a treasure that could only have come from one place. The quarry.

Fletcher waved too. Gabriel saw him through tear-blurred eyes and, filled with pain and resentment, he renewed his determination to keep Jessica from usurping his real mother's place.

Chapter 20

Firelight leapt to the cold night sky over Canajohari
sweeping an eddy of sparks upward with the flames. Weari
quill-worked and beaded buckskins, Fletcher sat cross-legg
in the circle of light and moved his eyes over the gather
celebrants.

Jade Akura and Nan Featherstone, who had fought a
brazened their way through London's mean streets, now sto
proudly in the wilderness of America. Clad in deerskin a
homespun, hair loose and eyes dancing, they embraced th
new life with a gusto that warmed Fletcher. Great Knife h
given them his heart and his home. In becoming his wive
they were giving him their future.

"This," Fletcher said to his grandfather, who sat besi
him, "is as it should be between the Mohawk and the E
glish."

"Yes, Shadow Hawk," Kayanere agreed, honing the hea
blade of a frow on a whetstone. "All people should be
sensible. The forest sentries tell me Emory Macon is scouti
around Two Rivers. . . ." Idly, Kayanere tested the keenne
of the frow. "Good." He grunted. "I have shingles to ri
tomorrow."

Fletcher smiled. Riving shingles for the village huts was
man's chore that could be done sitting down. Even in l
autumn years, Kayanere insisted on the dignity of work.

A burst of laughter reached them from the other side
the fire. Kayanere squinted through the smoke, then turned
wise and fathomless look on Fletcher. "You once told r
your wife pined for England," he remarked blandly.

Fletcher felt his color rise as his eyes sought Jessica. Fi

light cavorted in the curls escaping her braids and limned her face with golden warmth. Seated amid a circle of chattering Mohawk women, she looked at ease, as though she belonged. Her laughing eyes sparkled as she spoke to her new friends in animated gestures. She drew something on the ground with a stick, eliciting peals of mirth from the women. Even Adele Severin, sitting regally on a carved stump seat, smiled broadly.

Fletcher found himself likening his wife to a multifaceted jewel. Each time she moved, he saw something new in her, something that endeared her to him all the more. One facet remained dim, however. She had continued her correspondence with the duke of Claremont and hadn't offered to explain why. Fletcher decided to wait, to nurture their new love with patience, because it was still a fragile thing, vulnerable to words spoken in temper and in haste.

She looked up and caught his eye, and the quality of her smile changed from merriment to intimacy. Fletcher smiled back and found himself wishing they were alone together.

"Am I a fool, Grandfather," he asked, "to think I can make her happy?"

"You'd be a greater fool to deny the strength of the feelings that bind you to her."

Fletcher shook his head and furrowed his fingers into his hair. His eyes flicked to Kitty, who sat nearby gravely comparing Esme to the corn-husk baby that belonged to one of the little Indian girls.

A feeling of responsibility settled over him. He was deeply committed to his family, his clan, his wife. Perhaps that was why Gabriel's behavior troubled him so much. Lately the boy had been spending too much time in his room, banished there for infractions that even the indulgent Mohawk part of Fletcher couldn't bring himself to overlook. Only a few days before, Jessica had been helping Hilda clear the table after supper. "My real mother was a lady," Gabriel had taunted coolly. "She never did any work."

Fletcher recalled that scene, and too many others, with pain and anger. What was he going to do about the boy? He couldn't force him to accept Jessica, yet he couldn't sit by and let his son make his wife miserable. Jessica's patience had limits and Gabriel seemed determined to find them.

"Have you told your wife about the Great Council the Iroquois and the English will hold in the spring?" Kayanere asked.

"Not yet." The negotiations, to be debated at Fort Stanwix, would decide the fate of the Iroquois nation and were likely to occupy Fletcher for months. "Jessica does so love security," he said. "But I feel a wind rising, Grandfather, a wind that says I must commit myself to the clan as I did before. Can I subject Jessica to that uncertain life?"

"That is for you to determine. Do not act in haste, Shadow Hawk. Remember, it is the way of our people to pass all decisions through the flames of the council fire. You should do no less for your family."

Kayanere aimed a stream of spit at the fire. He put his shingle-splitting frow aside. "See with your eyes and hear with your ears, Shadow Hawk. But decide with your heart."

Barefoot and with his breeches hiked up around his knees, Gabriel stood frozen in the icy shallows of the Mohawk River. His feet ached with cold and his arm, holding a spear high above his head, trembled with tension. Although his eyes remained fastened on the swirling crystal water, he was aware of Kateri on the riverbank behind him. The frigid winter water would have driven him to dry land, but his stubborn will kept him waiting for a fish.

The silver flash of a trout's underbelly caught his eye. Damnation, the fish was out of range. Slowly, moving like the wind through the reeds, Gabriel edged forward, frozen toes curling over slippery rocks. As he moved his hand over the gut string binding the flint head to the spear and balanced its weight, he felt something inside him grow and change.

He was no longer an English schoolboy who ate his supper from china plates. Instead he felt he was a part of this wild land: clean, strong, driven by instinct rather than thought. For this moment he wasn't Gabriel Danforth. He had the substance to make a true man. He was Burning Sapling.

The spear felt like an extension of his hand. His eyes fixed on his quarry. The hovering trout idly waved its fins.

Blood hammered a message to his hand and his heart. The spear sped downward like a bolt of lightning and knifed into the water.

Gabriel lost his footing and plunged into the river. Water filled his eyes and nose, and for a moment he panicked because he did not know how to swim. Scrambling and spluttering, he righted himself and spun around.

Kateri had collapsed, laughing, on the bank. But Gabriel didn't resent her laughter, nor did he worry about the shock of cold that sent violent tremors through him. Because, writhing on the end of his spear in rainbow-hued glory, was his trout.

Triumphantly he slogged ashore and thrust the squirming fish under Kateri's dainty nose. "Well?" he said challengingly, teeth clenched against chattering.

"It is a good fish," Kateri said, still grinning. "Come, I will cook it for your supper." She draped a coarsely spun blanket around his shoulders while he donned his shoes, then led him along the path.

An hour later, Gabriel sat cross-legged at the open hearth in Great Knife's lodge, sharing the roasted trout with Kateri. He barely noted the absence of fine napery and plate as the smokey tasting juices ran down his fingers and chin. Amenities didn't matter. Not here, not now.

Wiping his mouth with his sleeve, he grinned at Kateri. "You didn't think I could do it, did you?"

"I think you could do anything, Burning Sapling, if you put your mind and your heart to the task. Think of all you have learned in only a few days. I used to be able to hide from you; now you are so skilled at tracking you could find me in a snowstorm."

Warmth suffused him. Feeling his ears burn, he looked around the lodge. "Does it make you angry to have to share this small space with Jade and Nan?" he asked.

She looked surprised. "No, Burning Sapling. I welcome my father's new women. They will be as mothers to me."

"What about your real mother?"

"Her spirit joined the stars three winters ago."

"But what about the part of her that you keep in your heart? If you accept Jade and Nan, you will betray your true mother."

"Betray?" The girl's brow wrinkled as she tasted the new word on her tongue. She made a face as if it displeased her.

"You'll drive your mother from your heart," Gabriel explained.

"Never. She will live in me always, only now she will have the company of two others."

"It doesn't work like that," Gabriel insisted. "I know. I've lived with it for half a year." As it often had in the past days, rancor burned a path to his gut.

"You have too much hate in you, Burning Sapling. I see it in your eyes when you look at Jessica and when you look at your father's Mohawk kin."

"Jessica is a thief," he retorted. "She stole my mother's place and she tries to steal my father from me. As for Papa's Indian kin . . . I do not know why he holds them in such high regard." He gave a derisive snort. "The old man Kayanere has hands too clumsy to light his own pipe."

"Those same hands can, with bow and arrow, fell a panther in the dark."

For a tense moment they regarded each other stubbornly. Gabriel surged to his feet. "We will never agree on some things, Kateri. I must go. My father says we're leaving tomorrow at sunrise."

Kateri followed him to the door of the lodge. "Then I will say good-bye to you now. You will learn someday that there is good in Jessica and in your father's people who are also your people. I hope you will learn it soon."

He shrugged and put his hand on the leather door latch. "Good-bye, Kateri."

Her eyes were wide and soft as they searched his face. "I will write you a letter as you have taught me. Then you will have my thoughts, even though we are far apart."

Gabriel's hand dropped from the latch. He felt his heart slam into his rib cage. She looked so pretty, with her black braids so neat and shiny, her smiling lips so soft and moist. "I'll write to you too, Kateri."

Her smile widened and her eyes sparkled. Placing her hands on his shoulders, she tilted her face toward his. Their noses bumped clumsily; their lips brushed in a whisper of a kiss. Kateri sprang back, coppery cheeks blazing. "Good-bye, Burning Sapling," she said.

Gabriel left the lodge, his mind buzzing and his senses swirling. In the space of a single day he'd speared his first trout and kissed his first girl. Glancing around the compound, he wondered if the people around him noticed that he'd grown at least an inch taller.

Following the wisdom of his grandfather, Fletcher pondered what his eyes and ears had told him in the days after the wedding of Great Knife. He'd seen Kitty cavorting like a bear cub in the rough-and-tumble games of the Indian children. He'd seen Gabriel setting a squirrel trap and Jessica grinding corn on a stone.

He'd heard much too: the songs of his people, the howl of the winter wind, the whistle of an elk, the lapping of the river. And always, Jessica's voice.

On the last evening of their visit, her soft laughter rippled from the open door of Kayanere's lodge. Curious, he stepped inside the stood unnoticed in the shadows.

Adele was weaving a willow-withe basket in one corner. Kitty and a half dozen other children sat around the fire beneath the bark shingles in the roof. Seven rapt faces regarded Jessica as she worked a pair of puppets fashioned from silhouettes mounted on sticks.

"And guess who this is?" Jessica asked, picking up the figure of a slim, elegant woman.

The children murmured among themselves, then looked at her, their faces happy but uncomprehending. "This is the new stepmother," Jessica exclaimed, brandishing the puppet.

Kitty thrust out her lip. "That can't be, Mama. That woman is beautiful, and all stepmothers are old and ugly."

Jessica laughed. "Nonsense, Kitty. Your head is too full of Monsieur Perrault's fanciful fairy tales. *This* stepmother happens to be exceedingly pretty and she is also most kind." The puppets pantomimed a merry dance.

"Oh," cried Kitty. "Just like you, Mama."

Fletcher grinned. Tales of wicked stepmothers would forever be banished from Kitty's mind.

If only Jessica could win Gabriel's affections as she had won Kitty's. If only his son were as open-minded and guileless as his daughter.

Sighing, he watched the story being played out for the children. The puppets danced, laughed, came together with comically voluble kisses. One figure tore, but Jessica discounted it with a laugh. "A dab of glue here . . ." she said. "There, it's all fixed."

A moment later, Fletcher saw Jessica gazing at him. She set her puppets aside and murmured something to Adele, who in turn led the children out of the lodge.

Fletcher stepped into the pool of flickering light cast by the fire. Jessica stood up and took both his hands, feeling her eyes brim with love and her heart quicken with desire.

He murmured something deep in his throat—Mohawk words.

Jessica let the strange, evocative language wash over her. "Is that as lovely as it sounds?" she asked.

Gently he lifted one of her braids and loosened its leather binding. As his fingers slowly plucked her curls free, he translated: "Your beauty graces the lodge as the stars grace the heavens at night."

Jessica sighed with contentment. "Thank you, husband," she said in halting Mohawk. She longed to melt into his arms and ask him to soothe the ache of her desire, but, glancing at the door, she hesitated. "Kayanere and the others might want to retire soon," she said.

Fletcher shook his head. He threaded his fingers into her unbound hair, then let his hands course downward, lingering at her breasts before moving lower. He reached around and untied the sash that circled her waist. He recognized the wild fibers and zigzag design as one woven by Mohawk women.

"Where did you get this?"

"It was a gift from Sabra."

"A gift to us both," he said, smiling. He stepped away and walked to the leather-hinged door. Opening it, he hung the sash on the outside and then closed it again. "The gift of privacy," he added.

Jessica tilted her head to one side, eyeing him curiously.

"To outsiders," he explained, returning to her side, "the belt upon the door is a symbol of our need to be alone."

Jessica's cheeks warmed with a misty blush. "Really, Fletcher, you mean we must announce to the whole village that we . . ." Her voice trailed off as Fletcher dipped his head and nipped lightly at her neck. "That we . . ." she began again, only to gasp with pleasure as his hands slipped her dress and shift down past her shoulders.

"That we are making love?" he inquired mildly, bending low to draw his tongue around her nipples in slow, lazy circles. "If you like, darling, I'll remove the belt and we can take our chances."

"No," she said breathlessly. "I would have you to myself tonight."

"You would?" he asked, looking up to flash her a smile.

"Yes," she said, fingering the delicate quillwork of his vest. "I've learned much about the Mohawk way of life in the past few days—the power of a shaman's dreams, the magic housed in every living thing of the wilderness, the dances and games . . . I can even ride a horse now. Great Knife says I'm very skilled."

"Oh, you are, love. You are."

She swallowed, inhaling the night-forest scent that clung to him. "But I've not yet learned what it means to be a Mohawk's woman."

"I can teach you that," he replied, and unfastened her skirt and petticoats, skimming his hands down her sides until her clothing fell to the earthen floor.

"A Mohawk woman comes to her husband eagerly, naked and proud of her beauty. She offers herself freely to her brave. She knows she has a right to feel . . . all the power of his love." As he spoke in a soft, soft whisper, he traced patterns upon her skin with his finger, circling her neck and breasts.

His touch felt like a feather skimming over her flesh, making her tingle and long for more. As he drew tiny arrows down her belly, she shivered and asked, "Is this some means of Mohawk torture?"

Quiet laughter rippled from him. "There is a legend," he continued, his fingers still light, still teasing, "of an Indian maid who so loved her brave that, when death claimed him, she turned into a swallow."

Feeling dizzy, Jessica asked, "Why?"

"So she could mate with his soul in the night sky."

Lulled by the softly spoken legend and the relentless wing-beats of his touch, Jessica felt a hot fountain of wild, wanton feeling bubble up in her. "You make me feel that kind of love, Fletcher," she whispered.

He grasped her around the waist and she arched backward, to feel his lips warm upon her breasts. "But," she continued shakily, as his mouth burned a trail even lower, "I would hold you earthbound tonight."

With that she straightened slowly, laying her hands on his cheeks and staring at the poetic beauty of his face. Eager to send him a message of her savage yearning, she reached beneath his breechclout and pulled at the leather thongs of his leggings.

"I think," she said, moistening her lips, "that these garments are ever so much more sensible than trousers."

"Aye, trousers are more difficult to make. Sewing through even the softest of hides with bone awls or thorns is hard work."

"I wasn't speaking," she said, "of the ease of *sewing* a breechclout." Her hand brushed his manhood and she heard him gasp. In moments he was as naked as she and they sank together to the hide-clad mat beside the fire, consumed by a fire of their own, generated by the shared heat of passion.

As she tilted her hips upward to received her husband, Jessica noticed the fan of their shadows on the bark-clad walls. The stark, overlarge figures heightened her desire; they melted together and became a single powerful image that only faded when the force of Fletcher's love embraced her in dark, velvet rapture.

Chapter 21

Jessica basked in late autumn sunshine as the *River Hawk* sailed down the Hudson toward Albany. Flame-colored leaves drifted to the water, spinning on the surface. Squirrels and martens scurried on secretive missions along the riverbanks, while overhead, flocks of honking geese winged southward. On either side of the river the mountains reared, dwarfing the sloop.

The splendor of the land enhanced Jessica's newfound contentment. Colors shone brighter, images stood out more vividly, sounds echoed more sweetly. This land had nurtured and challenged and shaped Fletcher Danforth into the man she loved, and it was fast becoming a part of her too.

She sat on deck, watching Fletcher as he took his turn at the tiller. A breeze that held the first chill breath of winter eased her bonnet brim. He had cast off his frock coat and waistcoat; his sleeves billowed in the light wind. Sunlight touched his face and the dark copper V revealed by his open shirt.

Their eyes caught and held; Fletcher flashed an easy smile. 'I thought you'd be below, napping the day away with Kitty and Adele.''

The warm undercurrent of his remark brought a blush to her cheeks. The previous night had afforded them much pleasure and little sleep. ''The day is too fine to waste napping,'' she said. But the weather was not all that kept her away from the well-appointed cabin. Gabriel was below too, playing chess with Mr. Elphinstone. Gabriel, whose narrow-eyed glances and hostile silences had become insupportable.

Jessica drew her mind from that worry, determined that

the troubled boy wouldn't ruin their trip to Albany. Lovingly she turned her attention back to her husband, eyeing the unruly cropped hair curling at the back of his neck, the relaxed set of his shoulders as he worked the jib sheets.

Since that day at the quarry, the strain between them had found a sweet, satisfying release. Yet the release gave birth to a new tension, a breathless anticipation of the honeyed shadows of nighttime, when daily trials and pressures gave way to the luxury of lovemaking.

With the naive eagerness of new love, Jessica had thought physical intimacy would heal all the wounds of betrayal and mistrust. She'd given all she had to him. She'd done things to his body that brought blushes to her cheeks and groans to his lips. She'd lavished him with tenderness and constancy and love from the deepest part of her.

In turn, Fletcher was an ardent, considerate lover whose inventive touch brought her shattering pleasure. Still, he remained a deeply troubled man. Even when their bodies were fused in ecstasy, when she whispered feelings too deep to speak aloud, he kept his worries to himself, hidden from her, as if he could not quite trust the depth of her love.

Looking ahead at the river, Jessica sighed. She willed herself to be patient. Deep scars took time to mend. Sybil's betrayal, Fletcher's imprisonment, Gabriel's rejection, the slow decimation of the Mohawk . . . none of these things were Jessica's doing.

Yet she wanted to share the burden, to shoulder it willingly, because she loved her husband. A sudden burst of affection propelled her to his side.

"How much farther to Albany?" she asked, dipping her head beneath the sheets.

He kept his eyes trained on the river. "We'll land in less than an hour."

"What is Albany like, Fletcher? I saw so little when we last passed by, on our way up from New York."

"A town like any other. Two churches, a library, a courthouse, warehouses." He paused and his jaw tightened. "A military post."

"Fort Orange," Jessica said. She understood his tension. "Fletcher, if you'd rather not go to town . . ."

"It's all right. I've business to conduct and it's about time you met our neighbors.'' One side of his mouth lifted in an ironic smile. ''Besides, my nemesis, Colonel Macon, has been transferred to Fort Niagara—as a 'reward' for his outstanding record of service to the Crown.''

He spoke easily and Jessica felt a welling of hope. Slowly, gradually, Fletcher seemed to be shedding the past. One day he might be free of those five lost years, the humiliation and isolation of imprisonment. She reached out and touched his sleeve.

At that moment, Gabriel emerged from the cabin. His eyes fastened on his father first, then on Jessica, and then on her hand on his arm. His burning look stayed there until, chagrined, she took her hand away.

''Have you shamed poor Mr. Elphinstone at the chessboard again, Gabriel?'' she asked brightly.

He seemed to look straight through her, then lifted his eyes to Fletcher. ''I was going to see if you needed any help at the tiller,'' he said. ''But I guess you're busy. . . .''

Jessica felt a jolt of anger. Of late Gabriel had turned manipulative, offering Fletcher his companionship, but only conditionally.

Her first impulse was purely selfish. She wanted to stay with Fletcher; their every moment together was precious, for every moment tightened the bonds uniting them.

Looking up into his face, she read conflict there and her heart constricted. She began to move away. ''I'd best go below and see if Kitty is up from her nap.''

Fletcher sent her a grateful smile and drew her against him. ''Not so fast, wife,'' he murmured, and kissed her lightly. ''I'm not sure I want to share you with Albany.''

''There's a part of me,'' she whispered, ''that I don't share with anyone but you.'' Turning toward the cabin, she brushed past Gabriel. The boy's scathing stare chilled her.

She tried not to resent him. He was a boy of twelve, still grieving for his mother. But, dear God, what would it take to make him see that their happiness as a family depended on his acceptance of her?

She had hoped that, with time, Gabriel would overcome his anger and grief. Yet of late he'd grown worse. His smoldering silences were no longer merely weighty; they were smothering. His rare comments were no longer pointed; they were poisonous. True, he was more open to Fletcher, but he'd slammed the door on Jessica. Meals were strained affairs. Daily lessons had become less pleasant than tooth extractions. Gabriel took offense at the mildest correction, the kindest criticism.

The deterioration of her relationship with Gabriel had everything to do with her new happiness with Fletcher, she knew. He resented the warmth that flowed between them, their intimacy, the little kindnesses Fletcher showed her.

Sighing, she renewed her determination to remain a steadfast wife to Fletcher. And if Gabriel continued to be obstinate, she would try even harder to be his friend.

Only when Jessica stepped from the *River Hawk* onto the Albany landing did she realize how little she'd missed city life. The river port was a far cry from the teeming, smoky bustle of London, but Albany was indisputably a thriving town.

The streets were long and wide, some paved, some crowded with livestock and market-goers, blanket-wrapped Indians and buckskin-clad traders. Built in the old Frankish way, with gable ends outward, neat houses with Holland tile slates lined the avenues. Two churches flanked the marketplace.

High on a distant precipice loomed the brooding citadel of Fort Orange, the Union Jack flapping in the autumn breeze. She cut a quick glance at Fletcher. His face hardened when his eyes lighted on the fort, but when he looked back at her, he seemed at ease.

"Shall we go to the town house?" he asked, offering her his arm. "It's but a short walk. I'll send for our things to be brought up later."

The porch-wrapped Danforth house nestled like a small, elegant jewel in the manicured finery of a tiny dooryard. Kept by an elderly Dutch couple, the house had been built by Fletcher's father.

"It's charming," Jessica said as they crossed the lime-washed porch and stepped inside. Privately she preferred the wild, endless acres of Holland Hall to the pristine order of the town house.

Fletcher smiled, then turned to Kitty. "You don't remember this place, do you, sweetheart?"

Kitty shook her head vigorously, sable ringlets bobbing. "Have I been here before, Papa?"

He knelt beside her and gave her shoulders a squeeze. "You certainly have. You were born in this house, right up those stairs in the front bedchamber."

Her wide eyes traced a path up the polished oak staircase. "Oh!" she exclaimed, throwing her arms around his neck. "I like it here already!" Seconds later she was pulling Adele up the stairs. "Madame, come see where I was born."

"I remember," Gabriel said, angling his shoulder against Jessica to make it clear he was speaking only to his father. "Mama always liked the town house better. You gave her an emerald ring the day Kitty was born."

Needles of envy pricked at Jessica's heart. It was not the first time Gabriel had made reference to Fletcher's devotion to Sybil. Deep down she knew the marriage had been unhappy, that Sybil's prejudice against Fletcher's mixed parentage had driven them apart.

Still, Fletcher had given Jessica few gifts, and those half jokingly: the bosom bottle at Bartholomew Fair, the mountain crystal at the quarry. She hated herself for wanting something as tangible as baubles. What she truly desired was a gift from the heart of her husband, something that spoke of love.

Fletcher cleared his throat. "Yes, well, I was very pleased to have a daughter."

Jessica's cheeks warmed. Was that the difference between herself and Sybil? If she gave Fletcher a child, would he then consider her worthy of gifts and praise?

She threw off her darkening mood and squared her shoulders. "I should like to freshen up and change my gown," she said. "Mrs. Fairfax expects me promptly at four."

A half hour later Fletcher joined her in the unfamiliar master bedroom. Jessica was struggling with the buttons of her crewel-worked dimity gown.

"Allow me, madam," he murmured as he fastened the row of buttons at her back.

"Thank you," she said, turning to him. "I suppose I could

have asked Nan to come from Canajoharie, but I didn't have the heart to tear her away from Great Knife.''

He rested his hands lightly on her shoulders, one finger toying absently with a stray curl. ''You're wise in not asking her to divide her loyalties.'' His handsome face grew troubled; the lines around his eyes deepened. ''I wish Gabriel would learn that from you,'' he finished.

Jessica nodded and leaned her cheek against the crisp front of his shirt. ''I simply don't know what to do about him, Fletcher. He's become so temperamental, so resentful of me.''

''Aye, he is that. The Mohawk view moodiness as a sign of the onset of manhood.'' The shadow of a smile appeared on his lips. ''You might be interested to know that he's gone to buy books to send to Kateri.''

She drew away, staring. ''Books? What sort of books?''

Fletcher laughed at her incredulous expression. ''A primer and a speller. It seems he's determined to teach the girl to read. He admitted they've been secretly working at it for some weeks now.''

Sudden affection for Gabriel surged through Jessica. For all his faults, he did possess certain endearing qualities. She shook her head slowly. ''I never know what to expect from him. Not so very long ago he detested Kateri.''

''She's a tenacious little thing,'' Fletcher said, chuckling. ''I couldn't say whether she's truly won him over or only worn him down.''

''I wish I knew how she did it,'' Jessica whispered. ''I am beginning to feel he will never get used to the idea that I'm a permanent fixture in his life.''

Only after the words were out of her mouth did Jessica realize what she'd said. Fletcher's quick, indrawn breath told her he, too, was affected by her remark. His hands strayed downward to span her waist.

''Jessica . . . are you saying you're with child?''

The dull, flat tone of his voice caused her heart to lurch. He did not want a child from her. ''No,'' she snapped, pulling away from him. ''I'm quite sure that I am not.''

He drew her back against him, his sigh of relief stirring the curls at her neck. ''Don't be angry, Jessica,'' he murmured. ''Much has changed between us; we've grown closer, aye, but a new child would complicate . . . matters.''

''It's Gabriel, isn't it?'' she asked.

He nodded. ''The boy's resentful enough as it is; he's not ready for a new brother or sister. The Indians stand to claim much of my attention too. I'll be going to Fort Stanwix in the spring to help negotiate a treaty with the English.''

Jessica couldn't fault his reasoning; neither could she still the yearning in her heart. ''What about you, Fletcher? Are you ready for a baby?''

He wrapped his arms around her and inhaled very slowly. ''I don't know. I just don't know.''

Pulling away, she swallowed the lump in her throat. ''I'd best be going,'' she said and picked up her reticule.

As she walked toward the door, she longed for him to pull her back, to hold her and tell her he wanted her to stay— baby or no baby, despite Gabriel's resentment and Fletcher's mission to preserve the Iroquois nation. But he merely held the door for her and followed her down the stairs.

Gabriel burst into the house, his face alight with boyish eagerness and his arms burdened with a stack of new books. The sparkle disappeared from his eyes when he spied Jessica.

She forced a smile. ''I'm off to the Fairfaxes', Gabriel. Would you like to come? You haven't seen Daniel since the wedding.'' Shrugging and lowering his gaze, he tried to look disinterested. ''We wouldn't expect you to take tea with us,'' she said coaxingly. ''You and Daniel will be free to concoct whatever mischief you please.''

Gabriel looked at Fletcher, who grinned and spread his hands. ''You're welcome to join me this afternoon, son, but I doubt you'd enjoy it. Elphinstone and I will be locked away in a roomful of corn factors, haggling over prices.''

Gabriel pulled a face. ''I suppose I could visit Daniel,'' he said at last.

Walking to the minister's house between Fletcher and Gabriel, Jessica felt proud. People here knew her husband and obviously respected him. Dutch burghers, merchants, and town officials called greetings and doffed their hats. The friendly acceptance warmed her. A person could start in America with a clean slate; success was not measured in terms of birth and bloodlines but in achievement and character.

Fletcher pointed at a stately brick house—a mansion, more rightly—at the head of the main street. "That's the Guyver house. You'll meet half the town there at tonight's soiree."

Jessica smiled up at Fletcher. Once, she might have balked at the idea of appearing before so many strangers, but as Fletcher's wife she could be confident of their welcome.

"I'm off to join Elphinstone at the counting house," he said when they reached the Fairfax house. He gave Gabriel's shoulder a gentle squeeze. "I'm sure you and Daniel will find plenty to talk about."

"Yes, sir," Gabriel replied.

"I'll see you at suppertime," he said. "Give yourself plenty of time to prepare for tonight." He grinned at Jessica. "Wear that gold taffeta gown Jade made you, love. It makes the most of your charms."

Pleased, Jessica turned her face up for a kiss. From the corner of her eye she saw Gabriel staring with a gaze wrought in stone. The look spoke of resentment and something more unsettling—something coldly calculating, perhaps. . . .

But as they mounted the steps to the minister's house, she chided herself. He was only a boy, after all.

A friendly looking butler greeted them. "Mrs. Fairfax is in the drawing room," he said and smiled at Gabriel. "If you'll wait here, young sir, I'll send for Master Daniel." Gabriel nodded curtly and gave Jessica a dismissive glance as she turned to follow the butler.

In the drawing room, the reverend's wife rushed toward Jessica with outstretched hands. "There you are, Mrs. Danforth. I wondered when your new husband would bring you to town. My, don't you look lovely."

"Thank you." Jessica touched her cheek lightly to Mrs. Fairfax's. "It's good to see you again."

"Lovely," Mrs. Fairfax repeated, stepping back to assess Jessica's gown. Although her glance was measuring, her light-colored eyes sparkled. "My friends were simply green with envy when I told them you'd brought your own mantua maker from London. Tell me, where *did* you find Miss—ah—"

"Akura. Jade Akura."

"Yes. Her name is as rare as her talent with the needle. Surely she must have trained in the best salons in Paris."

Jessica tried to keep the humor from her voice. "Jade has indeed had French training."

"I knew it," Mrs. Fairfax said, clasping her chubby hands. "Do sit down, Mrs. Danforth. I'll ring for tea."

Jessica sat on a delicate upholstered bench as Mrs. Fairfax lifted a tiny crystal bell and shook it.

"I hope you'll find Albany to your liking," she said. A maid in starched apron and cap brought a tray of tea and biscuits. "Of course, we must seem terribly provincial compared to London."

"I was never all that enamored of London," Jessica said.

"Well, I assure you we are a most upright community, nothing like the tumbledown trading posts one finds upriver." The lady shivered delicately.

Jessica poured cream into her teacup. "What is it you find so objectionable about the trading posts?"

"They are rife with Indians, dear, and—oh my." Mrs. Fairfax fussed with the lace of her fichu. "Well, of course I don't mean to say *all* Indians are objectionable. Your husband is a fine example of how one can rise above one's origins."

Instinctively Jessica readied a challenge to the remark; politeness held her back. "He is also a fine example of a Mohawk brave, Mrs. Fairfax. I happen to admire his people."

"Of course, and you're terribly loyal to do so. Good breeding shows, my dear. I daresay you'll soon learn there are many less admirable Indians. The men at Two Rivers drink to shocking excess and the women, well, they . . ." Mrs. Fairfax looked left and right to ascertain that no one was within earshot. "They *sell* their cheap favors to the fur traders."

Another challenge, and Jessica had to hold back her temper again. Her color rose high. "That's because the English have taken their lands and their men can no longer hunt to provide for them."

"I do think, Mrs. Danforth, that a Christian would find a decent way to earn a living."

"A person doesn't always have a choice."

The minister's wife fixed her with a keen look. "Well, I for one do not approve of such goings-on."

As Jessica cast about for a less volatile topic, a clatter of footsteps sounded in the foyer. She looked toward the doorway to see Gabriel run by, followed by a slender, light-haired boy. She smiled at them.

"Wait," Daniel said, "I should go in and pay my respects to your father's wife."

Gabriel scowled. "I don't know why you would want to. For that matter, I don't know why your mother's feeding her tea. Perhaps Mrs. Fairfax is not aware she's entertaining a whore."

Jessica's smile froze. Her heart stilled.

The words were spoken too loudly, too deliberately, to be directed solely at Daniel. Gabriel meant the minister's wife to hear as well.

Mrs. Fairfax gave a mortified squeak. Only vaguely aware of her actions, Jessica heard the rattle of her own cup as she set it in its saucer. Her mind screaming with outrage, she shot to her feet and stalked to the foyer. Gabriel was already darting toward the front door. Red-eared, hands shoved in his pockets, Daniel gaped at her.

"Gabriel." Her voice rasped with shock and fury. "Come here."

The boy stopped and turned stiffly. His eyes blazed. "Yes?" he inquired, malevolently polite.

"I demand that you apologize to both me and Mrs. Fairfax."

He squared his shoulders and sent her a defiant look. "No," he said softly.

Jessica's mind swam with turmoil. Gabriel's remark deserved more than a mild chastisement. And his refusal to apologize could not be tolerated.

"What you have said is beyond the bounds of propriety and foul beyond belief." She swallowed and tried to keep her voice from shaking. "You will make your amends and you will do it now."

Gabriel's jaw jutted stubbornly outward. "It's wrong to keep company with the reverend's wife and pretend to be something you're not."

He's only a boy, Jessica told herself. He's only a boy. . . . She forced the thought into her mind, repeating it over and over to stave off a blast of temper. But the chilling, vengeful look in Gabriel's eyes was not at all childlike.

"Come on, Gabe, you shouldn't have said that," Daniel stated, wringing his hands.

"Shouldn't I? Why don't we ask your mother?" Gabriel turned to Mrs. Fairfax, who stood in the doorway, her fan flipping agitatedly. "Don't you think, ma'am, that you have a right to know you're being deceived? She's a whore's bastard and a whore herself."

"Gabriel!" Jessica cried.

The lady's fan fluttered even more wildly. "Sweet merciful heavens . . . I feel faint. . . ." Looking more confused than ever, Daniel went and put his arms around her.

Dear God, Jessica thought, staring at Gabriel. *He knows.* She could see the truth in his gaze and in the confident tilt of his chin. How had he found out? She tried to speak, but all that came out was a half-choked sob.

"You see," Gabriel said, "she cannot deny it."

To Jessica's mortification, a scattering of servants began to gather in the hall.

The presence of an audience seemed to further ignite Gabriel's malevolence. "This woman trapped my father into marrying her. Had she not done so, she'd still be a London whore."

Jessica took a step forward. Her tongue felt thick as she tried to speak. "Gabriel, don't. Please, you don't know what you're saying . . ."

He swaggered on the polished wood floor. "Deny it, Jessica *Darling,*" he challenged.

"Oh my," Mrs. Fairfax said, breathing rapidly and leaning against her son. "What can this be about? Surely you'll not allow the boy to speak so, Mrs. Danforth."

"It's best you learned the truth now, ma'am," Gabriel snapped. "Before you gain the reputation of keeping company with a loose woman."

"Gabriel, for the love of God, hold your tongue," Jessica whispered urgently.

"I've held it long enough," he shot back. "You think you've managed to fool everyone, but you haven't. *I* know what you are. You're a London whore!"

"What a horribly outlandish tale," Mrs. Fairfax cried.

"Daniel, go to your room. I won't have you listening to such sordid talk." Reluctantly the boy shuffled away. At a stern look from their mistress, the servants did likewise.

Gabriel backed toward the door. "Mrs. Fairfax, it's for you to decide what to do about entertaining a whore in your home." As if sensing Jessica's burning impulse to slap the scathing look from his face, he turned on her. "You're not fit to take my mother's place!"

The sudden tears in his eyes burned away the violent impulse but not her sense of shock and betrayal. "I understand that," she said. "But I will not excuse your behavior."

"I don't care if you never forgive me!" he shouted and fled.

Jessica's throat was full of knots; her face was drained of all color. Woodenly she turned to Mrs. Fairfax. "I must go," she choked out, moving toward the door.

"Oh my, you cannot leave yet," Mrs. Fairfax pleaded. "Surely I deserve some explanation for being subjected to such foul gossip in my home. You must assure me Gabriel's accusations are false. I have a position to uphold in this community and cannot abide the slightest hint of scandal. . . ."

Jessica heard the woman's words as if from a long way off. One part of her clamored to deny Gabriel's accusations, to dismiss them as the vindictive rantings of a resentful stepson. Yet another part of her balked at addressing the issue with a stranger, even to save her reputation.

"I must go," she repeated. "Good day."

"But, Mrs. Danforth, if you cannot explain, then I can only conclude . . ."

Jessica didn't wait to hear the rest. Let the righteous Mrs. Fairfax conclude what she would. The need to deal with Gabriel was far greater than the need to reassure the minister's wife.

She found him in an orchard at the outskirts of the town. She stood several paces away from the boy, her nerves still too raw to step closer.

Staring hard at him, she folded her arms, hugging herself against the awful hurt that welled up from the pit of her stomach.

"I suppose you're going to tell Papa," he said dully, kicking at an old, wind-fallen apple.

Jessica gulped the cold, apple-scented air. Should she tell Fletcher, make him see his son for what he was? Could she deal the man she loved such a blow? "Why do you think that?"

"Why shouldn't I?" he shot back. "Mama always—" He broke off and turned away.

Jessica knew what he'd left unsaid because she was coming to know the sort of woman Sybil Danforth had been. Jessica didn't want to be like that; never would she use a child as a pawn in an adult power struggle.

"I expect you to tell him yourself, Gabriel."

He looked up. The pain in his eyes told her why he had maligned her. His unwillingness to share Fletcher's affections, his misguided loyalty to his mother, and his guilt over Sybil's death had driven him to it.

"I won't," he stated.

Although the refusal chilled her, Jessica tried with all the generosity of her nature to forgive Gabriel. But she could not. She had been forced to live with the boy's bitterness; now Gabriel would have to learn to live with hers.

Harvest time was a season for coming together, for distant neighbors to renew their friendships, for factors and farmers to meet and drive their yearly bargains on timber and wheat. After a six-year absence, Fletcher was back among them for their annual celebration. The whole family had been invited, but it appeared only Jessica and Fletcher would be going. The affair would run way past Kitty's bedtime, and Gabriel, who was welcome to go, had given no indication he would.

Jessica forced herself not to dwell on Gabriel's betrayal. Tonight should be a night of triumph for Fletcher. She was determined to give it to him. Her heart filled with pride and affection as he handed her into the coach that would drive them to the Guyvers' house.

She pushed back the leather curtain on the coach window to see Kitty and Adele standing on the porch waving farewell. Kitty dipped an adorable curtsy and Jessica felt a rush of warmth. The little girl had blossomed under the Frenchwoman's tutelage, just as Jessica had once done. Then, thinking of Gabriel, she realized how fragile things were in this family, how dependent each was on the others for security and happiness.

As if summoned by her troubled thought, Gabriel appeared, pressed and dressed for the evening, looking not in the least contrite but perhaps a little apprehensive. Jessica stifled an exclamation of surprise as a footman held the coach door wide for the boy.

"I was beginning to think you'd decided not to come," Fletcher said, smiling. "Where've you been, son?"

Gabriel shrugged. "Just . . . around." Relief was evident on his face. He stared, amazed, at Jessica. Despite her assurance to the contrary, he'd obviously expected her to report his misconduct to Fletcher.

"You look the perfect gentleman, Gabriel," Fletcher said. "Doesn't he, Jessica?"

"He . . . certainly does." She forced the words from her throat and settled back against the cushions. Gabriel sat in the opposite corner, pretending to be absorbed by the activity of the footman securing the door and signaling to the driver. She could not help admiring the fine figure he cut. In a snowy shirt and waistcoat of navy superfine, buff breeches and buckle shoes, he looked like a younger and more angelic version of his father. How ironic, she thought, that nature could favor such a child with outward beauty.

Gabriel caught her look and glanced sharply away. Darkness shadowed his face, but Jessica took heart from the fact that he could not meet her eyes. Perhaps, after all, he did have some scruples. Unfortunately, the boy's pangs of conscience came too late.

The coach lurched forward. The swaying motion sent Jessica careening against Fletcher. He put his arm around her shoulders in an easy motion. "Did you have a nice visit with Mrs. Fairfax today?" he asked.

From the corner of her eye Jessica saw Gabriel stiffen and realized how little he trusted her. No doubt he still expected her to betray him to his father.

"It was pleasant enough," she said. Until Gabriel informed the minister's wife that you had married a whore, she added silently.

"You're a poor liar," Fletcher said.

Jessica's heart froze. Had he found out already?

"I know you better than to believe you enjoyed an afternoon of tea and town gossip with Mrs. Fairfax."

Relieved, Jessica relaxed against him. Fletcher brushed his lips against her temple. "I wouldn't have subjected you to her, but her opinion holds sway over the entire town. Winning her favor will assure you of a proper welcome from our neighbors. I do want you to feel comfortable here."

"Of course." She slid a glance at Gabriel. "I'm sure by now Mrs. Fairfax has a very pronounced opinion of me."

"How did you and Daniel get on, son?" Fletcher asked.

Gabriel only shrugged and was spared from answering by their arrival at their destination.

Jessica offered up a silent prayer for patience as she entered the opulent brick house. She clung to Fletcher's arm and hoped the minister's wife had kept her counsel.

The Guyvers' ballroom was a whirligig of color, a symphony of sound. Candles blazed in glass and brass fittings, flickering against hand-painted walls and casting a glow of gold over the dancers. Ladies in their finery skipped through a reel, weaving among well-dressed men. Laughter and murmured conversation drifted in and out of the musical strains. Searching the room, Jessica could see no sign of the plump Mrs. Fairfax. She stifled a sigh of relief and fixed a smile on her face.

Gabriel sauntered off to a corner to join a gathering of boys. Nearby, a bouquet of girls peered at them and tittered behind their diminutive fans.

As their hosts, Chester and Olivia Guyver, greeted them, Jessica renewed her determination to make the evening a success for Fletcher.

"Shame on you, Mr. Danforth," Olivia chided, "hiding this lovely creature from us for so long."

"I can see why you wanted to keep her to yourself," Chester Guyver said, his glance at once good-natured and admiring. Briefly he clasped Fletcher's hand. "It's been a long time, my friend. Unfortunate, what happened to you. High-handed officers of the Crown treading on decent citizens . . . one day they'll go too far, by God—"

"Chester, please," Olivia murmured. "This is hardly the time to discuss politics."

Her husband looked chagrined. "Sorry, Livvie, but I don't like the militia breathing down our necks. Macon's like to start another Indian war."

Fletcher's face grew rigid. "Macon? I thought he'd been reassigned to Niagara."

Chester nodded. "The father was, but his son, Emory, still scouts around with his patrol, intimidating Indians."

"That will do," Olivia insisted. "Stop this talk so I can introduce Jessica to our neighbors." Both men bowed and swept aside to let their wives pass.

Jessica received a warm welcome from all the revelers, garnering compliments and bestowing greetings, feeling more and more at ease. When Fletcher came to claim her for a dance, her mood was light. "I practically had to fight my way to you," he remarked. "Every gentleman present is demanding the favor of a dance."

She laughed up at him as they whirled to the lively melody. "You're exaggerating," she accused.

His hand tightened around her. "Ah, Jessica, you seem so happy tonight."

"I am happy." In spite of your son. "Don't you understand what tonight means to me? These people want to be my friends. Aside from the girls at Madame's, I've never had friends before."

Behind his neatly drawn neckcloth, his throat worked convulsively. His eyes searched hers. "You ask so little, Jessica. I could almost believe—"

"You've monopolized her long enough, Danforth," Chester Guyver said, neatly stepping between them. "Give the rest of us stricken swains a chance."

Fletcher backed off good-naturedly. Intrigued by his unfinished statement, Jessica watched him over Chester's shoulder. Rather than seeking another partner, her husband took a glass of brandy from a tray and followed a group of men into an adjacent withdrawing room.

Long before all the guests had arrived, her feet had begun to ache from dancing. But the pain was welcome, as it attested to her acceptance. She smiled happily at her current partner, Clarence Little, a jovial man who owned a local rope manufactory.

"You'll have to bring the little girl around to play with my four daughters," Clarence said.

"Of course, Mr. Little, that would be . . ." Jessica let her voice trail off as she felt the prickle of a hard stare at her back. When they turned with the music, she found her gaze locked with the cold, disapproving eyes of Mrs. Fairfax.

She tried to keep her smile in place and her feet in step, but it was difficult, for Mrs. Fairfax began moving through the crowd with surprising speed, murmuring to this one and that one like a venomous creature spreading poison.

Jessica had no doubt about what was being said. At first the gossip was a vague ripple, a sinister undercurrent eddying beneath the music and chatter. But the ripple gathered strength and Jessica's prickly sensation grew more pronounced. Helplessly she danced in the arms of her new acquaintance as she witnessed her own social demise.

Jessica wasn't surprised when Mrs. Little, pale and tight-lipped, approached. Sparing only a curt nod for Jessica, she addressed her husband. "There you are, Clarence," she said. "I've been looking for you."

Nonplussed, he stopped but kept his hand covering Jessica's in formal minuet style. "My dance with Mrs. Danforth isn't over, dear."

His wife consumed him with a glare. "It is now, Clarence," she whispered fiercely and claimed his arm in a white-knuckled grip.

Jessica watched him being led away, his wife leaning up to whisper in his ear. A cold feeling of hopelessness settled like a block of ice in the pit of her stomach. All over the ballroom, outraged wives were murmuring similar tales into the ears of their husbands.

Dazed by shock, Jessica stumbled from the dance floor. Obviously Mrs. Fairfax had believed Gabriel's lies. Now they'd all heard; she saw it in the sudden flip of a lady's fan, in a gentleman's stiff back discreetly turned to exclude her from conversation. She heard it in the incessant buzz of whispers that began to sound like low thunder in her burning ears.

She snatched a cup of cider from the tray of a passing servant and drained it in two gulps. Casting her stinging eyes about the ballroom, she sought to bring her pain and shock into focus.

Laughing with Abel Cates, a wheat factor, Fletcher reentered the ballroom. She didn't want him to see her distress, for he would surely question her. Retreating into the shadows of a fluted wooden pillar, she prayed the gossip wouldn't reach his ears.

Apparently no one had the gall or courage to confront Fletcher Danforth. In fact, Jessica recognized pity on the faces of his friends. "Poor chap," she imagined them saying behind their hands, "trapped by a loose woman. . . ."

"And to think," said a female voice nearby, "I was going to invite her to our quilting bee tomorrow." Standing by the pillar, Jessica froze.

"The only place she ought to be invited," said another voice, "is on the next packet to London!"

Jessica fought the urge to face the women, to explain. But she couldn't answer the accusations because to bring them out in the open would be the same as admitting at least some of them were true. With a choked sob, she ducked her head and stepped down three stairs to the lower ballroom.

She found herself staring into the stone-blue eyes of her stepson.

Gabriel stumbled back, wary of Jessica's accusing gaze. Instantly her shock turned to fury, her pain to biting anger. Before he could retreat, her hand shot out and captured his wrist.

"You're coming outside with me, *Master* Gabriel," she said, pulling him toward a long bank of French windows. He must have sensed how close she was to losing control, for he made no resistance as she propelled him out into the autumn night.

"We have much to discuss," she told him once they stood alone on the verandah.

"I have nothing to say to you," Gabriel snapped, a caustic look in his eyes.

"Then stand there and listen. We are going to talk about what you have done to me—to this family."

"I've done no more than speak the truth when everyone else—even Papa—is living a lie." Gabriel leaned toward Jessica, his eyes narrowed to malevolent slits.

A chill breeze gusted across the verandah, picking strands

of curls from her coiffure. "How long have you known?" she asked, battling a sick feeling.

"Since we landed in New York. The day . . . of the gin. I pretended to be sleeping and I heard you and Papa talking about it."

"Oh, God." Jessica's shoulders slumped. Fletcher hadn't known about her virginity then; the scathing things they'd said to each other must have been branded on the boy's mind.

Angry as she was, she felt a ripple of sorrow for Gabriel. In addition to the turmoil of losing his mother, he'd carried this weight of misinformation about his stepmother as well.

"I wish you'd come to me, Gabriel. I could have explained—"

"I never needed an explanation. You condemned yourself out of your own mouth."

"It happens that what you heard is not entirely true. My mother was a courtesan, yes, but I was not." He snorted in disbelief. She flung her hands in the air. "Why did you say those things to Mrs. Fairfax today? Everything was getting better for us—for the whole family."

"Oh?" He lifted one eyebrow, looking much like Fletcher. And yet something about him struck Jessica as unfamiliar. His face was drawn in lines of anger and vengefulness. Sybil, Jessica thought, and a cold prickle shot down her spine. She was confronting Sybil's ghost.

"Kitty and Madame have each other, Jade and Nan have their redskin lover, and you and Papa . . ." He choked, screwing his face into a mask of disgust.

". . . both love you."

"That's a lie! He wants me to accept a stranger for my mother, and you . . . you want him to yourself."

"Gabriel, people don't love to the exclusion of all others."

"People in this family don't love at all."

"You're wrong, Gabriel. So very wrong. What did you hope to accomplish by blurting out a lot of unqualified indecencies to the minister's wife?"

"My mother taught me to speak the truth."

"Your mother taught you to hate!" A scalding rise of temper boiled away her control. "Sybil was not a saint, Gabriel, and it's time you stopped pretending she was. She betrayed

your father and took you and Kitty from him. What sort of
woman would do such a thing?''

Gabriel seemed not to hear. A bitter smile haunted his lips.
''You've always been jealous of her,'' he said softly. ''But
you'll never be good enough for Papa, not like she was.''

''Your father and I care for each other.''

''He doesn't care for you, and that's why you're so jealous.'' His eyes raked her from head to toe. ''Mama was my
father's wife, the woman he loved. But *you* are only his
whore.''

Goaded by his words and her own uncertainties about
Fletcher, Jessica felt reason desert her. She sucked in her
breath and drew back her hand. . . .

Fletcher propped his shoulder against a pillar and searched
the ballroom for Jessica. She wasn't among the colorful couples on the dancefloor, nor could he see her at the elaborate
buffet along one wall. She must be in the ladies' room, he
decided.

Pride filled his heart and an indulgent smile shaped his
lips. His adorable, clever wife had obviously enchanted everyone present; she'd probably danced her dainty little slippers off.

Triggered by affection, a jolt of understanding blazed
through his mind and left him shaken. It wasn't just pride,
or admiration, or even lust that made him feel this way.
Something much deeper had crept into his soul, warming him
in places he didn't know he had. Something a Mohawk called
orenda; something an Englishman called love.

His mind spinning with the impact of this new awareness,
Fletcher slumped against the pillar. He knew now that the
feeling had been building within him from the very start, that
he could no more stop it than he could stop the sun from
rising at daybreak.

All that remained was to tell Jessica what was in his heart,
to ask her to stay with him and be his wife and mother to his
children. Forever.

Nearby, a few men were gathered; through a fog of elation
Fletcher heard one of them mention Governor Amherst. He
blinked, remembering the letter he'd sent requesting to be
allowed to ship Jessica back to England. A slow smile spread

across his face. He didn't have to purchase the governor's cooperation now, because he'd won the right to love Jessica.

His mind clamored with impatience. His eyes stayed fastened on the figured walnut archway leading to the ladies' retiring room, but several minutes had passed and she still hadn't appeared. When Olivia Guyver stepped beneath the archway, he approached her.

"I seem to have misplaced my wife," he said, grinning at his hostess. He nodded toward the door. "Is she within?"

Looking discomfited, Olivia opened her fan. "No, Mr. Danforth, she is not. I believe I saw her step out on the verandah."

"Thank you," he murmured. He left her staring and walked quickly through the French windows into the chilly night air. He longed to shout his love to the moon . . . but he wanted to tell Jessica in private first.

Light from the ballroom slanted across the gardens illuminating Jessica . . . and Gabriel.

They seemed oblivious to his approach. They were leaning toward each other, speaking in low, strained tones.

He opened his mouth to greet them. The words died in his throat when he saw Jessica whip back her arm.

The slap she landed on Gabriel's cheek rang like thunder in Fletcher's ears.

Chapter 22

A cold wave of rage roared through Fletcher, scattering the sparks of warmth that had sent him searching for his wife. By the time he reached Gabriel's side, the imprint of her hand was already blossoming on the boy's cheek. Beneath that livid stain of red, his son's face was white as chalk.

"My God," Fletcher said, "what in hell is going on here?" He sharpened his stare at Jessica.

She stared back through wide, misty eyes. Her bosom rose and fell rapidly, her breath coming in painful gusts. Somehow she seemed just as shocked as he. "Gabriel and I had words, but—"

"Papa," Gabriel said in a choked voice, flinging himself at Fletcher. Through muffled sobs he cried, "Papa, she said such horrible things about me . . . and Mama."

Fletcher's eyes flashed to Jessica. "Is this true?"

He expected her to defend herself. Instead, she flinched. Her beautiful, troubled face had drained to paleness; her hands gripped the folds of her gown.

"She hit me!" Gabriel persisted, stepping away to aim his tear-drenched gaze at Jessica. "You saw her hit me."

Her eyes flared for an instant. "I'm sorry," she said, her voice a hoarse, throbbing whisper. "I lost my temper and for that I'm sorry."

"Don't bother saying you're sorry." Gabriel wheeled on Fletcher, eyes blazing. "Nothing has been right since you married *her*. Everything would have been just fine if *she* weren't around!" He backed away and disappeared into the ballroom.

Staring after him, Fletcher felt a huge welling of pain. Like a moonstruck fool he'd come to tell Jessica that he loved her. But she had undermined that feeling; she'd probably shattered any chance of a new closeness with Gabriel as well. The hurt gave way to an anger that seared Fletcher's eyes and throat. He turned on her. "I hardly trust myself to speak," he said very, very quietly.

She reached for his sleeve as if seeking something to lean on. He yanked his arm away.

"Then just listen, Fletcher," she said softly. "Please." Her eyes glimmered with tears. "Gabriel and I argued. I . . . I was provoked."

"Damn it," he snapped, tasting bitterness in his mouth, "what could a twelve-year-old boy possibly say to cause you to lose all control? He doesn't understand he's being cruel by comparing you to Sybil."

Jessica blinked. She drew a deep breath and straightened her shoulders. "What he said . . ." She paused, swallowed, and moistened her lips. ". . . is best left unrepeated."

Fletcher shook his head, despising himself for having ignored the problems between his wife and son. For weeks he'd cherished an image of Jessica, an image she'd shattered. There was a side to her he didn't know, a darker side she hid beneath her sweetness, her outgiving nature. His stomach clenched into a knot. "All along I imagined you were trying to understand the boy; I thought you knew how fragile he is."

"I do, Fletcher, but Sybil is the one who made him that way. Why is this my fault?"

"You've been feeding his resentment, confusing him, filling his head with destructive things about Sybil."

"I have not. I—"

"If you once had a chance of getting through to him, you don't now."

"For God's sake, Fletcher, will you let me speak?" Jessica's voice rose as she dashed away her tears. "I made a mistake, a serious mistake. Much as you did in London, when you blamed me for the welt on Gabriel's cheek."

He inhaled sharply. "A rather clumsy topic for you to bring up, my dear. Because this time you are indeed to blame. Gabriel got over Hester's slap and doubtless will survive yours, but he'll never forget that you maligned his mother."

"Perhaps it's time he faced the fact that his mother was not perfect."

"It is not your place to make that judgment," he said coldly, trying desperately to close his heart to her wide, moist eyes, her lovely mouth drawn into a sad, tender line. The woman he'd come so close to loving was a stranger now. A sense of betrayal gripped him . . . a betrayal all the more bitter because he'd tasted it before, and this time his emotions ran deeper.

Jessica wrung her hands. "Gabriel's more troubled than I ever suspected; he knows things—"

"He seems to know more about your true nature than I do," Fletcher snapped.

Jessica stumbled back, slowly shaking her head. "You know me well, Fletcher, but you just don't trust what you know."

Hope, gossamer thin and wavering in the chill gusts of anger, pushed its way into his mind. Gabriel had misbehaved in the past. . . . "What caused the slap?" he asked softly.

She avoided his eyes and said nothing.

Fresh anger sent his hope spiraling away. "Don't you owe me an explanation? You're denying me the chance to be a father to the boy."

She flung her head up. "Then talk to him, and give him a chance to be a man."

He turned away, loosening his stock. Of course he'd speak to Gabriel, but damn it, he wanted Jessica to talk to him too.

"Fletcher. I love you," she said.

The words barreled like dark thunder into his mind. Only moments ago his heart would have soared to hear her profession of love. Swiveling to face her, he clenched his fists in frustration.

"You use the phrase at your convenience," he told her, his voice icy.

She began to blink rapidly. "I do love you, Fletcher, and I have for a very long while—" She broke off and stared at his angry face. "Are you saying you don't believe me?" Her bewilderment hardened into anger. "Just what do you think has been happening to me these past weeks? Why in God's name do you think I've come to your bed, given you a part of myself I never thought to share with anyone, tried to be your wife in every way?''

''I never questioned it,'' he admitted gruffly. *I was too damned happy to question it.*

She let out her breath in a wavering sigh. ''Damn you,'' she said wearily. ''From the very start you've refused to listen to me; I see no point in trying to convince you of anything. Since you've allowed Gabriel to come between us, perhaps now he can afford to be magnanimous. Perhaps he'll accept you. That's all you've really ever wanted, isn't it?'' She swallowed hard. ''I think we should go home.'' Her voice was flat, barren of emotion. She began walking away.

Confused, Fletcher followed. A painful choice pressed on his mind. If he kept Jessica as his wife, he could lose the beginnings of love and loyalty he'd sensed in Gabriel. Yet if he let her go, he'd lose the only person who had ever made him truly happy.

But was his happiness an illusion after all? Reality was Jessica willfully driving his son from her; reality was the crack of his wife's hand against his son's face. Could he love a woman who, for whatever reason, had mistreated Gabriel?

Whether or not he could was no longer the question. Driven by five years of guilt, years he owed Gabriel, Fletcher admitted the commitment of blood ties was greater. All the laws of man and nature delegated his first responsibility to his son, the fruit of his loins, the heir to his fortune.

The next day as they returned home the weather turned, and autumn died on a gust of icy wind. Winter crept over the acres of Holland Hall, turning the grass brown, stripping the trees bare, chasing the birds to warmer climes. Seated in a window alcove, Jessica stared through the wavy panes of glass, feeling as bleak as the season. The night before had been filled with a strain beyond enduring, with silent pain over a hurt too raw for either to speak of.

She wondered if their love could withstand the rift. Would Fletcher close his heart, his mind, and his bedroom door to her as he had in the early days of their marriage? Or would he force an admission from Gabriel?

She put aside the silhouette she'd been cutting and drew her knees up to her chest. An early winter hadn't stripped the manor of its beauty, only transformed it, sharpened the lines of the hills and muted the colors of the river and fields.

But the wild splendor of the land seemed distant this morning, unapproachable. Before Gabriel's betrayal, Jessica had felt a sense of kinship, of belonging. Now she knew only a stabbing sense of loneliness for her husband.

Leaning back, she fought the urge to go to Fletcher and explain what had happened in Albany. A little more time, she cautioned herself. Just give Gabriel a little more time to give in to his conscience and talk to his father. Yes, she decided firmly, the admission must come from the boy; otherwise he'd learn nothing, except that Jessica was capable of informing on him just as Sybil had.

She picked up the silhouette she'd recently finished. As William Johnson had requested, she had created a crest for his family. An eagle volant soared above a sheaf of wheat; maple leaves surrounded the device. Although unofficial, the crest would please Sir William; it denoted strength and bounty and permanence. In lieu of a motto, Jessica had penned Johnson's Mohawk name beneath the crest: *Warrahiyagey*—He-Who-Does-Much.

A flash of sunlight glinted off the river. Setting her work aside, she rubbed the frosted window with the side of her hand. The masthead of a vlieboat appeared above the water. Glad for a diversion from her bleak thoughts, she fetched her cloak and went out to meet the mail packet.

Staring down from his window, Fletcher spied Jessica leaving the house. Her cloak flapping and her peach-gold curls tossed by the winter wind, she looked small and vulnerable, yet, oddly sturdy and brave. Unbidden affection surged through him, driving away the chill of last night's quarrel. He realized they'd both acted in anger and spoken rashly. Now that the initial shock had dulled, he knew he should have been willing to listen to her, even if it meant facing a disquieting truth about his son.

It was a truth he'd denied for too long. For weeks he'd been aware that Jessica and Gabriel weren't getting along, yet he'd buried his concern, telling himself that strain between a woman and her stepson was common.

After last night, however, he knew that their problems ran

deeper than that. Gabriel seemed determined to drive Jessica away, and Jessica was faced with the untenable choice of yielding to the boy or asserting her own place in Fletcher's heart. Fletcher considered the pain that must be causing her and he realized how difficult it had been for her.

Damn, his reaction last night hadn't made things any easier. He owed it to her to wrest an explanation from Gabriel, as much as he owed Gabriel the chance to face whatever it was he'd done to earn that slap.

A knock sounded and Mr. Elphinstone entered, bearing a packet of letters. "The vlieboat just brought these, sir," the clerk said.

Absently Fletcher took the letters and shuffled through them. A crest embedded in a green wax seal caught his attention. Tensing his muscles to keep his hands from trembling, Fletcher ripped open the letter from the duke of Claremont. Ignoring the bank draft that drifted to his desktop, he scanned the message.

His sudden burst of laughter startled Mr. Elphinstone, who jumped. "Mr. Danforth? What is it, sir?"

Chuckling, Fletcher handed him the letter and the draft. "For our paper mill," he said. "It seems Madame Severin wishes to invest." Relief trilled like liquid warmth through his veins. At last he understood Jessica's correspondence with the duke of Claremont. She hadn't been seeking a way out of her marriage; she'd only been trying to help Adele transfer her pension to his own keeping.

Fletcher's smile disappeared though, when he read the next letter—Amherst's response to his plan to send Jessica back to England. The royal governor was only too happy to accept the sum Fletcher had offered, to agree to Jessica's expeditious and discreet return to London.

Fletcher dropped the letter onto the desk. Amherst would have to do without the bribe.

"Where is Gabriel?" he asked Mr. Elphinstone.

"I believe he's in the conservatory, sir, building another kite."

Fletcher started for the door. They had something more important to build now.

* * *

A blast of winter air, sharp with the smell of cold, enveloped Jessica. The dock was already the scene of a small flurry of activity. Tenants eager for news and city-made goods gathered at the pier. Jasper stood ready with his lists and bills of lading.

Wide-cut sailor's trousers flapping in the wind, the skipper approached Jessica and doffed his woolen cap. "Good morning, *mevrouw.*" He held out a letter. "I forgot to give this to your husband's clerk a moment ago."

"I'll take it to him." She smiled, subduing an inner tremor at the idea of facing Fletcher after last night. "Mercy has a nice pot of soup on, and a crock of cider as well. You and your crew are welcome."

"Thank you, *mevrouw.*" The skipper turned his ruddy face into the wind. "Likely this is the last we'll get of Mercy's cooking until springtime. The river'll soon be iced over. You will have to rely on the foot post through the winter."

"Until next spring, then," she said and hurried to the house.

Fletcher's room was empty, his desk littered with the rest of the mail. Jessica laid the letter on the top of a stack of papers. She glanced down and her name leapt out at her.

Jessica's heart grew still as she recognized the signature of the royal governor. She hesitated, tried to pull her eyes away, but found she could not. Her fate could well be decided by the contents of Amherst's message. She had a right to know.

Phrases stared from the page, stabbing her heart: *a mutually agreeable arrangement . . . accept the sum you have offered . . . your wife's expeditious and discreet return to London . . . return to London . . . return to London . . .*

Sickness welled in her throat. Until this moment Fletcher's plan had seemed a distant threat, a storm hovering on the horizon, something that could be overcome by their newfound love. Yet now she had proof that she meant nothing more to him than a means to an end, a legal ploy to be abandoned now that her usefulness in securing his children was over.

Stunned and hurt, she felt the urge to hurl the letter into the grate. Then a cold and dreadful calm overtook her and she left Fletcher's room, unable to bear the faint forest scent of him that lingered in the air. Stiff and numb, she returned to her own room, where she gripped the bedpost and clung to it as if to anchor herself.

"No." She spoke with quiet resolution and the stillness of the empty room was shattered. "No," she said again more loudly. For months she'd allowed herself to be buffeted by Fletcher's commands. But not this time, she decided with chilling certainty. Not ever again.

She walked to the window recess and picked up the crest she'd created for Sir William. Although his desire for a resident artist in his self-made town had been half joking, his invitation had been sincere: *The trail's so clear a greenhorn could make it.*

Fletcher Danforth and London be damned.

Minutes later, a saddlebag stuffed with the barest necessities sat on Jessica's bed. Thoughts of Fletcher's plan left a bitter taste in her mouth, a hollowness in her breast. He wanted her gone, to be sure; he'd cold-bloodedly chosen her destiny. In that he would be disappointed. His pride sought to dominate; her pride rebelled.

The idea of leaving Adele and Kitty brought a throb of regret to her chest. She would miss her friend's Gallic good sense and her stepdaughter's buoyant good humor. Letters, perhaps occasional visits once she'd established her independence, would have to suffice . . . if indeed Fletcher would permit any contact at all. Desertion, she knew, was grounds for divorcement.

The thought sobered her. Resolution felt cold and hard. She would miss the feel of Fletcher's arms around her, the sudden flash of his smile. . . . Time and distance would free her of the pain.

As she tucked the fat saddlebag into a chest at the end of her bed, a loud noise echoed up from the entrance hall. Curious, she went downstairs to find a wide-eyed footman staring at a disheveled Indian youth.

"Billy!" Jessica hurried forward and clasped his cold hands between hers. "What is wrong?"

"I must see Shadow Hawk," he said in halting English. His troubled eyes darted wildly around the entrance hall.

Sensing his urgency, she led him on a quick search through the house. Fletcher and Gabriel were in the conservatory, speaking in low, hushed tones. A kite lay on the table between them and Gabriel was knotting a tail from a length of cotton.

Jessica swallowed a sudden lump in her throat. The guarded look on the boy's face told her he was keeping his secret well. Perhaps she'd been a fool to think last night's rift could be healed by the truth. Perhaps Gabriel's lies and manipulation were indeed more powerful than her love and commitment.

Billy strode forward and spoke rapidly in Mohawk.

Fletcher turned, stiffened, and spat something that sounded like a curse.

Jessica glanced at Gabriel. His eyes were locked on his father, his face pale. His hands worried the knots of the kite tail.

"There's trouble at the trading post at Two Rivers," Fletcher said to Jessica, his face grim. "Three Mohawks have been accused of murdering a white trader and the local militia is about to hang them."

He turned to Gabriel. "Son, I must go."

Gabriel blinked. The fabric made a rending sound as he ripped it with a savage tug of his hands. "You're always leaving me for those damned redskins." He shouldered past his father, past Billy, and nearly collided with Jessica. His tear-bright eyes shot sparks at her. "Nothing's been right since my mother died," he stated.

"Damn it, Gabriel, you're being selfish," Fletcher snapped.

An urgent plea erupted from Billy.

Jessica's heart melted at her husband's desolate face. Despite her anger at his plan to send her away, she couldn't bear that look of pain.

She stepped forward and touched his arm. "You must go, and quickly," she said. "You have no choice." She glanced at Gabriel, who was studying the floor. "I . . . I'll talk to him, try to make him see. . . ." She searched Fletcher's eyes for a message of affection, gratitude, anything to give her hope that he'd change his mind about Amherst. But she saw only determination in the harsh lines of his face.

"I'll be back as soon as I can," he said.

And I, she thought bleakly, will not be here when you return.

Gabriel leaned over the dock, staring at the reflection of his face in the river. He searched his tear-drenched eyes and blotched cheeks. There lived, hidden somewhere in that face, a flaw that made Papa leave him time and time again.

Standing, he picked up the new kite and told himself that Papa had to go; it was an emergency. But why did it always have to be Papa?

Scowling, he attached a ball of string to the kite and tossed it into the air. It drifted to the ground. If Papa hadn't left, he'd be here to help. Damn those redskins, Gabriel thought. Papa considered them more important than his own son. To Gabriel the Indians at Two Rivers were just faceless, soulless nonentities. He refused to think about the Indians of Canajoharie, who had taught him to hunt and fish and track. Because to think about them would be to give them faces, names, souls. To make them as human as he. Would they really be hanged? Could one of them be his kin?

"Gabriel?" a voice said softly behind him.

Oh, God, it was Jessica. Probably come to gloat. "Go away," he growled over his shoulder and pulled on the string to retrieve the kite.

She lingered behind him. "I was very disappointed that you made things so hard on your father," she said. "He didn't want to leave any more than you wanted him to go."

"Oh yes, he did. He always leaves me," he said hotly, still not looking at her. "If it's not the Indians, it's one of the tenants, or Kitty . . . or you."

"Not me, Gabriel. Not after what you did yesterday."

He felt something inside him grow soft. "You didn't tell Papa what I said to Mrs. Fairfax." He turned and she was wearing a long foot mantle and holding a saddlebag.

She took a step toward him. Holding his breath, Gabriel clutched the kite in front of him.

"I explained that I wanted you to have a chance to tell him yourself, Gabriel. You're mistaken about me, you know; what you overheard that day was a misunderstanding. Fletcher didn't know me then. . . ."

"You didn't deny it! Mrs. Fairfax would have believed you, but you never denied you were a—a—"

"A whore?" She spoke softly, yet a steely edge had crept into her voice. "Why don't you say it, Gabriel? You found it easy enough to say to the minister's wife."

He hunched his shoulders defensively. He hated the guilt

growing inside him. But it kept creeping around his feelings, strangling his bitterness until he no longer knew how he felt. "If I was so wrong, why didn't *you* tell Papa?"

"Because it would have hurt him . . . almost as much as it hurt me."

Gabriel found himself wishing she *had* told. Then it would be so much easier for him to lock her out of his heart. Instead she'd kept the secret, even when keeping it had driven Papa away from her.

A faraway memory stole into his mind. He recalled his mother, beautiful and stern and hard faced, bringing him before Papa to report the slightest transgression. Oh God, he thought, Mama would have told.

Jessica was trying to creep into his heart, into that soft, traitorous place that recognized her as good and kind, a woman who wanted to love him . . . just as he wanted her to—

"G . . . get away from me!" he cried. "I hate you! I hate Papa, and the Indians and . . . and everything!"

Jessica drew herself up. "Stop it," she said cuttingly. "I've had quite enough of your tantrums." Shouldering her saddlebag, she grasped his arm and began hauling him, the kite still clutched in his hand, toward the stables.

Oh God, he thought, what was she going to do now? Afraid and scornful, he said, "I'm not going anywhere with you."

"I have tiptoed around you long enough, Gabriel Danforth. You will come with me, and you will come now. We're going to Two Rivers; if we hurry we may catch up with your father. He's tried to shield you from the agony of his people. But they are your people too. It's time you accepted that."

Feeling grim, Fletcher rode up the stump-dotted main road into Two Rivers, where the waters of the Hudson and the Mohawk met and clashed. Billy hid upriver, away from the anti-Indian frenzy gripping the town.

Fletcher passed a jumble of thrown-together buildings and an assortment of loafing soldiers and frontiersmen and their unwashed women. The noonday sun leaked timidly through an iron gray bank of clouds.

He clenched his jaw. He knew better than to expect cooperation from the captain of the militia. Too many times the English forgot that they were allied by treaty to the Mohawk.

As he dismounted, a thudding sound like sentry drums wove through the gusting breeze. Suddenly he realized the rhythm was no trick of the wind but a distinct pounding.

With a stone-cold heart and iron-hard resolve, Fletcher approached a knot of people. In their center, a picket detachment was at work constructing a gallows.

"Where is your commanding officer?" Fletcher demanded.

A soldier jerked his thumb toward a shed. Fletcher saw the captain swaggering from the building. His heart seemed to stop, then began hammering with new force.

Emory Macon wore his ruined eye and white-streaked hair like badges of bitterness.

Fletcher stepped into his path. Recognition, then rage, darkened the redcoat's good eye. A mocking smile slid across his face. "Ah," he said, and his breath was sour with the reek of stale rum. "My gallant rescuer. Damworth, was it?"

"Danforth. Fletcher Danforth."

"Of course. Well, if you'll excuse me, Mr. Danforth, I've business to attend to." He nodded at the picket detachment. "Carry on."

Fury curled inside Fletcher. "If you string those men up," he said very quietly, "it'll be the last thing you do."

Macon made a clucking sound with his tongue. "You do enjoy acting the champion, don't you, Danforth? Well, save your damned half-breed breath. I know how to deal with Indians. They don't understand mercy."

Fletcher swallowed a gulp of bitter rage. He knew the sort of man Emory Macon was. Small-minded, terrified of the grandeur of the American wilderness and the ferocity of the Mohawks' code of personal freedom, he sought to subjugate through intimidation.

Fletcher forced himself to speak calmly. "I don't suppose you've bothered to hear their defense."

"They have no defense. The barbarians don't even speak the King's English. But it matters not. They tortured a man to death in cold blood. Have a look at them. They're spattered with English blood."

At a wave of his hand, guards brought forth the prisoners.

Fletcher saw three dazed and terrified Mohawks, chained together at the ankles, stumbling as they were prodded toward the gallows. Two were men of middle years; the other a boy no older than Gabriel. All three were indeed bloodstained. The sight seemed to whip the soldiers into a murderous furor.

"There they are, the heathen, the ones what done in poor Stiles," one man snarled, spitting on the ground. "Hangin's too good for 'em." Grumbles of agreement rippled through the crowd.

Pushing past Macon, Fletcher addressed the Indians in their own tongue. "I am Shadow Hawk. The English soldier says you have killed a man named Stiles. Is this true?"

The eldest thrust his chin high. "We did. He died a whining coward's death."

"Why?" Fletcher demanded, as angry at the Mohawk's fatal defiance as he was at Macon. *"Why?"*

The brave's shoulders sagged. "The white man flattered us, he promised us good trading, he fed us firewater. And when his evil drink made us sleep, he forced himself on my wife. Only her final scream of agony woke me." A single tear slid with lonely dignity down the leathery cheek. The brave spread his hands. "Yes, Shadow Hawk, I wear the blood of the Englishman. But I wear the blood of my wife as well."

Nausea buzzed through Fletcher's veins. "Does the English captain know this?"

"Yes. But he and the other one"—the brave gestured at a portly sergeant—"tossed my wife's body in the river." Grief furrowed his haggard face. "Now her soul will never join the sky."

Fletcher's throat burned with bile as he turned to face Macon. "So this," he said, "is your brand of justice."

Macon raked a hand through his silver-streaked hair. "These are savages, I tell you, barbarians. The atrocities they commit cause civil English blood to run cold."

Noble words, Fletcher thought, coming from a man whose people conducted public executions, paraded severed heads on pikestaffs, wore leggings made of Indian flesh.

"They all but stripped the man to his bones," Macon added.

"Aye, but what did you do with the body of the Mohawk woman Stiles murdered?"

The men nearby fell silent. The captain sucked in his breath and his face pinched into a furtive mass of scars. "What body?" he asked with elaborate nonchalance.

Confused whispers rose from some of the men. Knowing he'd touched more than one English conscience, Fletcher eyed the tradesmen and soldiers. "How many of you are aware of Macon's trick?" he demanded. "How many of you know about the other body, the Indian body, the body of a woman?" He fixed a merciless glare on the trembling sergeant. "These Mohawks did slay an Englishman, didn't they, sergeant? Because an Englishman raped and murdered a Mohawk woman." The soldier gulped audibly and stepped back. The murmuring grew louder.

"Restrain Danforth," Macon ordered urgently.

The guard who clamped his fingers on Fletcher's arm looked as mean and cold as any seasoned Indian hater. Fletcher forced himself to stand still, unresisting.

"So you'll risk all then?" he asked Macon quietly. "Your commission . . . your life?" His voice was cold with deadly promise.

A flash of uncertainty glinted in the captain's good eye. Then he conquered it. "The hanging is to proceed as ordered," he cried half hysterically. He spun toward Fletcher and brandished his sword. "And this Indian-loving bastard will never live to tell the tale."

Fletcher felt the cold bite of steel in his neck.

"But his son will." A quiet, resolute voice shattered the stunned silence.

A jumble of shock, pride, love, and fear surged through Fletcher. Only the captain's blade kept him from leaping forward.

"My God," he whispered hoarsely. *"Gabriel."*

Disheveled, wind burnt, and fiercely defiant, Gabriel stood facing the soldiers. Oddly, he held a somewhat ragged kite in front of him like a shield. Good God, Fletcher thought, he brought along the damned kite.

"Let my father go," Gabriel said.

Fletcher felt Macon's blade quiver. From the corner of his

eye, he saw the sergeant shuffle his feet. "Go on there, Cap'n, ye can't just do in Mr. Danforth, an' surely not his boy."

A few others mumbled agreement.

"Fools!" Macon shouted. "Would you have me send forth these devils to murder still more of God's Englishmen?"

A youthful private stepped forward. "You didn't tell us about the woman, Captain."

Fletcher aimed a frost-bitten glare at Macon. "The law is not on the side of the Mohawks you planned to murder, but it is certainly on my side," he said.

"Let 'em go," the sergeant pleaded. "All of 'em. We don't want no trouble."

Macon's eyes swung desperately to his men. "He's bluffing!"

Taking advantage of the captain's teetering control, Fletcher knocked the sword away with a huge sweep of his arm. Macon went sprawling to the ground; Fletcher was on him before he could right himself. Macon squirmed and produced the blade of a small, pointed spontoon from his belt. He stabbed upward with the short blade.

Fletcher caught Macon's wrist in a viselike grip and held it until the spontoon fell from his bloodless fingers. Still Macon struggled.

Full of remembered rage over Running Wolf's death and fresh fury at the murder of the Mohawk woman, Fletcher clamped his forearm across the redcoat's neck. "Just give me one more excuse, you bastard," he growled.

Macon's eyes bulged. "My father should have had you hanged when he had the chance," he rasped.

"You're alive today, Macon, because your father had the sense to show mercy. I may not be so reasonable."

A tear of frustration squeezed from Macon's good eye. "Enough," he whispered at last. "Please . . ."

Fletcher stayed long enough to see the three braves speed away into the woods, frightened but free. As the picket detachment dispersed, he turned to his son.

"Gabriel, how did you get here? Why did you come?"

"I wanted to fly my kite with you." Looking suddenly shy, he took Fletcher's hand. *"Rake'niha,"* he said in flawless Mohawk. "You are my father." Gabriel's solemn face glowed with relief at abandoning his anger.

His heart singing, Fletcher gathered his son close, nearly crushing the kite. "Ah, Gabriel," he said thickly, "I never thought to hold you again."

The boy pulled back, his eyes shining. "Jessica brought me, Papa. She made me come."

"Jessica's here?"

Gabriel nodded. "Not exactly here. She's waiting with the horses down at the ford. I . . . I wanted to do this alone." He took his father's hand again. "I was wrong about Jessica too, as wrong as I was about the Indians. I want her to stay with us."

A gust of wind whipped down from the mountaintops, but Fletcher felt warm inside. He didn't pause to question the boy; nor did he question the sudden upsurge of love for his wife. His feeling for her had never died, had only lain hidden under confusion and distrust. "Let's go," he said.

They left the trading post, Fletcher leading his horse and Gabriel clutching his kite. With a whoop of happiness, he tossed it into the air. The winter wind caught it and sent it soaring above the treetops, higher, higher, until it became one with the pale gray sky.

As she urged her pacer toward Johnson Hall, Jessica felt the agony of her bitter choice. Yet despite the hurt, she clung to the certainty that her choice was right: she would not accept Fletcher's form of banishment.

She'd stayed at the ford long enough to ascertain that Fletcher had averted the trouble at Two Rivers. Unnoticed by soldiers, traders, and Indians, she'd hovered at the periphery of the crowd and seen Gabriel run to his father. She'd witnessed Fletcher's victory over the captain's prejudice and cruelty. She'd watched the militia disperse and the Mohawks flee. And then she, too, had fled.

She slowed her horse and turned for one last look at Two Rivers. Squinting at the winter-dark sky, she saw a bird caught in a eddy of wind.

No, not a bird . . . a kite. A dry sob of joy and despair was wrenched from her throat and froze in the bitter air. Gabriel's kite. Although too disillusioned to cast herself in the role of fairy godmother, Jessica claimed the triumph for her own. A triumph to savor during the long, lonely years ahead.

Remembering the wild ride she and Gabriel had made to Two Rivers, she urged her horse to a gallop again. They'd spoken little, but apparently her tirade had jolted the boy into a new awareness of Fletcher—as a father, a man, and as a Mohawk as well.

Now freedom and a new life awaited her. Then why did she feel as if she'd lost everything?

Leaving the question unanswered, she studied the sky. The bank of gray clouds looked heavy and coldly threatening.

Hurry, she told herself, ducking her head over the pacer's neck to avoid a low-hanging branch. Cold air seared her lungs. Hurry. . . . Johnson Hall lay ten miles distant.

She put her riding crop to rare use. The pacer stretched its neck and surged forward, iron-clad hoofs striking sparks on the flinty path. Jessica offered a word of silent thanks to Great Knife, who had schooled her so well in riding.

An icy wind pricked at Jessica's eyes. A blurry shape appeared suddenly on the trail. Terror tore a scream from her throat as she recognized the arched spine and glittering yellow eyes of a wildcat, its mouth drawn back to expose its fangs.

The cat snarled. The horse reared and Jessica lost her seat. An equine scream tore through the wilderness as the horse bolted, leaving Jessica bruised and winded on the frozen forest floor.

Stunned and breathless, she watched the slinking shape of the wildcat melt into the woods. Above the pounding in her head, she heard the pounding of her panicked horse's hoofs and felt totally alone.

She lay still, assessing her body's damage. She discovered a few bruises and an aching coldness, nothing more. Dragging herself to her feet, she began walking northward, toward Johnson Hall.

Fletcher and Gabriel galloped southward, toward Albany. Fletcher fought a rising tide of panic and a plummeting sense of loss as images flickered through his mind like disjointed scenes from a stage tragedy. He imagined Jessica reading the letter he'd left carelessly on his desk, imagined her look of pain and shock, and pictured her fleeing, spurred by Amherst's letter and last night's quarrel. Albany was her logical destination, for there she could embark on the mail packet bound for New York.

Stung by the bitter wind, he cursed himself for having ever contemplated sending her back to London. Fool that he was, he'd styled himself master of her destiny, denying her any voice in her own fate, alienating himself from the woman with whom he wanted to spend his life. He could just as easily have ripped the heart from his own chest.

Sickened and feeling hollow, he glanced over his shoulder at his son. Gabriel rode as if driven, as if he, too, were terrified of losing Jessica. Pray God they would reach Albany before the season's last vlieboat bore her away, out of their lives forever.

Relief swelled inside Fletcher when, on reaching town, he spied the bobbing mast of the mail packet. Tucked into the harbor, the vessel was being laden with furs and winter stores. In the main square, people poured out of the English church. Belatedly Fletcher remembered today was Sunday.

As they approached the boat, Gabriel came abreast of him. "Do you think she's on board, Papa?"

"She has to be. She must be." Fletcher dropped to the ground and tossed his reins to Gabriel. Waving his hand, he strode toward the skipper of the vlieboat. Five minutes later he returned to Gabriel.

Worry gnawed at his gut. "She's not here," he said, remounting. "The skipper hasn't seen her since early this morning at Holland Hall." He glanced at the church, where people lingered to gossip after services. It was starting to snow. Little stinging flurries darted and danced through the air. Half to himself, he said, "Perhaps she'd ask for shelter from someone . . . the Fairfaxes . . ."

"No," Gabriel said, his voice so low it was almost swallowed by the wind. His face stained scarlet, his eyes bright and moist, he added, "She'd never turn to them."

Like the bitter wind, unease seeped into Fletcher. "Why do you say that, son?"

He swallowed hard. "Because they wouldn't welcome her, Papa, and it's all my fault." He became fiercely angry, accusing. "You should have made me tell you why she slapped me. I deserved it, and worse, yet she didn't tell."

"Tell me what? Damn it, Gabriel, Jessica's missing. We don't have time for chitchat."

His face desolate, the boy faced him squarely. "When we were in New York, I heard you and Jessica talking. You said she used to be a . . . whore in London."

"Oh, my God." Fletcher felt sick. It was hard to remember he had ever thought such a thing of Jessica.

"I know now it's not true," Gabriel said quickly. "but I believed you . . . before. Yesterday, I told Mrs. Fairfax you pulled Jessica from a whorehouse." Anguish etched his face. "I'm s-sorry."

A flash of understanding sped through Fletcher's mind. "By God," he muttered, "if ever a slap was earned . . ."

"I know, Papa," Gabriel said. "I'd do anything to take back what I said."

Anger and guilt settled over Fletcher. Anger at Gabriel for his cruel words, at himself for not trusting Jessica. Guilt, because now she was gone and the snow was beginning to fall harder, thicker. And he had no idea where to look.

He nudged his horse toward the church. "We'd best ask around. Perhaps someone has seen her."

The stoop was crowded with worshippers, gathered despite the weather for their usual round of Sunday gossip.

Awkwardly Fletcher explained that his wife was missing.

Avidly the townspeople listened. Mrs. Fairfax sniffed. "How terribly unfortunate for you, Mr. Danforth. But then, this cannot be too much of a surprise, considering the type of woman you married."

"The type of woman I married?" He spoke quietly, although anger roared inside him. "The type of woman who wouldn't lower herself to answer your spiteful gossip."

Gabriel leapt from his horse and ran forward. "She is good and kind," he shouted loudly enough for all to hear. Wheeling on Mrs. Fairfax, he declared, "You never should have listened to me, never! I was wrong about Jessica. Couldn't you see that?"

Olivia Guyver turned to Mrs. Fairfax. "Really, Margaret, you mean you credited the claims of a young boy?"

Chagrined, Mrs. Fairfax sniffed. "She didn't deny it," she said sulkily.

Gabriel burst into tears and suddenly he looked like a small child, bereft and frightened. "Help us find her, please, or she'll never know how sorry I am."

Fletcher watched as shock and shame crept over the faces of the people. His anger at Gabriel began to dissolve, to be replaced by pride. His son had done wrong, but he wasn't afraid to admit it publicly.

Spurred by the boy's outburst, the men sprang into action, bundling their families home and calling for their horses.

The thickening curtain of snow added urgency to the hastily launched plan to comb the area. Fletcher's heart pounded with fear; his throat tightened with regret. *Where had she gone?*

Hoofbeats sounded in the street. Fletcher turned. Through the slanting blizzard, he saw Billy on his pony, leading a riderless horse.

Jessica's horse.

Fletcher galloped to Billy's side. Shivering convulsively, the young brave spoke rapidly in Mohawk. "I found the horse north of Two Rivers, but I could not find your wife; snow has covered the path."

Fletcher dismounted and ripped open the saddlebag attached to the pacer's rig. With a lurch of his heart, he extracted a few articles of clothing, some biscuits, a hunting knife. His hand plunged deeper into the bag. The glass bottle he'd given her. The mountain crystal. She'd kept all the gifts he'd given her . . . and they were damnably few.

She'd planned very well indeed. But she hadn't planned on an unseasonable snowstorm. Or on losing her horse.

A London-bred woman couldn't know the viciousness of the upper New York winters. Storms blew in from the west, gathering force over the lake regions before dumping destruction on the river valleys. In such blizzards a man could lose his way on the path from house to privy.

His fingers fumbled through the rest of her belongings, seizing the familiar fruitwood case. She'd ridden out of his life. She might be racing toward death.

The thought made him tremble and he dropped the box.

Her silhouettes and scissors spilled onto the ground, scattered by the wind.

With cold, frantic fingers he retrieved them one by one. As the images flicked past, Fletcher's gut clenched. He saw pictures of himself and the children and the people of Holland Hall, idealized portraits of the life Jessica longed to embrace. Fragile paper, fragile dreams, dashed hopes . . . Shadows of what might have been.

Oh God, he thought, she dreamed of being happy with me.

The last of the pictures was a curious rendition of a family crest. The white light of winter showed an eagle volant surrounded by maple leaves. Beneath the crest, Jessica had penned the word *Warrahiyagey*—He-Who-Does-Much.

Something in Fletcher's mind locked into place. His heart pounding with hope, he thrust the silhouettes into the box and ordered Billy to take charge of the horse.

"Thank God," he muttered, mounting.

"What is it, Papa?" Gabriel asked. "Can you tell where she went?"

Fletcher nodded. "To Johnson Hall."

"But why would she go to Johnson Hall, Papa?"

"Because she was afraid I'd send her back to London." Fletcher squinted at his son through the driving snow. "You'd best get to the town house before you freeze to death."

Gabriel sat stiffly in the saddle. "I'm coming with you, Papa. I want to help find Jessica."

Fletcher understood the boy's aching need, a need that almost matched his own. As a father and son divided they had wronged her; as a father and son united they would find her.

"Come along," he said, wheeling his mount. "We've several miles of hard riding ahead." He glanced up at the snow-blurred sky. "And less than an hour of daylight, if that."

Jessica kept her eyes trained on the bleak light of the westering sun. West, that was the direction Johnson Hall lay. But was she really facing west, or was it some trick of reflected light that made her think so? The unexpected snow-storm obscured the sky. She forced the panic from her cold-numbed mind and commanded her frozen feet to trudge onward.

The wind tore at her foot mantle, defying her efforts to

eep it wrapped tightly around her. Snow stung her face until
he no longer felt her cheeks and lips, and her eyes were
early blinded. Doggedly she tucked her chin and nose down
nto the damp-smelling fur collar and pulled the hood for-
vard.

Nearby, the Mohawk River moved sluggishly beneath its
overing of ice. Rock edged its banks, but Jessica forced
erself to follow the uneven path. She kept walking even after
er feet lost all sensation. She continued even when her eyes
eased to see anything but white snow and vague shapes.
low far to Johnson Hall? How far?

Too far, her weary, frozen body decided.

She could go no farther.

Sinking to the ground, she marveled at the depth of the
owdery snow. Absently she plunged her gloved hand into
he whiteness, digging her fingers into a crevice. Her hand
merged holding the crushed remains of a wildflower. Staring
t it, she sighed. Only a few months ago this had been a
ummer garden of grass and blooming flowers; now it was a
vinter wasteland of snow and barren wilderness.

She buried her face in her cloak until a tingle of sensation
eturned to her cheeks. When she lifted her head, she found
er vision had cleared somewhat. The mountains reared high
ver the river. The scene of stark majesty captivated her.

How ironic, she thought, as a curious lethargy seeped over
er, that the land she'd grown to love would treat her so
arshly. She had embraced the mountains and the valleys with
ll her heart, only to feel now the icy kiss of winter. So, too,
vith Fletcher. She'd offered him her love; he'd driven her
way.

The thought made her angry. Shaking off the urge to suc-
umb to the seductive nothingness of the cold, Jessica jolted
› her feet, ignoring the pain. Defiance sent new warmth
ooding through her veins.

She refused to allow her life to end simply because she'd
iled to win a man's love.

Drawing strength from her resolve, she focused her snow-
lurred eyes, lowered her head, and hurried onward. Surely
was but a few more miles.

The wind howled and hurled great gusts of snow against
e rock face above her. A pile of snow dropped with a gentle

thud in front of her. Jessica looked up in time to see a large
shelf of snow coming loose, then falling. . . .

Her world went white. And silent. And still.

Their horses crashed along the frozen trail. Naked branches
whipped at Fletcher's face, but he barely felt the sting. His
consuming need to find Jessica overrode sensation, overrode
discomfort.

The trace grew indistinct, the forest forbidding. Finally the
trees and underbrush grew so thick that the horses could go
no farther.

"We'll have to continue on foot," Fletcher shouted above
the howling wind. They found a spot canopied by giant hem-
locks and tethered their mounts beneath the shielding boughs.
Spurred by cold and urgency and the waning light, they
plunged on through the forest.

When they'd covered some distance, Gabriel hesitated. He
plucked a bit of woolen fabric from a gorse bush. "She's
been here!" he said excitedly. Moving forward, he found a
few more fibers. "She went this way." Farther on they discovered broken underbrush, a small footprint clouded by
snow, a strand of peach-gold hair.

Fletcher frowned. The trail Gabriel had discovered led to
the east, not the west. Damn, he thought, she's lost her way.
They now had to search not only the route from Two Rivers
to Johnson Hall but the wide triangle of wilderness between.

Hearing a dull, thudding sound, Fletcher paused. But he
knew it wasn't a gunshot, the signal they'd agreed upon with
the men from Albany. Probably a tree limb falling. Fletcher
stared at Gabriel, who was squinting at a broken twig as if
reading a map. "Where the devil did you learn to track?"

Gabriel lifted his chin. "I am Burning Sapling," he said
in the language of his grandmother. "I am Mohawk."

Fletcher felt a sudden surge of admiration and pride. The
boy was tireless . . . and determined. Through terrain that
might strangle a greenhorn, the boy ran with his toes pointed
safely inward, in the Mohawk way.

Gabriel's sharp eyes and Fletcher's instinct guided them
through the woods. Just as the sky was darkening to the gun-
metal gray of winter twilight, they emerged from the tangle

of wilderness to a rocky path. White-clad cliffs jutted out over the river.

Fletcher saw a dark shape some yards distant. A dark, unmoving shape half-buried in snow.

"Jessica." Her name poured from his aching throat. He began to run.

Chapter 23

Fletcher's world narrowed to the four walls of Jessica's room at Holland Hall. Seated beside the canopied bed, he stared at his wife until his eyes blurred. Evening slid into night, then the bleak morning sun shimmered through the partially drawn drapes. Jessica lay still, silent . . . unreachable.

Mercy's poultices of bethroot and lemon balm had drawn the frostbitten whiteness from Jessica's face, hands, and feet. Blankets heated by brass warmers had thawed her body. But only Jessica's own will could revive her spirit and give her the strength to fight the deadly threat of lung fever.

His heart aching, Fletcher took her hand. He studied the chafed, delicate fingers and remembered that hand soothing Kitty's brow, shaping a silhouette, selecting a pocket knife for Gabriel at Bartholomew Fair, steadying Adele as they walked together in the garden. . . . It was the hand of a woman who knew how to love.

"Please," he whispered in a voice gravelly with despair and lack of sleep. "Please wake up, darling." But she slept on through the morning, into the afternoon. Mercy came with fresh poultices and draughts of medicine, and a tray of food for Fletcher. He could not eat, could only hope and pray to God and every Mohawk deity his weary mind could conjure.

Restless with fear, he moved to the window, flexing limbs that had grown tense during his vigil. Through the wavy window pane he saw the long fingers of twilight reaching across the snow-cloaked yard. Jessica's fruitwood box sat on the window seat. Absently Fletcher opened it and picked up the self-portrait Jessica had done in London. A year ago not even he threat of death had caused a stir in his prison-hardened heart. Now a mere portrait in shadows brought tears to his eyes.

The desperate, embittered prisoner was gone now. Jessica had turned him away from anger, had taught him the joy and the agony of love. He glanced at the slight, unmoving figure on the bed. Would she ever know? Or would she slip away before he could tell her?

He yielded to the pain of memories. The pale, shadowy figure became a laughing girl in a summer glade, her lips stained with berry juice and her eyes shining with love. How could he have driven that girl away?

Haunted by guilt for the many injustices he'd done and the many more things he should have said but hadn't, Fletcher returned to the bedside. With the power of all he felt for her he willed her to return to him.

Finally, just as the moon began to rise, she stirred. Fletcher sat forward. Her eyes fluttered open and his heart catapulted to his throat. Mute with relief, he watched her gaze climb to the canopy over the bed.

"How did I get here?" she whispered.

He squeezed her hand. "I carried you." He swallowed and his voice hoarsened. "We were all looking for you, Jessica, but none so desperately as I. How do you feel, love?"

She shrugged listlessly, her beautiful face an impassive mask. "I . . . hurt."

"I know, Jessica." Fletcher hardly dared to breathe as he tugged the bellpull to signal the household. The glassiness in her eyes disturbed him. Mercy had warned him to let Jessica revive slowly, to avoid startling her. "You've had frostbite." Gently pressing her hand, he added, "You'll heal."

Extracting her fingers from his, she struggled to sit up. Fletcher reached behind her to help. "I was going. . . ." she began, but her voice trailed off as if the effort were too costly. She lay still against the pillows and bolsters, her brow puckered in a frown. "Yes, I remember now," she said suddenly. The vague emptiness left her face and it became expressive, with a range of emotion that spanned everything from regret to resignation. "I was going to Johnson Hall."

A denial reared in his mind. Is that what she intended? To end their marriage? Is that what she wanted?

She sat forward and her eyes seemed to blur, then focus. "I've grown up, in case you haven't noticed, Fletcher. I'm no longer that shy spinster governess. I won't be sent back to London."

"No, love, you're not going to London."

"Good, because I thought to take up residence at Johnson Hall."

"That is your choice to make." Fletcher forced the words out; he owed her the decision. "Unless . . ."

"Unless what?"

He brought her hand to his lips, kissed each stiff, reddened finger. "Unless you want to stay here at Holland Hall."

Her teeth clutched at the rosy flesh of her lower lip. For a wild moment, Fletcher thought he recognized longing in her eyes. But her next words crushed his hope.

"That's impossible, Fletcher. After what happened in Albany it's become clear that I don't belong in this family."

A soft tapping at the door interrupted her. The door burst open.

Kitty ran to the bed and flung herself at Jessica. "Mama!" she cried, her small hands reaching out. "You left without telling us. Why did you do that, Mama? Esme and I were worried. They said you're sick."

Jessica closed her eyes and drew a deep breath. She stroked Kitty's hair. "I just did what I thought was best for all of us."

"Tiens." Adele Severin glided forward, her lips set in a severe pout. "You take too much upon yourself, copine." A sheen of tears belied her stern look. "I thought I taught you better than to go riding off into a snowstorm."

Fletcher made an impatient sound in his throat. Adele turned to him. "We shall keep our visit brief, monsieur."

A shadow fell across the bed. Jessica looked over Kitty's head, past Adele, past Fletcher. Gabriel stood at the foot, looking pale and oddly fearful. He took a step forward.

"Hello . . . Mama," he said.

Certain she'd heard him wrong, Jessica blinked. "Gabriel?"

He handed her a salver piled high with letters and calling cards. "The foot post from Albany just brought these."

Jessica frowned at the papers. She recognized Mrs. Fairfax's cream stock, Mrs. Guyver's embossed stationery. . . .

"I told them," Gabriel said desperately. "I told them they never should have listened to me. I'm sorry. Please say you'll forgive me. Please."

Awash with confusion and amazement, Jessica set Kitty aside and held out her hands to him. Instantly he filled her senses with the small, taut angles of his body and the warm, boyish scent of his hair. Hope flooded through her. If Gabriel had accepted her, then perhaps . . . She glanced up at Fletcher. To her dismay, he was turned toward the window, his shoulders stiff.

"You'll stay?" Gabriel asked.

Jessica took a long, unsteady breath. "I don't know, Gabriel."

"*Alors,* you are weak still," Adele said, her eyes moving from Jessica to Fletcher. "Come along, children. We'll return later, when your *maman* is stronger." Moving briskly, she propelled Kitty and Gabriel out the door. She aimed a meaningful look at Fletcher. "*Á vous, monsieur,*" she added and closed the door behind her.

He turned to Jessica, his face drawn, his hands clenching and unclenching at his sides. "Have you changed your mind now?"

Despite Gabriel's apology, she knew her decision lay with her husband, not her stepson. "Gabriel has said his piece," she told him slowly, "but you've not told me what you want."

Moonlight from the window shrouded him; the stubble of a beard softened the harsh, handsome lines of his face. "Give this wretched excuse for a family another chance," he said softly. "We need you, Jessica."

"Still you speak of the family and not of yourself." Suddenly restless and pricked by anger, she flung back the bedclothes, swung her feet to the floor, and stood. Pain bolted up her legs and she swayed, clutching at the bed-curtains.

Fletcher was at her side immediately. His arms went around her and he scooped her up against him, cradling her next to his chest. Stars of sudden movement dancing before her eyes, Jessica squinted up at him. He smiled and moved toward the window, settling on the ledge with her in his lap. She could see his face clearly now in the moonlight, could see every tender, volatile, vulnerable line.

"I speak of the family," he said, "because I'm afraid, Jessica, to speak of myself. You've every right to reject me."

A tremble eddied through her. "So I've tried to tell myself," she whispered.

Longing glinted in his eyes. Hesitantly he laid his hand on her cheek, circled his thumb tenderly at her temple. His breath disturbed her curls as he spoke. "Jessica . . . I want to keep you folded in my arms," he said, his voice throbbing with emotion. "And in my heart."

She held her breath, then let it escape slowly. "Why?"

He brushed his lips over the warm silk of her hair. "Because I love you," he said simply. "I love you. *I love you.* One day you'll grow tired of hearing it."

Jessica made herself speak over the wild hammering of her heart. "Not long ago you planned to ship me back to London. Now you profess your love. Forgive me, but I cannot find it in me to trust that."

"Then trust this," he murmured just before he kissed her. "Trust this, darling."

Her lips came alive beneath his. The taste of his mouth brought memories surging up from the shadows of the past. Always she had felt his passion when he kissed her, but now she felt his love, streaking like lightning through her veins, burning a path to her heart. A sigh slipped from her as he drew away.

"Tell me what made you change your mind," she said.

"Almost losing you," he said against her hair. "The prospect of never hearing your voice again, seeing your face, watching you shape a silhouette with your clever hands . . ." He shuddered. "I didn't let myself admit how much I needed you until you were gone."

"I love you, Fletcher," she told him.

He bent to nuzzle beneath the raucous spill of curls at her throat. "Enough to let me go to Fort Stanwix in the spring to negotiate for the Iroquois?"

She stared steadily into his eyes. "Enough to insist on coming with you." She put her finger on his lips to forestall his objections. "I love every part of you, Fletcher, the Indian part included."

He said something in Mohawk and she didn't need him to translate, for the sentiment was clear in his eyes. Joy burst inside her as she wound her arms around his neck and her mouth sought his again. He pulled back with a short, unsteady laugh. "I'd best put you to bed, love. I don't want to tax your strength."

"Nonsense," she said, lightly kissing his neck. "You say you love me. I would have you show me."

"But you're ill, you're—"

"Ill! What a terribly unflattering thing to say, Fletcher." She faced him squarely and laid her hand alongside his cheek. "At this moment I feel more love than I have ever felt before in my life, and you have the nerve to tell me I look ill."

His smile melted her heart. "In truth you look adorable, like a fairy princess borne on a snowflake."

She laughed and leaned back, realizing she'd never tire of his unexpected compliments.

Leaning her forehead against the frosty window, she smiled at the moon-shadowed splendor of the snowy yard, then back at her husband. His expression was soft, loving, completely open to her. With her finger she traced his brow, his nose, his lips, his chin, and knew she'd never look at him as a stranger again, because he'd invited her into his heart. "Perhaps at last I'll be able to make a decent portrait of you," he mused.

Smiling, he gently gathered her against him and carried her to the bed. "But not now, darling," he whispered. "Just let me love you. You've a lifetime to depict me."

SUSAN WIGGS

While living in Europe, SUSAN WIGGS made frequent imaginary pilgrimages into the past, sitting up all night in the fog on the boat train to England. She loved to climb the ruins of remote, crumbling keeps to smell the mustiness of the dank walls and wonder about the heroes who haunted the time-worn castles of the northern fells. "Stories leaped out at me from every echoing hall," she says. "I try to make my characters breathe life into the cobwebbed events of old. They lived and died and loved and hated as people have always done. It's fascinating to place them in their fabulous settings and test their grit."

She continues, "I've been asked how I can write after a day of teaching and caring for my young daughter, Elizabeth. The truth is, writing isn't a chore for me. My husband Jay doesn't mind that I'd rather have my nose buried in a history book than in a cookbook. He's not even startled anymore when, after a long, dreamy silence, I suddenly shout, 'God's blood!' and begin scribbling furiously in a notebook as a new story springs to mind."

Susan Wiggs is the author of the Avon Romances *Briar Rose* and *Winds of Glory*.

The Timeless Romances
of New York Times Bestselling Author

JOHANNA
LINDSEY

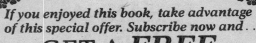